THE MIDNIGHT CHOIR

Gene Kerrigan is from Dublin. He is the author of a number of books, including *Hard Cases* and *Little Criminals*. He writes for the *Independent on Sunday* and has twice been named Journalist of the Year.

D1325173

GENE KERRIGAN

The Midnight Choir

VINTAGE BOOKS
London

First published in Great Britain in 2006 by
Harvill Secker

Vintage
Random House, 20 Vauxhall Bridge Road,
London SW1V 2SA

www.vintage-books.co.uk

Addresses for companies within The Random House Group Limited
can be found at: www.randomhouse.co.uk/offices.htm

The Random House Group Limited Reg. No. 954009

A CIP catalogue record for this book
is available from the British Library

ISBN 9780099483762

The Random House Group Limited makes every effort to ensure that
the papers used in its books are made from trees that have been
legally sourced from well-managed and credibly certified forests.
Our paper procurement policy can be found at:
www.randomhouse.co.uk/paper.htm

Mixed Sources
Product group from well-managed
forests and other controlled sources
www.fsc.org   Cert no. TT-COC-2139
© 1996 Forest Stewardship Council
FSC

Typeset by SX Composing DTP, Rayleigh, Essex

Printed in the UK by CPI Bookmarque, Croydon, CR0 4TD

This book is dedicated to Elizabeth Lordan

Like a drunk in a midnight choir
I have tried in my way to be free
          – Leonard Cohen

WEDNESDAY

I

GALWAY

It was just gone noon when Garda Joe Mills got out of the patrol car on Porter Street, looked up and saw the jumper sitting on the edge of the pub roof, his legs dangling over the side. Garda Declan Dockery was still behind the wheel, confirming to radio control that this was a live one. Looking up past the soles of the jumper's shoes, to the pale, bored face, Joe Mills was hoping the fool would get on with it.

If you're gonna jump, do it now.

Thing about people like that, they don't much care who they take with them. Mills had once worked with a garda named Walsh, from Carlow, who used to be stationed in Dublin. Went into the Liffey after a would-be suicide and the guy took him under, arms around his neck. Would have killed him if Walsh hadn't grabbed his balls until he'd let go.

The jumper was just sitting there, two storeys above the street, staring straight ahead. He looked maybe forty, give or take. The sleeveless top showing off his shoulders. Bulky but not fat. He paid no heed to the arrival of the police or the attention of anyone below. To the left of the pub there was a bookie's, and a motor accessories shop to the right and beyond that a branch of a building society, all with a trickle of customers. Passers-by slowed and some stopped. An audience was building. As Mills watched, several pre-lunch drinkers came out of the pub to see what was going on. Two of them were still clutching their pints.

Mills waited for Dockery to finish talking into the radio. He wasn't going up on that roof alone.

Thing like this, edge of the roof, all it takes is he grabs hold of you at the last moment, your arm, maybe, or the front of your jacket – and your balance is gone. You reach for a handhold and you're too far out and all you get to do is scream on the way down.

You want to jump, go ahead. Leave me out of it.

A man in his fifties, pudgy, balding and pouting, buttonholed Garda Mills. 'I want him off there, right? And I want him arrested, OK?'

'And you are?'

'The manager. I want him dealt with. That kind of thing – this is a respectable pub, right?'

Mills saw that the jumper was shifting around. Maybe his arse was itchy, maybe he was working on a decision.

'Oh, I dunno,' Mills said. 'Thing like this, you could have a lot of people dropping around to see where it happened. Tourists, like. Can't be bad for business.'

The manager looked at Mills, like he was considering if there might be something in that.

'I want him shifted, right?'

Dockery was standing at Mills's shoulder. 'Ambulance on the way. They're looking for a shrink who can make it here pronto. Meantime—'

Mills was thinking, traffic in this town, by the time a shrink gets here it'll all be over.

One way or the other.

Dockery was looking at the assembled gawkers. 'I reckon the most important thing is we cordon off down here. We don't want him coming down on top of someone.'

Mills nodded. That sounded like the sensible thing to do. Best of all, it was ground-level work. Dockery was already moving towards the onlookers when one of the drinkers said, 'Oh, no.'

Mills looked up. The jumper was standing.

Shit.

Mills said, 'We can't wait for the shrink.'

Dockery said, 'Wait a minute – there's—'

Mills was moving towards the door of the pub. He took the manager by the elbow. 'How do I get up there?'

'Joe—' Dockery was making an awkward gesture, caught between following Mills and moving the gawkers out of harm's way.

The manager, grumbling all the way, took Mills up to the top floor, where a storeroom led to an exit onto the roof.

Mills was trying to remember a lecture he'd attended a couple of years back. How to approach a possible suicide.

Reluctantly.

The roof was flat tarmac, with razor-wire barriers jutting out at a forty-five-degree angle on each side. The storeroom took up a quarter of the roof space at the back and there was a two-foot-high parapet at the front. Near the centre of the roof a green plastic garden chair lay on its side, next to a stack of broken window boxes and a couple of empty old Guinness crates. At the front of the building the jumper was standing on the parapet, arms down by his sides. Mills moved towards him at an angle, stepping sideways, keeping his distance. He wasn't going close enough to be pulled over, and he didn't want to startle the man.

From up here, the jumper looked like he was in his early thirties. Denim jeans, trainers and the dark blue sleeveless top. Well built, serious shoulders and biceps that didn't come from casual exercise.

Weights, probably steroids too.

What to say?

Mills couldn't remember much from the lecture, but he knew that there was no point arguing with a jumper. Logic didn't work.

Whatever it was had got him out here it'd be so big in his mind that there wouldn't be room in there for reasoning.

Get him talking. Draw him out. Make a connection. That's a start.

Maybe ask him if he's got kids?

No.

Could be domestic.

Mention kids and I might step on something that stokes him up.

It was mid-April and Mills could feel the winter overhang in the breeze.

Down there, touch of spring. Notice the wind up here.

'Cold out here. In that top.'

Fuck's sake.

The weather.

The jumper stared straight ahead.

'You a regular in this pub?'

Nothing.

Should have asked the manager.

'You want to tell me your name?'

Nothing.

'Don't know about you, but I'm nervous up here.'

Mills was trying to remember something that the lecturer had said. About how, more often than not, the subject is using the threat of suicide as a cry for help. Offer a way out, show them that you care.

Okay, fella, I hear you.

Well done.

Point made. Help on the way. Quit while you're ahead.

Say hello to the men in white coats and they'll give you all the little pills in the world and by tomorrow you won't remember what was bothering you.

Or what planet you're on.

The jumper turned his head just enough so that he was looking Garda Joe Mills in the eye.

Jesus.

The man's blank icy stare was unmistakable evidence that this was no cry for help.

There's something mad in there.

The jumper held Joe Mills's gaze as he turned completely around until his back was to the street and he was facing the garda.

Ah, fuck.

His arms still down by his sides, his heels an inch from the edge of the parapet, his expression vacant, the jumper stared at Joe Mills.

Now, he falls backwards, staring at me until he goes out of sight and the next thing I hear is the gawkers screaming and then the wet crunching sound that I'll be hearing in nightmares for years to come.

'Look, fella. Whatever it is – I mean, what you need to think about, give it time—'

Stupid.

Arguing – he can't—

The jumper stepped lightly off the parapet onto the roof. He stood there, chin up, his bulky tensed arms several inches out from his sides. After a few seconds he flexed his jaw in a way that made the tendons in his neck stand out. Then he took an audible breath and began to walk past Garda Mills. He was moving towards the storeroom and the door down from the roof.

'Hey, hold on—'

Mills reached out to grab an arm and the man threw a punch. Mills felt like his nose had taken a thump from a hammer. The jumper was turning sideways, instinctively positioning himself to block a return blow, but through the pain Mills was very deliberately suppressing his own urge to lash back. He was already ducking to the left, one hand snapping onto the jumper's right wrist, then he was twisting the man's hand and moving around him, keeping the arm taut, twisting it and pushing and the jumper made a *Hwwaawwh!* sound and Mills was standing behind him. The man was bent forward ninety degrees, immobilised by Mills's grip on his hand and his rigid arm.

Mills hooked a foot around the man's leg so that when he pushed the jumper forward he tripped and went down, his arm held rigid all the way. The anguished sound the prisoner made seemed to come in equal measure from the pain and from the realisation that he had no control over what was happening.

Mills could hear footsteps behind him and then Dockery was reaching down and seconds later the man was cuffed, belly down on the roof.

Mills felt the elation rush from somewhere in his chest, spreading out right to the tips of his fingers, blanking out even the pain in his nose.

Did it!

Situation defused.

Every move totally ace.

If Dockery hadn't been there, Mills might have given a whoop.

He wants to go off a roof, there's always tomorrow, and to hell with him, but for now—

Gotcha!

Mills took a deep breath and Dockery said, 'Jesus, look at that.' He was pointing down at the man's cuffed hands.

Mills could see dark reddish-black stains on both hands, across the palms, in between the fingers. The dried blood was caked thick around the man's fingernails.

Dockery turned the prisoner over. There were darker stains on the dark blue top. There were also dark streaks down near the bottom of his jeans. The man lay there, quiet, like the fight had drained out of him in that short frantic struggle.

Dockery was looking at Mills. 'He's not hurt?'

Mills shook his head. 'Can't be his blood. And it's not recent.'

That much blood – someone was carrying a hell of a wound.

Mills looked at his own hands, where he'd gripped the nutcase. He saw a smear that might have come from the stains on the man's hand. He rubbed his hand on his trouser leg.

He bent and looked at the man's trainers. There were dark

reddish marks ingrained in the pattern of the sole of one of them.

Might be, or maybe not.

Mills knelt, levered off both the man's shoes and held them by the laces.

Dockery said, 'What's your name?'

The man ignored the question. Lying on his back, cold eyes watching Joe Mills straighten up, there was a twist to one side of his mouth as though his face couldn't decide whether to scowl or smirk.

They got him to his feet and hustled him towards the roof doorway, from which the pub manager was emerging. As they went past, the manager poked a finger at the prisoner. 'You're barred, you are. You hear me? Barred.'

2

DUBLIN

On the way out to the Hapgood place Detective Garda Rose Cheney pointed out the house that had sold for eight million. 'Around here, the houses go for – what – pushing a million, and that's for your basic nothing special. One and three-quarters if they have a view of the sea, three if they back onto the beach. Any size on them at all and you're into four or five mil.'

Detective Inspector Harry Synnott wanted to tell her that he didn't much care about Dublin property prices, but this was the second time he'd worked with Garda Cheney and she was a bit of a yapper. If it wasn't property prices it'd be something else.

Cheney steered around a gradual bend and slowed down. 'That's it on the left, third one in from the end.'

It was a tall handsome house, glimpsed through a curtain of trees. Victorian? Georgian, maybe – Harry Synnott didn't know one period from another. Anything old that looked like a bit of thought had gone into it he reckoned was probably Victorian. Or Georgian. If not Edwardian.

'Eight million?'

'Eight-point-three.'

'Jesus.'

Rose Cheney snickered. 'Couple of rich men got a hard-on for the same sea view. Nice aspect, mind you. Worth maybe three million, tops. Not that I'd pay that for it. Even if I had three million. But the way the market is, I mean, place like that'd run to three million, there or thereabouts. But you know how it is, bulls in heat, and the bidding went up to eight-three before one of them threw his hat at it.'

Nice aspect.

Synnott wasn't sure what a nice aspect was, but it was apparently worth a rake of money. One minute the country hasn't an arse in its trousers, next minute the millionaires are scrapping over who gets to pay over the odds for a nice aspect. There were some who claimed the prosperity was down to EU handouts, others said it had more to do with Yank investment. There was a widely proclaimed belief among the business classes that they'd discovered within themselves some long-hidden spark of entrepreneurial genius. Whatever it was, the country had been a decade in love with its own prosperity and everyone agreed that even though the boom years were over there was no going back.

We might, Synnott thought, be card-carrying members of the new global order, but we're still committing the same old crimes. The working day had started for Synnott when he met Detective Garda Rose Cheney at the Sexual Assault Unit of the Rotunda Hospital.

Cheney had already interviewed the alleged victim and was waiting outside her room while a nurse did whatever it is nurses do when they usher visitors from a hospital room.

'Name is Teresa Hunt. Just turned twenty, doing Arts at Trinity. Family's from Dalkey, she has a flat in town. The doctor confirms she had recent intercourse, swabbed for sperm, so we might get something. She's not physically damaged, apart from minor bruising around her arms and thighs.'

'Who's the man?'

Cheney opened her notebook. 'Alleged assailant, Max Hapgood. They were an item some time last year, met again at a party a couple of weeks back. He called her a few days ago. Had a date last evening, ended up back at her flat, and you know how that one goes.'

Synnott shrugged. 'It'll be a she-says-he-says. How'd she strike you?'

'See what you think yourself.'

Teresa Hunt turned out to be a thin, wispy young woman who looked Synnott in the eye and said, 'I want that bastard arrested.'

Synnott's nod might have meant anything.

'You had a date,' Cheney said.

'I told you.'

'Tell the Inspector.'

The woman looked slightly resentful that telling her story once hadn't set the seal on the matter. She turned to Synnott. 'We had a date.'

'And?'

'We had a meal, a drink. It was good to see him again. I assumed maybe he was having second thoughts, you know.' She made a small dismissive gesture with one hand, like she was brushing away threads of illusion.

'You and he have a history.'

'It didn't last long – it was no big deal.'

Synnott heard something in her tone – perhaps it was a bigger deal for Teresa Hunt than she wanted to remember.

Cheney said, 'The relationship was sexual?'

Teresa nodded. 'We saw each other on and off, with other people – it's a small scene – but it tapered off. Then, when he rang, I assumed—'

Synnott sat back, let Cheney ask the questions. She did so gently but without skirting anything. There was no sign of the yapper now, just a capable police officer ticking off the boxes. Age of the alleged assailant? About the same as that of the alleged victim. He too was a TCD student. Business studies. Where it happened – in the woman's flat, on the floor of the living room. What time – between eleven and midnight. Yes, she asked him in for a coffee. Yes, there was affection, just a kiss or two. Yes, she consented to that. No, she didn't agree to have sex. Not in words, gestures or actions. Cheney took her through all the signals that meant one thing but might have seemed to mean another.

'It wasn't that kind of evening. It was hello-again, and that was that. I was happy to leave it that way. Then it was like he'd gone through all the right motions and it was time for the pay-off. He pushed me down—'

Again, Cheney methodically took Teresa through the moves that might have been taken for a signal of some kind. No, she'd just had a couple of drinks. Same for him, two pints. Yes, she had made it clear that she was saying no. Yes, she'd said the word. Again and again. Yes, she'd struggled. No, he hadn't threatened to assault her.

'I scratched him, his face, but he just laughed. He's tall, strong.' Quietly, with a twist of the lips. 'Rugby type.'

'Afterwards, what happened?'

'It was like, he was just normal, smiling, trying to make conversation.'

'You?'

'I went into my bedroom. Then he left, called in through the door, said goodbye.'

'This was about, what—'

'We got home, I don't know, maybe midnight, I wasn't keeping track. He didn't stay long.'

'His car, yours?'

'Taxi.'

A couple of questions later, Teresa went silent, her eyes and lips compressed. When it came, her voice was a hiss. 'He – just – I was *nothing*. Like it was something he wanted to prove he could get away with.' She wiped her eyes with the back of one hand.

Cheney said to Harry Synnott, 'I'll make the call'. They'd need Hapgood's address, and they'd have to request a preliminary check to see if he had a record.

Synnott shook his head. 'I'll do it. You stay with Teresa.'

When Garda Rose Cheney came out of the hospital room, Inspector Synnott was at the nurses' station, his mobile to his ear while he scribbled in the notebook that was open on the desk in front of him. Two nurses were chatting loudly about something that had happened the night before in A&E, while a doctor stood by a computer workstation, bent over the screen, clicking a mouse.

When Synnott finished he and Cheney found a corner where they couldn't be overheard.

Synnott said, 'No previous. Hapgood has an address in Castlepoint.' He nodded towards Teresa Hunt's room. 'What do you think?'

'We may have a problem.'

'I thought she was impressive enough.'

'After you'd gone I went back over how they came to arrange the date. Seems Teresa wrote to him, got his address from the phone book. Suggested they get together.'

'What she said was that *he* rang *her* for a date.'

'He did, but before that – she bumped into him at a party, a week later she sent him a note. He rang her the next day.'

Synnott said, 'Well.'

Both Synnott and Cheney knew that rape cases can fall one way or the other when they come down to a conflict of evidence. This one could be made to look like a young woman refusing to let go of a passing romance, pursuing the man to a sexual reprise. Depending on the sequence of events, the elements were there to create a defence that when Hapgood walked away, having no interest in Teresa Hunt beyond a quick roll, she made a revenge accusation. With a case that weak it wasn't in anyone's interest to let it go as far as a charge.

Cheney said, 'It doesn't mean she's lying about the rape.'

'No, but if Hapgood's kept the note and if what she wrote is in any way juicy, that's it as far as the DPP's office is concerned.'

'It's still her word against his.'

'The state doesn't like being a loser. If the odds don't stack up the DPP will pass.'

The Hapgood place in Castlepoint was way over on the Southside, on the coast. They drove there in Garda Cheney's Astra. It was a big house, set well back, but it was on the wrong side of the road. No beach access. Rose Cheney parked the car and said, 'What do you reckon? Two million, tops?'

Synnott said, 'Depends on the aspect.'

3

The American tourist put his MasterCard back in his wallet and took the money out of the ATM. As he slipped the notes into the wallet he heard his girlfriend make a frightened noise. He turned around Kathy was pale and rigid, staring off to one side. The mugger was four or five feet away, a woman in – what? – her mid-thirties. Thin legs in faded blue jeans, a shabby red jacket too big for her frame. Her long hair was blonde, tied back untidily, she was blinking a lot and holding one arm stiffly down by her side. What the American tourist mostly saw was the syringe she was holding in that hand, the blood inside it a darker shade than the red of her jacket.

'Give it,' she said.

'Take it easy, now—'

Neary's pub, where the tourist and his girlfriend had had drinks the previous night, was across the street. Down to the right were a couple of restaurants, customers sitting at the windows, people coming out of a fish shop across the road, others crossing towards the specialist kitchen shop, no one paying attention. It was pushing lunchtime and fifty feet behind the mugger, at the end of the side street, the usual throng of Grafton Street shoppers flowed by unheeding.

The woman stuck her chin out. 'You want the HIV?'

'Just—'

'Just fuck off – give me the money—'

'Thomas—' The American tourist's girlfriend was holding out a hand to him. 'Do what—'

The mugger said, '*She* can have it—' She waved the syringe towards the girlfriend.

The man made calming gestures, both hands patting an invisible horizontal surface in front of him. Thomas Lott, the manager of an upmarket sandwich shop in Philadelphia, had been almost a week in Dublin, Kathy's home town, her first trip home in four years. Thomas had long ago decided that the sensible thing to do if ever he was mugged would be to hand over whatever money he had, and that was what he intended doing. He just wanted things to calm down.

No room in Kathy's parents' house, so they'd stayed in the Westbury. After six days in the city Thomas found Dublin bigger and less folksy than he'd expected. Lots of sandwich bars and coffee shops, just like Philly. Lots of tall shiny glass buildings to provide the sandwich bars with their customers, just like Philly. Just as many shopping malls as Philly, just as many overpriced restaurants and just as many dead-eyed shoppers. And now, it seemed, just as many muggers.

The mugger's voice had a hysterical edge when she hissed, 'Give me the fucking *money*!'

Across the street an elderly woman and her middle-aged daughter, both raven-haired and wearing fur collars and dark glasses, were staring at the mugger.

'Sure, OK—'

Thomas Lott felt the strap of his black leather shoulder bag slip down his right arm and his left hand automatically reached up to catch it. He saw the mugger's mouth widen, her eyes move this way and that and he knew that she thought he was trying something and he thought for a fraction of a second that he should say *No, it just slipped!* But there wasn't time, so he caught the sliding strap in his right hand and he swung the bag hard. As

17

soon as he did he felt a dart of horror at his own foolishness – then he saw the bag connect, and the syringe was knocked sideways, flying out of the mugger's hand, and he felt a giddy rush of triumph.

Backing away, the mugger screamed a string of obscenities. Thomas Lott started towards her, but she was already turning, bent and running.

'*Thomas!*'

Lott gave up the notion of following the mugger. He roared, 'Stop her!' but she was already about to turn the corner into Grafton Street, slipping into the tide of unheeding pedestrians.

'Thomas.'

When he turned back, Kathy was standing very still, breathing heavily, like she was trying not to scream. Thomas Lott moved towards his girlfriend and he was within three feet of her before he saw the syringe, ugly against her dazzling white skirt, sticking up out of the front of her thigh at a forty-five-degree angle.

Stupid bastard.

All he had to do.

Stupid fucker!

Dixie Peyton's breath came in noisy gulps as she ran down Grafton Street. It was dangerous to run. Cop sees someone like her running – say goodnight.

To her left, a glimpse of a shaven-headed security man at the door of a shop, watching her, muttering into his radio.

Running, someone like me—

But the Yank – *fuck him* – might still be coming after her and she had to put some distance—

Half a minute later she ducked left, into a shoe shop. Two elderly women coming out of the shop stood to one side as she passed. They looked Dixie up and down and used their elbows to press their handbags closer to their sides.

Dixie stopped, aware that she looked out of place among the calm, well-dressed shoppers. She fought to control her breathing. She looked out through the shop window and saw a garda running awkwardly down the street. Young guy, moving too carefully to get up much speed, one hand holding his radio in place, the other touching his cap, glancing this way and that in search of the runaway mugger.

'Hey, you!'

Dixie turned and saw a big fat bastard coming up from the back of the shop, his stare fixed on her, his walkie-talkie held at chin height.

She turned and hurried towards the door. Behind her she heard the big fat bastard shouting something, as if it was any of his fucking business.

The two old women were still standing just outside the shop, watching Dixie as she ran out. Then she could hear the barking of the big fat bastard as he used his radio to let the whole street know.

Dixie turned right and ran back up Grafton Street. If it was just a thing of running, she'd have no problem leaving the cop or any of the fat bastards standing. But with the radios it was like the cops and the fat bastards had threads linking them all together, sticky threads. No matter which way she ran she left a trace.

To vanish in the anonymity of the crowd she'd need to stop running. To stop running, she'd have to get far enough away from the Yank and the garda and the big fat bastard, and all the other security men and their net of sticky threads.

All she wanted was for this to stop.

Didn't get any money. Keep it. Stick it where the sun don't shine.

All a mistake.

Stupid. All the Yank had to do—

Leave me alone!

She'd made eye contact with the Yank's girlfriend when the syringe hit her – *Jesus!* – talk about bad luck. Try that a hundred times, the fucking needle sticking up out of the prissy brunette's leg, it's never going to happen.

Ah, shit.

Twenty feet in front of Dixie.

Less than that.

One of the security men – tall guy in a black leather jacket, short haircut, chewing gum, was coming diagonally down the street, muttering into his radio, his gaze fixed on Dixie. She knew him. Potsy, something like that.

Dixie changed direction, headed straight towards Potsy, weaving through the shoppers. She saw Potsy stop and crouch, arms wide like he was a gladiator waiting for the lions to come out. Then – when she was three feet away from him – Dixie changed direction again and left him standing there like the gobshite he was, crouched, wrong-footed, one arm reaching hopelessly for her flying form, and she was past him and running towards the Westbury Mall and something hit her right shin hard, pain shooting up through her leg so that she screamed. Then her knees hit the ground, jolting her whole body, and she was rolling over onto her back, winded. She tried to sit up and she screamed as someone kicked her in the ribs.

'*Bitch!*'

It was the Yank, all excited, dancing around her, then Potsy was pushing him away and kneeling beside her. 'You OK?'

Dixie lay there, looking up. Everyone she could see – and there were dozens of people milling about – was staring at her. The Yank and Potsy, people standing around, people walking past, not looking where they were going, all of them staring at the woman sprawled on the ground. Curiosity in those eyes, excitement, contempt.

Leave me alone.

The garda was pushing his way through, younger even than she'd thought when she saw him first. He stood over her, making breathless noises into his radio.

Dixie's hands crossed in front of her chest, taking hold of the lapels of her red jacket, her fingers pulling the fabric taut. She tucked her legs under herself and curled up, turning her head to one side. She could feel the cold rough surface of the brick footpath against her cheek.

Dixie closed her eyes.

4

It was lunchtime when Detective Inspector Harry Synnott and Detective Garda Rose Cheney arrived at the Hapgood house, at Castlepoint. The Hapgood kid was chewing something when he opened the front door. Synnott looked at his face and knew two things.

One – *He did it.*

Two – *All going well, we'll have this wrapped up by close of business.*

'Garda Siochana, Detective Inspector Synnott. I'm looking for Max Hapgood.'

The young man's glance went from Synnott to Garda Cheney, standing four feet behind, then back again.

'Junior or senior?'

Harry Synnott said, 'Both.'

The kid blushed. There were two diagonal scratches on his forehead. He'd stopped chewing and Synnott guessed that right now the kid was suppressing an urge to spit out whatever was in his mouth.

He was big, six-two at least, broad and muscled. Across a courtroom from wispy little Teresa Hunt, even in his best suit, he'd come over as Attila the Rugby Player.

More often than not, Harry Synnott looked at a suspect and it was like a parent looking at a child – *Did you take those sweets?* And it didn't matter if the child denied it on granny's grave, the parent could tell by the way the guilt rippled through the kid's facial muscles. For a policeman as experienced as Harry Synnott, it could be the way a suspect stood or moved but mostly it came from what was happening in the face. It didn't work with the hard cases who could look anyone in the eye and rattle off a phoney alibi like they were saying a cherished childhood prayer. Lacking authority over his own face, Max Hapgood Junior couldn't prevent it betraying him.

There it was again. The flush rising up the cheeks.

It's not just that he did it. He knows that I know he did it.

The cling-film kids. Soft as mush, all wrapped up in themselves and you could see right through them. Smart-arses, but nothing to back it up. Synnott didn't even have to ask a question – all he had to do was turn up on the Hapgood doorstep, looking like he meant business, and a big neon *Guilty!* lit up across the kid's face.

He knows why we're here. He was gambling that Teresa wouldn't make a fuss, now he can feel the ground crumbling.

'My father's not here.'

'Your mammy in?'

A ripple of annoyance crossed the kid's features.

'My mother's not here at the moment.'

'You'll do. Can you confirm that you spent some time last evening with a young woman named Teresa Hunt?'

'Max? Everything all right?'

She was there at the other end of the hall. Black dress, thin as a rake, dark hair pulled back tight on her head.

'Mrs Hapgood?'

She didn't reply. She was looking at her son. She could tell that Synnott and Cheney weren't here to sell timeshares.

'Garda Siochana, Mrs Hapgood. May we come in?'

'Max?' She was ignoring Synnott and Cheney. The kid was chewing rapidly again as though he'd just remembered he'd a mouthful of food and he urgently needed to dispose of it.

'Detective Inspector Synnott, Mrs Hapgood. And Detective Garda Cheney. We have a few questions for your son. I think it might be better if we—' Synnott gestured towards the street, implying the hazard of neighbourhood gossips. Mrs Hapgood waved an impatient hand.

'Come in.'

She didn't know why exactly the police had come for her son but it was all over her face – *Whatever this is about, he did it.*

'Max?'

The kid looked from Synnott to his mother, then back, his face flaring. The stupidity of lying that his mother wasn't home had stripped away any possibility of defiance. He said, 'Please, I didn't do anything.'

'Then why don't we sit down and clear this up, sir?'

The mother spat the words. 'What's this about?'

'A young lady has made a complaint.'

The mother crossed to stand beside the kid. 'I'm calling my husband. I don't want you talking to Max until my husband gets here.'

*

The sergeant processing Dixie Peyton into a cell at Cooper Street garda station was grey-haired, with a grey face. After an initial glance at Dixie, he focused on the sheet in front of him, asking questions without looking up, filling in her details. Name, address, date of birth. Much of the sergeant's workday consisted of tending what he had come to think of as a production line in the crime industry. Stand there, fiddle with the ratchets and cogwheels and watch the never-ending stream of product pass through on its way to prison. It was a living.

'Any existing medical conditions?'

'I want to make a phone call.'

'Medical conditions?'

'No, I want to make a phone call.'

'Taking any medication?'

Dixie shook her head. She answered whatever he asked her and when the sergeant was finished he straightened up. Dixie watched him put down his pen, then she said, 'I'm sorry, I really do need to make a phone call.'

He turned and took the form back into an inner office. Dixie turned to the garda who'd arrested her. Standing a few feet away, he was somewhere off in text heaven, staring at the screen of his Nokia, his thumb dancing on the buttons. After a minute, the sergeant came back from the inner office and said to her, 'Do you need to make a phone call?'

Dixie was about to say something. Instead, she just nodded.

'Number?'

'Detective Inspector Harry Synnott. He's at Turner's Lane garda station.'

Dixie was taken through a doorway and down a corridor. She looked back and the arresting garda was still standing in the public area, his thumb tapping away at the Nokia. The sergeant opened a heavy metal door and led her through to the cells.

The sergeant went back to his desk and looked up the number for Turner's Lane. A voice at the other end told him that he didn't think Detective Inspector Synnott was here. As the sergeant hung up he saw another garda come through the door into receiving, leading a cuffed teenager with a bum-fluff moustache who was protesting loudly that he hadn't done any fucking thing wrong, right? The sergeant pulled another form from a tray.

*

Detective Garda Rose Cheney was thinking, not for the first time, that TV make-over programmes have a lot to answer for. Max Hapgood's mother had taken the kid off to some other part of the house, where no doubt he was being grilled. The two detectives were left sitting at the dining-room table. Cheney reckoned that the room had endured the attentions of someone deeply influenced by a variety of celebrity designers. The house was big and old, with high ceilings and tall windows, and the dining room looked foolish dressed in the kind of minimalist style more suited to a tiny riverfront apartment. Dark brown vertical blinds, bold whites balanced against various shades of grey, and more chrome than was good for any room that wasn't a works canteen. Cheney examined the artwork on the walls. She didn't recognise any of the signatures, but none of it came from a car-boot sale. On top of the fortune it cost to buy one of these houses, a lot more had been spent tarting it up. With that kind of earning power, Hapgood Senior might be a lawyer, though the name didn't ring any bells. Commercial law, maybe. The higher reaches of middle management in the Financial Services Centre, or perhaps a partner in one of the outfits that serviced the winners in the boom economy.

In the forty minutes it took the father to get home, Cheney exchanged maybe half a dozen sentences with Harry Synnott, all of them comments on the house. He made assenting noises, but offered no opinions. Probably that was because he didn't have any. Synnott didn't seem to have much to say about anything beyond the immediate matter at hand. His voice, measured and precise, with a soft Waterford accent, was at odds with his appearance. There were many gardai with his tall, wide build and large hands, and a few with the slight unevenness of his nose that was the legacy of a short-lived amateur boxing career. The stand-offish manner, however, was all his own. Maybe he had grown used to the cold shoulder and was out of the habit of making an effort. Unlike some in the force, Cheney had no problem working with the man. He wasn't easy to talk to but you wouldn't hang a man for that, and he hadn't caused her any grief. He was a shit, that was a given. But in the day-to-day, he was more than just a competent copper. She figured it couldn't hurt to work with someone whose name was attached to the Garda Sheelin murder case, as well as to the conviction of a serial rapist, to the Swanson Avenue murder and to two or three more of the force's biggest cases over the past twenty years.

The first thing the father said when he came home was, 'Sorry about the wait, Inspector. You don't have a coffee. Perhaps—'

'No, thanks, I—'

'Tea? A soft drink? It's no bother.'

Shirt-sleeved, he stood inside the door of the dining room, arms wide, palms up, as though he was ensuring that everyone was comfy before a meeting of the parish council.

'I'd love a Coke,' Rose Cheney said. She reckoned he wouldn't let them get on with the job until his hospitality had been acknowledged. Max Hapgood Senior smiled warmly. 'That's the ticket.' He turned to Synnott. 'Just give me ten minutes with Max – is that OK?'

'Of course, sir.'

The Coke arrived on a tray, in a glass with ice and lemon and with a little plastic sunflower gadget attached to the side of the glass. It was carried by a dark-haired woman in her mid-thirties. Rose Cheney smiled at the woman and said, 'Romania? Latvia?' The woman didn't acknowledge the question. She put the tray on a side table, turned and left the room. Obedience was a job requirement, Cheney reckoned, but familiarity with the people she had to obey would be discouraged. She'd be on a third of the minimum wage, sending money home to her family, her work permit held by the Hapgoods. If she had any time left after serving the family and their guests, cooking, cleaning and looking after Max Junior, she'd be sent to weed the flower beds or eradicate stray individual dust molecules from the master bedroom.

Cheney left the Coke untouched.

Almost half an hour passed before Daddy Hapgood came back, a surly Max Junior by his side, the mammy bringing up the rear. 'Now, Inspector, sorry to keep you waiting.'

Within minutes, it became clear that the shutters had come down.

Across the dining-room table Max Junior found something in the middle distance to stare at, while his mother was making no effort to conceal her hostility to the gardai. Max Senior maintained an impeccably polite and patently skin-deep air of cooperation.

Harry Synnott glanced at his watch and made a note of the time. 'As your son no doubt has told you, we're here in connection with a complaint made by a young lady.'

Max Junior opened his mouth and got as far as 'I—' before his father placed one hand gently on his son's arm.

'I've been onto my solicitor's office,' Max Senior said. 'He's in a meeting at the moment, but I've left word that we need his urgent attention.' He produced a small silver-coloured recorder, pressed a button and set the machine down on the table in front of Synnott. 'Until then, I think it's best if we just listen to what you have to say, and we'll reserve comment until we've had legal advice.'

'Of course, sir, that's a reasonable stance. In the meantime, it might help clear this matter up if we could establish some basic facts – for instance—' Synnottt turned to Max. 'You're acquainted with the young lady involved, is that right?'

Max Senior smiled. 'Inspector, I appreciate you have a job to—'

'Is this what the police force has come to?' There was contempt in the woman's voice.

Max Senior said, 'Please, Maeve—'

Max Junior said, 'Mum—'

Harry Synnott said, 'Why do you say that, Mrs Hapgood?'

'You come to my home, on the word of a silly bitch who has trouble keeping her legs closed, to accuse—'

'It might indeed help, Mrs Hapgood, if you have anything that might help explain—'

'Maeve—' Max Senior's voice carried a touch of annoyance.

Mrs Hapgood turned her head away, as though the very sight of Synnott was offensive.

Rose Cheney had her legs crossed, her notebook resting casually against one knee, her pen moving . . . *silly bitch who has . . . to accuse . . .*

Harry Synnott said, 'I appreciate your decision to await legal advice before making a formal statement – and, incidentally, I agree that that's what you should do – but there are certain technicalities we ought to get out of the way while we're waiting.'

'Such as?' Max Senior said.

'We'll need the clothes that young Max was wearing last night.'

'No chance.'

'I know it's an imposition, but I'm afraid it's necessary. And we'd rather do it quietly – no need to have hordes of uniformed members arriving in squad cars, all the hullabaloo of a formal search.'

Mrs Hapgood stared at Synnott. 'This is outrageous.'

'And perhaps, since it's an obvious matter of interest to us, young Max could explain where he got those scratches on his forehead?'

Max Senior shook his head. 'That has to—'

'He was drunk.' Mrs Hapgood said. 'It happens with young men. He was drunk, he tripped on his way in last night, he scratched his face on the bushes outside the front door. OK?'

Harry Synnott said, 'That's indeed a help, Mrs Hapgood. It's just that we have to clear things up, and if there's a reasonable explanation—'

Rose Cheney was scribbling away.

'As you can see, Inspector, my wife is upset. I really think, until my solicitor—'

Synnott said to Max Junior, 'Might I see the letter?'

Max Senior said, 'What letter?'

'This young woman, we understand, wrote to you recently.'

The parents were looking at young Max. 'It was just a note, last week. I binned it.' He shrugged. 'No big deal. Just a note. She's like, will I give her a ring, that's all.'

Synnott could hear the scratching of Cheney's biro. Teresa's letter wouldn't be a problem.

*

There was a different sergeant on the desk at Cooper Street when they took Dixie Peyton out into the yard of the garda station to board the bus to court. 'What about my phone call – the other sergeant was making a call for me?' The sergeant ignored her.

'You can call from Mountjoy,' a young garda said. There were three other prisoners ahead of Dixie, all of them women caught shoplifting. She stopped at the door of the Mercedes minibus and turned to the garda. 'He should have been here by now. Mr Synnott should have been here.' She looked back and through the doorway she saw the original desk sergeant passing behind the counter in the public office. He was wearing an overcoat. She said to the garda at the minibus, 'Look, I need—' He took her by the elbow and guided her firmly through the open door of the bus. 'Off you go, love.'

The sergeant saw the door of the bus close behind Dixie Peyton and he swore silently.

Memory like a bloody sieve. Meant to call Turner's Lane again.

He was tired, his back hurt, he resented having to use his lunch break to go to a bookshop to buy a study guide for his son who didn't fancy a trip into town because the traffic was shite. As the bus pulled away, he went back behind the counter and picked up the phone. He couldn't remember the number of Turner's Lane and he was about to say the hell with it. Instead, he swore and began thumbing through the station directory.

*

The garda who took the call at Turner's Lane was young, blonde and blue-eyed, just five weeks out of Templemore. She mentally shuffled the faces of the detectives.

Harry Synnott. The one with the bockety nose. Forty-somethingish. He just transferred out of here, right?

'Listen, hold on, I'll get someone.'

She'd seen Synnott twice in the days after she came here, then he'd transferred across the city to – where? – somewhere on the Southside.

There were three other uniformed gardai within earshot, and she chose to ask Sergeant Ferry. He'd been patient and helpful from the first day. Took her on a tour of the place, introduced her to everyone, showed her where everything was. When he told her, 'You're a right pain in the arse' he had a mock-irritable look on his face, then he patiently explained for the second time the back-office filing system. End of her first week at Turner's Lane, when the young garda was using her day off to paint away some of her new flat's shabbiness, Sergeant Ferry turned up at her door with a stack of pizzas, along with his wife and his thirteen-year-old daughter, and the three of them spent the evening helping her to decorate.

Now, when she asked if he knew where Inspector Synnott had transferred, Sergeant Ferry hesitated for a moment. Then he said, 'I'll take it.'

Into the phone, he said, 'Who wants to know?'

The sergeant at Cooper Street station repeated what he'd told the young garda – a prisoner, in on a mugging charge, needed to speak to Synnott. 'She seems a bit desperate. Probably an informer. Is Synnott around?'

Sergeant Ferry said, 'Never heard of the man,' and put down the phone.

The young garda watched as Sergeant Ferry turned and walked away.

5

'Trevor!'

Max Hapgood Senior spoke into his mobile as though welcoming the Seventh Cavalry coming over the hill.

'Thanks for ringing so promptly. We've got a slight problem here – I'm at home – it's Max, we—'

He was standing now. 'You'll excuse me, Inspector – solicitor.' He clicked off his little voice recorder and put it in his pocket. Moving towards the kitchen, he put the mobile to his ear, then turned back to his son.

'Not a word.'

With the father gone, and the mother upstairs with Detective Garda Cheney, collecting the clothes that Max Junior had worn the previous evening, Harry Synnott was alone with the younger Hapgood.

A couple of minutes, tops, before one or the other comes back.

'Daddy's right, you know. If you did what the girl says you did, the best course is to keep your mouth shut and hope you get a break from the jury.'

The kid's eyes widened. Synnott could see that his casual-seeming remark had delivered an almost physical blow. The kid was suddenly seeing himself standing in a courtroom in his best suit, watching a jury come back.

After half a minute, he said, 'What is she saying?'

'I think maybe you know that.'

'I didn't force her.'

As if he'd just remembered something, Synnott picked up his pen and scribbled in his notebook. He didn't look at the kid, just said, 'That means you shouldn't have anything to worry about.'

Max shrugged. 'I mean, it wasn't like she was a virgin.'

Synnott wrote that down, too.

'Did she say I hit her? I didn't hurt her. I swear, nothing like that. It was just sex. When we started, she wanted it as much as I did.' He leaned forward. 'I mean, you know what that's like – you can't turn it on and off like a fucking tap. I did nothing wrong.'

The kitchen door opened and the father was back, mobile in hand. 'Trevor's on his way,' he said to his son. To Synnott he said, 'My lawyer thinks it's best if you wait in your car until—'

Synnott had finished writing. He held out his notebook to the kid. 'You want to sign my note of our conversation?'

The kid looked from Synnott to his father. The man regarded his son with a mixture of surprise and contempt.

'What did I tell you?'

Max Junior looked like he might cry. 'I didn't tell him anything.'

The father turned to Synnott. 'What did he say?'

Synnott ignored him. He took his time writing down the exchange between the father and the son. Then he again pushed his notebook towards the son and said, 'It's normal, in these circumstances, to carefully read and then sign a police officer's notes of remarks made in—'

'He's signing nothing.' The father stood over Synnott. 'I know people, my friend. You screw with my family, you'll be lucky to end up waving your arms at traffic on the Aran Islands.'

The son, his face red from hairline to neck, pushed the notebook away. 'I said nothing.'

'Fair enough.' Synnott wrote some more, then looked at his watch and scribbled the time in his notebook. He stood up.

'And now, sir,' he said to the younger Max, 'I must ask you to come to the station with—'

'Like fuck!' The father's ostentatious charm was in shreds.

Garda Cheney came into the room, carrying a bundled evidence sack. The mother stood beside her, looking from the son to the father.

'What's wrong?' the mother said.

Synnott spoke to the kid. 'Mr Hapgood, I'm arresting you under Section Four of the—'

The father held up his mobile like it was evidence of something. 'My solicitor—'

'Tell him to go directly to Macken Road garda station and ask for Detective Inspector Harry Synnott.'

'You can't question – you have to wait until my solicitor—'

'No, we don't.'

Max Junior looked like he might throw up all over the shiny wooden floor. Harry Synnott told him that he had a right to remain silent.

Garda Cheney had her cuffs out, which was a cue for the mother to unloose a stream of obscenities. The cuffs were necessary. The kid seemed cowed, but he was a big lad and there was no telling what kind of panic-inducing effect the inside of a police car might have on him.

Max Senior was leaning towards Synnott and was speaking fast in a low, angry voice.

'The trouble with people like you – we give you power, and you're supposed to use it to protect decent people. Not to throw your weight around.'

He used his index finger a lot. He had it permanently cocked, and repeatedly used it to emphasise the importance of what he was saying.

'We're the public, smart boy. And you're a public servant.'

Synnott watched the finger jabbing a few inches away from his face and was tempted to take hold of it and give it a twist, just to watch the surprise on Max Senior's face.

'You know there's no case against my son – you *know* that – but you push your way into this house, you drag him away on the word of some little tramp.'

'You're not a robot, are you?' The mother didn't point her finger like her husband did, but her voice was louder. 'Have you *no* human feeling? Max did *nothing*, but mud *sticks* – this kind of thing could—'

In the hall, Rose Cheney draped the kid's blue jacket over the cuffs and when she opened the front door the mother's howling stopped. Synnott reckoned she feared attracting the attention of the neighbours.

Cheney led the kid down the garden path to the car, one hand on his elbow.

*

The one other time she'd been in the Joy, the screw with the bushy eyebrows had told Dixie his name but she couldn't remember it now. 'You OK?' he said. 'Jesus, Dixie, you look bloody awful.'

'You're looking fresh and well yourself.'

'What've you done?'

'Nothing.'

He nodded. She said, 'Any chance of a cup of coffee?'

An hour later he came to see her and said, 'Your blood, was it, Dixie – in the syringe?'

She didn't answer.

'You're not HIV, are you?'

She shook her head.

'That poor woman – she must have got an awful fright.'

Dixie said, 'What woman?'

'The woman you stuck.'

'I stuck no one. Yank bastard knocked it out of my hand.'
'Jesus, Dixie.'

*

First thing Harry Synnott did when he came into the interview room was tell Max Junior to stand up. Max had been sitting on the far side of a scarred metal table that was pushed almost up against one wall, with Rose Cheney facing him. Synnott pulled Max's chair into the centre of the room. He pointed at the chair and Max sat down. Synnott pulled a second chair into the centre of the room and sat down facing Max, a bare two feet away. Tell the subject what to do – doesn't matter what – for Synnott it was a way of emphasising the relationship between himself and the subject.

For a long time he had followed the standard practice of sitting across a table from the subject, but a few years back – the Swanson Avenue killing – he'd decided that there was a benefit in doing away with the table barrier. Subjects had nowhere to rest their arms, nothing stable to hold on to. It made them uneasy and they didn't know why. Getting closer, getting into the subject's personal space, unsettled them further. When Ned Callaghan, the man who had murdered his wife at their home on Swanson Avenue, moved his chair back a few inches, he wasn't even aware that he was displaying anxiety.

Synnott waited a minute or two before he moved his own chair forward towards Max. Trapped in his own unease, the subject makes mistakes.

Away from his parents, Max Hapgood Junior was so easy to open up that he might as well have had a dotted line marked across his forehead.

The dirty beige walls and the worn-out linoleum on the floor, the lack of pictures, calendars or anything else on the walls, the single naked bulb dangling from the centre of the ceiling, all were purposeful elements in creating distraction-free surroundings, to allow suspects to marinate in their own guilt.

Synnott sat silently for over two minutes, reading the notes he'd made at the Hapgood house. Max folded his arms. Synnott found a blank page and clicked his biro.

'Well, Max, you know what happened, and you now know that I know what happened. And we both know you're not a bad person – so what we have to do, we have to work out *why* this happened.'

Max stared.

Synnott said, 'I'd better do this formally – you have a right to remain—'

'You told me all that, I understand all that.'

'It's in your own interest, son. It might be you want to sit there with your mouth shut, leave it up to others to decide what happened. You have a right to do that. I just want to be sure you know.'

'I did nothing to be ashamed of. Whatever that silly bitch is saying – look, bottom line, this is a squabble between me and a bird I shagged. I don't know what it has to do with the police.'

Every few seconds as he spoke, Max's right hand flicked open in a throwaway gesture. Watching it, Synnott could see how a hand that size, backed up by the power of a shoulder to match, could hold down a slender, frightened woman.

'Teresa Hunt has a different view.'

Max made a dismissive noise.

Synnott leaned forward. Rose Cheney could still hear every word, but Synnott's voice was lower and his closeness to Max Junior suggested an intimacy that excluded the female. 'A lad like you, solid background – you don't do what you did unless you've got some kind of justification. I'm finding it hard, Max, to see you as some kind of mindless brute.'

'There was nothing wrong with what I did.' Max's voice, too, was quieter, though loud enough for Cheney to continue taking notes.

'I'm still not clear exactly what you did – from your point of view.'

'I did nothing.'

'When it comes to trial, she'll say different.'

Mention of a trial got Max animated. He cocked an index finger and poked it at Synnott, just like his dad had done. 'Explain this, then. Afterwards, how come she didn't make a fuss? How come she didn't think up an accusation until next morning? How come we chatted, we said goodbye, it was – *how come?*'

Synnott took a moment to nod.

She was scared shitless of you, you thick fuck.

Synnott said, 'That's a fair point, maybe. How do *you* explain it?'

'She wanted it. She got it, but maybe she was expecting more.' Max paused, his voice lowered again, like he was considering letting Synnott in on a secret. 'You know what this is about? It's about my big mouth. You know what I said to her? I said, *Thanks, doll, maybe we can do this again sometime.*' Max folded his arms. 'Maybe it was the way I said it. That's just the way it is – it's the way we talk, me and my friends. Maybe she got the message that it was no big deal to me and maybe it was more of a deal to her – who knows?'

'She said no, though? Before.'

'Bullshit. I told you, she wanted it, same as me, and she can't turn it on and off like a tap, right? Bottom line. There was no doubt in my mind, and there wouldn't have been in yours – she wanted it, and she got what she wanted.'

Harry Synnott could hear the scratching of Rose Cheney's biro. *Game, set, match.*

6

GALWAY

When they got the nutcase down off the roof he sat in the back of the squad car and said nothing all the way to McCreary Street garda station in the centre of Galway City. Garda Joe Mills put him into an interview room, while Declan Dockery did the paperwork and the prisoner sat there in cuffs, licking his lips and looking at the wall.

He wouldn't give his name when Joe Mills asked. He just sat there all afternoon. Wouldn't say where he was from, why he'd been on the roof.

'To tell you the truth,' Joe Mills told him, 'I'm not crazy about pressing assault charges. Not against someone with the kind of troubles that had him standing on the edge of a roof. Know what I mean?'

The nutcase didn't look at Mills. He just continued staring at the bare wall, like he saw something fascinating there. His eyes had lost the icy thing that Joe Mills had seen up on the roof.

'You pack a bit of a punch, though. We're looking at assault, resisting arrest.'

Silence.

'If you were to tell me what had you out there on the roof, maybe we could forget about the rough stuff.'

Nothing.

'My nose is a bit sore, but there's no harm done.'

Nothing.

Don't beat about.

'Where'd you get the blood on your hands?'

The nutcase looked down at his cuffed hands, then he looked up at Joe Mills. Then he shrugged.

'Come on, fella. You know this has to be sorted out, whatever it is.' That was when the shrink arrived, and a sergeant who told Joe Mills that was fine, he'd take over now, go type up a report. Mills was at the door, on his way out of the room, when the prisoner said, 'When it started out, there was no rough stuff. I'd never hurt a woman before.'

Mills turned and the prisoner was looking up at him, his expression uncertain.

The shrink, a slim brunette woman in chinos and a blue cotton shirt, looked like she'd been dragged here on an afternoon off and wasn't pleased about it. She caught Joe Mills's glance and inclined her head towards the door. Mills said, 'Okay, fella, these folks will look after you, right?'

Joe Mills and Declan Dockery spent the rest of their shift typing up reports on what happened on the roof of the pub. Mills added a paragraph on the nutcase's silence since they got him to the station. Then they went for a pint.

DUBLIN

The Hapgood solicitor, Trevor Egan, arrived at Macken Road garda station in the late afternoon. He demanded and received access to his client and when he emerged after twenty minutes he had a narrow smile on his wide face. Standing in the corridor, notebook in hand, Detective Inspector Harry Synnott inspected that face carefully. Plump and smooth and shiny. It went with the suit and the sculpted hair, the thick gold ring, the onyx tiepin and the heavy gold watch. Mr Egan's dark suit minimised his plumpness. He was carrying a black leather briefcase with his initials in gold letters below the combination lock.

How do you get a face to look like that?

The surface of the solicitor's face wasn't just washed, shaved and after-shaved, it seemed to have a veneer, like maybe every day when Mr Egan finished breakfast he took his face to a team of vestal virgins and they spent an hour buffing it with exotic leaves.

'Might I enquire when my client will be free to leave the station?'

Harry Synnott said, 'You can take him with you.'

Egan nodded as though he was pleased that the police had seen what should have been obvious all along. 'You've put the lad through a bit of a grind, Inspector. For no good reason.'

Synnott said, 'We're preparing a file for the DPP. I expect we'll be proffering charges at a later date.'

Egan looked Synnott in the eye for a moment, then deliberately looked away, staring at the wall, his jaw working. Either he was counting to ten or he was trying some intimidatory trick he'd picked up at lawyer school. When he looked at Synnott again his tone had an edge of anger. 'Inspector, come *on*. This is a young man and a young woman – the worst we're talking about is mixed signals. I mean, we've all been there.'

Synnott said, 'You've been there, have you?' He held up his notebook. 'Would you care to give me names and approximate dates and details of the occasions on which you held women down and forced yourself upon them?'

'Come on, Inspector, it's her word against his.' Egan made a snorting noise. 'If this ever went to court it'd be on the one hand, and on the other. And that, if I can be technical about it, is the definition of reasonable doubt.'

The solicitor stopped for a moment. When he spoke again, his voice had softened. 'Why put two people – and I'm sure that this young lady is quite sincere but the chances are that she's already having second thoughts – why put two people through such an ordeal?'

'Your client has a case to answer.'

'You know this isn't going anywhere.' Egan's voice took on an edge. 'Max's father is a man of substance – the firm of Hapgood & Creasy has done PR for some of the most important—'

Synnott said, 'I'll have someone get your client.' He turned and walked down the corridor to the public office.

The temptation was to argue with the lawyer, to wipe some of the gloss off his silly face. But Synnott considered Max's solicitor a poor opponent for such an exercise. When it came to commercial contracts Egan could no doubt spot a loophole at sixty paces. This was a criminal case, though, in which a slip of a girl would get up in front of a jury and tell one story and a brute in a suit would tell another. And what the jury would be looking for would be the bits and bobs of evidence that could tilt the scales one way or the other.

Synnott patted the pocket into which he'd slipped his notebook.

Actus reus. Mens rea.

*

Dixie Peyton woke, still smiling, sat up and Owen was gone. It was dark, but she hadn't dozed for long and the noises beyond her cell told her that the prison hadn't yet settled down for the night.

For a while, hardly a night had gone by that she hadn't dreamed of Owen, but that was in the first year after he'd died. These days, it happened now and then and it upset her and she welcomed the upset. If a dream was all she could have of Owen she didn't mind paying a price in wretchedness when she woke.

Stupid.

Ending up here.

Especially now.

'Christ, Dixie.'

Around teatime, the screw with the bushy eyebrows had tried for a heart-to-heart. 'Bit desperate, love, waving a needle around. Not like you.' His voice had sounded like it mattered to him. 'You on that dirty stuff now?'

'Not now.'

Dixie had asked him to ring Turner's Lane and ask for Inspector Harry Synnott. He had and he'd come back and told her that they'd said there was no Inspector Synnott there.

'Christ's sake,' Dixie had said. She had Synnott's card, with his mobile number, somewhere at home. If she got bail.

No chance.

Stupid thing to do.

Stupid.

Especially now.

Stupid thing to do.

What else was there to do?

Stupid.

She flinched from a thought, then relented, let it well up.

In the beginning, thinking about Owen had been too painful but she hadn't been able to help it. Then it became easier until she could remember him without the grief washing everything good out of the memory. Now, especially when things were as shitty as they'd become, it was where Dixie sought comfort. The last few days, she'd thought about him when she woke and when she tried to sleep, and in between she'd eased her stress sometimes by talking to him. Mostly she chose from an assortment of well-worn recollections, things that were nothing much until they turned into precious scraps when there was little else. She had four years of fragments from that life, from the evening they'd met to the morning she'd learned he was dead, and she had by now organised them in her head so that she could go to one bundle of remembrance or another as the mood took her. Anything that wasn't a comfort she could keep at bay.

Except for that night, Owen's last night. That night came at her sometimes when she wasn't careful and mostly she couldn't push it away.

She tried to put herself there beside him in the ditch, wondering if he managed to get past the pain and the fear, to find any kind of comfort in her and in Christopher, the son she'd been carrying when he died.

*

When he got home to his flat on the North Quays, Harry Synnott stood at the kitchen counter and flicked through his post. He threw away the garish advert for the German supermarket and the leaflet that insisted he wouldn't believe the difference that broadband would make to his life. He read the itemised bill for his mobile phone and then the leaflet that came with it. It boasted about the recent upgrade of transmission facilities. It told him how he should register to receive text messages of future improvements to the service. He stood for a moment and wondered who would have such an empty life that they'd sign up to receive such urgent news.

He read the invoice for his cable-TV service and the final demand that he pay his waste charges, then he wrote cheques for both and left them in envelopes on the table near the door. His mobile made the melodic sound that indicated the arrival of a text message. He opened the text.

Lunch tomorrow? 1.30? Colin.

After a moment, Synnott thumbed a reply – *OK* – and sent it back to Assistant Commissioner Colin O'Keefe.

It's on, then. Or it's not, and he wants to break it gently.

A classical singer, one of the fat guys who used to sing at the World Cup, was warbling in the flat below Synnott's. The woman who lived there didn't seem to have any other music and she played it every evening and sometimes joined in. Synnott had come to like the sound. He'd never particularly liked the fat guy's singing, and the woman's voice was no great shakes, but the combination had something about it. Synnott had never seen the woman and imagined her as a thirty-something, probably a civil servant. There were a few of them in this apartment block, or at least that was what they looked like on the rare occasions when he saw any of them. A couple of weeks back the woman had gone on a singing bender, the whole evening, her voice ripping through walls, soaring along with Luciano or Domingo or whoever it was as though she'd lost all inhibition. She hadn't done that before or since, and Synnott wondered if something had happened to cause the eruption. Maybe it had been her birthday.

In the six years since his divorce, Synnott had lived in three different rented flats, moving on for no reason other than boredom. Over the fifteen years of his marriage, he'd never warmed to the family house in Clonsilla. He remembered standing in the back garden one day, looking at the trellis he'd fixed to the wall, a profusion of green woven through it, thinking about the hours he spent on that and similar jobs. He remembered a broken strut on the trellis and how he repaired it with electrician's tape and Helen said no, that wouldn't do, they'd have to take it down and—

Staring at the trellis, Synnott concluded that it was the most idiotic, pointless contraption he'd ever seen.

What the hell is that about?

How do you end up doing so many things you don't care about, just because they're the things you're supposed to do?

Stuff like that had gradually transformed the house into the kind of place that Helen's magazines ordained a married couple ought to live in. That Sunday afternoon, under a blazing sun, he and Helen erupted into a screaming match over the broken strut on the stupid fucking trellis. It was around then that Synnott began seeing his marriage as something that he'd got into because it had seemed the orderly thing to do. It was what people did to make sense of their lives, and Helen had been the prettiest, brightest, bubbliest woman he knew. And when he began thinking that way, a whole section of his life – Helen and

Michael too – began to seem as pointless as a tacky trellis on a garden wall.

Now it seemed to him that a small central flat, easy to keep tidy, was the kind of place a single man in his forties needed to create a sense of order. No room for clutter. In his kitchen, without moving more than three feet, he could reach the fridge to get three eggs, the beaker to break them into, the fork to mix them with, the pan to cook them on, then the fridge again for some cooked ham to toss into the pan at the last moment. He opened the vegetable drawer. The two remaining tomatoes had gone off.

He made toast and sat in front of the television and flicked from channel to channel as he ate. He found an American sitcom, something about a man and a woman who shared a flat. He'd seen it before but he'd forgotten what it was about. The man was gay, maybe, or he and the woman had been lovers in the past and now they had to share the flat for some reason or other. The audience laughed every five seconds or so. After a while Synnott realised that the reason he was frowning at the screen wasn't just that he didn't think it was funny but that he didn't see how anyone could think it was. He reached for the remote and found BBC's *Newsnight*. It was doing something on a sudden renewal of an old conflict between two factions in some Middle Eastern country. Synnott watched for a minute or two before he decided he didn't need to have an opinion on whatever the trouble was. He found a channel with a soccer match. He didn't recognise any of the players. They were Italian teams and he knew nothing about them. He watched for a while and found himself willing on the side in yellow.

Synnott felt his head twitch and his eyes opened and he realised he had dozed off for a moment. He knew that if he continued sitting there he'd fall asleep and wake in the middle of the night with the television on and an ache in his neck. The plate with the remnants of the scrambled egg was on the floor at his feet. The morning would be time enough to deal with that. He reached again for the remote and a minute later he was undressing in his bedroom.

*

Dixie said to him, 'It's a dream, Owen. I know it's a dream.' He had Christopher sitting on his knee, bouncing him gently, and Christopher was giggling.

Owen held the son he'd never seen, smiling, shaking his head. 'Nothing to worry about, love, I know people.'

Dixie lay there for a while, staring at the ceiling of the cell, unsure if she was awake or asleep.

Going to be a long night.

She got out of bed and sat at the metal table, rubbing her upper arms for warmth. The only light came from a lamp that was out beyond the window high up on the cell wall. She wrapped her arms around herself and lowered her head until her forehead was touching the table and the chill of the cold surface seeped through, freezing her thoughts.

THURSDAY

7

Joshua Boyce was still fifty feet away when he heard the pounding music coming from his car. One of the stations where the style was rap and the morning DJ's chatter was peppered with *Yo! Bro!* and *Ma Maaan!* in an accent that swung wildly between Los Angeles and Mount Merrion.

The car was parked in the street next to his daughter's school and Joshua had just taken eight-year-old Ciara as far as the school's inner gate. His son, recently turned eighteen, was taking a lift with Boyce into town, where he worked as a trainee chef in an Italian restaurant.

Slumped in the front passenger seat, Peter had the window rolled down and was holding a cigarette between middle and ring finger. Joshua thought he probably got that from watching some MTV pimp showing the cameras around his crib.

Jesus. When I was that age, was I half as bloody obnoxious?

Joshua got behind the wheel and turned off the radio. He sat there a moment. Then he said, 'Come on.' He waited, staring ahead while Peter took a long drag from the cigarette. Peter pulled out the ashtray and made a big deal of tapping the butt. When he'd finished he folded his arms and looked out the side window, as though he could see something terribly interesting somewhere in the distance. A thread of smoke danced up from the crushed butt. As he moved the car away from the kerb, Joshua let the window down and threw the butt away.

He dropped Peter near the Custom House. The boy got out of the car and walked away without a word. Joshua continued on across the river and parked on the third floor of the Stephen's Green Centre and walked down two floors. He went into TK Maxx, walked about fifty feet into the shop, then turned back. There was no one of the right type between him and the entrance, so the odds were that no one had followed him in. He went up one floor on the escalator, switched to the descending elevator and went down to the ground floor. Everything still seemed OK. He went out a side door, then hurried around to the top of Grafton Street, crossed the road and got a taxi.

GALWAY

The manager came into the public office of McCreary Street garda station and said he wanted to speak to one of the policemen who'd got the nutcase down off the roof of his pub yesterday.

'We found a wallet,' he said, when Joe Mills arrived down.

'Congratulations,' Mills said.

'In the jacks, when we were cleaning out this morning.'

'And?'

The manager held up a black leather wallet and opened it. There was a yellow identity card tucked into one side. Staring out through the clear plastic was the dour and unsmiling face of the nutcase.

The manager said, 'It says his name is Wayne Kemp.'

DUBLIN

Each morning the routine was the same. The jeweller arrived at a minute or two to 10 a.m. and opened up. Each morning his assistant was waiting for him, leaning against the shuttered shopfront. The assistant, a young guy with silly hair, arrived by bus. The jeweller arrived on foot from the coffee shop a few doors down. He always carried his briefcase and a folded newspaper. Within a minute or two past ten, the lights went on, the steel shutters went up. Business was slow between ten o'clock and noon and somewhat better between noon and one o'clock. Joshua Boyce watched the shop just between the hours of ten and one. He didn't care what happened after that.

In the four weeks he'd been keeping watch no customer arrived before ten-fifteen, and on all but two occasions none before ten-thirty-five.

In the long-gone days when Kellsboro had been a centre of commercial and social activity for residents of the surrounding estates, there'd been two cinemas, three cafés and four excellent pubs. Now, with people travelling into Dublin city centre or out to the shopping malls, Kellsboro had the air of a run-down village. The stretch of shops on the south end of the main Kellsboro road was dilapidated, four of the fifteen shops gone out of business, their boarded-up fronts plastered with posters. Further down the street a row of buildings was scheduled for demolition, to be replaced by dog-box apartments with a Spar supermarket on the ground floor.

Joshua Boyce sat behind the net-curtained window of a flat diagonally across the road from the jeweller's shop, which he'd rented from an agency three months earlier. The flat had worn carpets and cheap furniture; nothing in it belonged to Boyce. The monthly rent was paid up front through a standing order from a false-name account. When the most recent payment had gone through, six days earlier, Boyce had closed the account. After the robbery, the police might or might not check out the buildings overlooking the shop, but Boyce always wore gloves when he came here, so it wouldn't matter.

He had a foolscap pad on his knee. There wasn't much to take note of, but he had a four-week daily record of anything that mattered. Timetables of openings, regular deliveries, rubbish-bin pick-up, daily post. Eleven-fifteen, every day, the jeweller's assistant fetched a take-out from the nearby coffee shop. The jeweller's shop was less than a mile from Macken Road garda station, but the only police activity around the area consisted of a couple of beat coppers plodding past the row of shops, never before noon and never after twenty past twelve.

Twice a week, Wednesdays and Fridays, always around eleven-forty, a Brinks van collected money from a building-society branch office two doors down from the jewellery shop. A gobshite in a security guard's uniform stood at the door of the building society. Young man, lanky, with a big chin and a shaven head. He was already there each day when Boyce arrived and he was there when Boyce left. His job seemed to be to stand in the doorway all day, occasionally scratching his arse but mostly just looking bored. Bugger-all use to anyone if there was a serious attempt at robbery, but his presence would keep the insurance people happy.

After four weeks watching the jewellery shop, Boyce planned to take it shortly after it opened the next day. He'd leave the stolen getaway car in the small car park off to the side of a twenty-four-hour shop about a hundred yards up the street. He reckoned he'd have fifteen minutes to do the job safely without interference.

There couldn't be a guarantee, but Boyce had put enough work into the job to give him a very good chance of getting in and out without any trouble, and to finish up with enough jewellery to choke a whale.

Boyce checked his watch. It was pushing noon. Another hour, and that was that. Seeing as this was his last day watching the shop, and as the robbery would be long over well before noon, there was really nothing to be gained by staying until one o'clock. But Joshua Boyce liked to do things right. He watched a pair of cops walk past at ten minutes past noon, and he waited another fifty minutes. Then he had one last look around the flat, made sure that he was leaving nothing behind, and left it for the last time.

He walked for ten minutes, then got a taxi across the city to the Northside. He bought a sandwich in a deli near the small garage he owned. He spent a while at the garage, chatting with the two mechanics he employed. Between the three of them, they made a good living and the garage also served as a cover for the kind of work from which Boyce couldn't declare an income.

He left the garage at two-twenty-five and after a short walk he was standing outside the school in plenty of time to collect Ciara.

8

It was called preparing a file for the Director of Public Prosecutions. Harry Synnott had been working on the task for a couple of hours since lunchtime. At first the work involved nothing more than scribbling on a notepad, occasionally scratching out a thought, adding to the list or subtracting. He read his own notes three times, and he read the statement that Rose Cheney had already typed up from her notes.

The file would have to convince a lawyer from the DPP's office that Max Hapgood Junior had raped Teresa Hunt. Then it had to convince the lawyer that the evidence was strong enough to persuade a jury of Max's peers to send him to jail for it.

Synnott began typing his own statement, using just the index finger of each hand. The fact that this was slow had never bothered him. He could type as fast as he could think of what he needed to write. It would take him a couple of days' writing and revising to get his own statement right.

The DPP's office wasn't into idealism. It was no use knowing that someone did something. Prosecute everyone who the police believed had committed a crime and the courts would seize up within a month. Worse than that, the state would look inept when juries threw out cases they couldn't be sure of, or when judges kicked out evidence without which the case was threadbare.

There would be no case against Max Hapgood Jr without the

victim's own statement and the remarks that Synnott had winkled out of the young man. But the element that would make the file a runner would have to be Synnott's own account of his inquiries.

Nail down the *actus reus*, the performance of the criminal act, then stitch in the *mens rea*, showing that the accused was aware the act was wrong.

Synnott was six paragraphs into the statement when he got a phone call. He glanced at the caller ID and recognised the number of his old station, Turner's Lane. The voice was young and female and unfamiliar. She wouldn't give her name. 'This may be none of my business, but I think you should know.' Synnott waited. 'There's a woman who's been trying to get in touch, needs to speak to you. Dixie Peyton? She's in Mountjoy.'

*

They brought Dixie Peyton to a small room in Mountjoy's administration block to meet Harry Synnott. She looked like she hadn't seen sunshine for a few months, and if she'd tried sleeping recently it hadn't taken. No make-up, her eyes sunken, her cheeks thin. She moved to the front of the desk across from Synnott and let the chair catch her as she slumped.

'I've been calling you for two days.'

'I transferred out of Turner's Lane. Just heard an hour ago that you were looking for me.'

She examined him like she knew he was lying,. Then she looked down at the desk.

'Can you get me out of here?'

There were lines around her eyes that Harry Synnott didn't remember being there.

'Come on, Dixie, this is not shoplifting. A syringe full of blood, for Christ's sake.'

'Whatever it takes, I have to get out. Christopher. My kid.'

'The procedure—'

'I can give you something.'

'Not for this, Dixie. Needles and blood, that's serious stuff.'

'It wasn't blood, it was ketchup.'

'It was a needle. They tell me you scared the shit out of a couple of tourists. You know what that's like.'

Mug a tourist and if you came up in front of the wrong judge you'd get a far longer sentence that you'd get for the same crime against a native. Judicial sentencing policy wasn't supposed to give priority to protecting the tourist industry, but some judges didn't see it that way.

Synnott shrugged. 'Besides, what could you possibly trade – something this heavy – I'm sorry, love, I'd like to help you.'

He was already leaning back in his chair, the first move towards levering himself to his feet, knowing that the gesture would unsettle her enough to speed things up.

'I want money, too.' The pitch of her voice was higher.

Synnott smiled. 'And a cherry on top. Come on, love, you're not exactly dealing from a position of strength.'

'I want five hundred.'

Synnott put his hands flat on the table. In the years he'd known Dixie Peyton, she'd given him four good tips that had led to arrests and convictions, another half-dozen that helped foul up criminal projects and a dozen scraps that hadn't taken him very far. Some informants were one-offs, the product of an arrest and panic, ready to sell whatever and whoever they could in the hope that it would ease the weight coming down on them. Others, like Dixie Peyton, were there or thereabouts among the grifters and the shifters, not close enough to the action to produce the inside dope but picking up enough to give a friendly garda the occasional steer towards a worthwhile arrest.

'You want a dig-out on this needle thing, and you want five hundred?'

'It's good.'

'You know where they buried Shergar, then?' Pushing away

from the table, Synnott stood up. It was probably bullshit, but he'd listen to it. Making like he was about to walk away was part of the expected dance.

'Five hundred.'

'If there's any message you want me to pass to anyone outside, maybe something you want sent in—'

'I'll do whatever they want, for the thing with the needle, I'll plead guilty, whatever they say. But right now I need to be out. My kid—'

Dixie looked up at Synnott and stopped, as if suddenly aware that he wasn't interested in her problems.

Synnott had one hand on his hip, the fingers of the other hand splayed on the table. Standing there looking down at Dixie like he was working something out in his head. Finally, as if he'd totted everything up and the answer came out just about right, he rapped his knuckles on the table and sat down.

'Tell me.'

'Do you promise?'

'Scratch my back.'

She told him about the warehouse on the Moyfield Industrial Estate, how it had been motoring away for six or eight months, producing bootleg DVDs. It had everything – the machines for churning out the discs and the printers for the labels and inserts. 'All top-quality. They bring it over from the States months before the movies are released here. They can charge top rates for that kind of stuff.'

'Who?'

'Do I get what I want?'

'Who's running it?'

It was one thing to get fifth-rate copies of movies shot on a Handycam by someone sitting in the stalls of a New York movie house. Making duplicates from a genuine advance copy of the movie needed good criminal contacts in the States. That, and manufacturing good-quality copies, took an investment way beyond the means of the usual quick-buck artists selling dodgy DVDs for a fiver at car-boot sales.

'Lar Mackendrick.'

Thought so.

'I'll tell you exactly where it is, but they're moving out – they've got a new place set up down the country, miles from anywhere. If you want this you'll have to hurry.'

'How do you know this?'

'It – I can't say where I got it, but I swear it's good.'

Synnott said, 'Three hundred.'

9

GALWAY

The yellow identity card said that the nutcase was named Wayne Kemp and he worked for Paladin Security Solutions, a Dublin firm. It took Garda Joe Mills five minutes to get the number of the company and discover that Kemp was currently on a week's holiday. It took him another fifteen minutes to coax an executive in the security company to fax him a page from Wayne Kemp's personnel file. There was little in that except the standard details of DOB, address and phone number. A start date told Mills that Kemp had worked for the company for six years. In a box at the bottom there was a handwritten note stating that Kemp had served two years in the army, then spent several years working in Britain before he had returned to Dublin. Mills rang back the executive and found out that the firm paid Kemp's wages into a Bank of Ireland account in Ranelagh.

The bank would tell him nothing on the phone, so Mills rang Ranelagh garda station and they sent someone around to the bank and an hour later he knew that Kemp had had an account there for six years. It was a standard account that never went too much into the red, and never accumulated more than a few hundred. He had only once taken a loan, five grand, which he'd paid back scrupulously. The guarantor was his older sister, Mina Moylan, who was married and had an address in Bushy Park, Galway.

I'd never hurt a woman before.

On the way out to Bushy Park, Declan Dockery said, 'I have a bad feeling about this.'

No shit, Sherlock.

Joe Mills was driving. The neighbourhood had a fine view of Galway city but Mills wasn't in a humour to be impressed by the scenery. It could be that the sister had information that might lead them to wherever the blood had been spilled. Or—

I'd never hurt a woman before.

The Moylan house was in a cul-de-sac. Like most of its neighbours, it had a well-tended garden behind high hedges that maintained privacy. A three-year-old Isuzu Trooper was parked in the driveway.

'Not short of the odd penny,' Dockery said.

Joe Mills was reaching to press the bell when he saw the blood on the round brass handle in the centre of the door.

'Declan.'

The blood had dried to the same brownish colour as that on Wayne Kemp's hands.

Dockery winced. 'Told you I had a bad feeling.'

Joe Mills used a knuckle to push against the door but it was closed. Instead of pressing the bell, he used his baton to rap hard three times on the door. He waited a minute, then did it again. Nothing.

'We should call it in,' Dockery said. 'Preserve the scene.'

Joe Mills shook his head. 'There could be someone in there needs help.' While Dockery spoke into his radio, Joe Mills used his baton to lightly tap the glass in the door, near the lock. Then he swung it sharply and the glass shattered.

They found a dead man lying on his back in the hallway, his blue shirt pushed upwards, baring his chest, his arms spread wide, his eyes and mouth agape. His torso looked like it had been opened by several strokes of a blunt axe.

I'd never hurt a woman before.

Joe Mills took a deep breath. He wasn't looking forward to the next few minutes.

Declan Dockery's voice quivered slightly as he got on the radio again and called in the murder. Joe Mills looked into the living room, then the kitchen, then he went upstairs and checked out the four bedrooms. All neat and shipshape upstairs and down. Imaginatively decorated, good-quality carpets, solid furniture. When he opened the bathroom door he immediately smelled the blood. Even with the door half open, Mills could see there were splashes of red everywhere. On the white-tiled walls and the white rug, on the ceiling, on the pebbled-glass window, on the toilet and the washbasin, on the mirror – even on the narrow porcelain frame around the mirror – there were red streaks. Several of the bottles of shampoo and skin cream on the three glass shelves above the washbasin were splashed with blood. Mills opened the door wide. He didn't go inside. He saw blood on the floor. He noticed a bloody shoe-print. Looking around the door he saw that blood had pooled in the bath around the body it had come from.

The corpse was small, slender, face up, dressed in black shorts and a white shirt. The shirt was open and the torso had been repeatedly slashed. The pale face was serene, streaked with blood, the eyes wide open. It was the face of a teenage boy.

I'd never hurt a woman before.

Joe Mills called down the stairs, 'Second body. Another male.' He moved more quickly now, retracing his steps and opening every bedroom closet and finding just clothes and shoes and shelves with neat boxes. Then he went downstairs, where Declan Dockery was standing pale-faced in the hall and looked inside the ground-floor bathroom. Nothing. He pulled back the shower curtain and saw a long wide-bladed knife lying in the shower tray, the blade blood-streaked, a single large bloody handprint on the pink-tiled wall.

Mills found the back door unlocked and went out into the

garden. It was about fifty feet long, bounded by a wooden fence. There were garden chairs and a table to one side, a shed to the other, no sign of anyone. He broke open the padlock and hasp on the wooden garden shed. There were only garden tools and old tins of paint inside.

There was no woman – alive, dead, injured or otherwise – in the Moylan house.

10

DUBLIN

Detective Inspector Harry Synnott had already driven through the gateway of Garda headquarters in the Phoenix Park, shown his ID, and was past the security barrier before he realised that he'd ignored the monument. There'd been a time when he couldn't come through those gates without looking to the right and paying a silent tribute to what it represented – the forty-three gardai killed on duty since the foundation of the state. Since the murder of Garda Maura Sheelin he had self-consciously tried to resist taking the monument, and what it represented, for granted. Back in Templemore he'd learned the stories behind the Roll of Honour but it was dry stuff, names and dates from the history books. Not half as interesting as learning how to take a watertight statement or how to make a suspect come quietly. After Garda Maura Sheelin's murder, Harry Synnott had seen the Roll of Honour as an emblem of something that had to matter deeply to any serious police officer. He believed it was that murder, and his part in what followed, that had shaped his life over the past two decades.

Sheelin's murder was part of the third wave of police killings. The first wave was in the 1920s, when the Garda Siochana was in its infancy. The war of independence and the civil war had left a lot of guns around, and almost as many old scores to settle. One poor bastard in an ill-fitting uniform was shot dead because he'd been too energetic in his pursuit of *poitin*-makers. The second wave of killings was short-lived, a product of the unrest during the Second World War, as the IRA realised that their old buddy Eamon de Valera was well settled into power and was more likely to hang them than to nod and wink at their capers. The third wave came with the resurgence of the IRA after 1970. In 1987, Garda Maura Sheelin walked into a bank during a Provo hold-up. She was in civvies, looking to cash a cheque before heading off for an afternoon's shopping with her sister. It was a time when Mickey Mouse bank security dovetailed with the needs of paramilitaries eager to top up their coffers.

The two bank robbers came running out, hauling holdalls stuffed with cash and waving revolvers. Maura Sheelin could have stood aside, played civilian, she could have waited and called it in, given a description. Instead, she stood firm in the doorway, shouted 'Garda Siochana!' and grabbed hold of the first robber. He shrugged her off, slamming her against the porch wall, leaving her winded, her right hand grasping at the second robber, who shot her as he ran past. She lasted five hours in hospital, doctors patching up her insides and the subsequent complications tearing her apart all over again.

Harry Synnott knew her slightly, her fiancé having been in Synnott's class at Templemore. The Maura Sheelin murder turned out to be the case that put Synnott's foot on the first rung of the promotion ladder, pleasing some within the force and pissing off a whole lot more.

'It's not that time?'

Colin O'Keefe was one of the few who had applauded Harry Synnott's performance in the Sheelin murder case. Now he was standing by the open boot of his car, his arms full of R-Kive boxes, watching Synnott approach.

'One-thirty,' Synnott said.

'Look, let me dump this lot, wash my hands. Meet you in my office in half an hour?'

Harry Synnott nodded. Another cheapskate lunch.

Detective Inspector John Grace was in the copy room, off a corridor between reception and the Commissioner's office, when he heard, 'So, this is what they have you doing?'

He turned and saw Harry Synnott with a big smile on his face.

'Don't tell me they're letting the likes of you into the inner sanctum?'

'Another working lunch with O'Keefe.'

'Hope you're not hungry.'

They shook hands and Synnott said, 'You're finishing up this week?'

'Tomorrow, lunchtime. You'll be at the retirement party do? Sunday evening, The Majestyk?'

Synnott grimaced. 'Turner's Lane – it's not a month since I transferred out of there. I don't think it's best.'

'That old shite. Forget it.'

The two had worked on several cases together over the years, a couple of big ones but mostly routine. Grace, six years older than Synnott and now on the point of retirement, looked more tired than his age warranted.

Grace said, 'You see much of Helen these days?'

'We talk on the phone. It's OK.'

'Michael?'

'He's thinking of dropping out of college. Figures it's a waste of time getting an education when there's money to be made.'

'What's he want to do?'

'The detail changes from week to week, but he reckons he's a born entrepreneur.'

Grace grinned. 'You hear a lot of that these days. They say *I'm an entrepreneur* like it's a trade – like someone might say they're a nurse or a mechanic.'

Although both men got on well enough, it was the Swanson Avenue murder case – four years earlier – that had bonded something like a friendship. Synnott had been a detective sergeant then, just arrived at Turner's Lane, Grace had been one of the station's senior detectives. Although there had been little contact since that case, the bond remained.

Harry Synnott gestured. 'This place, it didn't work out? So dull that you prefer retirement?'

Harry Synnott had last seen John Grace almost eighteen months earlier, two and a half years after the Swanson Avenue case, at the funeral of a colleague murdered during a kidnap. Severely affected by the killing, Grace went on sick leave from Turner's Lane and never came back. The administrative work at the Phoenix Park HQ was a last resort, after drifting through several assignments.

Grace smiled. 'Dull is one word for it. Traffic, sports events, immigration. Mostly admin. I went out on two immigration raids, then I couldn't do it any more. The second one, kicking out a planeload of Nigerians who'd overstayed their welcome. You ever involved in that kind of thing?'

'Not yet. It's a thriving business.'

'This country, everyone used to have a relation who worked himself to a stump on a British building site. Poor lonely bastards, sending home the money that made the difference, drinking the rest.' He shrugged. 'You'd think—'

Harry Synnott decided to keep his mouth shut. There's a reason for the law being the way it is. Send out the wrong message, you lose control – floodgates and open doors.

'Anyway, since then I've been shifting pieces of paper from one desk to another. By and by, it gets like you're doing things out of habit. So—'

'Perhaps it's for the best.'

'O'Keefe was good to me. I didn't have to explain, he arranged the paperwork, it's all painless.'

Synnott said, 'Why don't you come around to my place, Saturday night? I'll cook something, we'll open a bottle in honour of the next twenty years.'

Grace laughed. 'If I want chicken nuggets I'll go to McDonald's. Come out to Sutton. Mona's got tickets for some musical thing, herself and her sister. I'll order in, you bring the bottle.'

'You're on.'

On their way back down the corridor, John Grace said, 'What I'm hearing, O'Keefe has offered you something?'

'There's nothing solid, but he's been sussing things out. Something very different, he said. And Christ knows I could do with a change.'

Grace raised an eyebrow. 'We could be celebrating, come Saturday evening?'

'It's possible.'

'It's long overdue.'

Assistant Commissioner Colin O'Keefe didn't seem to be aware that he'd lost a crumb of chicken from his sandwich and that it had found refuge half an inch above his left jawline.

Harry Synnott, sitting on the other side of O'Keefe's desk, chewing on his own chicken sandwich, made a gesture towards his own face and O'Keefe flicked the offending particle away.

'It's more than a maybe,' O'Keefe said. 'If you decide you want it, the position's there for the taking.'

The 'position' had yet to be fully explained to Synnott, but the very real prospect that he might soon be stepping away from the mess of his garda career had lit a small, hopeful light somewhere inside him.

All he knew about the job on offer came from a similar lunch appointment with O'Keefe two weeks earlier, a lunch of ham sandwiches from the canteen, eaten at the assistant commissioner's desk.

'The Minister makes the final decision,' O'Keefe had told him, 'but I'm headhunting and all I need to know is if you're in the market?'

'For what?'

'Can't say. But it's not a small move, and it's very different. No point going any further if you're happy as you are.'

Happy as I am.

Now O'Keefe looked at him from across his desk and said, 'To be honest, Harry – I think you'd be mad to say no, but I know how much it means to you, being at the coalface.'

A desk job, then.

Or continue as I am – wondering how long it'll be before there's another stretch of turbulence and everyone decides it's best if I move on again.

Synnott tried not to let the disappointment show on his face.

Happy as I am.

Two days after the funeral of Garda Maura Sheelin, Garda Harry Synnott, aged twenty-three, was on duty at Cheeverstown garda station. What happened that day would define Synnott as a policeman and shape his career over the next two decades.

He was fifty minutes into his shift when he was ordered, along with another garda, to take a prisoner from the cells and bring him to Interview Room 3, where two detectives would question him. The station had been buzzing since the prisoner, Conal Crotty, had been brought in that morning.

'He's one of them.'

They hadn't got their hands on the other bank robber – he was said to have left the country – but this little shit was the one who'd pulled the trigger. The intelligence lads had thrown their weight around, squeezed their Provo touts, and come up with Crotty. He was pulled in under Section 30 of the Offences Against the State Act, so they had him for twenty-four hours, and they could renew the detention for another twenty-four. During that time, with no lawyer to get in the way, teams of detectives could take turns breaking down his denials.

The prisoner was a weedy little shit, with a sparse moustache and thinning hair. Little beads of sweat stood out across his face. He was wearing a red sweatshirt and black jeans. Harry Synnott was told to stay and guard the prisoner. The second uniformed garda left the room.

'I've done nothing.'

There was a tremor in Crotty's voice. Synnott didn't answer.

After a few minutes, two detectives arrived, neither of them from the Cheeverstown station. Detective Sergeant Joyce and Detective Garda Buckley.

'Hello, Conal.'

Buckley stood in front of the prisoner, looking down at him. When the silence got to him, Crotty pushed back his chair and stood up. The defiance in his face was struggling to control his fear.

With one hand, Buckley took hold of the front of the Provo's red sweatshirt and with the other he slapped his cheek. The prisoner made a noise that might have been an obscenity and Buckley backhanded him, then slapped him again, twice, three times around the ears, the man shouting, 'Hey! *Hey!*' and trying to back away.

Buckley twisted the Provo's sweatshirt around his hand, pulled him forward and spat in his face.

Sergeant Joyce grabbed Buckley by the shoulder. 'Hey, wait now,' he said. 'Hold on a minute.'

Buckley turned and looked at Sergeant Joyce, then looked back at the Provo and made a disgusted noise. He let go of the sweatshirt and stood back.

The Provo, spittle on his cheek, scowled at Joyce and said, 'Yeah.'

Crotty's face was reddened where he'd been slapped. He used the sleeve of his sweatshirt to wipe his lips. 'Good cop, bad cop, right?'

Sergeant Joyce straightened the man's sweatshirt. 'Something like that,' he said. Then he gestured towards Buckley and said, 'He's the good cop' as he punched the Provo very hard in the stomach.

The Provo yelled and bent sharply and Sergeant Joyce grabbed his hair, forced his head down and at the same time drove his knee into the side of the Provo's face. The prisoner gave a muffled scream as he lost his balance and went down on his back. Joyce stood over him. He lifted his right foot and stamped on the Provo's chest and stomach, again and again. Then he kicked him in the side as he rolled over, howling.

Leaning across Sergeant Joyce, Detective Buckley bent forward and aimed a punch at the suspect's face. Unbalanced, as Joyce jostled him, Buckley's punch missed. Joyce lashed out and kicked the prone man twice in the back.

Harry Synnott ran from the room, hurried down the corridor and up the stairs to the station superintendent's office. He opened the door to the outer office, found the superintendent talking to a secretary and blurted out, 'The prisoner, sir – they're beating him up, they're out of control!'

The superintendent looked at Synnott. He made a soothing gesture.

'Calm down, garda. Take it easy.'

'No, sir, it's—'

The superintendent's tone was even, a slight flush to his cheeks. He said, 'Return to your duty, garda.' He held Synnott's stare. 'You have a job to do. Pull yourself together and do it.'

Synnott was panting. He took a breath and said. 'Sir, I don't think—' but he was speaking to the superintendent's back. His superior slammed the inner-office door behind him.

The secretary didn't look at Synnott. He was very carefully inserting a yellow form into his typewriter, twisting the roller slowly, adjusting the paper so that it was perfectly square.

Synnott left the office and stood in the corridor. He leaned back until his shoulders were touching the wall. Then he lowered his arms, palms flat against the wall, aware that his hands were trembling.

If Harry Synnott felt anything for the Provo prisoner it was loathing. Unless garda intelligence was way off target, this was the piece of shit who'd put a bullet in Maura Sheelin. Synnott had been at the funeral, he'd watched the parents, pale and wide-eyed, Maura's three younger brothers and the teenage sister who adored her, all of them trying to hold themselves together and failing.

It wasn't the prisoner's welfare that mattered to Harry Synnott. It was secondary that Synnott himself might get into trouble if it came out that he'd stood by and watched a prisoner being beaten. What was working away inside his gut was the blatant use of naked violence, the contempt not just for the prisoner but for Harry Synnott and anyone else in the station who might see or hear what was going on. It was the assumption that membership of the force automatically tied him into that shameless wielding of unbounded power.

He knew that running to the superintendent had already marked him as a weakling. *You're one of us or you're not.*

Harry Synnott went back downstairs.

In the canteen, Synnott found three uniformed gardai around a table near the window. He sat down and told them what he'd seen.

'Fucker deserves whatever he gets.'

'That's not what worries—'

'These are the boys from downtown, right? Buckley and Joyce. Later, when they get tired, some of their mates will be up to keep that bastard company. In the meantime, they'll do what they're good at and when it's all done and dusted another piece of Provo shit will be locked up for the rest of his natural. What's the problem?'

Synnott stood and left the canteen.

In the corridor, Buckley was headed towards the canteen, lighting a cigarette. He passed Harry Synnott and didn't acknowledge him by word or glance. He seemed not to see him.

In the interview room, the prisoner was crouched by the far wall, wiping his face with a towel. Sergeant Joyce was standing near the table. Joyce turned to Harry Synnott.

'About time. Keep an eye on this bastard. He's got twenty minutes to decide how he wants to play this.' To the prisoner he said, 'That's for openers. And we've got another twenty-two hours before we have to renew the detention. And after that it starts to get rough, OK? You think you're up to it?'

The Provo said nothing.

Joyce turned away. As he opened the door he said over his shoulder to Harry Synnott, 'Don't talk to the little shit.'

Harry Synnott stood near the door. The prisoner threw the towel away, then sat down on the floor, his back to the wall.

It was more than ten minutes before either of them spoke.

'You're a bit young to be a party to torture.' The prisoner's chin was up, his head tilted back to rest on the wall.

Synnott said nothing.

The prisoner said, 'Those bastards don't believe in the law.' Synnott looked across. The prisoner was staring at him, his lips trying for a sneer, but let down by an unmistakable tremor. 'Great men altogether, those two. When they've got one man in a room, and a cop shop full of hard men to back them up.'

Synnott took out his notebook. He wrote down a few words.

'Keeping a note?'

Synnott said, 'I'm not supposed to speak to you.'

'You going to report those bastards?'

Synnott said, 'I knew her, the garda you shot.' He made eye contact. 'I met her once. It was a terrible thing to do.'

The prisoner said, 'I didn't do it.'

'The fuck you didn't.'

'I'm a soldier,' the prisoner said. 'I follow orders. I fight the Brits. I don't shoot Irish women.'

When Joyce and Buckley came back, Harry Synnott went to the canteen. He had a cup of tea and sat at a table on his own, looking at his notebook. The notes were spaced out, two or three sentences per page.

I'm a soldier, the Provo said. Soldier of the Republic. And that made it OK, whatever he did. How come, Synnott wondered, not one of them ever stood up in the witness box and said *Yes, I did it and I'm proud I did my duty as a soldier?* How come every fucking one of them's innocent?

Harry Synnott stared at his notes, at the lines he'd scrawled and the gaps between them, until his tea was cold.

He went off duty that evening at 7 p.m. and called in sick next day. When the radio alarm went off the following morning the news came on and David Hanly announced that a man named Conal Crotty had been charged at a special sitting of the District Court with the murder of Garda Maura Sheelin.

*

When the trial of Conal Crotty came to the Special Criminal Court seven months later, Harry Synnott wasn't on the list of witnesses in the garda file. His role in the case, guarding Crotty for a short time, had been peripheral and he hadn't expected to be called, but he was nonetheless relieved.

Crotty pleaded not guilty and claimed that he had been forced to sign a statement implicating him in the bank robbery and the murder. The chief prosecution witnesses, detectives Joyce and Buckley, gave evidence that he had made a voluntary confession.

'When I came back in the room,' Joyce said in the witness box, 'the accused remained silent. After a while, we had a general conversation. I knew he'd played a bit of hurling at county level and I'd played a bit myself with a cousin of his, so I asked him about that. After we'd talked for about half an hour, give or take, he suddenly said he wanted to get something off his chest. That's when he made the statement.'

It was Crotty's senior counsel, Desmond Cartwright, who buggered up the confession.

With little material to work with, other than his client's

protestation of innocence, Cartwright cast his net wide. Apart from those who had made statements, Crotty and his lawyers didn't know the names of any of the uniformed gardai who had been present during his detention. So Cartwright asked the court to call every garda who was on duty during the forty-six hours his client had been held prior to him signing the incriminating statement. It was a tiresome process, lasting several days, with a procession of gardai confirming their insignificant roles in the events, or their complete lack of involvement in the case, and swearing that they'd seen and heard nothing to substantiate the accused's claims of being beaten up. After sixteen such witnesses had given evidence, with number seventeen on his way to the witness stand, one of the court's three judges leaned forward and asked, 'Mr Cartwright, are you certain this is necessary?'

Cartwright, a small man, broad-faced, with a receding hairline and an air of natural superiority, put on a smile that was as ingratiating as it was blatantly spurious. 'What I'm certain of, My Lord, beyond any doubt, is that Your Lordship will be absolutely scrupulous in protecting my client's right to a full and fair ventilation of all aspects of these most serious charges.' Everyone in court knew that this was a barrister's way of telling a judge to go fuck himself.

Harry Synnott was garda witness number twenty-four.

'In the course of your duties that day, Garda Synnott, did you see or hear anything out of the ordinary?'

Two days before he was due to give evidence, Synnott had considered resigning from the force.

Commit perjury, or help that murdering bastard walk free?

Helen, his then girlfriend, later his wife, told him that he'd been talking in his sleep, pleading with someone not to do something. 'Walk away from it,' she told him. 'They're no good, any of them.'

On the witness stand, Harry Synnott said, 'I saw the accused being assaulted.'

A ripple of murmurs and feet-shuffling swept through the courtroom. To Desmond Cartwright's credit, he didn't do anything more than raise his eyebrows. 'You did?'

'Yes, sir.'

'By whom?'

'Detective Sergeant Joyce, sir, and Detective Garda Buckley.'

Cartwright took off his glasses and looked down at the table in front of him, absorbing the prospect of victory after several days of assuming that he was fighting a dead one. He'd handled a number of these Special Criminal Court trials and made no secret of his contempt for the ease with which the three judges, sitting without a jury, accepted garda evidence. There had been a steady accumulation over the years of allegations of brutality, confessions later repudiated, suspects who emerged from interview rooms with bruises that were explained with a claim that they fell down stairs or bumped into a door. On occasion, the explanation was that defendants, in order to cast doubt on incriminating statements, had beaten each other up. Or, when alone in cells, that they had beaten themselves up. A similar explanation had been given for the bruises found on Conal Crotty when he'd been subsequently examined by a doctor. He had, for one crucial hour, been kept in a cell with another Provo.

Aware that he'd been given an unprecedented gift, Cartwright took his time. The judges seemed to be sitting straighter on the bench, and the detectives gathered at the back of the court were exchanging whispers. Three newspaper reporters were taking down every word. Sitting on a bench off to one side, Detective Sergeant Joyce was looking down at the floor. Detective Garda Buckley stared at Synnott as though he was something nasty that Buckley had found on the sole of his shoe.

Cartwright put his glasses back on and made eye contact with Harry Synnott.

'And what did you do when you witnessed this, Garda Synnott?'

'I reported it to a superior, sir, but he wasn't interested.'

'You made a contemporaneous note of all this, I hope, Garda Synnott?'

'Not contemporaneous, sir. I made a note of what happened, immediately afterwards, in the canteen.'

'And you have that note?'

Harry Synnott took a notebook from a side pocket.

The prosecution made noises about having this sprung on them, while Cartwright pointed out that it was all news to him, too.

The prosecution went through the motions of seeking to suppress Synnott's notes, knowing that no judge would dare do so. One of the judges leaned forward. 'This notebook that you have, Garda Synnott – that's the original?'

'It's not detailed, My Lord. It's just a note I made immediately afterwards, in the canteen – it says, *DS Joyce and DG Buckley beat and kicked the suspect, Mr Crotty, in my presence*. That's all it says. I just thought, My Lord, I just thought I should make some kind of note. I wasn't sure what to do, My Lord.'

Cartwright then took Harry Synnott minute by minute through his contact with the accused, stitching the description of the assault into the court record. He listened to every account of a punch or kick and then brought Synnott back at it from several angles.

'When this particular punch connected, Garda Synnott, did my client scream?'

'He made a noise, yes.'

'An exclamation of pain?'

'Yes.'

'Extreme distress?'

'He was distressed.'

'Distraught?'

'I suppose so.'

'Agitated?'

'Yes.'

'He cried out? Screamed?'

'That's what I heard.'

'Was it a loud scream?'

'It was a scream.'

Cartwright was speaking to Synnott but he was looking up at the judge who had questioned the need for the lengthy trawl through the police on duty during Conal Crotty's interrogation. The judge kept his gaze fixed on the back of the court.

'Not a mere yelp, Garda Synnott, certainly not a restrained expression of protest?'

'He screamed.'

'And when he was kicked, did he scream then, too?'

After a while, Synnott mostly looked down at his notebook and when he looked up he didn't look at Cartwright but at the stenographer, a middle-aged man with wavy grey hair. He could hear the thump of the heel of the man's hand repeatedly hitting the bench in front of him as his fountain pen scurried down page after page, putting every word on the record.

Cartwright took Synnott through Conal Crotty's statement, in which he alleged he had been beaten.

'This passage, where my client alleges he was lying on the floor when one of the detectives – he's not clear which one – stamped on his chest, did you witness that?'

'Yes.'

The senior counsel for the state was sitting behind his table, his gaze cast down on an empty page of the foolscap pad in front of him.

When they got to the period when Synnott had been alone with the Provo, Cartwright took a minute to read silently through a passage of his client's statement. Then he looked up.

'Did my client make any complaint to you?' Cartwright asked.

'He did. He said I was a bit young to be a party to torture.'

'As indeed you are, Garda Synnott.'

'He said that the other gardai, Sergeant Joyce and Mr Buckley, were bastards.'

'And what did you say?'

'I said to him something like, *I knew her, the garda you shot. I met her once.*'

Synnott looked down at his notebook again. 'He said, *I had to do it.*'

Cartwright jerked his head up so sharply that his glasses rocked on his nose.

Synnott continued. 'He said, *I'm a soldier.*'

Cartwright's stare was boring into Synnott's face. Synnott said, 'Then he said, *And my orders were to do the bank. She got in the way. It was nothing personal.*'

Cartwright, more than anyone else in the courtroom, knew exactly what was happening. His voice was clear and bleak.

'You say he said that, do you?'

'Yes, sir. I asked him if he meant to kill Garda Sheelin. He said, *I've said too much.*'

Cartwright said nothing for a while, one foot resting on the bench behind him. Like a chess player, he was thinking through the next few moves – if he said this, if Synnott said that – his tongue occasionally wetting his lower lip. Finally, he demanded and was given Synnott's notebook. The court adjourned for ten minutes while photocopies were made of the relevant pages for the three judges and the other lawyers.

Synnott watched Cartwright examine the pages. There was no way to tell the lines written in the canteen that day from the lines added since.

Eventually, because he couldn't do otherwise, Cartwright asked the obvious question.

'And you told nobody about this? And you made no statement?' His voice rose. 'You had a confession, you say, implicating my client in the foul murder of a young woman garda, a colleague of yours, a heroic young policewoman who put the defence of the state ahead of her own safety – her young life whipped away in an instant – you have a confession to this vile crime and you quietly close your notebook and put it away?'

Looking at the judges, Synnott said, 'I did and that was wrong, My Lords. When Detectives Joyce and Buckley secured a confession from the suspect, I was sure that was enough, that he would be charged and convicted. No one approached me, no one asked for a statement. After I reported the assault on the prisoner, and that was ignored—' Synnott looked across at the bench. 'I don't like saying this, My Lords, but I was afraid.'

One of the judges leaned forward. 'Of what, garda?'

Synnott said, 'I was afraid that if I came forward and said what he had told me I'd have to tell the truth about the assaults on the prisoner – or perjure myself. Frankly, My Lords, it was a choice I was hoping to avoid. I was hoping that Mr Crotty would be found guilty without my having to say anything. I knew he did it, he told me so. Then Mr Cartwright had me called – I had to tell the truth, My Lords, all of it.'

Cartwright intervened. 'And what do you say, Garda Synnott, to the fact that my client denies ever making any incriminating remarks such as those you have related here? What do you say to the charge that you're simply making this up?'

Cartwright knew he had to ask the question, and he knew it was pointless. Synnott's voice was steady. 'Mr Crotty killed a garda, My Lords – he told me so. I'm not surprised he's ready to commit perjury.'

The trial continued for another two weeks, but the outcome was decided before Harry Synnott left the witness stand. The court ruled that Crotty's confession to the detectives was inadmissible, but found him guilty of murder on the basis of his verbal admission to Garda Harry Synnott. The court found that Crotty had been assaulted while in custody, and one judge – the one who had asked Synnott why he'd beem afraid – made scathing remarks about detectives Joyce and Buckley. The same judge said,

'The fact that Garda Synnott admitted, here and on oath, that he witnessed the assaults on the prisoner, thereby causing potentially ruinous harm to the prosecution case, marks him as a witness who must be taken very seriously indeed. When it comes, therefore, to assessing his own evidence implicating the accused in the murder, we cannot but assign to it the utmost significance.'

Crotty got the death sentence, with the subsequent customary commutation to life in jail. The day after the guilty verdict, one of the tabloids had a picture of Harry Synnott on the front page, walking from the court. The headline was 'The Man Who Told The Truth'.

12

Happy as I am.

'For every colleague who admires what you did, ten of them will despise you.' Colin O'Keefe had been an inspector at the time, peripherally involved in the Sheelin murder investigation, and he sought out Synnott to offer congratulations and a word of warning. His prediction had proven accurate. Synnott's role in the Crotty trial defined him to his colleagues as untrustworthy. It didn't matter that senior officers knew about the beating of suspects, it didn't matter that politicians knew and that some had privately given their approval. Synnott's betrayal meant that two experienced detectives ended up taking early retirement because a colleague had ignored the unwritten rules. Several years later, when Synnott reported a garda for shaking down a pub owner, the estrangement from his colleagues increased. The garda was suspended, then sacked.

'You're a back-stabber. No matter where you go, no matter how much brown-nosing you do with the brass, that'll be your epitaph.' Sergeant Derek Ferry, a colleague at Turner's Lane, had never been more than cool to Synnott. Hostilities came into the open when Synnott gave evidence at a disciplinary hearing against another sergeant at the station, a man accused of misappropriation of petty cash. The tension within the station became a part of the daily routine, on several occasions erupting in shouting matches.

On the advice of Assistant Commissioner Colin O'Keefe, Harry Synnott had recently transferred out of the Turner's Lane station.

Happy as I am.

Over the eighteen years since the Crotty case O'Keefe had maintained contact, being helpful whenever possible. Synnott was slightly shocked to be seriously considering the possibility of a move away from the kind of policing that had been the centre of his life for more than two decades. When O'Keefe had first asked him if he was in the market, Synnott had said only, 'I'm interested.' O'Keefe changed the subject and they hadn't talked since then. Now, finishing off the glass of milk that came with his chicken sandwich, O'Keefe said, 'How's your French?'

'Rusty schoolboy.'

'Good enough, with a crash course to bring you up to speed.'

'You're offering me a job in France?'

'The Netherlands at first, Paris eventually. You've heard of Europol?'

Synnott could feel the hope inside him dim.

'Vaguely.'

'It came out of the Maastricht Treaty, started off coordinating anti-drug strategies for police forces across Europe. Now, as these EU things will do, it's grown and grown. Over three hundred souls based in The Hague, and countless more employed in liaison bureaus, one in every country in the EU, and more outside it, all liaising away like rabbits.'

A niche in the bureaucracy.

'Sir—'

Over the years, O'Keefe had given up on telling Synnott to call him Colin. Now he shook his head.

'I know what you're thinking and you're dead wrong.' He took a sheet of paper from a file and passed it to Synnott. It was an organisational chart. 'That's the structure. Bureaucracy galore – then there's the Information and Technology Department and the Department of Corporate Governance. That one there, in the middle, the Serious Crime Department, that's where I want to put you. The criminals are international, and what we're trying to put in place is a structure that efficiently confronts that.'

'Doing what?'

'There've been conferences, seminars, the usual bullshit, but serious people have been talking on the sidelines. About structures and about bringing the best people together. We can't stop the bureaucracy weaving its usual web, but we *can* build something from the ground up that can make a difference in confronting organised crime, fraud, terrorism, currency forgery.'

Despite his doubts, Synnott could feel the hope flicker again.

O'Keefe said, 'It's cutting-edge stuff. The world is changing and policing has to change with it. Everyone you work with will be as serious about policing as you are. It's solid, useful, hands-on work. It's well paid, with generous expenses. And it gets you out of the corner you've painted yourself into.'

Synnott sat silently for several moments. He tried to keep his tone flat. 'I didn't know I'd painted myself into anything.'

O'Keefe finished the last of his sandwich. 'Clear away the bullshit, Harry, and what you've got is this – you told the truth in a garda murder, and there's no more serious case. You told the truth and you took the heat. Since then you have put away some of the most dangerous people this city has had inflicted on it. Wilkinson – we don't know how many kids were spared that bastard's tender mercies since you took him out of circulation. Or how many women escaped having their lives torn asunder by Hartigan. Swanson Avenue – there you closed down a cold-blooded killer who might have walked. I don't know one other garda who has single-handedly done more public service for this city than you have.'

Synnott waited for the but.

'And if you haven't got the sense to turn a blind eye when your colleagues cross a line – well, you've paid the price for that.'

'You think I should have turned a blind eye?'

'That's not what I said. Any police force, it has ways of doing things – and when things go wrong we tend to sort it out quietly.'

'Circle the wagons?'

'If you like. There's a lot of fucking Apaches out there. Apart from the scum we have to deal with, there's the newspapers and the television, the politicians and the civil-liberties people, Uncle Tom Cobley. Whenever they get a taste of victory, they lose respect, start sniffing everyone's trouser leg.'

'I thought you saw it my way.'

'You did what you thought was right and I admire that and I'll back any man who does what he thinks is right – but, like I said, you pay a price. And we end up with one of our best detectives moving from station to station because other good coppers won't work with him.'

Harry Synnott suddenly felt like he was in an argument that he didn't care about any more. O'Keefe was doing what Synnott knew had to be done from time to time. Stand outside the problem. See things coldly and clearly, do what had to be done.

O'Keefe rapped his knuckles on his desk. 'Enough of that. How do you feel about kissing the minister's arse?'

Synnott smiled. 'There had to be a catch.'

'You have to meet the minister. Impress him. He wants a nomination from me, but he has the final say.'

O'Keefe wiped his mouth with a paper napkin, then flicked imaginary crumbs from his shirt-front and straightened his tie. 'He just needs to see that you don't drool down your chin. Maybe throw a few statistics at him, a little slang so he feels he's had a whiff of the streets. And smile and shuffle your feet a bit, so he knows you're nervous to be in the presence of a man of substance. It's a doddle.'

'When and where?'

'Sunday morning, Haddington Road church, after eleven o'clock Mass. Some politicians natter on about post-Catholic Ireland, but our lad likes to be seen saying a quiet prayer. He'll be in man-of-the-people mode.'

Synnott felt his usual unease with the civilities. 'Look, I ought to say thanks – I mean, over the years, you've—'

The phone rang. O'Keefe picked it up and held a hand over the mouthpiece. 'I've never done anything that wasn't what I thought best for the force.' He put the phone to his ear and said his name.

After a few seconds he said, 'Have they been identified?'

O'Keefe listened for another minute, occasionally saying things like 'And?' or 'So?' Finally, he said, 'Jesus *Christ*.' Then, 'Keep me informed, minute by minute. Whatever you need.'

When O'Keefe hung up he said, 'Galway.' He shook his head. 'Like something you read about happening in the wilds of Kansas, somewhere like that. Two people, adult male and a teenager, also male. Dead in a house in Bushy Park. Knifed, maybe. Some kind of edged weapon, anyway – maybe a hatchet. The locals have a man for it – and they think he might have done another one, a woman, but they can't find the body.'

Harry Synnott stood up. 'I'll leave you to it, so.'

O'Keefe said, 'Remember, smile, street slang and shuffle your feet for the minister.'

*

My name is Detective Inspector Harry Synnott, c/o Macken Road Garda Station.

On the afternoon of Wednesday 13th April I attended at the Sexual Assault Unit of the Rotunda Hospital following a call from the station informing me of an alleged sexual assault. There I met Detective Garda Rose Cheney and together we interviewed a Ms Teresa Hunt, who made an allegation of sexual assault against one Max Hapgood Jr. Detective Garda Cheney took down the details of Ms Hunt's allegation and the complainant signed the statement in my presence. Garda Cheney also made notes of the complainant's remarks, which the complainant signed.

The statement from Harry Synnott would be a general outline of the allegations made and the consequent steps taken by the police. The heart of the file for the DPP would include the victim's statement, a report from the doctor at the Sexual Assault Unit, Cheney's statement and Synnott's own account.

Having obtained an address for the alleged assailant, Detective Garda Cheney and I drove to Castlepoint, where—

Harry Synnott figured he'd be spending the rest of the afternoon at the keyboard. He had the elements needed to make his own statement strong. First, the *mens rea*, starting with Max Junior lying that his mother wasn't home. Then the mother's insistence on getting her husband to come home, the husband immediately reaching for a lawyer, the family conference before Max Junior was allowed to speak to the police. The Hapgoods were entitled to do what they had done, but a good lawyer could bring out the subtext of guilty knowledge. Then the father recording part of the interview, the mother's aggressive remarks about the complainant being a silly bitch who couldn't keep her legs closed. There was no evidence of what had been said at the family conference, but it wouldn't be too difficult for the jury to guess. Nothing conclusive, and the jury would be warned to make its decision on hard evidence, but laying out an account of the family's conduct was the kind of thing that bolsters a jury's confidence.

The core of that part of the case was that Harry Synnott at no point, in the Hapgood house, detailed the complaint made by Teresa Hunt. All the Hapgoods knew was that a young lady had made a complaint. Yet, after the family conference, it was clear that the family knew of the sexual nature of the complaint.

'. . . *A silly bitch who has trouble keeping her legs closed* . . .'

Stitching Max Junior into an admission that the sex wasn't consensual would be more difficult, being entirely verbal and implicit in the notes, some made by Synnott alone, some by Synnott and Rose Cheney. Their credibility on the stand would be crucial.

'When we started, she wanted it as much as I did.'

'You know what that's like – you can't turn it on and off like a fucking tap.'

'She wanted it and she got what she wanted.'

It remained a she-says-he-says, but Synnott reckoned that the clear evidence of guilty knowledge would add sufficient weight to the verbal admissions to help a jury tip the scales.

13

GALWAY

When Joe Mills arrived back at McCreary Street station the place was buzzing with the news about the two bodies he'd found in the house at Bushy Park. An inspector met him in the public office and said, 'The nutcase, he hasn't said a word to the shrink. He wants to talk– the way he puts it – to the copper from the roof.'

The sergeant and the shrink were still with Wayne Kemp when Joe Mills arrived. The sergeant was looking pissed-off, and the shrink might have been disappointed but she was hiding it well. Once word came in about the find in Bushy Park, the chief superintendent had asked a solicitor to represent Kemp. The suspect shrugged. It wasn't assent, but it wasn't rejection, so it would do. The solicitor, a young man with long sideburns who looked like he'd rather be doing a bit of conveyancing, sat just inside the door, looking nervous. Wayne Kemp was puckering his lips and doing that flexing thing that made his neck muscles stick out. He didn't look up when Mills came in.

Mills stood a few feet from Kemp and looked down at him. 'They said you wanted—'

Kemp looked up at him. 'Did you ever live in Blackpool?'

'Blackpool?'

'Blackpool, England.'

'No.'

'Where are you from?'

'What's this about?'

'Up on that roof, I turned around – I can tell you, one more second I was going off, backwards flip – you know what I mean? – like in the Olympics. Then, I thought I knew you.'

'No, I don't think so.'

'Then I said to myself, no, maybe not. For a minute there I could have sworn you were a fella used to work in the clubhouse bar. He was from Drogheda. Every Saturday morning, I went there. Nice people. Anyway, it doesn't matter now.' Kemp was staring at the shrink. 'It was like I was waking up, standing on the roof. I knew why I was there, and I kind of remembered – maybe not. Anyway, that was that.'

'And?'

The nutcase looked again at Joe Mills. 'I was just curious. Thought you might be the guy, after all. Just wanted to ask you.'

'There was no woman.'

Kemp raised an eyebrow. 'Of course there was.'

'I looked all over the house, the garden, front and back.'

Kemp looked confused. Then he closed his eyes for a few seconds and when he opened them he was smiling. He understood. 'No, not Mina's house – Christ, no, what do you think I am? She's my sister.'

'What did you mean – *I'd never hurt a woman before?*'

The suspect shook his head. 'Different thing altogether. Not here. Not Galway.'

'Blackpool?'

'What about it?'

'This woman, whatever you did to her – did it happen in Blackpool?'

'Do you think I could get a cup of tea? Milk, no sugar.'

Wayne Kemp got his tea and he didn't say another word for three days.

DUBLIN

When he closed the front door of his flat, before he switched on the light, Harry Synnott saw the little yellow light blinking on the answer machine. He grimaced. The day's work might not yet be done.

Synnott pressed a button on the machine.

'Harry—'

It was OK – his ex-wife.

Synnott pressed another button and the message aborted. He crossed to the kitchen table, set down the Chinese takeaway, and hung his jacket on the back of a chair. When he'd spooned the food onto a plate he sat at the table and began eating. After a couple of minutes he switched on the radio. A man was talking about classical music, explaining the background to someone's masterpiece. After a while he stopped talking and played the music. Synnott listened as he ate and when he'd finished eating he switched off the radio and dumped the remains of the meal in the bin. Then he went to the answer machine and played Helen's message.

'Harry, maybe it's nothing, but I had a call from Michael this afternoon. Nothing wrong, but he casually dropped the fact that he intends quitting college. Just like that. Has he said anything to you? You know how these things go, it could be he's just being cranky, but, anyway, I think maybe you should give him a call, see if he's serious. Let me know if there's anything to worry about. Take care.'

Synnott had spoken with his son a week earlier. He'd taken Michael to dinner in the expensive city-centre restaurant that his son had nominated. The food was all right, the servile waiters a pain in the arse.

When Michael ordered something with a French name he leaned heavily on the appropriate accent. Synnott didn't know why that irritated him so much, but it did. His son was pushing

93

adulthood. He was just three years short of the age that Synnott had been when he had given evidence in a murder case. Synnott found his son's pretensions no longer cute, just irksome.

Michael chattered about some opportunity that had come up. He and two friends were hoping for some venture capital from the father of one of the friends. 'We're thinking of opening a brand consultancy.'

Synnott tried to keep the scepticism out of his voice. 'Michael, what do you know about—'

'Suppose you've got a business – a product or a service you really believe in. It's only as good as the image your potential customers have of it. That's where we come in.' Michael leaned forward. 'Everything from letterheads to launches, from the design of the product to the look of your offices, the packaging, the clothes your people wear to work, the music the customers listen to when they're put on hold. We enhance your presence in the market, using the sensibilities of the artist.'

Michael paused, as if suddenly aware that he was giving his father a ready-made marketing line. 'It's cool, dad. We take a humdrum business, we give it all the style of a brand, we make it stand out from the herd.'

Synnott said something about college and Michael waved that away. 'That's for drones – initiative and blue-sky thinking, you can't learn that kind of thing in a lecture hall.'

Now Synnott lifted the phone and tapped in the first four digits of Michael's number before he hung up.

Not tonight.

Synnott had had similar conversations with Michael over the past year. Never a product, never a skill, never a consumer service at the heart of the latest plan, always a fresh angle on how to interface with something, or how to get in on something, or behind it or intervene or connect or transform. Synnott found such conversations difficult. It was as though they were speaking the same language, but in different dialects.

Not tonight.
He'd call his son tomorrow.

*

Joshua Boyce wasn't crazy about La Pontchartrain, but Antoinette got to choose the restaurant tonight. The lighting was too dim, the food was too – *fussy* was as close as he could come to putting a word to it. Boyce didn't like places that made a drama out of producing a meal.

'To us.' Antoinette was drinking white wine, and Boyce returned her toast with mineral water.

It had become a custom for Joshua Boyce and his wife to dine out the night before he did a job. If something went wrong tomorrow it would be a long time before they did anything together. And although the jewellery shop was a safe enough job, once there were guns involved things could get hairy very quickly.

Antoinette was the prettiest woman in the room, no doubt about that. Long straight hair, pale blue eyes. She was wearing her newest dress, a dark blue Marc Jacob that she had picked up on a weekend trip to New York with a couple of friends. It used to be London for shopping trips, but New York was better and cheaper and more fun. Joshua Boyce didn't see the need for such excursions, given the arrival in Dublin of every consumer delight from Harvey Nichols to Louis Vuitton, but Antoinette got a kick out of her shopping adventures.

Things are as they should be.

Boyce allowed his fingertips to brush the walnut handle of the fork in front of him. *Touch wood.*

*

As Dixie came awake she could feel the pulse in her neck, as strong as if her heart had pushed its way up into her throat.

Stay calm.

Panic attack's the last thing we need.

Stupid. In here. Trapped in a box.

She pressed her face into the pillow. The monotony of the day and a half that she'd spent so far in Mountjoy had left her exhausted, but her sleep was shallow and repeatedly broken. She turned over onto her back.

'Friday will tell the tale.'

Tomorrow.

Another prisoner, a woman with a sing-song voice, was talking somewhere not too far away. Just the one voice, no reply, and occasional hoarse laughter from the same voice. Dixie welcomed the diversion that the noise provided. A long time later it stopped: the woman must have dozed off and that made it easier to think, which Dixie didn't want to do.

Tomorrow would be the end of everything there was and everything there was to be, and from this cell Dixie could no more change that than she could fly to the moon.

'Friday will tell the tale.'

In search of distraction and comfort, Dixie said one prayer and then another.

Oh my God, I am heartily sorry for . . .

Our Father, who art . . .

Hail Mary, full of grace . . .

In the name of the Father . . .

14

The first time Dixie saw Owen Peyton, he wasn't the hand-somest man in the pub – that was Paul, the long drink of water she was seeing at the time – but he was the coolest. Owen didn't live on the Cairnloch estate – he was in the Bird's Nest that evening, in company with a dozen others, because he hung around with a brother of one of Dixie's friends. Shaggy dark hair, a bottle of Heineken in his hand, and a smile that lit up his deep dark eyes. She was aware that she wanted him to like her and even more aware that she didn't want him to know she gave a damn.

Back then she was Dixie Bailey. Deirdre to her father, Dixie to everyone else. The most important thing in her sights was the health-and-fitness course she was doing. A diploma would open all sorts of doors – a job at a fitness centre, maybe freelance work as a trainer. She didn't speak to Owen that night, but towards the end of the evening, just before he left with a couple of friends, he met her gaze and raised the Heineken in a toast.

Two weeks later she broke up with Paul and phoned Owen. He said, 'You took your time.'

Owen drove a white van. 'Deliveries,' he said. He didn't have set hours, he didn't take the van home with him – it was garaged, he said, somewhere out in Coolock. It wasn't his van, but he had the full-time use of it from his boss. People that he knew, he said, recommended him to people who wanted stuff moved.

He'd spent a year at DCU and quit, because he could earn more doing what he did than he'd ever earn when he got a degree.

It was a few weeks later that Owen's van was stopped with a stack of stolen tyres inside. Standing at her front door, Owen's brother Brendan telling her what happened, Dixie felt like a layer of ice had been placed across her scalp.

'He'll be all right. Don't worry.'

Owen rang Dixie as soon as he got bail and they went to The Merchant Prince. 'It's something I do from time to time, it's not a big deal. Some of the stuff I move, it's not the kind of—'

He stopped, took a breath. 'It's not how the millionaires do their business. But, I mean, that's the way things work in this country. There's the official way, right? And there's VAT and receipts and accountants and all that shit. Underneath that there's the real businesses, the ones that most ordinary people make a living out of. I mean, do you know anyone who pays full price for anything?'

People do deals, he said, and maybe they don't do all the paperwork, but it's how the world works, and when people do deals they have to have stuff shifted, and that was what Owen did.

Dixie asked him if he'd ever been arrested before.

He looked her in the eye for a few seconds. 'A couple of little things. Probation. Doesn't count.' Then, he said, he got two months for receiving, but that wasn't a serious thing and, besides, he got out after six weeks.

This time he did fourteen months.

While Owen was in jail, Dixie had a miscarriage. When he came out they got a three-bedroom flat in Santry and spent a week fitting it out. Dixie thought it looked like something from a magazine.

*

Owen's brother Brendan was best man. He was the older brother, pudgy and dour, but Owen said he was just shy.

At the reception Dixie came across Owen in conversation with a chubby middle-aged man in an expensive suit. The man looked at Dixie and turned to Owen. 'You did well, kiddo.'

Owen introduced him as his boss. The man stuck out his hand to Dixie. 'Lar Mackendrick. Best thing ever happened to this scallywag, when you took him on.'

Later, Lar Mackendrick danced with Dixie, sang two songs and when he left he handed Owen an envelope. When they opened it that evening they found tickets for a flight to Paris, a voucher for a week's stay at a hotel and two grand in cash.

'What business is he in?'

'Whole lot of stuff.'

'He must think well of you.'

'I told you, I know people.'

'Never?'

'No.'

'Not even tempted?'

'At parties, now and then, the odd joint, that kind of thing. I wouldn't touch the hard stuff.'

Owen laughed. 'Coke isn't hard stuff. It's just – it gets you there.'

'I like to keep a clear head.'

'Nothing clears your head like a Bacardi Breezer?'

'That's different.'

'I know. This is better.'

Dixie told him about the guy who worked with her brother Fiachra, how he overdosed on heroin. 'They all got the day off work for the funeral.'

'Heroin is shit. Only losers mess with shit.'

She watched the plastic card slicing the white powder.

He said, 'You don't mind?'

'To each his own.'

*

When they raided the flat for the first time, the police weren't gentle. Everything that could be moved was turned over, every drawer and door was opened, every shelf was cleared, they emptied shoeboxes and cabinets. Dixie said, 'What gives you the right—' They ignored her.

They found nothing. Afterwards, Dixie asked Owen, 'How often is this going to happen?'

'They're just fishing – they've nothing solid.'

The police came back three weeks later, on an afternoon when Dixie was alone in the flat, and again they found nothing.

This time Dixie stood in front of a detective and watched him poke through a kitchen cabinet.

'You're just doing this to fuck us up, aren't you?'

'Our job is to inquire into the activities of criminals.'

'I'm not a criminal.'

'You're married to one.'

'My husband isn't a criminal. He's a driver. He drives a van.'

The detective opened a cabinet below the counter, bent over and began pulling out saucepans.

Dixie's father hadn't worked for years. His kidneys went bad early on and he needed regular dialysis. Jack Bailey didn't show any fear when things got bad. His wife had died a year after Dixie was born. He seemed neither surprised nor upset by his own sudden decline. Dixie was with him every day in the hospital. Her big brother Fiachra came home from London for the funeral.

Fiachra had never said a bad word against Owen, but a couple of days after they buried their father he repeated what he'd said the night before she got married. 'I'm always there for you, remember that.'

One evening, two or three weeks after the funeral, Owen was slicing lines of coke on the kitchen table when Dixie said, 'I'd like to try.' Owen looked at her for a moment, then nodded. He passed her the tube from a biro and she bent over the table and snorted.

It wasn't the big deal she thought it would be. She was waiting for a rush inside her head, and when it didn't come she thought maybe she'd done it wrong. After a while, when she'd stopped thinking about it, she noticed she was laughing loudly, in the middle of a very funny, very fast conversation with Owen about something her friend Shelley had said.

From the morning of her father's death, it was like some kind of invisible weight had attached itself to Dixie. Now the coke seemed to flood through her, cleansing her head of the cheerlessness that dominated her days. She felt it made her who she was again.

Owen held up the Tesco Clubcard he used to slice the lines. Dixie took it, licked it and in seconds her tongue was numb.

The health-and-fitness course was a doddle. Dixie was slim, fit and eager to learn, the practical end of it was a snap and she immediately got into the rhythm of the lectures. The middle-aged man who ran the course – whose nickname, for some long-lost reason, was Obi-Wan Kenobi – told Dixie one morning that once she had the diploma he'd introduce her to contacts in the gym business and she'd have no bother getting a job.

When Dixie opened the door and saw the detective who'd led the last police search, the one who'd called her husband a criminal, she said, 'Oh, for Christ's sake.' He didn't have a warrant in his hand and there was just one other garda with him, a younger man with red hair and freckles.

'Showing him the ropes, are you? A few tips on how to push people around?' Dixie had one hand on the door, the other on her stomach. She was two months pregnant.

The freckled cop seemed embarrassed.

The detective didn't display the cold manner he'd shown during the raid. When he said, 'Mrs Peyton—' there was a softness to his voice and Dixie said, 'No, please—'

The policeman said his name was Detective Sergeant Harry Synnott. Dixie was looking at his nose, where it thickened in the middle like something inside had been knocked out of shape and it hadn't healed right. He was sitting across the kitchen table from her. The freckled cop was carefully placing a cup of tea on the table.

'He wasn't being chased at the time,' the detective said.

Owen had been driving the white van when he was pursued by a garda squad car. 'They lost him. He was free and clear.' He wanted her to understand that the police weren't to blame.

No one knew that the van had gone into a ditch on a narrow twisting road beyond Balbriggan until an early-morning walker found it not long after dawn.

'How long was he lying there?'

'It happened sometime after 10 p.m. – that's the last the local guards saw of the van, and – they don't know, sometime after that.' His voice was low, reluctant. 'A few hours.'

When he offered his sympathies Dixie knew that he meant what he said.

She cried when she woke up alone and she cried when she lay down at night. When she did things she used to do with Owen – even shopping or watching a favourite television programme – she felt guilty. Doing things that Owen could no longer do felt like a betrayal.

Dixie convinced herself that crying would be bad for the baby inside her; it would fill him with sadness before he was born. So she stopped crying.

The baby was born seven months after Owen's death, and Dixie called him Christopher as she and Owen had agreed they would. Sometimes when Christopher slept Dixie stared at his face and tried to see Owen there, and tried to imagine how the child's features would mature and strengthen and evolve. Every night of his life, she kissed his forehead, touched his cheek and whispered, 'You and me.'

FRIDAY

15

The detective sergeant in charge of the raid on the DVD factory was a thorough sort. He had unmarked police cars set up on all three exit roads from the small Moyfield industrial estate, and half a dozen uniforms were already posted around the back of the target warehouse, cutting off any runners. He wasn't above seeking advice, either.

'You see any loopholes?' he asked Harry Synnott.

Synnott was sitting in the front passenger seat of an unmarked Ford minibus, four other officers in the back. In one hand he had a photocopy of the industrial-estate layout. In the other hand, in a long, narrow envelope, he had a search warrant for the warehouse. He said, 'Looks good to me.'

This early in the morning, just past dawn, there was little sign of life on the industrial estate. Here and there, lights showed in premises where there was a night shift. A glow could be seen through the windows high up on the near wall of the target warehouse.

The detective sergeant looked at his watch, made a note in a small notebook, returned the notebook to the inside pocket of his dark blue jacket, and said, 'Let's get this over with.'

It was a part of the job that Harry Synnott never liked. The physical stuff, where maybe twelve stone of semi-hysterical criminal is hurtling in any direction that might take him away from captivity. Anyone caught in an operation like this faced the probability of several years of living in a small room with barred windows, locked into a suffocating prison routine, the boredom overwhelming even the anger, fear, nauseating smells and limitless sexual longing. With that kind of a future coming towards them, too many gurriers were seized by the kind of reckless panic that could leave a garda in hospital for a couple of weeks. In the raid on Lar Mackendrick's warehouse there were enough uniforms – members who had volunteered for the job – to handle anything that might happen, so Harry Synnott felt at ease about hanging back. Two of the gardai on the raid were armed in case there were guns inside, though that was unlikely. Harry Synnott's role was to serve the search warrant and assess whatever might be found on the premises. If whoever was in there was smart and could hold their nerve they'd skip the physical stuff, call their favourite mouthpieces and play the odds in court.

The warehouse was set back off the main road that ran through the industrial estate. There were buildings on every side, making it easy to approach without announcing the raid. The warehouse admitted daylight through the windows of pebbled glass set just below the roof line, through which the glow of lights could be seen. Such windows were useless for keeping watch. The CCTV cameras that looked down from high on the front of the warehouse could no doubt be used to keep tabs on the outside, but it was unlikely that Lar Mackendrick's crew was that conscientious. The way in was a small door around the side, steel-reinforced but vulnerable to the nudge of a garda ram.

The sergeant in charge of the raid nodded to the four gardai in the minibus, waited until they dismounted, then walked quickly towards the building, his men following, one of them carrying the ram. Harry Synnott got out of the minibus and followed about twenty feet behind. He noticed a visibly increased tension in the gardai posted on watch around the warehouse.

Things speeded up once the crash of the ram on the warehouse door echoed off the surrounding buildings. The uniforms ran inside, while those stationed around the building moved forward, narrowing the area that any agitated suspects might have to play with if they made it outside.

When Harry Synnott entered the warehouse he found the sergeant standing with his hands on his hips, his men standing idly around him. Apart from a heap of something hidden under a dirty tarpaulin in a near corner of the warehouse the floor was bare of anything or anyone, right down to the far wall. The light from the four fittings that dangled from the roof beams showed that the warehouse was entirely empty.

Synnott walked quickly across to the heap in the corner. His gloved hand pulled the tarpaulin back. There was a wheelbarrow lying on its side and about a dozen bricks spilled onto the floor. A Marks & Spencer plastic bag lay on top of the bricks. Synnott opened it and found a half-empty bottle of Diet Coke and a plastic pencil case with a picture of Buzz Lightyear on the side. He unzipped the pencil case; there was nothing inside.

The detective sergeant was standing beside him.

'Don't worry. It happens.'

Synnott let the pencil case fall to the floor and kicked it away.

Dixie.

He didn't understand what she could be up to.

Ought to know better than to fuck me around.

16

Lar Mackendrick finished his warm-up on the stationary bike, climbed off and took a long breath. He looked around the spare bedroom that he'd converted into a gym. He always felt this bad starting off, and it was always worth it when he was done. In the old days, he'd be tucking into a solid breakfast about now. Instead, he'd had the juice, the tea and the wholemeal toast and much as he'd have liked to take a break he had a routine to follow. He went to the bench and after fifteen minutes he felt warm and loose.

The chest stuff, maybe he could skip that.

Maybe not.

Lying on his back on the bench, a weight in each hand, he began the flat bench presses, counting down the repetitions. After a couple of dozen he put down one weight and clasped the other in his cupped hands. A lot of this stuff was a bore, but Lar enjoyed the dumb-bell pullovers. Arms stretched back over his head, he liked the way the weight created a balance against the pull of his restraining chest muscles. he stopped counting and continued the pullovers until he had to grunt to make the return lift.

A year earlier, six months after the tragedy that had left him alone to run the family business, Lar Mackendrick had got a warning from his doctor. Lose the weight, quit the fags and get fit, or he'd be joining Jo-Jo in the tasteful surroundings of Sutton cemetery.

'There's any number of possibilities, the state you're in. My money's on a stroke.'

Fear was the great motivator. In the months before the health warning, Lar Mackendrick had had to struggle to keep his mind from seizing up with despair. Pushing sixty, the settled life he'd been living crumbled around him when his elderly mother and his younger brother Jo-Jo had been murdered in their home. If he'd been able to think clearly he'd have realised that such a possibility was always there for anyone living a successful criminal life, envied and feared by their competitors. It had been a possibility for Lar and Jo-Jo from those early days when they'd been working their way up through Dublin's rapidly maturing criminal network. But after the shock of the murders Lar Mackendrick was on automatic. Later, he didn't remember ordering the killing of a brother and a couple of friends of the man the newspapers confirmed was responsible for the murders, a man who was himself in hiding abroad. Revenge, Lar concluded, was necessary but empty.

Lar couldn't imagine life without his brother's guidance. Jo-Jo had been the brains. He'd handled strategy for the family's various criminal enterprises, while Lar was the hands-on type. Lost without Jo-Jo, Lar thought of jacking it in, but retirement would only give the emptiness more room to wear him away.

So, fitfully managing the business, he let himself drift, indulging every whim, impulse or craving, half aware that he was sliding towards something from which he wouldn't be able to come back. An unrestricted intake of food and drink added a layer to his already dangerous bulk. Some evenings he had people around to his home in Howth, sometimes May had a couple of drinks with him, but mostly he watched television alone, all kinds of shite, and sipped vodka. Sometimes he talked to Jo-Jo, just told him how things were going, gave him the drill on people they knew, what was happening. He woke up in the A&E of Beaumont Hospital one afternoon, having passed out at the foot of the escalator on the ground floor of the Jervis Centre.

'I can't force you to do anything,' the doctor told him, 'but this isn't something we can fix with a course of antibiotics. Bottom line – things stay as they are, you've a good chance of a stroke within a year or two.' Lar spent a week in the Mater Private, his every moment dominated by fear.

Ten months later, three stone lighter, Lar Mackendrick lived according to the diet drawn up by a nutritionist called Tammy and the regime laid down by a fitness instructor called Dave. First thing every morning he swallowed his daily seventy-five-gram dose of Nu-Seal, last thing each evening he took the Lipitor that kept his cholesterol down. Before long his doctor told him to forget the daily Tritace dose, his blood pressure was stable. He hadn't had a drink since the night before his collapse.

Upper abs.

Lar's breathing was steady. A few months back, he would have been puffing just from the effort of opening a bottle of Stolly.

His back was flat on the floor, arse tucked into the skirting board, legs pressed up against the wall. Slowly, drawing in air, he bent up from the waist, upper body lifting from the floor, fingers reaching towards his toes, then exhaled as he sank back, five, ten times, fifteen. Twenty repetitions. His breathing heavier now, he stood up and his mind felt as clear as his body felt invigorated.

Jesus, Jo-Jo, who'd have thought it. Lump of lard like me doing a Schwarzenegger.

The fear that motivated Lar had over the months turned to pride. He still had a bit of a belly but he was trimmer, stronger than he'd been since his twenties. Clear-headed and aware of the world around him, he'd applied himself to the family business with a passion that he hadn't felt in decades.

Six weeks ago, for the first time in twelve years, Lar had personally carried out a killing and found he enjoyed it. The subject was a mouse of a man, had to be done. Years ago Jo-Jo and Lar Mackendrick set this fella up in a small neighbourhood mini-market, let him keep a percentage. A lot of funny money went in one door of that shop and came out the other end smelling sweet. Recently, the guy had been pulled in for an insurance fraud on a failed garage he'd owned with his brother-in-law. Two days later, the whole thing was dropped. The mousy man – name of Johnny something, just turned fifty – turned up back at his home as casually as if he'd just spent a long weekend at the races in England.

'The cops had me by the balls,' he told anyone who asked. 'Then they screwed up the paperwork.'

The Lar Mackendrick who struggled to keep sane after the death of his brother might have missed what was happening, but the wide-awake Lar could read this one from a mile off. This had to be some cop bastard turning Mr Mousy, setting him up as a channel into the Mackendrick business.

It made sense. Over the past while, it had become obvious that someone was whispering in the law's ear. Maybe more than one someone. Over a year or so, several jobs had to be aborted when the cops tightened security. A bookie shop and a building firm, well insulated from association with Lar, had to be closed down after the Criminal Assets Bureau raided them. Lar figured the bastards had targeted the Mackendrick businesses once Jo-Jo was off the scene. Johnny Mousy Man knew the scene, now he was walking free from a sure-thing conviction.

'One thing I can't stand', Lar told Matty Butler, 'is a tout.'

This wasn't really true. Lar Mackendrick knew that sometimes people get caught up in something and they can't find a way out and they do what they think is best, and sometimes that involves squealing to the law. Lar didn't take it personally, but it wasn't something that could be left unattended. He sent Matty off to arrange things and a week later Johnny Mousy Man was shoved into the boot of an Avensis and driven to a derelict house near Ballybough.

When Lar walked into the house, Johnny was slumped on a broken-down sofa, his hands tied behind his back, his face bloody,

Matty and one of his people standing over him. He struggled to sit upright and said, 'Lar, I swear—' and Lar said, 'It's OK, I know, I know.' He looked down at the mousy man. 'Don't worry, Johnny. I understand your situation. Everything's OK.'

'Please, Lar—'

Matty handed Lar a .22-calibre Ruger pistol and Lar shot Johnny in the forehead. Johnny fell back on the sofa and lay there, his eyes open, staring at Lar, still breathing. His lips moved, a whisper came out, too ragged to make sense. Lar sat down beside Johnny on the sofa and looked at the small black wound in Johnny's forehead. The bullet hadn't come out the back of his head, which was only to be expected with a .22, but you could never tell with bullets.

'I'm in no hurry,' Lar told Johnny Mousy Man. 'Take your time.' He felt maybe Johnny expected him to say something, so he said, 'Nothing personal, Johnny. A problem has to be closed down. Someone fucks with someone, they get fucked right back. It's expected. Otherwise, what's the point?'

For a moment, he thought maybe Johnny was going to answer back. But Johnny just kept looking at him, a thin dribble of blood, no more than an inch long, coming from the black wound.

Lar sat back and watched Johnny Mousy Man dying. The smell of the gunshot was strong in the small room. Lar wondered if Johnny could get it.

'Can you smell it, Johnny? The propellant, that's what they call it.'

Johnny just stared.

'Strong smell,' Lar said. 'People think it's cordite, but it's not. Cordite, that was a bugger of a smell, but they don't use it any more.' He wondered if Johnny could hear him, or see him. Probably his senses were all messed up. Get a really hard thump in the face, in a fight or playing football, Lar reckoned, and you're not sure where you are. Probably more or less the same with a bullet in the forehead, only more so.

'The same,' he said to Johnny, 'only more so.'

He leaned over to the left, out of Johnny's line of sight, and Johnny's gaze didn't follow him. All jumbled up in there, Lar reckoned.

It was hard to tell when Johnny Mousy Man let go. His eyes stayed open and his breath was so hardly there that Lar couldn't tell if he'd stopped breathing. Lar looked over at Matty and the fella he had with him – Lar didn't know his name, Troy, Toddy, something like that, a bit of a cowboy. 'What do you think?' Lar said. The fella said, 'It's hard to tell.' His voice sounded like his mouth was dry and his tongue was thick. Only to be expected. Young guy.

Lar nodded.

After ten minutes, Lar thought that the mousy man was probably gone, but he couldn't be sure so he told Matty to do something final before they brought him up the Dublin mountains to bury him. Then Lar gave Matty back the Ruger and went home.

These days, Lar could touch his body and feel his ribs. He could stretch and sense the muscles flexing over his belly. He felt more in touch with everything. He was no Slim Jim, but he didn't have to connect to the world through a pillow of fat around his body and a cloud of despair around his mind. Things would never be what they were before his brother and his mother were so cruelly taken away, but Lar Mackendrick felt as though he'd been pulled back from the brink of something bottomless.

He was on the landing, coming out from his shower, wearing a purple bathrobe, when the phone rang. It was Matty.

'They bought it.'

'Which one?'

'Moyfield.'

Fucking cops.

Not as smart as they think.

Lar ended the call. The warehouse on the Moyfield industrial estate was one of three locations from which Mackendrick businesses supposedly operated. Fishing for touts, he'd fed the locations to three people he wasn't sure of.

Moyfield?

Supposed to be a dodgy DVD factory.

Who'd I feed that one to?

Standing at the top of his wide staircase, looking down at the marble-floored hall below, the staircase wall decorated by two Graham Knuttells and a Charlie Whisker, Lar swung his arms forward, back again, and forward, ten times, twenty times, thirty times. Light on his feet coming down the stairs, feeling his body strong, pliable, sensing the energy in his legs, the strength in his arms, the tang of life on his lips.

17

Dixie Peyton wasn't lying. Her face was frightened and angry and mostly puzzled. Harry Synnott knew that whatever was going on she wasn't lying about the DVD factory.

'I swear, I know it's true.'

Less than an hour after the failed raid, Synnott arrived at Mountjoy prison and confronted Dixie in the same small administration-block room where she'd sold him the information. It took him seconds to know she wasn't lying. Probably she'd picked it up wrong. Or she'd got it from someone who'd got it garbled from someone else.

'Who told you about the warehouse?'

'That wasn't part of the deal.'

'What deal? You make up a story—'

'I made nothing up!'

'– and you put a premium price on your lies—'

'I wasn't lying!'

'Who told you about the warehouse?'

Dixie's breathing sounded like she'd been in a serious struggle.

'I want to get out of here. I want my three hundred.'

'Who told you about the warehouse?'

Her head was down, her elbow on the table in front of her, her forehead resting on the rigid fingers of her right hand. She spoke without looking at Synnott, her voice barely controlled.

'Please. I *need* to get out of here. And I need the *money*.'

His voice was soft. 'Always, Dixie, going right back, you know I've looked after you. But fair is fair. You give me something, I do what I can. And when you give me shit, like you did – it's embarrassing for me, I have to wonder if you're messing me about. See it from my point of view.'

'Please.'

'What I'll do, the best I can do, I'll have a word, bail shouldn't be a problem. The three hundred – I mean, we have to be sensible.'

Dixie sat there, and as her head tilted forward the fingers of her right hand went back through her hair, slowly, rigid like a claw. She took hold of a handful of hair and held it tightly, her forearm shaking, the hair straining at the roots. When she looked up at Synnott she'd managed to keep the tears from coming out.

Twenty-what – Synnott did a mental sum and came up with twenty-eight, maybe twenty-nine. The look of her, she might be five years older. Dixie wasn't holding up well.

She'd looked so offended, that first time he'd raided her house, on a tip that Owen Peyton was holding a gun for a gang member with whom he'd once shared a cell.

'I'm not a criminal.'

'You're married to one.'

'My husband isn't a criminal. He's a driver. He drives a van.'

Then, her face had been toned and soft, the jawline firm and the skin had had the colour and texture of youth that no amount of cosmetics could replicate. Her skin now was pale, blotchy, her arms, once slender, were now merely thin.

The first time he'd seen her after Owen died was when she'd been getting out of a patrol car in the yard of Sundrive Road, where Synnott was stationed at the time. She was handcuffed, drunk and she had a satisfied smile on her face. Despite her circumstances, she had the bounce and spirit he remembered. He recognised her immediately.

I'm not a criminal.

Synnott found out from a sergeant what the charge was.

'Pissed out of her head, standing outside a house on Wicker Close. She arrived with a dozen cans of Heineken from the off-licence, had one left when the lads got there.'

'She drank eleven cans of beer?'

'Didn't drink any beer. She was pissed on vodka long before she ever got there. She was throwing the full cans at the windows of the house. They bounced off the windows – double glazing – one of them smashed the glass on the door.'

'Why?'

'According to the neighbours, she stood there, screaming at the house – something about Obi-Wan being a bastard. Over and over. And when she felt like it she threw a can of beer at the house.'

'Obi-Wan?'

'Nickname of the guy who lives there. Obi-Wan Kenobi. Middle-aged guy, family man.'

'This a sex thing?'

'I don't think so. All she'd say was Obi-Wan was a bastard.'

'What does he say?'

'Not home. Himself and his missus were out, left the lights on. I'll send a lad out later to talk to them.'

Harry Synnott said he'd go and see Obi-Wan.

Obi-Wan turned out to be a reasonable man – he knew Dixie, he said, they'd had a falling-out, he didn't want her to get into trouble. Back at the station, Synnott squared it with the sergeant.

'You can go home,' he told Dixie. 'I've had a word.'

'Thanks.'

'How are things? The kid?'

'Bastard promised me.'

'Obi-Wan?'

'Know what he said? *It wouldn't look right, Dixie. Nothing against you, Dixie,* but Owen – he didn't know about Owen until the accident. If he recommends someone, people trust his word.'

Dixie smiled at Harry Synnott. 'And we don't want the local gangster's widow messing things up, do we? A wallet goes missing, the petty cash doesn't add up – oh, it must be the bitch that Obi-Wan recommended. You know – the gangster's widow.'

'Where are you living now?'

'I'm staying with Shelley Hogan, she's a mate from Cairnloch. Has a flat. She's looking after Christopher.'

Synnott gave Dixie a lift to Shelley's place. He paid her a visit a week later and made admiring remarks about the baby and after she made him a cup of coffee he said, 'You could help me, Dixie, maybe help yourself at the same time. It's not like there's a big budget, but—'

She looked him in the eye.

He said, 'Nothing formal. Just, you know, you see something, hear something. The kind of people you know.'

'I'm not a tout.'

'I wouldn't want you to be. It's just, if there's something – look, I'll leave a number.'

'No point.'

It was almost a year before she called him the first time.

'Please, Mr Synnott.'

The bastard was looking at her like she was something in a test tube.

'You embarrassed me, Dixie.' His voice was soft. 'Organising a raid, it involves other people. I end up with egg on my face. OK, I know you didn't mean that, but all the same – you give me nothing and I do you favours, pretty soon that's all we have. All take, no give.'

'Please.'

'I'll sort out the bail arrangements – it's the best I can do.'

'The three hundred – could you—'

'We've been through that.'

'Just two hundred—'

Synnott was on his feet. 'Take care, Dixie.'

'Fuck you!'

At the door he said, 'I know you don't mean that.' And he was gone.

18

Joshua Boyce went into the jewellery shop with a baseball hat on his head, a big false moustache on his face and an empty holdall over one shoulder. When he took a nine-millimetre Sig-Sauer P226 automatic out of his anorak pocket the jeweller and his assistant looked for a moment as though they might be about to run somewhere, then they thought better of it. The assistant was a guy about twenty-two, short dyed blond hair gelled into thorny shapes like something designed by an unemployable architect. He won the race to put his hands up.

'I'm not going to scream at you,' Joshua Boyce said in a casual voice. 'I won't threaten you. But you should know that I'll do what I have to do to get what I want done. Is that understood?'

Neither of the two said anything.

'Good,' Boyce said. 'If we all know the rules, let's get started.' He walked straight over to the assistant and hit him on the nose with the butt of the Sig-Sauer.

Boyce stood back as the blood spurted down the guy's front. Nothing like a bloody nose to subdue the civilians. The young guy held his face and tried not to blubber, the blood splashed all down his dazzling white shirt.

Boyce turned to the jeweller. 'You can have some of that.'

'Please, no.'

The jeweller was a ball of putty. Small guy, young, maybe

thirty, fat, thin lips and a tremor in his voice. Having seen what had happened to his assistant just for cooperating, he put a lot of effort into avoiding eye contact with the gunman. He kept his face averted, showing that he didn't want to even guess what the guy looked like behind the big fake moustache. He immediately offered Joshua Boyce a heavy ring of keys.

Boyce shook his head. 'Lock the front door, then we go inside,' he said, gesturing towards the back room. 'The safe first.'

When they got into the back room the jeweller offered the keys again. 'Take what you want.'

Boyce threw the holdall at the jeweller's feet.

'*You* do it.'

The bag was a lot heavier when he got it back. Boyce checked the safe and found a leather folder with a thick wad of banknotes inside. He put it into the holdall, turned and found the jeweller taking a step back, one hand clutching the front of his shirt. 'Do anything like that again', Boyce said, 'and I tie you up and set fire to the place when I go.'

The assistant was making moaning sounds. He tried to say something but the words were muffled. Joshua Boyce went to him and examined his face. 'Broken nose. Not to worry, son. It'll add a little mystery to your image.'

There were tears brimming in the assistant's eyes. Joshua Boyce waved his gun.

'Let's go out front.' Again he threw the bag at the jeweller's feet and this time it gave a prosperous rattle. 'Fill it up from the display cases. Just the merchandise, dump the trays and the packaging.'

In the front of the shop, the assistant picked up a black cloth from behind the counter and tentatively held it to his nose.

'No,' Boyce said. The assistant dropped the cloth. The blood was still dripping onto his white shirt. Amazing how a nose dripping blood takes the pep out of someone who might otherwise give in to the prompting of his testosterone and do something stupid.

Boyce pointed at the display cases. 'There, there, and that one, first. No shit, no trinkets.'

It took the jeweller little more than a minute to empty the selected display cases. Then Boyce pointed out several more, directing the jeweller mostly to the display cases behind the counter.

'Go, please.' The jeweller was holding out the holdall.

Joshua Boyce looked around, then gestured with his gun hand towards a long narrow display case on the far wall. 'Be generous.'

After the jeweller spent another couple of minutes filling the bag Boyce said, 'That'll do.' He gestured towards the back room. 'Inside.'

Watching them shuffle through the doorway, Boyce was looking forward to this part. Once inside, he waited, let a few seconds pass with them just standing there. Then he watched the jeweller's face when he said, 'Now we'll do the floor safe.'

The man's mouth opened, his eyes flared and died and Boyce could hear him breathing from across the room. He could see the man was about to say something stupid about there not being any other safe, so Boyce used the gun to gesture at the assistant and said, 'Take up the carpet, that's a good boy.'

The assistant held the back of one hand to his nose while he bent and used his other hand to pull up one of the flecked grey carpet tiles, revealing a small circular metal door set in the floor, about nine inches in diameter. By the time the assistant stood up the jeweller was moving like he'd abandoned any hope. He knelt and tapped in the combination. There was just one thing in the floor safe, a black velvet bag, not big but heavy. The jeweller clasped the bag in both hands, holding it against his chest like he was hoping there might be something he could do to hold on to it. Boyce threw the holdall on the floor. 'In there.'

He took their mobiles, ripped the phone line out of the wall, and told them that anyone coming out of the shop in the next fifteen minutes could count on being shot.

*

The street was as it always was, nothing worrying going on. Turning right, heading towards the car park of the twenty-four-hour shop, Boyce maintained a natural unhurried stride. *Nothing offbeat so no one gets excited.* If the jeweller or the assistant got a dose of heroics and came barrelling out after him he'd have to speed things up, but the smashed nose and the dripping blood had almost certainly taken care of that.

Nice and easy does it.

The stolen getaway car was a blue Honda Accord. Joshua Boyce was twenty feet away from it, with the key in one hand and the holdall of stolen jewellery in the other, when someone shouted, 'Stop, thief!'

Jesus, fuck.

Boyce stopped, stood, and for a moment he couldn't imagine who it was. Then it dawned on him who the fool had to be. He turned and saw the lanky, shaven-headed security man from the building society next door to the jewellery shop.

Had to be him.

Had to be a clown who imagines himself a tough guy – had to be, to brace someone with a gun.

Not a cop, none of them that dumb. ERU, maybe, waving their Uzis, but if it was that lot Boyce would be dead by now.

Had to be the tall bald Dumbo in the uniform.

He'd been lounging as usual in front of the building society when Boyce came out of the jewellery shop. Boyce had paid him no more attention than he'd paid the nearest lamp-post. Maybe Boyce had missed something. Maybe Dumbo had heard something during the robbery. Maybe, once they'd given Boyce time enough to get a good distance from the shop, the jeweller or his assistant had run out, looking for help.

Whatever it was, Dumbo got to play the scene he'd fantasised about since the first time he'd put on his pale blue uniform.

'Stop, thief!'

The guy's not for real.

Joshua showed him the gun. Didn't point it at him, just let him see it. Looked him in the eye.

The gobshite kept coming, the twist in his lips displaying contempt, his large shoulders flexing under his blue uniform.

Joshua raised his gun and Dumbo stopped.

He kept his hands down by his sides and straightened his back and Boyce knew what he was about to say and then he said it.

'Big man,' Dumbo said. 'Wouldn't be such a big man if you didn't have that fucking thing.'

Boyce turned and walked quickly towards the car. When he looked back Dumbo hadn't moved. Boyce got the door open, threw the holdall inside. He could hear running footsteps and he turned and pointed the gun at Dumbo's chest and this time Dumbo didn't stop. Boyce raised the gun to fire over Dumbo's head but that was no good. At that angle, a shot might hit any one of half a dozen second-floor windows of the building at the other side of the car park.

And then it didn't matter, because Dumbo was running right through Joshua Boyce, clutching at his shoulders, and they were both bouncing off the Accord and going down onto the tarmac.

Boyce swung his body so that Dumbo landed first and when Boyce came down on him Dumbo made a whooshing noise that ended in a squeak.

Dumbo was stupid, but he was as strong as he looked. He had one hand curling up around Boyce's shoulder as the other gripped the elbow of Boyce's gun arm.

Stupid, maybe, but Dumbo was getting to be a problem. Enough passers-by around for at least one of them to be reaching for a mobile.

Boyce let his gun arm give in to Dumbo's pull, letting it move towards the fool, holding back just enough so that Dumbo thought it was all his own doing. Then Boyce let the arm go slack, then immediately jerked it forward, breaking Dumbo's grip.

Dumbo made an excited grunting noise and Boyce rolled over and got one foot flat on the ground, the knee angled for leverage, keeping his gun arm out of Dumbo's reach.

Dumbo's free hand didn't go for the gun – it wrapped around Boyce's neck, and it felt like a metal restraint locking into place. Then Boyce lost his tentative footing and he was coming down on his side, both Dumbo's arms holding him from behind.

Boyce rocked his body from side to side, testing the firmness of Dumbo's grip. There wasn't much give. Dumbo had fastened himself onto Boyce's back like he was a steel trap.

Boyce raised one foot and lashed back. Dumbo grunted again as Boyce's heel connected with his shin. It was a glancing blow, and next time Boyce lashed out there was nothing there – Dumbo was holding his legs back out of harm's way.

It stays like this, it's all over.

If Boyce wasn't well away from here in the next minute or two, chances were he'd still be held down like a struggling bug when the police showed up.

Boyce reached down with his gun hand, feeling his way until the gun was resting against the side of Dumbo's thigh.

'Let go.'

'Fuck off!'

'Right now,' Boyce said, 'and we both walk away.'

Dumbo's voice came in ragged bursts. 'Not such a – big fucking man – now, are ya?'

Boyce stretched both his legs forward as far as he could. They were out of the firing line but you could never tell, once a gun went off, what it might hit and where the bullet might go afterwards.

Dumbo made an aggressive noise through clenched teeth and when Boyce squeezed the trigger the noise turned to a high-pitched scream.

As the security man's grip slackened, Boyce rolled clear and stood up, stepping away from Dumbo, who was rolling, clutching his leg above the knee, making a muted gasping noise now. Boyce opened the door of the Accord and climbed in. He started the engine and closed the door but saw there was no way of driving off without running over Dumbo.

Boyce got out of the car and got behind Dumbo. He bent and held him under the arms and backed away, pulling him towards the side of the car park.

Dumbo screamed, 'You bastard!' Then he began making threats, his squeak rising in pitch. One of his shoes had come off. He was wearing yellow socks decorated with some kind of cartoon character

Boyce dropped Dumbo and got back into the Accord. No sound of sirens. As he gunned the motor, he saw half a dozen people across the road, looking his way. Two of them were talking into mobiles.

Great.

As Boyce swung the car out of the car park, he glanced back and saw that Dumbo was leaning on one elbow, trying to stand up.

*

Detective Garda Rose Cheney finished typing up a long-overdue report on a child abuse case just in time to leave for the courts. The way traffic was, it meant adding half an hour to the usual driving time, just in case. Better that a copper be an hour early than keep a judge waiting half a minute. She pulled on a jacket and was reaching for her handbag when her mobile rang. The caller introduced himself as a detective from Earlsfort Terrace. 'You're dealing with an alleged rape, I'm told?'

'Who said?'

'A colleague mentioned it, knew I'd an interest, put me onto you. The name of the alleged rapist is Hapgood, I'm told?'

'You know him?'

'We should talk.'

19

The Kellsboro Shopping Arcade was barely a six-minute drive from the jewellery shop and Joshua Boyce decided that was as far as he could go in the hot Accord. The small collection of shops, jam-packed under a perspex roof that badly needed hosing down, had been opened in the 1980s. It now had too many scuff marks, too many faulty light fittings, too few customers. Like everything else around here it was losing out to the new shopping centre a couple of miles up the main road between Kellsboro and the outer suburbs. Boyce needed a minute of privacy and the shopping arcade would do.

Once the cops got into gear there wouldn't be a garda in the country who didn't have a description of the car. The plan had been to use the Accord to get to a second getaway car, but Dumbo had blown that. Boyce would have to improvise.

He took his holdall and left the Accord in the shopping arcade car park with the door slightly open and the keys in the ignition. There was a chance that some loser would steal it and give the police something to keep them occupied.

Fucking Dumbo.

An armed robbery at a poky little jewellery shop would make the news, but way down the list. A shooting, even a nick in the leg of a gobshite security guard, raised the ante.

Inside the Arcade, Clara's Coffee Shop had cheap mugs,

scarred Formica tabletops and a dyed-blonde waitress with the disposition of someone doing community service. All five customers were pensioners killing time, two of them eating belated breakfasts, the others nursing cups of something brown. Walking past the waitress, Boyce's smile was all sunshine and roses as he ordered a coffee and continued on through to the tiny toilet down the back. He took off the anorak and stuck the baseball hat in one of its pockets along with the false moustache. He put the lot into the holdall along with the jewellery.

He looked at his watch. Almost ten-thirty.

When he came out of the toilet he noticed an emergency exit at the end of a short, murky corridor. He went to it and pushed down on the bar. The yard the door opened onto had a metal gate with large bolts, no lock, and when he opened it he found himself in a laneway. At the end of the laneway he crossed the road. A bus was just approaching a stop thirty yards further on. The jewellery in the holdall rattled as he ran.

Boyce got to the stop as the last of the four or five people in the queue shuffled aboard. He put some coins into the machine beside the driver and waited for his ticket. He had no idea where the bus was going.

*

Detective Garda Rose Cheney was in her Astra, on her way to the Circuit Criminal Court, when her mobile rang. She pressed a button on the hands-free and the car filled with a voice she recognised as a lawyer from the Chief State Solicitor's office.

'Detective Garda Cheney?'

Cheney said, 'Bollocks.'

'I'm afraid so, garda.'

'What is it this time?'

'He's claiming that all the publicity makes a fair trial impossible. His high profile, and the resultant media comment is prejudicial – he wants it put back indefinitely, to create a cordon sanitaire. The papers went in this morning.'

'But, he's – ah, Jesus!'

'I know, he's the one who created most of the publicity. If he gets a judge with the balls of a performing flea he'll be told to take a running jump, but – in the meantime.'

'Bollocks.'

This was the fourth legal motion designed to postpone or sabotage the trial of a prominent accountant accused of several varieties of corruption. The attempts to find a loophole had precedents in various high-profile trials, and the accountant had the money to employ enough lawyers to trawl the books in search of fresh punctures in the law through which he might wriggle. Cheney's only involvement in the case was that she had accompanied several members of the Criminal Assets Bureau in a raid on the accountant's home. Her evidence would be formal and routine, but the defendant's lawyers were conceding nothing. It had already cost Cheney several wasted days hanging around the courts, waiting for the trial to get into gear.

'How long will this one take?'

'Depends on the testicular condition of the performing flea. Anywhere from a week to several months – and if he gets his cordon sanitaire, who knows?'

'The Yanks could put Michael Jackson and OJ on trial, the Brits could put Jeffrey Archer in the slammer – Jesus, this is a joke.'

Cheney turned onto a side avenue that would eventually allow her to double back towards Macken Road. She stopped and left the engine running while she called the station to let them know she wasn't on court duty after all. The sergeant on the other end told her about the robbery at a jeweller's shop in the Kellsboro area.

*

When Detective Inspector Harry Synnott arrived at the jeweller's shop, there were two uniforms there and a third maybe a hundred yards up the street, holding traffic back as an ambulance, siren shrieking, came out of a car park and sped away. A young man with a peculiar hairstyle was standing outside the jewellery shop, his head held back, his white shirt streaked with blood, a couple of civilians looking solicitous.

'What's the score?'

The older of the two uniforms pointed out the shop where the hold-up had happened, and told him the guy with the bloody nose was an employee. 'The jeweller's down the road, having a coffee to steady his nerves.'

'The call said shots fired – in the shop?'

'There was a security man – from the building society, had a go. That was him in the ambulance. Flesh wound – up the street it happened, there's a car park.'

Synnott looked in the direction the uniform was pointing and saw that the garda who had directed the ambulance onto the roadway was walking back towards the jeweller's shop.

'Anyone securing the scene of the shooting?'

The two uniforms said nothing.

Synnott spoke to the younger of them. 'Tell that fool to go back, you go with him. Nothing more goes into or comes out of that car park – no one gets in, no matter how urgently they need to get their car.'

The younger uniform moved away in a hurry.

To the other one, Synnott said, 'Have we got a description?'

'It's been called in. Early thirties, five-ten or so, moustache, baseball cap, jeans, anorak – driving a dark blue Accord. Two witnesses got the reg – but they disagree on the last two numbers.'

'We're going to need enough members here for control and search and to canvass for witnesses.'

As the uniform spoke into his radio, requesting support, Synnott crossed the pavement and went into the jeweller's shop. Most of the businesses around here hadn't seen a lick of new paint in ten years, and never would. The area had redevelopment written all over it. The jeweller's shop was lit like an operating theatre, with bevelled glass everywhere and walnut casings for the display units. It managed the trick of looking expensive and tacky at the same time. Sometimes it seemed to Synnott that over the past few years half the city had been redesigned and built by the people who make those crappy little earphones that cost a small fortune and still leak tinny music. There were some drops of blood on a glass-topped counter. *That'd be from the assistant.*

When Synnott came out, he saw Rose Cheney's car pull up across the road. She parked with two wheels on the pavement.

*

The bus took Joshua Boyce through Rathmines, where he got off and spent twenty minutes in a taxi, crossing the city to Dorset Street. After a minute waiting on the footpath, he flagged down a second taxi and got into the back.

'The airport.'

The driver glanced at the mirror. 'Travelling light?'

Boyce had the holdall on his lap.

'Just the weekend.'

'Going over for the match?'

'Ahuh.' Boyce had no idea who was playing.

He looked at his watch. Eleven-seven.

The driver gave his opinion about Chelsea. Boyce made appropriate sounds.

A little over twenty minutes later he got out at Dublin Airport's departures terminal, then took a five-minute taxi ride back to the long-term car park and went directly to the Hyundai he'd parked there three days back. He opened the boot and lifted the mat. Leaning in, his body concealing his actions from any casual observer, he put the Sig-Sauer into the empty spare-wheel bay and then the jewellery. He dropped the mat back on top, put the anorak and the empty holdall on the mat, then threw his gloves in. Keeping his fingers inside his sleeve, he used his forearm to slam the boot shut.

He looked at his watch. Eleven thirty-nine.

20

The jeweller looked like someone who'd lost a winning lottery ticket. If he wasn't patting his pockets he was rubbing the side of his face, pinching his chin or using his nails to scrape something invisible from his forehead.

He was sitting in a booth in the coffee shop a few doors down from his place of business. A waitress gave him a sympathetic tut-tut and refilled his mug.

Harry Synnott said, 'We'll need a list of everything stolen – you have photographs?'

The jeweller nodded. 'Except the cheap stuff – though he didn't take much of that.'

'Any idea of the value?'

The jeweller shook his head.

'You recognise anything about this guy? The voice? The accent?'

Another shake of the head

'Anything he said strike you as odd? Maybe a turn of phrase, something you've heard someone else say – a customer, maybe?'

The jeweller had nothing helpful to say. Synnott went back to the jeweller's shop and found a detective there named Costigan. He told him to take custody of the shop's CCTV tape.

'Then take a walk down the street, fifty yards down to the left, then back the other way, all the way up as far as the car park where the shooting happened. Take a note of every CCTV, get hold of the tapes.'

By the time a second ambulance arrived at the scene, a passing civilian had worked on the assistant with the peculiar hairstyle and had managed to staunch the flow of blood from his nose. The kid didn't want to go to the hospital but the ambulance men insisted. Rose Cheney went with him. He said his name was Stephen.

'Take your time, Stephen. Let's go through everything, step by step.'

Sitting in an administrator's office, sipping a glass of water, Stephen told Cheney about the shock he got when he saw the gunman coming into the shop. When he told her about how the gunman used the gun to thump him in the face she put on such a motherly look that Stephen felt it might be OK to let go of the tears he'd been holding back. When he'd arrived in the A&E he'd asked a nurse to call his mother at her workplace, let her know what happened, and the message back was that she'd call him at home at lunchtime.

A thing like this, you get your nose smashed, everyone's supposed to be all over you, but so far this cop – she was way older than Stephen, but not bad at all – she was the only one to act like he deserved a little consolation. After the gunman left, Stephen had expected his boss to fuss over him, instead of which the stingy bastard had stood there, thumping the counter and making grief-stricken noises.

'My nose,' Stephen said, and the jeweller got him a dirty towel from the midget bathroom at the back of the shop. Stephen threw it on the counter and held the sleeve of his white shirt against his nose.

'Do you think,' Stephen asked the policewoman now, 'I could claim for this? It's destroyed.' He looked down at the bloody stains on the front of his white shirt and on the right sleeve and said, 'It's from Thomas Pink.'

'I'm sure your employer will make good. After all, I'd say it's a work-related injury.'

'Tight bastard.'

Apart from the grief-stricken noises all the jeweller said to Stephen was, 'Say nothing about nothing, right? You know what I mean.'

The policewoman took Stephen through the sequence of events as the gunman directed the collection of jewellery. 'Did he say anything? Did he know much about jewellery? Did he suggest particular pieces?'

Stephen could tell that she *cared*. It wasn't like he was just a flunkey in someone else's world: she listened to him like he was someone who mattered. So he told her everything.

After about twenty minutes she gave Stephen a big smile and said, 'You're terrific. Could I just ask you to hold on a minute? I need to make a phone call.'

*

When Joshua Boyce left the long-term car park at the airport, he crossed the Swords Road and walked for almost fifteen minutes and when he reached the short-term car park he got into a Nissan he'd arranged to have parked there that morning. He drove the two miles up the road to the Northway Retail Park, where he went into the furniture section of the Perry Logan superstore.

He looked at his watch. A minute past twelve.

After strolling around for a couple of minutes he saw Antoinette. He casually joined his wife in the middle of a row of beds. They didn't greet each other.

'Which one?'

Antoinette said, 'The one with the curved headboard.'

'You don't think it's a bit colonial?'

'They're delivering it next Tuesday.'

'That's quick.'

'You like it?'

'It was your choice, I thought it was a bit colonial, but I went along.'

He kissed Antoinette, then said, 'See you back here in a minute.'

He went through the store to the electronic section, where he immediately took a Canon photoprinter to the pay-point and used his Visa card.

After the 'guess what' phone call from Rose Cheney, Harry Synnott went back to the coffee shop, sat down across the booth from the jeweller and said, 'Tell me about the safe in the floor.'

The jeweller sat very still.

Harry Synnott said, 'You ask me what safe and twenty minutes from now a half-dozen policemen will be digging up your floor with pickaxes. Then I'll charge you with obstruction of a criminal investigation. Tell me about the safe in the floor.'

The jeweller's name used to be Murphy and his parents named him Patrick, a decision he came to bitterly resent as an adult. In a society in which image mattered, where a cosmopolitan tinge could justify a premium price, the jeweller didn't see himself as a Paddy Murphy.

When, at the age of twenty-six, Paddy Murphy received a considerable inheritance from a grandfather who had never said two kind words to him when he was alive, he bought a half-share in a small and faltering jeweller's shop owned by an old fool. The old fool had accumulated a fortune from his decades in the jewellery business, but he was a conservative, out-of-touch fossil who had no understanding of the possibilities open to a businessman attuned to modern Ireland's need for the proper fashion accoutrements. For a couple of years, Paddy Murphy made himself a nuisance, constantly questioning stock decisions, pestering his partner with queries and demanding explanations for the most routine business judgements. When he offered to buy him out, the old fool hurriedly accepted.

At twenty-nine, Paddy Murphy had taken a crucial step on what was scheduled to become a legendary rise to the summit of Irish moneymaking. The shop would be modernised, applying all the marketing principles he'd learned at the business school. He would seek out young designers in touch with the *Zeitgeist*. He referred to the shop sometimes as a launch pad and at other times as a cash cow. It would finance his initial foray into property. That was the business where anyone with a million to invest at breakfast time could be sure of a million and a half by lunch.

Believing that his name was inappropriate for the class of person he intended to become, Paddy Murphy adopted and adapted the names of two of his favourite Hollywood stars, Julia Roberts and Andy Garcia, and for professional purposes became Mr Robert Garcia. It was the name above his shop, and it was printed in gold on the faux-leather jewellery boxes in which he sold his goods. The professional name soon became the name he used in his personal life.

Within a year of taking over the shop, he had borrowed heavily to invest in his modernisation and marketing plans. The shop's internal lighting scheme alone cost €60,000, the new display and counter modules another hundred and thirty grand, while the revamped exterior, the translucent wrapping paper and the faux-leather jewellery boxes cost only one sixth of the amount he spent in advertising during that year. On top of all that, he now had a wife with a serious Prada habit and the upkeep of his two kids cost so much that he briefly considered downsizing from his VW Tuareg 4×4. The redevelopment of the cash-cow shop came to fruition just in time for the business to collapse, as customers flocked to the new shopping centre two miles away. The centre had three jewellers' shops, all staffed by extraordinarily thin young women with long straight hair.

Robert Garcia cut his staff to the bare bone, just himself and the kid he thought of as his idiot assistant, and still he was losing money. More than once since getting into the business he'd been approached to buy jewellery that he reckoned was of doubtful provenance. With incoming cash flowing like treacle, and the bank threatening to take his shop if he didn't do something to make up the payments he'd missed, Robert Garcia made a phone call.

What was required was terribly simple. Through previous transactions, one of them questionable but probably legal, he already had a trade contact in Leeds who could shift the stuff for him. He had the expertise to price the dodgy jewellery. He had the money belt in which it could nestle on the flight to Leeds and Bradford airport. He had the trade knowledge to deal with the buyers at the other end.

He had the floor safe installed for extra security. That was supposed to ensure that the special merchandise would be OK. The possibility that some thug might rob the shop came with the territory but the floor safe was supposed to safeguard the uninsurable commodities.

It mattered. The man who'd approached Robert Garcia about the special merchandise had prefaced everything with a warning. 'You fuck up, you pull a fast one, you even think about it, well—' And the man had used his thumb and forefinger to make the shape of a gun.

The first three transactions had gone swimmingly and one client led to another. That part of his business flourished and the generous commission he negotiated made the difference. Sooner or later the property people who'd been snapping up premises around this part of Kellsboro would make an acceptable offer. So far, the vultures were trying to get the place on the cheap. Mr Garcia suspected that they knew he was in hock to the banks – all those fuckers gang up against the small businessman, he knew that. They'd make a realistic offer, though, if he could just keep afloat long enough.

Now this.

His thoughts wouldn't stay in line. He tried to think it through – the police didn't know what was in the safe, so as long as he kept his mouth shut – the people he was shifting the stuff for, what if they thought he – the police might think – but there was no—

Jesus.

The people who owned this stuff – what if they thought he was in league with the— Ah, Jesus—

With red friction marks on his chin, cheek and forehead where he'd been rubbing his face since the man came into his shop with a gun, Mr Paddy Robert Garcia Murphy looked across the café table at the detective who was threatening to have his shop floor dug up. He said a line he'd learned not at the business school but from dozens of TV cop shows. 'I want my lawyer.'

21

Dixie got bail just after ten o'clock and it took her an hour to get home. She waited a few minutes at a bus stop near the courts, then got restless and began walking up along the quays.

On O'Connell Bridge, she took off her red jacket. It was clean enough but it was cheap and she'd washed it too many times – the material looked tired, the colour anaemic. She folded the jacket over one arm. Her jeans were OK, her black T-shirt was a little light for the April weather, but she felt cleaner, less conspicuous among the shoppers.

Across O'Connell Bridge and down the south quays. The sky around here had been full of cranes for the past few years, office buildings and hotels shooting up. Beyond the Custom House, either side of the river, there were times when Dixie thought it looked like something from a science fiction movie. She'd crossed the bridge to the North Quay one afternoon and taken a walk through the Financial Centre, past discreet bars and restaurants with French and Italian names, past chrome-clad shops that looked like the de luxe versions of similar ones elsewhere in the city. She felt as though she'd wandered across an invisible border into a foreign country.

Now she took a right through the Grand Canal area. More offices, apartment towers, and bars that looked like upmarket staff canteens, where expensively dressed young office workers with assisted tans made connections over drinks that had humorous names. Eventually, in the area between Grand Canal and Ringsend, Dixie reached South Crescent, a curving network of one- and two-storey houses, where she had lived for the past three years. The land was reclaimed from the bay, the small houses built for the employees of the docks and the factories and mills that had grown up around them more than a hundred years before. Now some working-class families remained, but increasing numbers of the little houses had been bought up by the young executives working in the glass monuments to prosperity that dominated the area. The doors and windows of many of the houses had been modernised, with wooden blinds behind double glazing, the interiors all polished floors and off-white walls. Extensions had been affixed to the backs of some of the houses, some of the extensions bigger than the original dwellings.

Dixie lived on Portmahon Terrace, halfway down a row of two-storey terraced houses, no front gardens, narrow pavements separated by a roadway that wasn't much wider. When she got there old Mr Jordan was sitting on a kitchen chair on the pavement in front of his house, directly across from hers. Mr Jordan, who had lived in the same house since childhood, had retired from work after he got a few thousand in a pay-off for losing his left hand in an industrial accident. That money had long since gone on groceries. Mr Jordan, unmarried and apparently content in his solitude, lived for the sun. As soon as a day worked up a blush of sunshine he brought a kitchen chair to the pavement out front and sat there for several hours. Sometimes he brought a newspaper and held it at arm's length, reading it through glasses perched on the tip of his nose. He held the folded newspaper with his remaining hand and occasionally tucked it between his chin and his chest to turn a page awkwardly. Mostly he just sat there, one knee crossed over the other, face tilted towards the sky.

Today, in weather that still had a touch of winter about it, Mr Jordan was wearing the black jacket and trousers that weren't quite close enough in shade to pass for a suit. He sometimes wore a black felt hat but today he was bareheaded. On a sunny day, he'd leave the jacket off and roll up the right sleeve of his shirt, leaving the other sleeve pinned up over the stump of his wrist. Dixie had never seen him without a tie. She sometimes wondered how he put it on.

He nodded a silent greeting to Dixie as she approached her house. She nodded back.

Inside, she had a shower and lay on her bed. She hadn't got much sleep in Mountjoy but now she spent an hour just staring at the ceiling. When she felt hungry she went downstairs, opened a tin of ravioli, poured it into a saucepan and put the stove on a low heat. Then she went back upstairs. She avoided looking at herself in the full-length mirror beside the wardrobe. The brown skirt and the tan blouse she'd worn on Monday were on the floor, where she'd flung them after the meeting with the bitch.

Four days ago? Is that all?

She took down a white blouse and a pair of light blue jeans. There would be a time for nice clothes, a time for dressing up, a time for more than getting through the day. She had no idea when that might be, and she accepted it might never happen.

After Owen died, the thought that Dixie tried to connect with was *Get back on the rails*. It took a while to accept that there were no rails any more, no certainties. The only thing she could be sure of was the purity of the moments that she shared with Christopher. It didn't matter where they were or what happened before or after, or what was going on in the rest of her life – the certainty of what she felt for the child and the warmth that was reflected back from him created a kind of sanctuary. Now that too was in danger of crumbling.

Get through this.

Money.

Dixie sat on the bed and went over the possibilities, as she'd done a hundred times over the previous few days. There was nothing in the house she could sell. The radio was a cheap piece of junk, the television was a small portable. No clothes worth shit. The jewellery that Owen had given her was long gone, the stuff left was the kind of thing they sold from the stand near the register at Penney's.

Five hundred would get her free and clear and on her way. Even the three hundred that Inspector Synnott had welshed on. In her pocket she had less than a tenner.

Maybe get twenty for her watch. Fifteen, more likely.

Twenty-five, total.

Today was collection day for the Widow's Pension. She got the pension book from the kitchen drawer and put it in the back pocket of her jeans. She'd bring back a hundred and fifty from the Post Office.

Not nearly enough.

There was a camera somewhere. It was a Kodak, Brendan's. Worth bugger-all.

Nothing to sell, nothing easy to steal. The thing with the bloody syringe had been a disaster.

Synnott—

Bastard – all he had to do—

Dixie went downstairs and was halfway through the ravioli when she had an idea. She spent several minutes rummaging until she found Brendan's Kodak, then left the house and crossed the street. Although Mr Jordan's chair was still on the pavement he was gone. Dixie knocked on the open front door.

'Mr Jordan?'

When he came out it seemed to Dixie that he didn't recognise her. She hadn't been up this close to him since a couple of Christmas Eves ago when she'd brought him a small Christmas cake that she'd bought in Tesco. Up close now, she could see specks of hardened food on the front of his jacket.

'Mr Jordan – it's me, Dixie Peyton.'

He just stared at her.

'I've never – Mr Jordan, it's just that things are a bit tight at the moment. I'm not asking – it's just, would you like to buy a camera?'

He looked at the Kodak she held out.

'It's a good one,' she said. *Push him to fifty, eighty – not worth a fraction of that, but how could he know?*

Mr Jordan said, 'I don't – I haven't taken a picture – not since—'

'Mr Jordan, I – please, I really—'

She stopped.

It was like talking to a fucking lamp-post. She looked past him, down the hall to his kitchen, where she could see a saucepan on the stove, the lid bobbing as steam escaped.

Has to be something in his house worth real money.

The only thing that made sense was to just walk past him, into the house, have a look around – *fuck him* – see what there was to be taken. Old people like that – all those years to accumulate stuff – and if he tried to stop her, that wouldn't be a problem. Besides, once she got the money she needed she'd be long gone and he could tell the police and it wouldn't matter. Anything she got, he was probably insured, he'd get it back.

Mr Jordan was still staring at Dixie. His right arm was crossed over his chest, the left hanging down by his side, nothing below the cuff of the sleeve. His mouth was open, his eyes wide and fixed and it suddenly occurred to Dixie that it wasn't that he hadn't recognised her. He was terrified.

'I'll be, later,' he said, 'my pension – maybe—'

'Listen, Mr Jordan – I'm not – I'm OK, it'll be fine.'

'Are you sure?' The concern in the words was contradicted by the relief on his face.

For a moment, Dixie felt a surge of desperation – *just fucking do it – what's he going to do?*

One thump in the face and he'd be – go in, reef the place – there has to be—

Dixie turned and walked back across the road.

What was left of the ravioli was lukewarm.

Shelley?

Shelley had bugger-all to spare. Shelley was the kind of friend you got drunk or stoned with, told secrets to and in their teens she and Dixie had shared clothes, boyfriends and whatever money they had.

No matter what fix Shelley Hogan got herself into, down through the years, Dixie never had a doubt that her friend would wriggle out of it. Right now, though, there was little room to manoeuvre. Her husband had left Shelley with two kids and his heroin connection when he got a five-year sentence for armed robbery. Shelley had divorced him and her parents were looking after the kids until she got her shit together. These days she was living in Sunnyfield Apartments, a city-centre building east of O'Connell Street. She had the use of the place rent-free from the owner, a man named Robbie, with whom she'd had an on-off thing over the previous eighteen months. Robbie was her ex-husband's drug connection. He gave Shelley a discount on whatever she wanted – cocaine, cannabis, mostly heroin.

'I'm using it,' she told Dixie, 'it's not using me. I need it to get through a bad patch. Soon as I deal with this, I'll pull it all together again.'

Dixie had no doubt that was true. Shelley was as tough as stone. One of her other friends had nicknamed her Tight Corners because of the number of scrapes she'd got herself into and out of. These days, as though dispensing with unnecessary frivolity, Shelley had her hair cut tight and dyed deep black. Whatever her own problems, she never turned down Dixie's appeals for help. Money, though, wasn't something she could spare. Most of the money Shelley got her hands on went straight into the hole in her arm.

Three hundred. Jesus, there were times when Owen was flush and we'd spend that in an evening.

The noise at the door wasn't someone knocking to let her know they were outside. It sounded like someone had punched the door, twice. Then someone put a finger on the buzzer and kept it there.

The first thing Dixie thought was that the old bastard across the road had called the police.

I did nothing.

When she opened the door there were two men outside – she knew one of them, Matty Butler – and the younger one was already walking into the hallway, passing her, raising a single finger in warning, then taking the stairs two at a time.

Matty didn't raise his voice – he just stood in front of Dixie, one hand flat against the wall to the right of her head, his lips inches from her face when he said, 'Where is he?'

Matty Butler could see that the bitch was close to tears. All choked up. Not worth a fuck. He walked past her, stuck his head into the front room, then went into the kitchen. No one.

He could hear young Todd making noise upstairs. There was a loud crash as something got turned over. Todd liked to throw his weight around. No finesse. But that was OK sometimes, when an impression needed to be made.

Todd was making a lot of noise coming down the stairs and Matty went back out into the hall just in time to see the bitch running out the front door.

'Will I fetch her back?' Todd asked.

Matty shook his head. He went back into the kitchen, pulled out a couple of drawers, had a look at a noticeboard on the wall in a corner. There was a coupon for the neighbourhood Apache Pizza pinned to the board, a printed recipe for pancakes, a flyer for a local taxi firm and a little calendar announcing the dates of the monthly recycling collection. No scribbled notes, nothing like that on the small kitchen counter, nothing on the telephone table in the hall.

On his way back towards the front door, Matty saw that Todd

was standing in the middle of the front room, unzipping his fly. Todd liked to piss on things.

'Leave it,' Matty said. 'Come on. Places to go.'

As he got into the car Matty had his mobile to his ear. He heard Lar Mackendrick pick up and he said, 'Me.'

'Yeah?'

'No sign of him.'

22

Jesus.
  Matty Butler.
  Has to be Lar.
  They want Brendan.
  They found out.

Dixie knows about big brothers. Her brother Fiachra came home twice to ask her to move to London. He's fitting out apartments over there, he says, taking them over from builders, making them ready for the clients to move in. Good money.

'I can get you a place, a bit of work, you'll love it over there.'

Should have gone then.

Shaking her head, telling Fiachra *no* – this is where she belongs, she'd drown in a sea of strangers. Fiachra worried. 'You know where I am.'

Brendan Peyton is Owen's big brother. Not the same thing. A moocher. Chubby and cheerless. 'It's just that he's shy,' Owen used to say. 'He has a good heart.' Dixie thinks that's probably true but she doesn't really care.

Lar Mackendrick takes her aside at Owen's funeral.

'Good lad, Owen, the very best. I'm really sorry.' He calls around to the flat three days later and she makes him tea and he says this and that and when he's leaving he gives her an envelope containing five grand.

Two years later, a few bills overdue, Christopher's shoes too tight, Dixie goes visiting.

When Lar shakes his head she asks him again, begs him this time, and his face flares. 'I mean, fair is fair. Coming here like this, you're taking advantage.' He leans forward and says, 'Jesus, woman – some fucking nerve – I mean, I did the right thing when your fella died, right?'

'You were great, Lar, but the funeral, by the time I paid – Owen died doing a job for you, don't forget that—'

And he bares his teeth. 'Owen went into a ditch with two dozen twenty-eight-inch television sets in the back of my van, cost me a fucking fortune. Did I make a big deal of that? Did I?'

'Please, Lar.'

But he's shaking his head like he can't believe the hard neck.

Paying back an overdue loan, a cup of coffee for lunch, there are weeks when it's about choosing what to skimp on. Dixie prowls the bargain bins at Penney's and keeps an eye on the *Reduced to Clear* shelves in Tesco. She haunts the pound shops for Christopher's toys, has the Santa stuff bought and stored away by September.

Maura Holt – Dixie knows her from school; they had their first cigarette together and though Dixie didn't take to the fags Maura is up to twenty a day. Maura tells her about the butcher who sells white mince. 'Cheapest minced beef you can get, lots of fat in it – it's not really white, but you know what I mean, and it tastes OK if you don't spare the chilli powder.'

When Christopher is three, Shelley Hogan takes him for two mornings a week and Dixie gets a few hours on the checkout at a Spar. She finishes her health-and-fitness course and gets her diploma, then she seeks out Obi-Wan Kenobi from the fitness classes. She could really do with a few hours' work a week.

'You know I know my stuff.'

'Dixie—' and it's all over his face, the fear of association with the gangster's widow and she wants to spit but her mouth is too dry.

'Don't be bloody mad,' Shelley says that evening. But Dixie goes to Obi-Wan's house, throws cans of beer at the window and the police come and it's all over the neighbourhood and that's how she loses the job at Spar.

It just happens, Dixie and Brendan. On the first night Brendan stays over, Dixie tiptoeing over to Christopher's bed to check he's asleep, then back to the bed where Brendan is waiting, his eyes wide and urgent.

She and Christopher have been living in a one-room kip. Sometimes when she's alone Dixie notices that she's talking to herself, telling herself what happened today, what she's got to do tomorrow, how she feels about something, what she hopes might happen. She keeps the radio on, listens to music she doesn't like and discussions of things she doesn't care about. When she switches off the radio the silence is worse.

The best thing about Brendan staying over is the mornings, when they're getting dressed and Brendan's in good humour and they're chatting about nothing much. Sometimes Dixie catches herself laughing out loud.

Brendan can be funny in a soft, sad way. Owen was right about his older brother. It's Brendan's shyness that makes him seem dour, though sometimes he's just moody. After that first night he stays over a couple of times a week and when he asks her two months later to move into his place she can't think why not.

A couple of times a week the kid next door babysits and Dixie and Brendan go to the pub or the cinema. Dixie could do without either, but Brendan likes them to do things as a couple.

They never mention Owen.

Brendan calls her 'darling' from the beginning and the word sits awkwardly on his lips. It's like he chose it because he thinks it's the right word to use to express something that he doesn't feel but wants to.

There's a lot of that about Brendan – awkward affection, a hug that never quite connects, always an elbow or a shoulder or a misplaced knee and the embrace is diminished.

Brendan does an occasional delivery job for Lar Mackendrick and some others in the same kind of business, gets regular work shifting stuff from one place to another and things are looking up so they rent the house on Portmahon Terrace.

One evening, while they're watching *EastEnders*, Brendan goes upstairs and when he comes down he sits on the edge of the sofa, opening a wrap. He looks across at Dixie with pride and nervousness in his face.

That stuff hasn't once crossed Dixie's mind in all the time since Owen died. Now, seeing it, she feels the elation surge inside her, as if she's come across an old friend.

'Only now and then,' Brendan says, 'it just – you know—'

Dixie smiles and says nothing.

When Brendan is pulled in on suspicion of assault, the police come with a warrant and mess the place up. One of the coppers finds his stash at the back of the cutlery drawer. 'What have we got here?'

That's the one night Dixie spends in Mountjoy, before Inspector Synnott comes to see her and has a word in someone's ear and the drug-possession charge goes away.

'Smart man, Lar. Look at the gaff he's got. Fucking palace.' Like Owen, Brendan wants people to know that he hangs out with people who matter. He drinks with the people who drink with Lar Mackendrick and Tommy Farr and Bill Ridley. Brendan knows what's going on and he talks about it. In the weeks when money is especially tight Dixie sometimes makes a phone call.

'Inspector Synnott?'

It's business, but sometimes there's a personal edge to it. Dixie feels good when she's making a call about something that Lar Mackendrick's up to.

What goes around comes around.

23

The CCTV camera inside the jeweller's shop took in a good three-fifths of the retail space. Harry Synnott watched the gunman appear at the bottom of the frame, back to the camera, gun in hand, just standing there. Could have been anyone.

Then the gunman walked forward, showing the gun to the jeweller and the assistant, and Synnott said, 'Joshua Boyce.'

Rose Cheney said, 'You can't see his face.'

They were in what was known as the Comms Room, in Macken Road garda station. It was called that probably because the room was once used for radio transmissions, though now it was more of a storeroom. On a table against one wall there was a television set and a video player. There were no chairs, so Synnott and Cheney stood in front of the television, bent slightly forward towards the screen.

From somewhere down the corridor they could hear incoherent shouts. The first of the late shift's customers, no doubt collared somewhere in the vicinity of a pub, was getting stroppy.

Synnott said, 'I've had that bastard in my sights for ten years – sat outside his house, followed him for days, had him in several times.'

Although the baseball hat and the anorak made the figure anonymous, Synnott had no doubt. Perhaps it was the way the gunman moved, the way he stood, the inclination of his head, the gestures he made with one hand as he said something to the jeweller and the assistant.

Boyce, beyond question.

On the screen, the gunman suddenly strode across the shop and used the pistol to smash the assistant's face.

Cheney winced. Even with the strained colours of the CCTV tape, the flecks of blood down the front of the assistant's white shirt were garish and shocking. She noticed the drops of blood that landed on the glass-topped counter. The lack of sound somehow emphasised the assistant's terror.

Poor kid.

Then the screen emptied as the gunman took the two jewellers into the back room.

'It's not just fingerprints that set us apart,' Synnott said. He was leaning forward towards the screen and Cheney felt like he was eager to teach her something. 'You switch on the telly and there's a football match. And before the commentator says anything, even when it's just a dot running in the distance, you know that's Ronaldo or Beckham or Lampard, you know without having to think about it, from the way he turns or runs or just the way he holds himself.'

Cheney said, 'I guess.'

'Boyce,' Synnott said. 'Four or five other jobs, he did that, hit someone, made them bleed. It's his way of closing everyone down.'

'Has he done time?'

Synnott shook his head. 'Not since he was a teenager, stole a car. One job, a bookie's, we got back a bundle of cash from a lock-up that Boyce rented a few weeks earlier. The guy who rented it to him, he identified Boyce from a picture, then chickened out. That was all we had, so the DPP wasn't buying.'

On the screen the gunman and the two jewellers had come out of the back room and the gunman was directing the older man to take pieces of jewellery from the display cabinets.

Rose Cheney watched Synnott staring at the screen. His features seemed to lose a struggle to suppress the loathing inside. His voice was so low that she barely heard the words.

'People like that.'

On the screen, Boyce was sideways-on to the CCTV camera and Harry Synnott stared at the image of the baseball hat, the fake moustache, the slight arrogance of the stance. He could see himself sitting up in front of a jury, with his best suit on, telling them that he knew Boyce did it because – he knew.

Juries don't believe in a policeman's intuition.

'It's a start,' Cheney said.

Synnott continued looking at the screen. 'He didn't expect to be tackled, he didn't expect a shooting, and that's made more of this job than he planned for. His fence will be expecting the stuff, but now someone's got shot he won't want to take it until things cool down.'

'See if the jeweller can make an ID?'

Synnott turned towards the door. 'I'll make up a spread of mugshots, Boyce included. You show them to the jeweller and his assistant, I'll bring them to the security guard. Long shot, but something might ring a bell.'

The security man's name was Arthur Dunne and he was aged twenty-four. He was insulated from the world by a cushion of painkillers but when he moved in the hospital bed he winced. There was pride in his voice when he said, 'I'm going to join the force myself.'

Standing at the bottom of the bed, watching a nurse scribble something on the security man's chart, Harry Synnott figured this was the event that Arthur would bore his grandchildren with thirty years from now. How he got shot trying to stop an armed robber getting away with a bag of jewellery from the shop next door. Synnott wondered whether the grandchildren would tell him to his face that he was a fool.

Arthur Dunne's face right now had an expression that said he was looking forward to having a medal pinned to the front of his hospital gown.

The pillows aren't the only thing puffed up around here.

Which, Synnott conceded, might be fair enough. There was bravery in what Arthur did, even if a more accurate description was stupidity. The professional thing to do was also the smart thing – let it happen, deal with it later. It was what Arthur should have done, but it was what Garda Maura Sheelin should have done too, all those years ago. Arthur went at the robber like a train and he got lucky, coming away with a wound instead of a headstone.

The shooting had made headlines in the *Evening Herald*. Arthur would be all over the dailies tomorrow and no doubt he'd be talking to the television reporters when he got out of here. The publicity couldn't hurt the investigation. The *Herald* described the 'callous, cowardly shooting of a have-a-go hero', thereby ensuring a certain level of police overtime. Although the robbery had nothing to do with Arthur's official duties, the building society had put up a reward of ten grand. That would bring out the busybodies, pointing fingers at every thug who ever smashed a street light. But sometimes it worked – a reward encourages a criminal's friends and neighbours to sell him out.

'You didn't notice a second man?'

'Just the one.'

'No one else driving the Accord?'

'The bastard drove himself, once he took me out of the picture.'

'No one keeping lookout?'

Arthur said, 'I know you can't give a commitment, I'm just asking – but do you think they'll take this into account when I apply?'

'Sorry?'

'To join the guards.'

'To be honest, that's not—'

'I applied about three years ago, got a form letter – never even got an interview.' Arthur shrugged. 'I know they get a lot of applications. But, a thing like this, I mean, I've shown my mettle, right? That should count, do you think?'

Harry Synnott didn't know if getting shot in the course of a robbery would count in an applicant's favour – but he wasn't here to pop the bubble of a potentially crucial witness.

'I don't see why not. You tackled him, you got up close – did you notice anything significant, anything that might help identify him?'

When Arthur spoke it was with the tone of a security veteran. 'Holding onto him – I reckon the moustache was a phoney. Baseball cap, it changes the shape of the face, but I'd definitely recognise him if I saw him again. Anytime, anywhere.'

Synnott nodded. 'You did well. Any scars on his face, on his neck, his hands, marks, whatever?'

Arthur thought about it, then shook his head. 'I don't think so.'

'Anything distinctive about his accent?'

'Just, you know, ordinary.'

Bugger-all use.

Synnott opened his briefcase and took out a dozen mugshots. He laid them out in three rows of four on the cantilevered tray at the bottom of the hospital bed. He put the picture of Joshua Boyce in the middle row. Synnott moved the tray up the bed and Arthur leaned forward.

'The shape of the face,' Synnott said, 'the shape of the head, shape of the mouth, the eyes – anything ring a bell?'

The security man spent a couple of minutes carefully examining the photographs before he said, 'I'm ninety per cent, maybe ninety-five.' He pointed at a photo on the extreme left of the bottom row. 'That's him.' He was pointing at the picture of Ronnie Carey, a burglar that Harry Synnott knew was currently into the second year of a four-year sentence for aggravated assault.

*

As Harry Synnott arrived back at Macken Road, Rose Cheney was coming out of the station. 'Nothing,' he said.

'Snap. The jeweller's assistant spent five minutes deciding that he didn't recognise anyone. The jeweller looked at the mugshots for all of two seconds before he said it was pointless.'

Synnott said, 'There's nothing more we can do tonight.'

Cheney said, 'The Hapgood thing, the rape?'

'Little Max and Big Max.'

Cheney gestured across the road to Derwin's. 'I'll tell you over a drink.'

Synnott shook his head. 'I don't – I'm tired, I should—'

She was already walking out to the kerb, talking over her shoulder. 'It'll help you sleep.'

24

It was about more than the Hapgood thing, as Harry Synnott knew it would be. Sooner or later, anyone he worked with got around to asking how he'd managed to make enemies of so many colleagues. And, if they had the guts, they followed that up by making it clear that they intended to guard their back while he was around. Cheney came at it sideways. Arriving back at the table with a vodka in one hand and a whiskey in the other, she said, 'I hear you're not long for Macken Road?'

Synnott took the whiskey and put it on the beer mat in front of him. 'Doesn't take long for word to travel, does it?'

Cheney shook her jacket from her shoulders as she sat down on a low stool at the other side of the table. She folded the garment onto the stool beside her. 'This town, everyone knows someone who knows someone. You went to see Colin O'Keefe at HQ, right? Lunch with the Assistant Commissioner.'

'He's an old friend. Way back. But, as it happens – and please, I mean, I'd rather this—'

Cheney said, 'I'm not as big a mouth as you might think.'

'Anyway, there's nothing in the bag yet, but there's a possibility of a kind of promotion. Nothing to get excited about.'

They were sitting at a table close to the front window. The long imitation-leather seat on which Synnott sat stretched the length of the window. Derwin's was a neighbourhood pub that had recently been tarted up. The shiny black bartop matched the shiny black backdrop behind the bar. The backdrop was decorated by three large rectangles of coloured glass lit from behind. Anything that wasn't coloured glass or shiny and black was matt chrome. It was pushing nine o'clock and custom was still fairly light.

'A kind of promotion? What's that.'

'It's a way out of a cul-de-sac.'

'Macken Road is somewhere to keep you busy while you wait, then?'

Synnott shook his head. 'It wasn't like that—'

'What happened?'

Sooner or later they all ask. There was nothing aggressive in Cheney's voice, just curiosity.

Synnott picked up the whiskey and looked into the glass as he gave the ice a swirl. Then he put it down. 'No offence, but—'

'It's your business – I just thought, if you wanted to talk.' She was looking him in the eye. 'Myself, I don't care. I've nothing to worry about, working with you.'

Synnott tried to keep the harshness out of his voice. 'I've a clear conscience. I did what I knew was right, every time.'

'Fair enough.' Cheney used a blue plastic stick to rattle the ice in her drink.

She's just curious. She's not having a go.

I'm pissing her off.

Sooner or later they all asked, and always he finessed the answer. He didn't remember ever wanting to talk about any of it. He took a sip of whiskey.

'The Garda Sheelin murder—'

Cheney shook her head and said, 'I've no problem with that.' She stirred her drink again with the plastic stick. 'You were young, Joyce and Buckley – I know all about that case, and they were shits. What I don't understand is Wyse. And then this thing at Turner's Lane? People you were working with?'

J. J. Wyse was a uniformed garda, a sergeant, well settled and well thought of. His run-in with Harry Synnott began during a stag night for one of the lads from the Kilreddin town station, to which Synnott had recently been attached. Wyse poked his head into the private room he'd arranged for the stag party at a pub called Black Benny's, a kip with sawdust on the floor and a dubious traditional band playing dismal *chéilí* music. There was hardly a function involving station personnel – stags, weddings, first-communion lunches, retirements – that JJ didn't make the arrangements for.

'They looking after you, lads?' The groom-to-be, a man named Ryan, invited JJ to sit down and have a drink.

'Can't stay – some of us have to keep the wheels turning.'

As the door closed behind Sergeant Wyse, Harry Synnott almost didn't hear the exchange between two of those present. 'JJ's off to collect the pension.' The other garda made a remark about it being well for some.

'Everyone knew,' Synnott told Rose Cheney. He took a sip of the whiskey. 'It was like it was no big deal. Friendly Uncle JJ, one hand washes the other.'

It didn't affect Harry Synnott directly until he was on duty late one night when a local Nosy Parker called in with a complaint that a pub was serving drinks an hour after closing time. Sergeant Wyse smiled. The local drama club, he told Harry, was having a bit of a night out.

In a sing-song voice, as though reciting a piece of folk wisdom, he said, 'The sociability of a community is in direct ratio to the flexibility of the authorities.' He tapped the counter lightly. 'We don't rule the people, we serve them.'

Synnott couldn't stop himself. 'You're not getting your usual back-hander, then?'

The smile slid down Wyse's face and he turned and walked away.

It was three weeks before Synnott decided to make a formal complaint to the superintendent. Another sergeant took him aside, explained that JJ never asked anyone for money, it was just that he steered a bit of business towards a couple of pubs and they were occasionally grateful. 'It's not like he ever threatened anyone with a raid if they sold after hours and they didn't give him a few shillings. It's just – there's people who appreciate the service, that's all.'

When nothing had happened a month later, Synnott wrote to headquarters in Dublin.

'He lost his job? Wyse?' There was sympathy in Rose Cheney's voice. Synnott wasn't sure if it was for him or for Sergeant Wyse.

He said, 'The way I see it, if you know about it and you stay silent you become part of it.'

'What happened at Turner's Lane, what made you leave?'

Synnott shook his head. 'I know you mean well, but it doesn't matter any more. If things go the way I think they will, I'll be gone from here before too long.'

'OK. I'm not judging you. It's just—'

'I know.'

'It's just that it's what people talk about when they hear you're at Macken Road, and I wanted to hear your side.'

Synnott realised he was about to ask her what she thought of it all, but he decided he didn't want to know. He wondered when he'd last had a drink with a woman. He hadn't had a relationship for almost a year – and that had been no more than an awkward couple of months with a woman he'd met at the wedding of a nephew. Studious sort, pretty and droll. They'd nothing in common except their need for company.

He knew nothing about Cheney's personal life. He noticed she wasn't wearing a ring.

Synnott's whiskey was all but untouched. There was nothing in Cheney's glass except ice.

'Vodka, isn't it?'

'I better not.' She made a face. 'Driving. Haven't taken the time for a drink after work since – probably before Christmas. It's all go at the moment. Our eldest is making her First Communion this year – another six weeks.'

Synnott wondered if something in his face had betrayed his thoughts. Then he decided that was self-centred nonsense. He remembered why Cheney had insisted that he come to the pub.

'Big Max and Little Max?'

'I got a call this morning from a detective at Earlsfort Terrace. He came looking for me once he heard the Hapgood name. Fifteen months ago, he handled a complaint against Max Junior – sexual assault. Two weeks later the victim withdrew her complaint, walked away, wouldn't say why.'

Synnott said, 'Paid off, maybe, or frightened.'

'He talked to her – he seems a good guy, sensitive enough to do it right – but she just said no, she didn't want to go any further.'

Synnott made a disgusted noise. 'So, young Max is making a career of it.'

'Do you think I should talk to that woman – see if she has anything useful?'

'Fifteen months on? Probably wants to forget it happened.'

'No harm trying.'

Synnott nodded. 'No harm trying.'

Cheney was on her feet. She gestured towards his whiskey. 'You take your time.'

'Right.'

She took a step away, then stopped and said, 'Look, it's not like I've any right to judge – it's just, maybe you were right, about Wyse and the other stuff, and maybe you weren't. But I just thought – it was in the air, best to clear it away, OK?'

Synnott realised he was smiling. 'OK,' he said.

When she was gone, Synnott finished his whiskey and called the Asian lounge boy across and ordered another. It was the first evening in a long time that he hadn't gone from work to home to sleep. He took his time over the second whiskey, then he caught a taxi home to his flat.

He was getting into bed when he remembered that he'd meant

to ring his son. The jewellery robbery had kept him so busy he hadn't thought of it. Anyway, by now Michael had probably changed his mind again about the attractions of leaving school for the delights of business. Lying back on the pillow, Synnott thought for a moment about reaching for the phone. He wondered if he had the mental energy to conduct a difficult conversation. He stared at the ceiling, knowing that calling Michael was about fulfilling a duty and he didn't for a moment believe that anything he said would influence him one way or the other.

Tomorrow.

*

Dixie had a key to Shelley Hogan's flat at Sunnyfield Apartments. She found Shelley asleep on the settee, the television showing some American shite.

Dixie switched off the television and went into the spare bedroom. The place was a mess, clothes scattered across the bed and onto the floor, a pile of magazines in one corner, tipped over and strewn across the carpet. She straightened the duvet and puffed up the pillow. She found a blue sweatshirt that looked reasonably clean and decided to use it as a nightdress. As she changed she heard a noise and went back into the living room. Shelley was awake and standing up.

'You OK?'

Shelley nodded, still groggy, still stoned. There was a syringe on a coffee table, next to a small wooden music box.

'I wanted—' Shelley said. She stood there, her face blank, as though she was trying to remember something. She pushed one hand through her short black hair. Then she said, 'I'll see you in the morning.' At the door of her bedroom she turned and said, 'Help yourself.'

Dixie said, 'No, I'm all right.'

Halfway there. Not nearly enough.

There was around a hundred and fifty in the right-hand pocket of her jeans, the pension she'd collected from the post office after she'd fled from Matty and his thug friend.

Too late now.

Dixie was still awake an hour later. She went out to sit on the living-room settee. There was just the light from the spare bed-room and the room was cold.

She had used a syringe a couple of times, but although she knew Shelley was clean she'd never got over the fear of what a needle might carry. Shelley kept the tea candles in a kitchen drawer and Dixie brought one back to the living room, along with a box of matches and some aluminium foil. She went to the bathroom and unspooled a nearly-finished roll of pink toilet paper. There was a lot more on the roll than she thought. She made a ball of the loose toilet paper and stuffed it into the small metal bin under the sink. She brought the cardboard tube back to the living room.

Five months.

She hesitated for a moment.

Stupid. Five months of proving to herself and to them that she didn't need it.

Throw that away?

It wasn't like that.

Just once.

Relieve the pressure.

Control the pressure.

The music box played 'Clementine' when she opened it. Dixie tore a square from the aluminium foil, then lit the candle. She crumpled some of the heroin onto the foil and held it over the flame. When it melted, the liquid drops of heroin rolled this way and that across the silver surface, leaving trails of dark specks. She moved the foil to try to keep the liquid above the heat of the candle and was rewarded by ribbons of smoke rising from the drug. She bent forward, holding the cardboard tube to her lips, and seconds after she inhaled the smoke she felt it hit her lungs. She chased the smoke, anxious not to waste any.

She could feel the strength of it, the warmth of it streaming through her blood, easing its way around everything that hurt and filling all the empty spaces in between.

Dixie lay back on the settee and it was like everything weighed less. It was all going already, all the shit that overloaded her mind through the hours she lay awake. The fear and anxiety that had crushed her insides over the past few days was still there, but at a distance, blunt, unfocused, harmless. She knew it would come back, as strong and as inevitable as a tide, but maybe by then she'd have the strength to deal with it. For now, her blood was singing with relief. She let her head loll on the arm of the settee and she stared without blinking at the tiny core of red at the centre of the yellow flame of the tea candle.

25

Friday will tell the tale.

The bitch has dropped the blazing smile she usually uses, like she wants Dixie to understand this is serious. The bitch should be fat and warty, an old hag with a voice like emphysema, but she's about the same age as Dixie and her face has a glow and her teeth are perfect as though someone designed them. Her sweet voice can do the tone that shows how caring she is and when she says that Dixie can't have Christopher back she does so with tenderness.

Five months since that day at the Prunty. Five months without Christopher.

Monday, when Dixie went to the meeting with her, the bitch walked her to the edge of the cliff.

'Friday will tell the tale,' she says.

Friday. Today.

Over.

Too late now.

The Prunty Shopping Centre is fifteen minutes' walk away, but it takes longer when Christopher is in a mood. Dixie promises him a lolly.

She's thinking things through. Health-and-fitness clubs — everywhere you look, people running and stretching and hoisting weights, trying to shed the fat so that they'll look good when they got to the pubs and restaurants. She's made a list. She'll start with the clubs nearest where she lives, work her way out until she finds one that has a few hours' work to offer.

She buys Christopher the lolly in the Sweet Factory, and he runs ahead to Marie's Big Little Toy Shop, off to the left of the supermarket, where he'll browse until Dixie's finished shopping. He's good with toys, no whining, no demands – he knows money doesn't grow on trees, but he likes to take the toys down from the shelves and examine them at length, his serious little face appraising them like the expert he is.

The supermarket has changed the aisles around again. Just when you're used to the layout they change it. They try to stop customers getting used to where everything is, so that you have to check out every aisle and end up buying stuff you don't need. Dixie has no problem ignoring the temptations. She knows how much she's going to spend. She finds the tinned tomatoes, the tuna, the sliced pan, the porridge.

At the checkout there's a kid in the togs of the local GAA team helping to pack bags. Dixie throws a few pence in his bucket. Her head is singing. Half an hour before she decided to go shopping Dixie was slicing a line of coke, bent over her bedside locker, a small, solitary celebration of the possibilities she's decided to chase.

Get work – stay clean.

She feels an enthusiasm that she hasn't felt about anything for a long time. She's wondering if she should swallow her pride, go see Obi-Wan Kenobi, see if he's changed his mind about helping her get work in the fitness business. It's been two years since the trouble – if she's respectful, contrite – it's not like she wants a full-time job, just a couple of hours here and there – mornings, when Christopher's at school – all it would take would be a word from Obi-Wan and—

Then—

It's like something electric has zapped through her chest.

Oh—

And it comes out in a howl.

'Oh, *Jesus*—'

Dixie is five minutes from her home and she drops the plastic bag of groceries on the pavement and turns, running, trying to keep the panic from swamping her.

The woman from the shopping centre is smiling, she's got Christopher in her arms and he has a thumb in his mouth and there's a security man and he's saying, 'Sorry, love, he was running all over the place looking for you – we'd no idea where—'

'It was just a mistake—'

Dixie is aware that she's sweating, a twist of hair is stuck to her cheek, she's trying to keep the fear from her eyes. She can feel the muscles in her face pulling against the smile she's trying to create.

'Come on into the office, love, and—'

'No!'

But the shopping-centre woman is already walking away with Christopher in her arms.

Dixie says, 'Please.' She has Christopher by the hand. She takes a step backwards, she smiles at the garda, she says, 'OK?'

The garda says, 'Well—' and the Prunty security man says, 'You can see she's stoned, you can't let her walk out with a child.'

Dixie makes eye contact with the garda. He has dark eyes and they're uncertain.

'Please.'

Dixie is backing away and Christopher gives a little squeal. 'Mammy, you're hurting me!' and Dixie looks down to where her hand is coiled tightly around Christopher's little wrist. She lets him go.

She says, 'Oh, please.'

In that second, as she finds the young garda's eyes again, she can see it all. The police station and the doctor, the tests, the drug charges, child neglect, the social workers, the court and the massive black hole that waits beyond.

'No, *please.*'

The garda says, 'I'm sorry—'

The shopping-centre woman has Christopher in her arms again and he's making high-pitched noises and lashing out with his feet and she's going, *There, there, it'll be all right.*

Social workers who begin every meeting with a smile and when they cross their legs and lean forward the smiles go away.

Five months of meetings.

'I'm not an addict. I use the stuff – I *used* to use the stuff – I don't – I won't.'

'We're not judging you – it's not like that. Today, it's what's best for the child, that's all that matters.'

They ask Brendan to come to a meeting along with Dixie. He answers questions politely. When it finishes the bitch puts on her best smile and next day Dixie calls her and the bitch says there'll be a case conference shortly and she can't say anything, but she'd like to see Dixie again on Monday morning. 'We can do a final progress assessment.'

Please.

Sunday afternoon, Dixie irons her brown skirt and the tan blouse she wears when she goes looking for work.

Christopher.

She has to struggle to keep herself from losing control when she thinks of him. Swelling love colliding with sliding despair.

Sunday night, Brendan says let's go down to Keating's and Dixie limits herself to one gin and tonic, after that she sticks with Ballygowan. Brendan keeps glancing towards the door. Dixie wants to go home early but he's waiting for someone and he orders another pint.

Dixie doesn't talk to Brendan about tomorrow's meeting. He knows it's happening and if they get Christopher back, that's OK with Brendan, if they don't, that's OK too. He sips his pint and tells her what this mate of Lar Mackendrick told him about Lar's DVD factory out on the Moyfield industrial estate. 'There's a pile of money in that caper. Smart man, Lar.'

Dixie nods and decides she doesn't want to think about Lar.

Piece of shit.

Brendan rabbits on about how clever Lar is, the connections he's got. 'That's the business to be in.'

When they get back from the pub Brendan is complaining about the gobshite who didn't turn up with the twenty-five he borrowed two weeks ago. The dishes from the teatime meal are still sitting on the kitchen counter. Brendan makes a remark about the state of the kitchen and Dixie thinks he's joking, so she bows slightly and says something about her lord and master and Brendan gives her the back of his hand.

He's all apologies, offering a towel to wipe the smear of blood on her upper lip.

Jesus, darling, I've never, listen, it was just—'

Dixie looks at her face in the mirror.

Aw, Christ.

Monday morning, eleven o'clock. The bitch says nothing about the bruising on Dixie's left cheek. Dixie has applied foundation, then concealer on top, staring into the mirror, touching up the camouflage. The make-up both hides the damage and draws attention to it.

The discussion is about Dixie's work prospects and she sits with her legs crossed, her knees turned to the left, her head tilted slightly away from the bitch. She knows it's pointless but she can't help it. She knows the smile she's fixed to her face doesn't look right but she can't do anything about that, either. After less than ten minutes she suddenly says, 'I bet you're wondering what happened,' and she touches her cheek. She makes up a story about helping Shelley shift a sofa and how Shelley's elbow—

The expression of sympathy on the bitch's face agitates Dixie and she assures the bitch she isn't lying.

'Am I going to lose Christopher – is he going to be adopted?'

'Believe me—'

'Five months—'

'We're not near a definitive decision.' The bitch smiles. 'A final decision.'

I know what 'definitive' means.

I fucked it up.

She's taking him for good.

The bitch babbles on about Friday's case conference, about how it's essential that they're convinced that the situation has been progressed, before they can move on to the next stage. The bitch puts on her best smile when she says, 'Friday will tell the tale.'

Dixie spends the rest of Monday trying to contact Fiachra in London. It's that evening before there's an answer at his flat, an unfamiliar male voice saying Fiachra hasn't lived here for two months. She tries his mobile but a recorded voice says the phone is out of service. She gets the same results the next day, Tuesday.

It's Shelley who faces up to what needs to be done – *get out, take Christopher, walk away, leave it all behind, go to Fiachra.* Shelley spends half an hour on the phone, comes back with a figure for air tickets for Dixie and Christopher, a B&B in London for three nights, food, odds and ends, and no matter how close she cuts it there's no way it'll take less than four hundred, more like five.

Come Friday, collect the Widow's Pension at the post office. A third of what she needs, and leaving it late—

She tries Fiachra's mobile again on Wednesday morning but

there's still just the recorded voice and Dixie pulls on her jeans and her red jacket and takes one of the syringes from Shelley's flat and brings it into town.

Total fucking disaster.

Water and ketchup mixed in an eggcup, suck it up into the syringe, there's no telling it from the real thing. Off to Grafton Street, mooching, find somewhere quiet, the syringe in her pocket.

A few fucking hundred.

Jesus.

The Yank and his tweety girlfriend walking past, chattering away, then the Yank is taking his wallet out of his pocket and he's sticking his card in the hole-in-the-wall and the money coming out is in fifties and there are several of them and it's too good to be true.

'Give it.'

'Take it easy, now—'

Ah, fuck.

The flame on the tea candle is tiny and wavering. Dixie realises she's holding her breath in case the least puff of air blows the flame out. She inhales, then turns her face away and lets the air out slowly and when she turns back a quivering twist of pale smoke is rising where the flame was. She makes a small involuntary noise.

Killed it.

SATURDAY

26

Joshua Boyce watched his children chase a ball, Peter taking advantage of the ten-year start he had over eight-year-old Ciara, contesting the game like he was fighting to keep out of the relegation zone. At the table in the decking area just outside the French windows, Boyce's wife Antoinette poured Tropicana into four long thin chilled glasses.

Back in Cairnloch, when he was growing up, Joshua Boyce used to organise races with his mates, in the back garden of his family's council house. Later on, when he thought about it, he reckoned the garden couldn't have been more than a glorified yard, with scraggy grass and relentless weed. Back then it had seemed like a prairie.

Boyce watched Peter throw back his head and laugh. There wasn't a hint of the teenage moodiness that too often got between them.

It was Antoinette who insisted from the beginning that Saturday morning was family time, whatever happened during the rest of the week. Working around Ciara's weekly basketball sessions, and levering Peter out of bed when he insisted that it was his God-given right to spend every free morning lying in until noon, Antoinette always organised something the kids could do along with herself and Joshua. Maybe something as simple as a trip to a shopping centre or a visit to granny. Mostly it was just a board game or a romp around the back garden. What mattered was that they did something together. In summer it might be a drive down to Wicklow, a stroll around Howth Head or a swim at Portmarnock. This morning, the weather being excellent, it was an old favourite, a version of football in the back garden, what Ciara called boys versus girls. The game continued between the kids while the adults took some time out for refreshments.

The long wide garden was what had sold Joshua Boyce on this house off the coast road in Clontarf, when he and Antoinette had bought it nine years earlier. This kind of thing wouldn't last too much longer, the Saturday family mornings, the closeness with the kids, first Peter and then the late miracle, Ciara, now both together. But when it ends, Boyce told himself, there'll be other things. Holidays alone, self-indulgence, all the kinds of things he and Antoinette had happily sacrificed when the kids came along. They'd have the kind of money they'd never had in the early years.

Boyce went to the table near the back window and picked up a glass of Tropicana. He turned in time to see Peter dart forward to intercept a wayward shot from Antoinette. The boy flicked the ball from toe to knee, bounced it up to head height, then nodded it forward, stuck out a foot and did the toe-knee-toe thing again, then back up to his forehead.

Ciara was laughing, urging him on. Joshua smiled and took a slug of juice and—

Oh Christ.

In the kitchen, through the open doors, the radio was playing in the background.

Joshua Boyce stood facing his family, not seeing them.

He hadn't noticed the end of the music programme. As a newsreader continued with the eleven o'clock bulletin, Boyce felt his fingers grow too weak to hold the glass of Tropicana. He stood with his head held back, eyes closed, his concentration blocking out the childrens laughter and the sound of his glass breaking on the concrete.

'– *the dead man, who was employed by a branch of the Cooperative Building Society, witnessed the jewellery robbery and was attempting to apprehend the fleeing robber when he was shot in the leg. A spokeswoman for the hospital told RTE News that the man's death followed a sudden deterioration in his condition in the early hours of the morning.'*

'Are you OK, Dad?'

*

Poor bastard.

In the Comms Room, Harry Synnott and Rose Cheney watched Joshua Boyce and the security guard – Synnott had to think a moment to remember the man's name – Arthur Dunne wrestle on the ground in the car park. The quality of the CCTV footage wasn't great. Just two anonymous figures down at the bottom left of the screen, perspective distorted. The footage was from a camera positioned high up above the car park of the twenty-four-hour shop where the gunman had parked his Accord. The car wasn't visible except for a couple of seconds of footage at the end, when it drove past the camera and out onto the street.

Synnott watched again as the security guard silently screamed on the screen and rolled to one side, clutching his leg, and Joshua Boyce – no doubt in Synnott's mind it was him – jumped up, holding the gun, and moved out of the camera's range.

Synnott was woken by the call at around six in the morning, thirty minutes after the security guard died. No point going to the hospital. He was at Macken Road station before seven, pulling together the scant information. He phoned the hospital and an hour later a consultant rang back and said that he couldn't give a definitive cause of death until after a post-mortem. 'Off the record – some kind of cardiac failure.'

'At that age?'

'It happens. Footballers, kids at the peak of fitness – your guy, perhaps ischaemic heart disease but far more likely hypertrophic cardiomyopathy. In the vast majority of cases involving young people the diagnosis happens at the autopsy.'

'He was shot in the leg, about fifteen hours earlier.'

'Trauma could be a factor.'

Ten minutes later Synnott was on the phone to the state pathologist's office. 'We need to know if there was cause and effect between the shooting and whatever caused the death.' A direct causal effect was the difference between aggravated assault and a charge of murder.

*

The security man's death had upgraded the case. Word came through that Chief Superintendent Malachy Hogg was now supervising, but the investigation would proceed much as before, with Harry Synnott directing daily tasks and initiatives. The major difference was an increase in available manpower and overtime resources. After a brief assessment meeting with Harry Synnott, Hogg endorsed Joshua Boyce as the most likely suspect.

Four CCTV cameras on Kellsboro's main street had caught elements of the jewellery robbery. Technical had copied the relevant sections of the footage onto a single tape and already Synnott and Rose Cheney had watched it through four times. It had to be done, but it didn't leave them any wiser. In one shot, the robber could be seen for a few seconds as he passed a garage on his way up the street towards the jewellery shop. In another, the roof and one side of the Accord were captured for less than a second as it drove away. The other two shots showed the robber in the distance, an indistinct figure walking away after the robbery. The footage from inside the jeweller's shop and the images of what had happened in the car park, which Synnott was reviewing now, were all that were worth a damn. And then only to someone familiar with Boyce. With the robber's features hidden by the anorak and the baseball hat, the tape was useless as evidence.

'The security man, was he married?' Rose Cheney said.

Synnott nodded. 'One kid, another on the way.'

On the screen, two ambulance men were kneeling in the car park beside the security guard.

Do you think they'll take this into account when I apply?

Poor, sad bastard.

*

Dixie had met Mrs Dobbs several times during her visits with Christopher, always with a social worker. She'd never liked the woman, but she knew that wouldn't look good so she was always overly polite.

She put a big grin on her face now. 'Hiya, Mrs Dobbs, I was in the neighbourhood.'

Mrs Dobbs held the front door half open, her fat face caught between a weak smile and a grimace. 'I don't think—'

'If I could just see him for a minute?'

'I'm sorry, Dixie, you know—'

'Please!'

Dixie's smile was gone. She felt like she was begging, but she knew her voice was coming across as an aggressive croak. She tried the smile again, but she knew it didn't sit right.

Whatever.

Just so the old cow understood this was important.

'I have to see him. I *have* to see him.'

Mrs Dobbs looked for a moment as though she was about to give in. Then she said, 'Dixie, love, the little fella's fine, and Seamus and I, all we want is to help out until you're—'

'I'm not going away until you let me see him.'

'Ah, Dixie—' The door was closing.

'I need to see him!'

'I'll call the police.'

Dixie was leaning on the door. Up close, she could see the little piece of skin that jutted up permanently from Mrs Dobbs's left eyelid, sticking straight out like the handle of a tiny saucepan. Mrs Dobbs planted her substantial body behind the door. There was a tremble in her voice.

'Seamus!'

Dixie used a shoulder to push against the door and Mrs Dobbs made a wet sound and moved back. Then her skinny little fucker of a husband was standing there, his mouth all pinched up, his eyes blazing and he was pushing back against the door. For someone who looked like he'd blow over in a stiff breeze, there was strength behind his shoulder and the door was moving towards Dixie like there was a bulldozer behind it. He was squawking at his wife, 'The phone, Lucy, get the phone, get the police, Lucy, go *on!*'.

Dixie was halfway down the garden footpath when she turned back, 'Look, I'm sorry. *Please!*' The skinny little fucker was already shutting the door.

27

Standing at the top of the incident room, speaking to the eleven detectives squeezed into a space that usually accommodated six, Harry Synnott switched off the television and said, 'I'd bet my pension on it.' Technical had provided stills from the CCTV footage and three of them were pinned to the board behind him. Synnott tapped one of them,

'Joshua Boyce. Careful, thorough. One job a year, two if it's something very tasty.'

Officially, the robber had netted around sixty grand's worth of jewellery and three grand in cash. As yet, the jeweller was keeping his mouth shut about what had been in the floor safe. Harry Synnott suspected the dodgy merchandise had to be worth a multiple of the legitimate stuff.

'Joshua Boyce is in the frame, but that's just my opinion. We don't limit this investigation in any way. Chief Superintendent Hogg has already put the message out to every station in the city – all touts get their cages rattled over this weekend.'

Four of the team, including Rose Cheney, were from Macken Road. The rest had been brought in by Chief Superintendent Hogg.

Synnott introduced Cheney. 'Detective Garda Cheney has a list of the fences who we believe could handle this kind of merchandise. If you know of anyone not on the list, give her the name. Every one of them gets a visit today – Cheney's handing out assignments.'

Cheney said, 'We tell them the man who was murdered was a security guard. He had lots of friends on the force – they don't need to know any different – we tell them anyone who hides anything gets his balls in a wringer.'

'The Super has a team doing a fingertip search of the car park this morning. The security man taking him by surprise, it's just possible he left traces behind – though Boyce is a careful bugger. We go back to Kellsboro main street, we canvass every shop again in case the uniforms missed anything.'

A detective was assigned to check any cars stolen in the past month that turned up abandoned anywhere in the city over the weekend. They'd found the stolen Accord at the Kellsboro Shopping Arcade and it was possible that Boyce had picked up another car close by.

One of the detectives leaned back in his chair. 'I take it we'll be paying Mr Boyce an official visit?' He was an older man, a detective sergeant named Tidey, with whom Synnott had worked briefly on the Swanson Avenue murder.

Synnott said, 'I'm expecting a search warrant any minute.'

*

The four uniforms and three detectives were going through the house room by room. It would take a while. It wasn't likely that Joshua Boyce had the jewellery or the gun in his house, but the shooting might have rattled him and it was possible that he'd panicked and left something somewhere he shouldn't have – the anorak, maybe, or the baseball hat. The searchers would take their time.

'Where were you yesterday morning?'

'Yesterday?' Boyce looked at his wife.

'Shopping,' she said. She spoke to Synnott. 'Shopping. I think.'

Boyce said, 'Any particular time you were interested in?'

Synnott was writing in his notebook, recording the exchange. 'Where did you do your shopping?'

Joshua Boyce smiled. 'That's a very personal question, Inspector.'

'What time did you leave the house. To go shopping?'

Boyce said. 'Is it important? I mean, what's this about? Should I have a lawyer here?'

'What time did you get to the shops?'

'What time did this happen, whatever it was?' Boyce was relaxed. He might have been asking about a television programme he'd missed. 'What is it, someone nicked the Garda Commissioner's poodle?'

'What time did you leave here?'

'I'd have to think about that. I wasn't keeping track. Next time, maybe whoever did whatever they did, you could get them to let me know in advance. That way, I can keep a note.' Boyce pressed a button on the mobile he was holding. When someone answered he said, 'Joshua Boyce – tell Connie the boys in blue are all over the shop. I'd appreciate a little service.'

He waited and when someone spoke at the other end he said, 'Hi, Connie, no big deal, but the shades are here, asking questions about the Garda Commissioner's missing poodle.' After a pause he said, 'Yeah, they have a search warrant.' Twice he answered 'No' to a question at the other end. Then he said, 'Thanks a lot, Connie' and ended the call.

'Connie Wintour. He's already revving up the paperwork. He says to tell you to search away, then arrest me or piss off.'

Synnott offered his notebook to Boyce. 'Would you care to sign my note of our conversation?'

Boyce looked Synnott in the eye. 'Take a hike.'

The search took two hours and they found nothing.

*

When the taxi came into the cul-de-sac Garda Joe Mills perked up. On duty at the front gate of the murder house at Bushy Park, he was three hours into the shift and bored witless standing alone outside a crime scene that was yesterday's news. For two days the media had been all over Bushy Park, salivating about a juicy double murder and conjuring all sorts of theories as to why a man and a boy should end up butchered in a quiet Galway suburb. Had they known that police believed the killer might also have killed a woman, as yet unknown, the papers would have gone apeshit with delight.

Since Thursday, Mills had done two other shifts here, always with another garda for company. Mostly the work involved shooing away sightseers and nosy neighbours or standing up straight whenever photographers came within range. On the Thursday evening, after the discovery of the bodies, Joe Mills's mother had called from Navan to say she'd seen him in RTE footage on the nine o'clock news. Today, two days since the discovery of the bodies, resources were stretched and Mills was here alone. Besides, nothing was likely to happen. It was like the murders were something that had happened on a television show that was already fading from memory. The neighbours had their Saturday shopping to do and the media had got all they needed from the scene. Reporters from the daily papers were off duty, those from the Sunday papers who were dealing with the murders were at their desks, busy cajoling garda contacts for last-minute information, of which there was very little.

The shrink was still trying to get Wayne Kemp to talk, but despite periods of lucidity he hadn't said anything helpful since his arrest. Once Kemp had been identified, the Dublin police checked his flat in Ranelagh. Joe Mills expected to hear that they'd found blood-streaked walls and a decomposing female body. Instead, they reported back that Kemp's flat was neurotically neat. Mills was tempted to conclude that Kemp had made up that stuff about hurting a woman.

The woman who got out of the taxi was plump, with dyed red hair. She stood, the taxi door open behind her, looking at Garda Mills as the driver heaved a suitcase out of the boot. The driver brought the suitcase around to the side of the taxi and stood beside the woman. Her face was pale. Her voice was fragile.

'He said,' she spoke to the garda and gestured to the driver, 'he said there'd been—'

She went silent. Her breathing was fast and shallow.

Joe Mills crossed the pavement slowly and spoke gently. 'Do you live here, Mrs—?'

'Oh, Jesus, what has he done?'

*

It took more than an hour to walk from the old cow Dobbs's place to Portmahon Terrace. As Dixie Peyton came around the corner she saw two men standing outside her front door. She stopped, turned and stepped back around the corner.

Matty.

She stood for a moment, her back to the wall of the corner house, then poked her head out to have a look. Matty and that little piece of shit with him. They were wearing dark overalls and baseball hats. Their car was parked a few feet away, the boot open. Matty had his finger on the doorbell. Dixie pulled her head in and leaned against the wall, trying to stop her legs from trembling.

It was a whole day since they'd come to the house and Dixie had fled. They couldn't have stayed around all that time.

There was a shout of anger that turned into a yelp of fear. When she risked another look she saw that her front door was open and the two men were grappling with Brendan.

Matty had him in a headlock – Brendan's arms were flailing. The other little shit punched him once, twice, in the kidneys, then Matty jerked Brendan off balance and dragged him around to the back of the car. Brendan yelled a string of obscenities as the other bastard grabbed his legs and they dumped him into the boot.

The little shit leaned over and swung his fist, then stood back as Matty slammed the boot shut.

The car made a screeching noise as it accelerated. By then, Dixie was walking quickly away from Portmahon Terrace.

28

The overalls that John Grace was wearing were paint-streaked and dusty. When he opened the front door to Harry Synnott he had a document wallet under his right arm and a sandpaper block in his left hand.

Synnott grinned. 'If you whip out a pair of overalls and hand me a paintbrush, I'm out of here.'

'Don't worry, I'm almost finished.'

Grace dumped the document wallet on the stairs and accepted the bottle of Johnnie Walker that Synnott offered. 'That ought to do the job.'

Grace stepped around a filing cabinet in the hallway as he led Synnott towards the kitchen. 'I'm converting my office back into a bedroom – Jess is moving in.'

Jess was Grace's daughter. 'She's just starting a full-time job with an advertising outfit. The price of childcare, it makes more sense to move back in here for a while, until she's settled. Me retiring, that makes it easier. Frees up the home office – used to be Jess's room, anyway.'

There were four box files on the kitchen table, three red, one blue and white. Synnott saw that they were marked with the names of cases that John Grace had worked on.

'Souvenirs?'

Grace shook his head. 'Mindless hoarding. Whenever a case

ended, I'd stick a copy of the papers on a shelf. Most of them I junked last week. Those four, the big cases, I figured I'd look them over, see if they're worth holding on to.'

Harry Synnott had never collected such keepsakes. He remembered what mattered, and he reckoned that what wasn't strong enough to stick in his memory probably wasn't worth remembering.

John Grace put on the kettle, then moved the old case files onto a corner of the kitchen counter. 'The big cases, the ones that mattered.' He smiled. 'Until you look at them.' He opened one of the box files. Most of the statements and reports were held together by a loose fastener. There were two slim court transcripts in comb bindings.

'A man named Wallace – crippled his neighbour in a fight over a hedge. It was a big deal at the time, all over the papers. Columnists waffling on about the shocking lack of values in modern society. I saw myself on the nine o'clock news, walking into the court carrying an evidence sack with the garden shears that did done the damage.' He dropped the file on the table. 'Pathetic gobshites, both of them. The victim was a loudmouth who'd bullied his family for years. Couldn't have happened to a nicer scumbag. The other fella, Wallace, was the neighbourhood nice guy and he'd taken all kinds of hell from the scumbag before he let loose. He shit himself in the van on the way to Mountjoy. Hasn't worked since he got out of prison.'

'No one said life was fair.'

'And that was one of my big cases.' Grace picked up the file again and held it for a moment. Then he dropped it into a large cardboard box on the floor at the end of the counter. The file sat on top of an accumulation of documents, newspapers and magazines obviously destined for junking.

'Let's not get bogged down in that shit.' Grace picked up the Golden Pages. 'Chinese or Indian?'

'You're, what, now – forty-five?'

John Grace said, 'Forty-eight'.

'Young to be a grandfather.'

'We started early, Mona and me.'

Grace had always looked younger than his years. Harry Synnott knew that at forty-four he looked older than Grace. He was always surprised when he caught a sudden glimpse of his reflection. The lines that defined his face were deeper than he remembered, while the tinge of grey made his hair look not so much distinguished as tired. He knew two people around his own age who had died suddenly and John Grace's premature retirement was another unpleasant milestone. O'Keefe's offer of the Europol job had at first seemed like the interruption of a career in mid-flight. Now he was thinking of the move as the natural end of one career and the start of something else.

Could be it's a blessing. Stick too long at the one thing, you don't notice the slide into repetition, habit, passing the time until retirement.

'Have you figured out – I mean, at forty-eight, this is going to be a long retirement.'

They were sitting in the kitchen, the table cluttered with their dinner plates and various tinfoil containers of food.

'Financially I'm OK,' Grace said. 'The mortgage is paid off, the pension's not bad, Mona and I don't need much, apart from the odd week down the country. Later on, maybe I'll pick up the occasional nixer. The security business is wide open to a former detective inspector. Nothing's certain, but however it works out I've gone as far as I'm going in the policing business.'

Synnott spent some time on his King Po Beef. Then he said, 'How much does this have to do with Nicky?' Synnott had never spoken to Grace about the incident in which Grace had seen another policeman shot dead. At the funeral, Grace had still been too traumatised to exchange more than the usual clichés with commiserating colleagues. That case wasn't among the box files John Grace had kept.

Grace took his time over a forkful of rice. When he spoke his voice was flat. 'Nothing. Everything.'

When they were moving from the kitchen into the living room, John Grace put his three remaining case files side by side on the kitchen counter. After a moment, he picked one up and dumped it in the waste box. He tapped another and said, 'That was a sad one – two young lads, just a bit wild, got into a fight with a couple of hard men. Both kids got a kicking, one never recovered consciousness. We got one of the hard men for murder, his mate got off. He was dead within a year – an uncle of the dead lad caught up with him.' Grace dropped that file, too, into the waste box. The remaining file was marked *Swanson Avenue*.

Harry Synnott said, 'Where did you put the whisky?'

They sat in the living room, with the curtains pulled back. Beyond the back garden, the landscape curved up towards Howth. 'Even that one,' John Grace said, 'all it was – end of the day – the Swanson Avenue thing was no more than an ambitious loser who couldn't keep his zip shut. Pissed off at the missus because she found out and might take his comfy little life away. We were smarter than he was – which, when you think of it, is no great compliment to us. Pathetic.'

Synnott said nothing.

'I'm not saying it didn't matter – the work we did.' Grace swirled his glass and the ice made a noise. He sipped the whisky. 'Bastard deserved what he got. All I'm saying is, looking back, even at the ones that were big at the time – they don't amount to much more than sweeping up the shit in the crazy house.'

John Grace was pouring Johnnie Walker over ice and talking about a detective he knew who'd retired and moved to the country and he'd never been happier. Sitting a few feet away, Harry

Synnott made an agreeable noise. He'd been distracted ever since the conversation about Grace's retirement plans.

I wouldn't know what to do.

Without the job of policing, there was no end of things that Harry Synnott might take up to fill his time, but there wasn't anything that had the sense of—

What?

Substance? Power?

More than that.

Reality.

– that policing brought to his life. Other people found their own way of pinning things down, dealing with the chaos and the chance and the randomness of it all. Family, hobbies, games, community work – they were fine for those who could settle for that kind of thing. In Harry Synnott's mind, none of those things would even survive without the pattern laid down by law enforcement. It was what mattered, and he couldn't imagine existing without being part of it.

Law and order. The means and the end.

The means are defective, so the ends are arbitrary.

The law is a swamp patrolled by alligators in wigs and gowns. They operate by rules that others hardly know exist, let alone understand.

Even when you think you know what the law says, some smartarse in a wig finds a new wrinkle in an old rule and you watch some sniggering thug waltz out of court.

When the law is a bouncing ball on a spinning wheel, all that a righteous man can aim for is order.

Harry Synnott looked down at the ice cubes sliding around the bottom of his glass. He'd downed the last whisky without even noticing.

John Grace was right. When you stood back from the detail, even the big cases were just the pathetic flopping about of blundering humans trying to find a short cut to a slice of something better. The police couldn't stop it happening: at best they could try to find an acceptable pattern in which to rearrange the debris.

Maybe that was precious little, but it was still something.

Maybe in a thousand years.

John Grace was talking about another detective who'd retired, a man embittered by a lack of promotion. 'He seems a lot calmer now.'

Harry Synnott said, 'He was never very good at the job.'

Harry Synnott knew that what good policemen do is make order from chaos. Without order there's no meaning. He knew that the day when he stopped being part of that would be the day he stopped living. His life might still have days and nights in it but nothing else.

I wouldn't know what to do.

*

At first, Shelley Hogan didn't notice Dixie arrive in The Bronze Bean coffee shop. One assistant was clearing tables, another hadn't turned up this evening. Shelley was making two cappuccinos for a couple at a window table who were making no secret of their impatience. Meanwhile, Shelley was half-listening to a slim young woman in tight jeans and a halter-neck top who had a complaint about the quality of her latte. Shelley wondered how anyone could have so much to say about a cupful of anything.

Stay calm. The customer is always right, even when she's a cow.

The woman said, 'It's the principle of the thing. It's about respecting the customer.'

Shelley noticed Dixie standing behind and to the left of the mouthy young woman.

'Hi, sweetie.'

The woman looked from Shelley to Dixie and back again. Then she said, 'Christ, what's the point.' She left the latte on the counter and by the time she got back to her table her friend, an equally slim young woman with a large ring on every finger, and on both thumbs, was getting to her feet. The two walked out without looking back.

'How are ya? Coffee?'

Dixie shook her head. Shelley felt a surge of tenderness towards her friend. She seemed more frayed than at any time since the old days, after Owen died. Her looks were buried under the fear and the worry, she wasn't taking care of herself, her clothes were shite. Today she was wearing jeans and a dark green top that she'd borrowed from Shelley's flat, and they did nothing for her. The sparkle, the bounce, all the things that made her Dixie had been drained out of her.

Shelley served the cappuccinos and returned to the counter. Dixie said, 'I spent the afternoon wandering around. Brendan's in trouble, two guys came and – look, I can't go home.'

'You've got a key, sweetie, you know you're welcome. When I get out of here tonight I'm going to Robbie's gaff, then I'm back here at lunchtime tomorrow. You've got the place to yourself for the weekend.'

Dixie hesitated. Then, 'Any improvement – moneywise?'

Shelley made a face. 'I'm going to have to get somewhere that pays better than this kip. I've ten or fifteen in my bag, that's about it.' There wasn't anything that Shelley hadn't already considered – nothing to sell that would fetch what Dixie needed, no one to try to borrow from who wouldn't back away. Shelley herself was as close to the edge as she'd ever been. Robbie would keep her supplied with enough smack or blow to keep her head together, and until the next pay day came her mother was good for the price of enough groceries to make the difference.

Dixie said, 'I had to ask, just in case something—'

'What's your name?'

The voice came from the left, over by the cash register. Shelley turned and saw that the cow in the halter-neck top was back.

'Sorry?'

The woman said, 'I want an apology.'

'For what?'

Dixie was heading towards the door.

'Dixie?'

Dixie turned and shrugged. 'See you tomorrow.'

'If I don't get an apology—'

Shelley turned to the complaining woman and said, 'I'm sorry – for whatever – OK?'

'I can always take my custom elsewhere, you know.'

On her way out the door, Dixie passed the complaining woman's companion, the woman with rings on each finger.

When Shelley spoke her voice was low, without anger. 'Just piss off, will you?'

The woman stared at her for several moments, then turned and held her shoulders back as she walked quickly towards the door. Shelley made a dismissive noise with her tongue and her teeth. Several customers looked like they were pretending not to have noticed the squabble. The cappuccino couple at the table by the window stared at Shelley, making their disapproval plain. She gave them the sweetest smile she could manage.

*

The bottle of Johnnie Walker was still half full when Harry Synnott stood and stretched his arms over his head.

'Mona should be home soon,' John Grace said.

'I've got an appointment in the morning – about the possible job. Better get my head down.'

'Coffee?'

'I'll wait until I get home.'

John Grace rang for a taxi and they waited at the front door. The wind was picking up and overhead the dark clouds were low. Down to the right there was a narrow view, between a line of trees and the side of an apartment block, across a stretch of water to the distant lights of the city centre.

'You were blessed, moving out here.'

Grace said, 'It worked out. Mona will be sorry she missed you.'

'You're retiring, not emigrating – I'll probably see more of you than ever.'

'Tomorrow night, The Majestyk – will you be there?'

'I don't think it would be appropriate – Turner's Lane, all that shit.'

'The hell with that – it'll be a good evening. Do your best.'

Synnott's nod could have meant anything.

By the time the taxi arrived the rain had started. Synnott got in and as he closed the door he saw John Grace coming from the house, something in his hand. Synnott rolled down the window and Grace handed him a red box file with the words *Swanson Avenue* scrawled along the side.

Grace said, 'Without you, he'd have got away with it.'

29

The apartment was dark except for the pool of light around the kitchen table at which Harry Synnott sat. He'd shut the windows because of the rain, so there were none of the late-night city noises, just the patter on the glass. He opened the Swanson Avenue box file, grimaced and felt an urge to close the lid. The statement on top of the case documents was a psychiatric counsellor's assessment of Carmel Callaghan's son, Donny. Synnott hadn't seen the report in the four years since the Swanson Avenue murder but he could remember everything it said.

Poor little bastard.

Synnott remembered sitting next to three-year-old Donny Callaghan on a sofa at his granny's house, giving him a smile, asking him what Santa brought, how he liked playschool. There was nothing inside the kid except terror as he shrank away to the other end of the sofa. A week previously, three days before Christmas, he had watched his father murder his mother.

Perhaps John Grace was right, perhaps police work amounted to little more than sweeping up a never-ending supply of debris. But there was a reason why the Swanson Avenue case meant a lot to Harry Synnott. It was high-profile, a big deal in the media, but what mattered when it was all over was the certainty that he had done right by Carmel Callaghan and her devastated son.

This is what makes all the shit worthwhile.

Harry Synnott took the statements out of the box file and spread them on the kitchen table. He could remember the content of every document. It had taken Synnott and John Grace less than two weeks to break the case.

It had seemed obvious at first that Carmel Callaghan had come home with her son from playschool and interrupted a burglar at work. She was killed in the conservatory. Harry Synnott flipped open a two-page report by a detective inspector, pointing out that there'd been four similar break-ins in the area over the previous three weeks, all mid- to late morning, all detached houses, entry gained in all cases by the burglar breaking a window at the back or side. And in the Callaghan house there was a broken pane in the back door. As in the other break-ins, money, small pieces of jewellery, a couple of cameras and the like were missing.

Synnott found the autopsy report, but didn't read it. Three or four blows to the face from a heavy object, the pathologist said. A statement from an officer from Technical identified the bloody weapon, found near the body. The heavy brass statuette of Molly Malone was a wedding present from someone Carmel had once worked with. Although her pants had been pulled down the pathologist reported there was no evidence of sexual assault. The inspector with the theory of a burglary gone wrong suggested that the burglar pulled down the pants in a half-hearted effort to mislead police into rummaging among the city's registered creeps, looking for someone with a sexual motive.

Synnott opened the book of photographs taken by the garda technicians. The pictures were a superficial representation of the desolate atmosphere in the house that day. When John Grace saw the victim he said, 'Ah, *Christ*' and turned away. Synnott forced himself to look at the mess that had been Carmel Callaghan's face. From the bloody midst of that shambles her lifeless eyes stared at the ceiling. Her jeans and pants in a clump around her ankles added indignity to the woman's devastation.

'I'm still not used to it,' John Grace said. He hunkered down beside Synnott and looked at the dead woman. 'The waste.'

She was twenty-six, small and tubby. There was a photo of her in the box file, a head-and-shoulders taken in a studio. The plainness of her features, the fading chin and the chubby cheeks, didn't detract from the warmth of the face. The photographer had got her to attempt a glamour pose. Instead of showing her at her best, the photograph caught the timidity in her eyes as she tried vainly to be something she wasn't.

Her father was Billy Bonds, one of the city's best-known publicans, owner of three pubs. Carmel and her husband Ned owned a pub, The Old Jar, on the nearby Kilmartin housing estate. Ned was at work when Carmel's older sister arrived at the house for a lunch appointment and used her spare key. She found the body on the floor of the conservatory. She could hear Donny sobbing. When she traced the sound to a kitchen closet and opened the door the sobbing turned to a scream. A long time passed before the screaming stopped.

'What's that?' John Grace pointed.

Synnott leaned over and saw there was something on Carmel's lower stomach, an inch or two above her pubic hair. A round mark, perhaps a small healed wound. Synnott bent closer and saw that it was a tiny tattoo, maybe an inch in circumference. It was a finely detailed rosebud. He felt a slight twinge of guilt at being an uninvited witness to the dead woman's hidden sexual playfulness.

Technical identified urine on the floor of the dining room, just beyond the archway from the conservatory. They concluded that it was where Donny had been standing when he'd witnessed the murder and pissed himself.

There was no statement in the box file about the first hint of suspicion that things were not what they seemed. It was the kind of thing that a police officer would never write down. Passing through the hallway two days after the murder, on Christmas Eve, as garda technicians cleared up after examining the floor and walls, John Grace caught a glimpse of the bereaved husband, alone in the living room, the door half closed. Ned Callaghan was checking his hair in a mirror. It was a mundane action but was being carried out with inappropriate concentration at such a time, so much so that Grace back-pedalled and checked what he'd seen. Callaghan was standing, stooped slightly forward, his right hand teasing some tufts of hair above his temple.

As Grace stepped into the room Callaghan heard him and turned, his expression sombre. He pursed his lips and raised his chin in an enquiring gesture.

Grace said, 'Everything OK?'

Callaghan hunched his shoulders and nodded, as though too preoccupied to speak. He was medium height, thin-faced, his features earnest and boyish. Grace said later that Ned Callaghan put him in mind of an unreliable waiter. Whatever the circumstances, his face never lost its touch of impatience, as if he believed he ought to be elsewhere, doing something that mattered.

Grace said something meaningless about Christmas and loss and children. Callaghan said yeah, he and Donny would spend Christmas at his own mother's and they'd do their best to make it mean something to the kid.

Harry Synnott was sceptical. 'Some people can't help checking themselves out when they pass a mirror. It's automatic.'

'Five minutes earlier he was the grieving husband,' John Grace said. 'Then he's John Travolta, primping up for the disco. If you'd seen it – it just looked – callous, I suppose.'

The husband was always a possibility. Discreet inquiries established that Callaghan had spent all morning at the pub that he and his wife owned. Checking the preparations for the lunchtime food, serving behind the bar, working on the books in the office, checking stock in the cellar. He arrived just after nine o'clock and didn't leave until he received an urgent call to go home. The murder happened sometime around midday – body temperature suggested Carmel had been killed not much more than an hour before her sister had discovered the body at twelve-fifty.

The main emphasis of the investigation remained on the possibility of a burglary gone wrong. A trawl of fingermarks in the house, when compared with a range of prints taken for comparison, turned up a number that didn't match any member of the family or known visitors. That wasn't unusual, and none of the marks were on record. A couple of local crowbar specialists were pulled in, questioned and released.

When John Grace voiced his suspicions, Harry Synnott interviewed the pub staff himself. Initial reports from uniforms said that one or other of the employees saw Callaghan at the pub between 9.05 a.m. and 1.10 p.m., when he was called home. Pushed to be more specific, a barman qualified his earlier story that he saw Callaghan carrying a crate up from the cellar at eleven o'clock. 'I wasn't clock-watching, it could have been maybe fifteen, twenty minutes either way.' A cook, who earlier described talking to Callaghan during a coffee break at noon, was taken patiently through her memory of the morning. She recalled that she'd had a minor problem with the base of the soup kettle and she always got that ready for the lunch trade shortly after twelve noon. So she couldn't have taken the coffee break until perhaps ten or fifteen minutes later. By the time Synnott was finished, he had established a minimum forty-five-minute period in which Ned Callaghan hadn't been seen at the pub. The murder scene was a ten-minute drive away.

Synnott questioned Ned Callaghan about that forty-five minutes. He said his memory of the morning was confused. 'Once I got that call – Jesus, the world just went all crooked. I can't remember who I talked to or when.'

'It'll take a few days to get all the phone records – landlines and mobiles,' Synnott told a conference. 'Canvass the neighbours again, talk to their friends, family, employees – there's a housekeeper comes in three mornings a week – how loving were the loving couple?'

Harry Synnott spent a minute leafing through the box file looking for the statement from Petra Maguire. He found the typed-up version as well as the notes he'd made, ten days into the investigation, when she turned up at the station, aged nineteen, all smiles and swishing blonde hair. She worked part-time at The Old Jar and she'd just remembered that she'd seen Ned in his office at the pub at eleven-forty-five that morning.

'I went in to ask him for Saturday night off.' They talked for ten minutes. That eliminated the time gap in which Callaghan could have done the murder.

Synnott looked at his note of Petra Maguire's interview now as he'd looked at it then. She'd remembered none of this when he'd interviewed her several days earlier. He recalled the surge of satisfaction he felt when he finished with the silly bitch.

Stupid move, Ned.

Synnott smiled at Petra as he stood up. 'Thanks a million for coming in, Ms Maguire. You'll be hearing from us.'

It's shame that matters.

The sentence was scrawled at the bottom of a page of Harry Synnott's notes. He remembered now when he wrote it as a reminder, before he began the interrogation with Ned Callaghan. It was something he'd learned early on in his career. Use the suspect's shame. Make the stink of unacknowledged guilt unbearable.

Find his weakness, humiliate him with your knowledge of his secrets, pile it on until there's only one possible relief – to explain why he had to do it, to seek understanding and forgiveness. And there's no forgivenes without admission.

After a while, the shame seeped out of Ned Callaghan's every pore.

They invited him in twelve days after the murder, two days after Petra Maguire's silly attempt at providing an alibi. There were just some things that they needed to clear up, they told him.

He was glad to help – 'Whatever I can do.' He was determined to be sensible. 'I know you have to check out the husband.' As they pressed him, that changed to 'What worries me, I mean – look, you're barking up the wrong tree.'

Eyes wide, the complaint conveyed more in regret than vexation.

John Grace sat off to one side, one elbow on the table. Harry Synnott sat in the middle of the room, several feet from the table, almost knee to knee with the suspect. He watched Callaghan first fold his arms, then rub his hands on his thighs, then fold his arms again.

They took him over the jumps. Callaghan denied that he and his wife were having problems. He denied that he'd ever had an affair during his marriage, he denied that he'd had an affair during the year prior to her death. No, he and his wife hadn't had arguments recently, he hadn't threatened her. He'd never left the pub that morning. Harry Synnott wrote it all down in his note-book, then he read it back aloud and asked Callaghan if he would sign the notes. Callaghan did.

Then Synnott and Grace watched him fall apart as they unreeled the evidence they'd gathered of his sham marriage, his bullying, his lies.

It was all in the box file, the statements from four of the women he'd had affairs with since his marriage, one of them – located through his mobile-phone records – in the months prior to him murdering Carmel. The witnesses who saw Callaghan and his wife arguing, the neighbours, the housekeeper. The statement from Carmel's sister – how Carmel came to her in tears and showed her the photo she'd found in Ned's desk at the pub, a holiday snap of a young brunette, taken on a beach. The sister was there as Ned screamed at his wife that she'd had no fucking business snooping. The insults, the open contempt, the three times he left her in the evening and didn't come back until next day.

'Don't tell daddy,' Carmel begged her sister.

Daddy would have snapped the bastard in two.

'Your current girlfriend, Ned – does she know about the dumb blonde?'

Callaghan just sat there, looking at John Grace.

'Blondie? Petra Maguire? Affair number five. We took her in last night. Petra's in a cell right now.'

Ned Callaghan was rubbing his hands on his thighs again.

Synnott said, 'She crossed her legs and tilted her head and gave us a great big smile and we told her she was going to jail as an accessory to murder. Within two seconds she was blushing, within five minutes she gave us everything – the affair, how you told her you didn't have an alibi and you were afraid the police would stitch you up, so could she please say she saw you at the pub mid-morning.'

Ned didn't say anything for a while, then he said, 'I swear, on my son's life, it's true, the whole morning—'

'As true as the shit you told us about how you never had an affair?'

At that stage, Ned began admitting things he knew they could prove – the affairs, the rows – though he still denied he ever physically hurt his wife. 'I never laid a finger on her, *ever*.' Which was when they read him the statement from the friend who had tried to convince Carmel to see a doctor four months earlier, when Ned had twisted her arm so badly that she couldn't use it for a couple of days.

'That was an accident.'

'It's not your pub, right?'

'It was a wedding gift, from Carmel's dad.'

'He kept it in your wife's name, right?'

'That's a technicality.'

'Not if she told you to pack your bags and bugger off with your dumb blonde. That's what she said, that last argument, right?'

When Ned Callaghan looked up at Synnott the confirmation was all over his face. All Synnott knew was that Callaghan's next-door neighbours had heard a very loud argument in the driveway the night before the murder. There had been previous quarrels, but this had gone beyond the usual shouting.

'We know everything, Ned.'

When Callaghan began crying, Harry Synnott glanced at his watch. Just fifty-three minutes had passed since the interview began.

'I didn't do it.'

Ned Callaghan's voice was weak.

Synnott wrote a line in his notebook.

The fear of public shame was the last barrier. It would crumble if they had long enough to work on him.

'Ned, I've been making notes.' Synnott peeled the pages back towards the front of the notebook. He stopped and began reading aloud: *'I lied when I said I never had an affair during my marriage to Carmel. It was also a lie when I said that Carmel and I didn't have any rows.'*

Synnott took his time reading the details of the affairs and the rows Ned had admitted to.

'I lied about being in the pub all morning.'

'That's not true. I didn't say that.'

'When I arrived at the house at around eleven-thirty, Carmel wasn't home yet and—'

'Fuck off, I didn't say that.'

Synnott put pity into his eyes when he looked up at Ned Callaghan. 'I know it's not easy – what we're trying to do here, we're trying to help you find the truth. If that isn't exactly how it happened – OK, maybe we've got some of the detail wrong. Tell us how it went down.'

'I'm not under arrest – am I?'

'Ned, you'll just make it worse for yourself, for your family, for Donny.'

'No—'

'What's it going to look like when it all comes out – the affairs, the rows, the physical stuff—'

Callaghan's mouth was open, his breathing was audible. For a moment Synnott was certain that he was about to cave in. Then the scraping noise as Ned pushed his chair back and stood.

'I'm not under arrest, right?'

'You said you wanted to help us find your wife's killer.'

'Go fuck yourself.'

Ned Callaghan, face sweating and red, was unsteady on his feet, shaking his head, his movements awkward. He left the door wide open behind him.

John Grace said, 'We should arrest him now.'

Harry Synnott disagreed. 'We don't have enough – he's signed nothing incriminating – but we're not too far off. We need a lever.'

As his guilt weakens him, the fear of public shame strengthens his resistance. Find the piece of evidence that tips the balance, sends him tumbling into the self-hate that allows him confess the truth and to seek to justify.

Donny would help. Ned Callaghan could fool his friends and his relatives, and in time he might fool himself. But his son was something else. Donny wasn't at ease in his father's presence. That one time when Synnott had talked briefly to the boy alone, at his granny's house, the kid hadn't responded to the questions about Santa or playschool. Synnott had been about to stand up when Donny had said, 'My mammy—'

Synnott had no idea how to respond. The kid was too young to be asked what he'd seen that morning. The counsellors said it and the police agreed. To question him, no matter how sensitively, risked shattering an already damaged boy. Anyway, nothing a traumatised three-year-old might say was of evidential value.

Synnott didn't reply to Donny. He just put what he hoped was a comforting expression on his face. He lifted his chin, inviting the kid to continue.

Donny's eyes were brimming. Synnott could barely hear him when he spoke, but the repeated words were unmistakable.

'*My daddy, my daddy—*'

A moment later the grandmother, Ned Callaghan's mother, swept into the room and took Donny away.

Callaghan was on the edge. One push.

First thing in the morning, arrest him at his mother's house – let him watch her crying while he's handcuffed. Ask him if he wants to say a final goodbye to his son. The memory had to be gnawing away inside him – looking up from his wife's dead body and seeing his son's terrified face. The trauma of the arrest would connect with the guilt, his defences would melt.

An hour later they were back on Swanson Avenue. Not at the Callaghan house but at a builder's skip, a hundred yards further down the street. Witnesses heard Ned Callaghan's car accelerate as it tore past his house. Two of them were close enough to see him wrench the wheel to the right and drive diagonally across the road at high speed. When the car hit the skip Gallaghan came out through the windscreen. The police found him in a garden. Looking down at the shattered face, the throat gaping open, Harry Synnott couldn't help thinking of Carmel Callaghan's bloody features.

The newspapers called it a tragedy. The next weekend, someone leaked several of the documents from the police file to a tabloid and Ned Callaghan was christened 'The Monster of Swanson Avenue'. The notoriety of the murder, the shattered child, the proximity to Christmas, all heightened the profile of the case. Synnott found himself being congratulated. When he thought of Donny, the child's pain now and in the years ahead, the plaudits faded to nothing.

The rain had stopped. Synnott stood at the window, in the dark, looking down at the lights and the revellers across the river.

John Grace was wrong. Maybe it was about cleaning up the crap, but it was also about something else. There were enough times – and the Swanson Avenue case was one of them – where they managed to find some kind of justice.

And that matters.

Amid all the disappointments, the numbing routine and the faltering ambitions, some things matter. Synnott realised he was clutching the box file, one arm holding it to his chest, the way a kid holds onto a favourite old blanket.

SUNDAY

30

Nothing but pain.

No memory, no anger, no resistance. No fear except fear of more pain. No hope.

After they put Brendan Peyton in the boot of the car they drove for maybe an hour. Then they parked and he could hear them slamming the car doors and walking away. There was no sound of people or traffic.

After a while he kicked the lid of the boot and shouted for help. He stopped when he ran out of hope that anyone would hear him.

He tried to keep a measure of time but he had no idea how many hours went by solid with fear. It had to be into the small hours of Sunday morning by now.

Brendan kicked and shouted again, but this time only for a minute. He was cramped and tired. For a while he just lay there and let the tears come.

He tried to think of what this might be about – with Matty involved, it was something to do with Lar Mackendrick – but he'd done nothing wrong. He hadn't stolen anything or bad-mouthed anyone, and he didn't owe money to Lar or anyone else.

He had no idea that he'd fallen asleep until he heard the car start up. As he struggled back to consciousness, he didn't know if it was the cold or the fear that was making him shiver so violently. He shouted Matty's name but there was no response.

If they were going to kill me they'd have done it when they took me.
He could feel how weak his grip was on this crumb of hope.

An hour, two hours – he couldn't tell how long it was before the car stopped and the engine cut out. When they helped him out of the boot the bright daylight made Brendan squeeze his eyes shut. He squinted as they moved him along and he saw that he was in some kind of yard, with building materials scattered around. He searched their faces for comfort.

'Matty—'

'Speak when you're spoken to.'

They took him through a doorway and across bare floorboards to a room with an echo, where a hand on his arm told him to stop. The room was dark, the window boarded up, just enough light to see the cracked walls and a ceiling torn open. He could see the floor joists of the room upstairs.

Matty pushed him in the chest and something caught him behind the knees and he gave a high-pitched squeal as he went down on his back.

Before Brendan could stand up one of them held his hands together while the other tied them tightly in front of him with a plastic loop. They bound his feet together and some kind of cloth was fastened over his eyes. Then he heard them walk away.

After a long time just lying there, Brendan started screaming. He knew they had left him to die. Thirst or starvation, rats – his body jerked and twisted in panic and he passed out.

Brendan was conscious when they came back, a long time later. They said nothing as they untied his feet. They left his hands tied. One of them pulled the cloth roughly from his eyes.

He saw Matty standing over him, his face blank. No aggression, just a man doing a job. That was always how Matty—

Jesus!

The other one hit Brendan across the face with something

hard, maybe something wooden, slashing at his cheeks and nose. Brendan didn't see it coming and as he twisted and hid his face he felt blood trickle from one nostril.

'Jesus Christ! What the fuck! Matty!'

Wherever they were, these yobs weren't worried about noise.

'Matty, what—'

After the next blow to his face, from the heel of Matty's hand, Brendan Peyton lashed out, his back on the floor, his legs kicking in rage. When they pulled a plastic Tesco bag over his head he shrieked, certain he was about to be suffocated. But they left the bag loose around his neck. The idea seemed to be to leave him blinkered so that he wouldn't know when the next blow was coming, or where it would strike.

Mostly they hit him in the belly and the back, at first. One of them kicked him in the side, over and over, making a little high-pitched noise to accompany every kick.

When they pulled his trousers down he begged them. He tried to roll himself into a ball and begged them to tell him what this was about. They turned him over onto his back and one of them held his feet down. Then the other one began to hit him across his shins, both shins at the same time, with some kind of metal bar, and Brendan screamed and never knew there could be such pain.

He squealed as cold water struck his face and he felt like he was struggling to the surface and he realised the bag was off his face and he'd passed out, and the agony in his shins filled him up. Then they put the bag back on his head and hit him again, the bar on the shins, and again, and he screamed, and screamed again, over and over and gulped in air between the screams, sucking the plastic bag taut against his open mouth.

After a long time, they pulled the bag off his head. Matty sat him up and put one hand around Brendan's throat. Brendan sobbed. He looked down at his legs and felt something heave inside his chest.

The younger one leaned forward and used an index finger to flick at Brendan's nose.

'Muppet,' he said.

Matty was speaking into Brendan's ear. 'The DVD factory – right? I want the name of the copper you talked to. Lie to me, and it starts all over again and I won't ask you another question for a whole hour.'

Brendan remembered one of Lar Mackendrick's mates telling him about DVDs – *Jesus, that was just in one ear and out the other* – and he wanted to say that he'd never whispered a word to the police about that or anything else. He wanted to say that he hardly remembered anything the fella had said about a DVD factory, but he knew that was the wrong answer.

'Look, I swear I didn't—' Brendan said, trying to think as the waves of pain rolled up from his burning shins. 'All I—'

'Time's up,' Matty said.

And the bag went on Brendan's head again and he was down on his back and someone was holding his feet and he screamed even before the bar came down on his shins. When the second blow came it felt like his tormentors had smashed through to a deeper, more sensitive layer.

After a while, incapable of thought, his mind abandoned to agony, a flash of memory connected and held and Brendan screamed that he'd told her, he'd told the bitch.

'The bitch! The fucking bitch! It must—'

But the blows continued and he passed out again. Then they took the bag off and threw water on his face once more and when his head cleared Matty took him by the throat and said, 'Tell me.'

*

It was about five minutes from the end of the Mass when Harry Synnott's phone vibrated silently in his pocket. He took it out and the screen showed *Withheld*. A man kneeling in the pew across the aisle was staring at him like he'd farted in church. Synnott thumbed a button to accept the call, then held the phone down by his side as he rose and walked quickly towards the back of the church.

'Mr Synnott, you're my last chance.'

Standing in the church porch, Synnott closed his eyes for a couple of seconds and when he opened them his voice was flat and hard. 'I'm not a bank, Dixie, and you've got no collateral.'

'Things are – Brendan is in trouble, apart from – two hundred, I'll get the rest somewhere, but you can afford—'

'You're dreaming, Dixie. What we have is a business relationship and you haven't been doing the business.'

'There's things I know, there's things you'd—'

As Dixie yapped away, a possibility occurred to Synnott. He stepped out of the church porch and moved a few feet to the left of the front door. When she paused, although there was no one within yards, Synnott kept his voice low.

'Joshua Boyce?'

'What?'

'You remember him? He grew up in Cairnloch, he was still there around the time you and Owen—'

'I haven't seen Joshua in years. He was never, he was older than me, I'd nothing to do with him, I barely knew him.'

'Think about it, Dixie. Something someone said, maybe something about who's fencing for Joshua these days. Maybe he's got a lock-up somewhere, keeps his stuff there, maybe anything.'

There was silence for a while and then Synnott said, 'No?'

'I'm sorry, Mr Synnott, I just haven't seen him in years.'

'No play, no pay.'

'Mr Synnott, I need—'

Synnott ended the call.

Long shot. Dixie and Joshua Boyce, they move in different circles.

The early leavers were already trickling out of Mass. Synnott decided not to go back inside. It was nearing midday and

Haddington Road, a long straight street lined with trees, looked pretty in the sunshine. The ministerial Mercedes parked at the kerb outside the church railings fitted in with the feel of the street. Tall, handsome houses, expensive offices, and it was warm enough for some of the Sunday-morning strollers to sport their favourite rugby shirts.

Synnott approached the Mercedes and nodded to the detective behind the wheel, whose return nod indicated recognition. Synnott leaned down. 'He got any other appointments this morning?'

The detective – Synnott remembered his name, Brannigan – shook his head. 'Lunch at home with the family, then a speech this evening.'

'Speechifying on a Sunday? Busy man.'

'In his business, you can never shake too many hands.'

'How many Masses has he been to this morning?'

Brannigan smiled. 'Two, in the constituency, plus this one. The constituency Masses are so's he can meet the grass roots. Was a time he'd go right through the race card, but you don't get the crowds any more.'

'What's he doing here? It's not his constituency.'

The detective said, 'This is the kind of gig where he might run into the nobility.'

Synnott watched the Minister for Justice standing outside the church door when Mass ended, shaking hands with a succession of fellow worshippers. Mass attendance mightn't be what it was, since the child abuse scandals, but Synnott reckoned it was on the up. In recent years, as the economy surged, Synnott had noticed a significant revival of Mass-going among the more affluent. He wondered if it was some form of thanksgiving, or maybe an offering to the gods who could stave off a return to the relative penury of old.

He noticed one couple being greeted by the minister, the man with a puffy red face and a well-cultivated moustache, the woman at least two decades younger. The man's face was familiar. Then Brannigan said the name and Synnott remembered – something to do with horses. People in that business had the kind of money that gets a politician's close attention. The minister held the horsy man's elbow as they spoke, their heads close together.

Brannigan started the Mercedes's engine. When the minister strode across the pavement, his smile wide, his cheeks shiny, he clapped Synnott on the shoulder and said, 'Off we go.'

Brannigan was right. A dour bastard.

The minister adjusted his backside into the Merc's leather and smiled across at Detective Inspector Synnott. Good man, exemplary record of service, but hardly the type to fit comfortably into the upper echelons of the force. No social skills.

'Thanks for taking the time – it's just a matter of touching base before we take this Europol thing any further.'

'No bother, sir.'

'Brannigan will take you wherever you wish, once he's dropped me home.'

The minister noted Synnott's ready-made smile. No hint of genuine appreciation at being singled out. The Europol job was the ideal slot for a capable high-profile copper with compatibility problems. Promotion, but to a position that required more concentration and application than political shrewdness.

'There was a time, Harry, when a job like this Europol thing would go to whatever police officer was next in line for a favour. As long as he had the proper connections and he'd played the game the right way.' The minister had a file open on his lap. He stopped skimming through the file and continued to speak as he assessed a buff-coloured document.

'Not any more. These days it's quality that counts. That's the hallmark of the new Ireland. These days, when we step onto the world stage we set an example.' He closed the file and looked across at Synnott.

'Whatever the task, the new Ireland puts its best people forward. Look at Bono. Shaking the conscience of the globe. That gives us a kind of credibility you can't buy. Geldof, too. He has a mouth on him, that man, but his heart's in the right place.' The minister turned towards Synnott and leaned forward. 'Name a field, we're shining in it. Ryanair, Jesus – they started from nothing, they end up practically running the European airline industry. Our horse breeders – we've got Arabs coming cap in hand to get our stallions to knock up their flea-bitten nags. There was a time, if we came third in the Eurovision Song Contest we were creaming ourselves for months. These past few years, Booker Prizes, Nobel Prizes, Olympic golds, the rugby team kicking the arse off the lot of them, the native games stronger than ever. The soccer lads – well, we'll rise again.'

The minister could see that Synnott was beginning to understand the compliment he was being paid in being considered for the position.

'That's the level of excellence you'll be aiming for, Harry, if you take this job. You're representing your country. I said to Colin O'Keefe, I said – I want someone with the street smarts and the intellect, someone who can represent a country that doesn't settle for second-best. And he gave me you. Are you up for it, Harry?'

Harry Synnott tried not to look at the tiny piece of spittle that had landed on the left lapel of the minister's jacket during his speech. He hoped his own expression appeared sincere enough to cloak the resentment he felt at being expected to perform for a politician. Either he was a good enough policeman for the job or he wasn't.

'I think I've shown, minister, that—'

'Have you ever met any of these bang-bang merchants yourself, personally?'

Synnott tried not to look puzzled.

'The gangsters. The hard lads. The General, he's long dead, of course. The Viper, the Coach, John Gilligan, Tommy Farr, the Mackendrick brothers – those toughies. What are they like? What are their ambitions?'

Same as yours, minister, same as your horsy friend's. They want position and wealth with the least amount of sweat possible. They do whatever it takes.

Synnott wondered for a moment if he should answer honestly. Then he decided that the truth didn't matter, just the performance.

Shuffle your feet for the minister.

'Very determined people, very dangerous.'

Synnott said something about the geographical spread of the gangs, the ruthlessness of the young guns and the resilience of the older outfits.

If they had the connections to get in on a stock option or to front a sure-thing property deal, that's what they'd do. Instead, they know how to import coke, organise bank raids, bully a string of prostitutes and wallop the shit out of anyone who looks crooked at them. They're the brightest and most enterprising people in their community.

For a passing moment Synnott was tempted to drop the word 'entrepreneurs' into his patter, just to see how the minister would take it.

'They're strong, but we're making inroads. It makes a difference when a police force knows that it has a minister who's genuinely interested in the problem.'

Synnott hoped he wasn't blushing. The minister was nodding, seeming to accept the compliment as no more than a statement of fact.

'Weaknesses?'

Same as yours, minister, same as your horsy friend's.

'They reach a stage where they feel free to stamp on anyone who gets in their way, even their own henchmen, and that leaves a lot of damaged people who sometimes talk to us about them.'

The minister nodded. 'This gangster that shot the security guard—'

Synnott had to make a quick adjustment. Joshua Boyce had nothing to do with the gangs – it was a different kind of crime, but there was no point trying to explain that. The minister saw crime as one big problem, instead of the accumulation of diverse wickednesses that Synnott dealt with.

Synnott said, 'We're pursuing several lines of inquiry.'

'I've heard you've got him in your sights. What kind of man are we talking about?'

Synnott said, 'Well, it's early days—'

Jesus.

Talking to a civilian, even the Minister for Justice, about operational matters – *fuck that.*

The minister's mouth made a pursing movement after every sentence. 'A public-spirited young man, cut down by a gangster. This is one we're all watching, Harry. And from what I hear, you've got the bastard teed up and ready, that right?'

'I'm hopeful. We have a lead or two, we're working hard.'

The minister crossed his arms. He was staring ahead when he spoke.

'These days, Harry, we get things done. On the streets at home, or on the world stage. I'm counting on you.'

The Merc turned onto a short street, both pavements shaded by lines of trees. The houses were mostly three-storeyed, with basement flats and steep steps up to the front doors. Fifty feet along the street, the car pulled in to the kerb.

The minister said, 'On the world stage, we're punching above our weight.' Synnott watched another tiny piece of spittle arc away from the minister's mouth, towards him, falling away below his eye-line. He forced himself not to look down to see where it landed. 'This country used to specialise in moral victories, Harry. We'd take a beating, slink away, tail between our legs, and then we'd brighten up and we'd say it was a moral victory for such a wee nation just to be allowed on the pitch.'

The minister leaned forward, one hand on the door handle.

Synnott looked down, saw the minuscule white bubble on his left knee. He forced his eyes to look away. The minister's voice was passionate. 'To hell with moral victories, Harry. These days we have victories, full stop. Nothing moral about them. We stomp right out into the centre of the ring and we don't stop punching until the ref is holding our hand up high and fuck the begrudgers.'

Brannigan had the car door open. The minister had one foot on the pavement when he said, 'Soon as you've wrapped this one up – this animal, what's his name, Boyce – we'll have the Europol paperwork ready and you'll be on your way.'

Synnott arranged his face and said, 'Thank you, minister. I won't let you down.'

Brannigan waited until the minister was up the steps of the house and through the front door before he got back behind the wheel of the Merc and put the car in gear.

'Where to?'

'Macken Road garda station.'

As they pulled back onto the main road, Harry Synnott used the cuff of his jacket sleeve to brush his knee.

31

Lar Mackendrick was standing in the lobby of the Four Seasons Hotel, waiting for his wife May to come out of the Ladies' and join him for lunch. His nutritionist would tut-tut if she knew he was indulging in hotel food, but it was May's birthday, so sod the nutritionist. If he couldn't celebrate the sixty-first birthday of the woman who'd shared his life, what was the point of all the effort to protect his health?

Lar nodded to a builder he knew, a man for whom he arranged waste disposal at an unlicensed site in Wicklow. The man didn't return the nod. He steered his two companions towards the bar. Lar didn't mind the snub – the guy had to be careful about who he was seen with.

Lar's mobile rang. He answered and listened for a few moments.

'You believe him?'

Matty said, 'We pressed our case very hard.'

'Fair enough. Better find her, then. Thing like this, I'd like to attend to it myself.'

*

Sunday lunch was the one guaranteed sit-down family meal of the week and Rose Cheney's husband was dishing out the roast lamb when the phone rang.

'Your mother,' Rose said.

'Your boss,' David said.

Eight-year-old Louise picked up the phone. 'Mammy,' she called. David smiled. Rose breathed a silent curse.

Harry Synnott said he was ringing from Macken Road.

'I'm just about to have lunch with my family.'

Synnott said, 'No problem – you know Chief Superintendent Hogg has called a conference at four-thirty? On the jewellery robbery?'

'Yes.'

'The Kellsboro Arcade – Boyce dumped his car there after the robbery – a waitress in the coffee shop saw someone pass through, did a runner out the back door – we can assume that was him. No one's run a photo display past her – how about, an hour before the conference, we see if she recognises his picture?'

Rose knew it made sense, but she'd been looking forward to an hour of nothing much, maybe chasing around the garden with Louise and Anthony.

Bugger.

'Three-thirty, not a minute before. Where'll we meet?'

*

Dixie Peyton was in the kitchen at Shelley Hogan's flat, rinsing the saucepan she'd just cleaned, when Shelley arrived, slamming the door behind her. There was rage in the way she tore off her yellow jacket and threw it at the armchair.

'I thought—'

Shelley went into her bedroom, slammed that door too. It was fifteen minutes before she came out. She slumped onto the settee and grimaced at Dixie. Her voice was calm. 'Bastard gave me the sack. He was waiting when I arrived in at noon, big gob on him—'

She suddenly shrieked, '*Bastard!*' and lashed out with her right foot, connecting with the side of the coffee table. An empty cup rattled on its saucer and Shelley shrieked again, '*Fucking bastard!*'

'Why'd he sack you?'

That stuck-up bitch from last night. Whining about how her coffee didn't come the way she'd ordered it. She rang this morning, telling him the customer expects certain standards these days.'

'Ah, Jesus—'

'She wasn't the first. He's been looking for an excuse, that bastard. I told him to fuck off – I wasn't—' Her voice was lower now, her words coming more slowly. 'Last night, Robbie – fuck it, one thing on top of the other.'

'I thought you and him—'

Shelley shook her head. Leaning forward, elbows resting on her knees, she cupped her face in her hands. Dixie busied herself pouring two mugs of coffee.

Shelley sounded more tired than angry now. 'The thing about Robbie – he liked me being – Jesus, he's a bastard. He liked it that I depended on him, it was part of the kick. And showing me how easy he could fuck me over, that too.'

'I thought—'

'He was OK for a laugh and he had a good connection. The stuff he was moving, he gave me a discount. Last night – he's a shit, just a shit.'

Dixie removed the empty cup and saucer from the coffee table and brought Shelley a mug of coffee.

'One thing on top of the other.' Shelley's eyes were closed, her head resting against the back of the settee.

'You were going to try for another job anyway, right?'

Shelley opened her eyes and leaned forward. 'Suppose so. It'll take a few days, and there's nothing coming in and without Robbie's discount – fucking wonderful.'

'I wish I could help.'

Shelley smiled. 'Look at the two of us, right pair of whingers.'

She raised her mug. 'We've survived worse, sweetie, and we'll rise again.'

Dixie held up her own mug in a toast.

'Tight corners.'

32

The waitress from Clara's Coffee Shop at the Kellsboro Shopping Arcade reluctantly let Synnott and Cheney into her home. When they told her what they wanted her to do she said, 'Why?'

The waitress was in her mid-thirties. She'd put a lot of effort into her hair. There was something in her wide, dark eyes – mischief, Synnott decided – that compensated for the rounded shoulders and the lines around her mouth. Her house, in a cul-de-sac in Dolphin's Barn, was small, clean and the front wall and windowsills were freshly painted. The front garden was tiny, the grass trimmed to within an inch of its life. There were rows of daffodils under the window and the borders consisted of assortments of small blue, pink and yellow flowers that Synnott didn't recognise. The front room was little bigger than the garden, and there were two kids under ten slumped on a two-seater sofa in front of the television. In the kitchen the woman offered Synnott and Cheney coffee, which they declined. She didn't bother to pretend to seriously consider their request. All she said was, 'Why?'

Synnott answered. 'This man killed a young security guard. He left his getaway car at the shopping arcade where you work, we know he ordered a coffee from you, didn't stay to drink it. Apart from the victims of the robbery, you're the only witness to see him close up.'

She looked at Synnott as though he was speaking another language.

Rose Cheney said, 'Perhaps he'd taken the false moustache off, perhaps he'd changed his clothes. You may be able to identify him.'

'Why should I?'

'All we're asking is that you look at the photographs.' Cheney touched one of the eight pictures she'd laid out on the table in two rows, squaring it up with the others. Joshua Boyce's face was second from the left, second row.

'No point. I saw nothing.'

There was an edge to Synnott's voice. 'Perhaps you'll recognise a face. Sometimes people don't know that they've—'

The waitress leaned forward, hands flat on the table and when she spoke her voice was gentle. 'Five days a week, love, I work breakfast and lunchtime serving sausages and chips and pots of tea. I take orders from people who have the manners of pigs. Five nights a week, eight to eleven, I clean offices. Don't ask me whose offices or what business they're in. All they know is that when they come in next day the dirt fairy has taken away the mess they left. Saturday and Sunday afternoons, I do five hours behind the counter in a pub on the other side of the estate. Altogether, what I get, it almost adds up to a wage.'

She stood upright, folding her arms across her breasts.

'If I want to take holidays, or get sick, I do it on my own time.'

'If you're afraid—'

'I'm not afraid. I don't care.'

Synnott said, 'A young man lost his life. A decent working man with a family. Every one of us has a duty to ensure that the killer is put where he belongs.'

The waitress took her time lighting a cigarette and her chin jerked as she blew smoke towards the ceiling. 'The things you're paid to care about, they've got nothing to do with me when I'm scraping what's left of someone's sandwich off the floor.' She looked from Synnott to Cheney. 'Nothing to do with me now.'

*

'That's a pity,' Chief Superintendent Malachy Hogg said. 'We need a break.' He was standing at the far end of the room, making the odd comment, but allowing Harry Synnott to run the case conference. One of the detectives had offered Hogg a seat in the crowded room, but the Chief Super shook his head and stood against the wall, hands in the pockets of his jacket.

The conference started with a review of the physical evidence, or lack of it. Nothing in the Accord, not even a partial. Nothing in the car park where the shooting happened. No second car that could be linked to the robbery. The Kellsboro Shopping Arcade had no CCTV.

'We need the gun, the jewellery or the money,' Harry Synnott said. 'We've got bugger-all from the fences we've rousted, but we can go back to the likeliest ones. They won't give us anything, but we may frighten off whoever he has lined up, so he can't offload the jewellery.'

Chief Superintendent Hogg asked if they'd got anything useful from touts. Synnott shook his head. 'Not a whisper – Boyce keeps things pretty tight.'

'Keep at it. He'll come up with an alibi, somewhere close to home. It's imperative we get a sighting somewhere over on the Southside, on the way to or from the robbery scene.'

A detective that Synnott didn't know said, 'What if it wasn't Boyce?'

Chief Superintendent Hogg took a moment before he replied. 'If we get a lead elsewhere, we follow it – meanwhile, if Harry Synnott says he's certain the man on the CCTV tape is Joshua Boyce, that's where the emphasis is going to be. We're pressing all the buttons, and we'll get a break or we won't.'

*

Rose Cheney left Macken Road immediately after the conference. It had taken her two days to track down Donna Wright and she'd already gone twice to the flat on the third floor of Carlyle Buildings where Donna now lived. Third time lucky. The door was opened by a small dark-haired woman in her early twenties. When Rose Cheney introduced herself the woman said, 'What's wrong?'

'Nothing's wrong, and I may be wasting my time, but I think you can help me. I've been talking to a detective from Earlsfort Terrace. You talked to him, fifteen months ago, about a man named Max Hapgood.'

Donna Wright closed the door partially. She waited.

'I wonder, could I come in and talk to you about that?'

'I've nothing to say.'

'I've seen the detective's notes. I know what happened.'

'Look, it's Sunday evening, I'm getting ready to go out.'

'Donna, can I suggest something? No notebook, nothing on the record, nothing official at all – just one woman talking to another. Nothing can come from it, you won't be compromised in any way – but it might help, just so I know we're not wasting our time.'

'There's nothing to say, that's all in the past.'

'He's done it again.'

The woman stood silent for a few moments, then opened the door wide.

*

At first, the doctor in A&E thought that Brendan Peyton had been in a car accident. Bruises on his face and torso, multiple severe contusions and abrasions on both legs, the right shin fractured. Then one of the nurses told him that Mr Peyton had been brought in by ambulance after a strolling dog owner found him moaning in some bushes in St Anne's Park.

'What happened to him?'

'He says he doesn't remember.'

The doctor told the nurse to call the police, and when two tired uniformed gardai arrived and pulled the curtains around the cubicle Brendan Peyton repeated that he just didn't remember. One policeman snorted and left to get some coffee.

'Do you have a mobile?' Brendan asked the other policeman.

'Yes, why?'

'I need to make a call.'

'You can remember phone numbers, then? No bother with that part of your memory?'

'Please?'

The garda was looking through Brendan's wallet. 'They didn't take your money, whoever gave you a going-over?'

'Just one call?'

'I'll tell you what. I'm going to join my mate for a coffee, and when we come back, if your memory's any better, maybe—'

'Bastard!'

'You need to do a course in making friends and influencing people, you do.'

When the garda was gone, Brendan told a nurse he needed to make a phone call. She said what he needed was a bed and they didn't have one available. Brendan Peyton, held together by pain-killers, spent the evening on a trolley in the A&E corridor. The police came back. When he said again that he didn't remember what had happened they stared at him with a mix of sympathy and contempt.

'Don't be stupid. Whatever animals did that to you – let us deal with them.'

'Yeah, right,' Brendan said.

After a while, he borrowed a mobile from a man on another trolley and called home, but Dixie didn't pick up. He rang Shelley Hogan's flat but there was no answer.

33

Harry Synnott had just pulled into the car park of The Majestyk Inn when his mobile rang.

'Please, I have to talk to you.'

'Dixie, it's Sunday evening, I'm off duty, and we don't have anything to talk about.'

'I'm begging you, now, begging you. If I don't – look, this is more important to me than anything, *ever*, and you know I've been a help to you, you know I'll give you stuff again, you know – *Jesus*, Mr Synnott, I'm begging you, and it's hardly any money, a few hundred, I'll get it back to you, you know—'

'Look, Dixie—'

'– *Please*, Mr Synnott, I'll do anything, anything, and if—'

'Dixie, I'm late for an appointment.' He cut her off, put the mobile in his pocket and got out of his car.

*

It was a gorgeous house and Finbarr was an attentive host. He wouldn't do business until the jeweller named his drink and accepted a heavy crystal brandy glass that was generously laden with Courvoisier. Paddy Robert Garcia Murphy was here to get the opinion of one of the most expensive barristers in the country, and the hospitality was a welcome extra.

'I don't want to know what was in the floor safe,' Finbarr said, 'but I assume it was legal.' His smile gave his ample face a benevolent glow. 'Since there's nothing to show it wasn't – the proverbial empty stable – the police must in legal terms make the same assumption. Ergo, no problem.'

'They threatened me – obstruction, concealment of a crime – the detective was an obnoxious bastard.'

'They're entitled to their suspicions – and you're entitled to tell them to bugger off. Evidence is what matters. They find a secret safe, empty after a robbery, and you don't wish to tell them what was in it.' He shrugged. 'It might be photos of your mistress, for all they know, and you don't want the embarrassment. They may speculate, they may bluster, but you're on safe enough ground.'

Robert Garcia felt better. He'd had the same advice from his solicitor, but it meant more to him when he had to pay top rates to hear it from a senior counsel. He sipped his brandy and listened to Finbarr rephrase the same reassurance in various ways, giving value for money.

He liked being in Finbarr's house, the walls of this reception room heavy with selections from Finbarr's renowned and very expensive collection of paintings. He liked being able to share his problem, he liked the warmth he got from Finbarr's fellowship, even though he knew that he wouldn't get an invitation to attend at Finbarr's home on a Sunday evening unless there was a hefty bill attached.

'Is there anything else arising from this robbery that might be a problem?'

Robert Garcia shook his head and put on a smile. 'No, that's it.' The problem of how he'd break the news to the owners of the jewellery stolen from the floor safe wasn't something he could discuss with a lawyer, even at Finbarr's rates.

'Well, then,' Finbarr said, swallowing his own whiskey and giving Robert Garcia another benevolent smile. He gestured to the brandy glass. 'Take your time.'

*

Someone had strung a banner across the top of the room. In black letters on a pink background decorated with stars and streaky-tailed comets, it said *Amazing Grace!* There were posters on each side of the banner. One said, *Good Luck, John!* The other said, *Life Begins at Retirement!*

Turner's Lane station had booked the biggest function room the Majestyk Inn had to offer, and when Harry Synnott arrived it was already filling up. There was a bar down one side of the room and the centre was a forest of tables and chairs. On a raised dais in one corner a fat red-haired man with freckles was sitting behind a stack of speakers and a keyboard programmed to sound like an orchestra. He was halfway through the theme from *Hill Street Blues*.

Bob Tidey was at the bar, a whiskey in one hand, the other hand waving in the air to attract Synnott's attention.

'What are you having?'

'A pint.'

'He's well on already.' Tidey nodded towards John Grace, who had one arm around the shoulder of a young red-headed woman and the other around the shoulder of a grizzled ex-sergeant who'd had a similar party when he'd retired a couple of years back. Grace's wife Mona, sitting at a table in the middle of the room, caught Harry Synnott's glance, smiled and raised her eyebrows.

Synnott looked around. There was no one he wanted to talk to. When he was young, this kind of crowded pub was standard for a night out, but now he couldn't understand how he'd ever put up with the noise and the crush of it.

Most of the drinkers were Turner's Lane people, with a sampling of members from stations around the city who had worked with John Grace in the course of his career. There was a Chief Superintendent from Turner's Lane, and a couple of senior officers from the Phoenix Park HQ. Tidey said, 'O'Keefe left a little while ago. He made a speech about life after crime-fighting. Apparently, we've all got a lot to look forward to.'

'Is that it then, for the speeches?'

'Dream on.'

The freckled man with the keyboard was working his way through his repertoire of television cop shows. As the last notes of *The Rockford Files* died, the Chief Superintendent from Turner's Lane took the microphone. 'Order! Quiet down the back! Bit of order, or I'll have to call in the heavy gang!'

When the hubbub died, he spoke for a few minutes about civic duty and how easily it was taken for granted, about pride and honour and integrity. 'John Grace, in his time as a policeman, has taken more than his share of knocks. But he came through it, and we're proud to be here with him tonight, and to wish him and Mona all the very best in the years – the long years – to come. He's getting out when he's still young enough to thrive in some other field, and the rest of us can only hope that when we leave the force we'll have a career as worthwhile as John's to look back on.' After the applause, it took him a minute of coaxing to get John Grace, shaking his head and making hushing gestures with his hands, to come up to the microphone. Holding on to the microphone stand with one hand, the other tugging at the side of his shirt collar, Grace waited for the applause to end.

'Listen, all I want to say – to all of you degenerates – is thanks. It's been – I won't say I'm not glad to be getting out. Some of you know that wouldn't be true. But I made a lot of friends on the force, and I think, over the years, we managed not to let ourselves down. We did the job.'

A couple of people near the dais began clapping and the rest joined in. Beside Harry Synnott, Bob Tidey's piercing whistle soared above the applause.

'There were shitty times.' John Grace paused. 'Good people gone. But we're not here tonight to mourn. What I still – I know everyone says this, but it's true – you think you're just getting the hang of something, and you look up and notice your hair is grey and there's young bastards like some of you lot, sniffing at your heels. Then you know it's time to shut the fuck up.'

There was applause as he stepped down off the dais, and several people stood to shake his hand as he walked back to his table. By the time he sat down, Sergeant Derek Ferry from Turner's Lane was holding the microphone. 'There's something not yet said, but it ought to be.'

Sergeant Ferry looked around the room. His gaze passed over Harry Synnott, then came back again. Then he looked down at Grace.

'John Grace is a gentleman who served the public with distinction. I'm proud to call him a friend. He and Mona – and I know she wouldn't want to be—' There was a flurry of applause. 'It's a life well spent. A life of service, comradeship – as the Super said, honour, integrity – and a life of trust. The public trust us, we trust each other.' He paused. 'Trust. And when you can't trust the member of the force next to you, when you have to watch your back—'

Bob Tidey said, 'Ah, for fuck sake.'

Harry Synnott looked down at the bar in front of him. His pint glass was almost empty.

'– when you know the member next to you is waiting for the kind of mistake that – everyone, if you're human, everyone sometimes does something, maybe in a moment of weakness – and when you *have* a moment of weakness, what you need is your colleague, your comrade – someone you trust, there beside you, to see you make it back to the straight and narrow.'

The Superintendent was standing beside Sergeant Ferry, reaching for the microphone. 'Derek, it's not the time or the—'

'Judas!'

There was a smattering of applause, a few boos. The Superintendent took the microphone from Ferry's hand and shook his head. He gestured for him to step down. Ferry stood there, his hands on his hips. The Superintendent spoke into the microphone, his voice subdued. 'This is John Grace's night, Derek. Don't spoil it.'

Sergeant Ferry tilted his head back, stood there for another moment, then stepped off the dais and went back to his table.

After a moment, Harry Synnott looked up. The room was filling with chatter again. There were people glancing his way, but they turned away when they saw him looking. Beside him Bob Tidey was gazing into his empty whiskey glass, his face flushed and sweaty.

Harry Synnott walked towards the door. No one said anything to him. Behind him, the fat freckled man on the dais was starting to play the theme from *The Sweeney*.

34

It was the rhythm that mattered, not the speed. Get into the rhythm and then it's just one foot in front of the other until you get where you're going.

The double murder at Bushy Park had screwed up the week for Garda Joe Mills. The overtime wasn't to be sneezed at, but his erratic work hours meant that he hadn't been out for an evening run since the previous Monday. It was past evening now, only the odd pedestrian on the dark residential streets of the Livermore estate where he lived.

There was a time when Joe Mills had taken his running seriously. Breathing 3-2, then 2-2, start the count on the first fall of the left foot, five minutes moderate pace, three minutes fast, then five minutes moderate, keep it going, fast and then moderate and fast again, for an hour. Pretty soon he decided the hell with that. It was like trying to remember a piece of elaborate choreography and that took the fun out of it. Now, usually three evenings a week, he enjoyed his run through the Livermore. Back straight, head up, body slightly forward, the steady beat of his cushioned feet – the rhythm of the run made him feel like he was reclaiming every ounce of flesh that had been deadened by the routine of the day.

Late though it might be, after today's developments with the nutcase he'd been looking forward to the run, to feel his body loosening, to feel the tendons and ligaments take the strain while he let his mind shut down.

More of that Blackpool shite.

It was like the nutcase had figured that a couple of bodies in his sister's house wasn't a big deal. And whatever the story was with the missing woman he'd assaulted, he could care less. What was important was working out where he might have seen Mills before.

'*Did you have a brother, maybe? In Blackpool?' The tone suggesting that he believed he'd finally solved the puzzle.*

'*One brother. Lives in Long Island, has done for six years, doesn't look a bit like me. Neither of us has ever been to Blackpool.*'

Wherever this Blackpool thing was coming from, Joe Mills knew it was fantasy. Whatever it was about, it meant that Mills was called into the station shortly after noon to let the nutcase ask him more questions. If that was the only thing that got the nutcase talking, the Chief Super said, so be it. Maybe once his lips started flapping he'd answer the odd question about why he'd killed two harmless males in the house at Bushy Park, and who – and where – was the woman he'd harmed, and how badly had he harmed her.

As it happened, after three days of stubborn silence it took no more than twenty minutes of gormless chatter with the nutcase before he opened up a little, just for a few minutes. Then he seemed to wander back into whatever fog he lived in. It was all go after that. It was like when the nutcase spoke he'd thrown a switch and the station came alive. Nine hours later, Joe Mills ended up sitting in the office of the Chief Super, who had his feet up on his desk, his chair tilted back so it almost touched the wall behind. The wall had pictures of the Chief Super with his class at Templemore, at various official functions, and one of him standing, with a huge cheesy grin on his face, beside Chris de Burgh at some charity do. There was a bottle of Jameson on the desk. Joe Mills usually took ice in his whiskey, but he thought it better to take the drink as it was offered, neat.

'I've arranged for you to go to Dublin tomorrow,' the Chief Super said. 'You've done good – haven't put a foot wrong since you brought this butcher down from the roof.'

'We sent on everything, sir, do they—'

'They want to hear it, step by step, what happened, what he said, what he sounded like when he said it. They know what he said, they need you to tell them how convincing he sounded. I've e-mailed all the notes but they'll want the A-B-C of it and you can only do that in person.'

The Chief Super reached for the bottle again, held it up, tilted it towards Mills. 'Help you sleep.'

Joe Mills was about to say that he shouldn't, that he was hoping to get a run in tonight, but he figured it wouldn't hurt, hanging out with the Chief Super. He sipped the whiskey, looking forward to the rhythm of the run.

And now it wasn't working. Usually he could count on the pleasing monotony of the rhythm to obliterate everything else. Tonight the debris of the day, the surprises and the worries, stubbornly elbowed their way to the front of his mind, and just as stubbornly Mills tried to push them back again.

No point carrying on with this.

Mills took a sudden left and headed down a laneway that would take him back towards his digs and cut the distance of his run by more than half.

*

From the window of his flat overlooking the Liffey, Harry Synnott could see across the river to the ebb and flow of the night-time crowds moving into and out of the Temple Bar drinking quarter. The window was open as wide as the safety bar allowed, the street noises were audible even from three floors up.

From directly beneath the window, down on the boardwalk on his side of the river, he could hear the chatter of young men, occasionally erupting into shouts that might have been either anger or play. Synnott looked down and saw half a dozen young lads on the boardwalk, some of them holding beer bottles, a couple of them horsing around.

Across the river, Temple Bar would be busy into the early hours. Synnott occasionally ate in one restaurant or another over there, but always earlier in the evening, before festivity turned to oafish drunkenness.

He noticed that the boisterousness down below had muted. He saw two uniformed gardai strolling slowly along the footpath beside the boardwalk, heading upriver. The exuberant young men concealed their bottles of beer. When the gardai passed, one of the lads did a silent monkey dance behind their backs, holding up his bottle of Bud and making faces.

Synnott smiled. The lads' pretend rebellion did no harm. What mattered was that they understood that there was a line they shouldn't cross, and an agency that patrolled that line. They might mock that authority, but they understood its power. They knew that if it didn't exist they'd be prey to anything that was stronger or more ruthless than themselves. Living in the centre of the city, Harry Synnott could look out of his window any day of the week and see the shifting, capricious forces down below, the innocent and the hustlers – the innocent who in the blink of an eye became the hustlers. Every day of every year they stole from each other, committed rape and assault, abused and disrespected and defrauded one another. Every year dozens of them murdered someone, and sometimes they killed the ones they claimed to love.

Maybe in a thousand years—

Shortly after the Maura Sheelin murder case, Synnott had taken a week off and gone back to his home village in Waterford, unsure if he wanted to continue as a policeman. He went to see an old friend, a priest for whom he'd served Mass as an altar boy. It was Fr Padraig who had first steered him towards the force. The priest still received from his parishioners the regard that used to be the birthright of all priests, before the scandals broke the Church.

His private encouragement of individuals and his tireless engagement with the public affairs of his parish gave him a unique position of trust.

'You did the only thing you could.'

'I perjured myself.'

'Are you looking for absolution?' Fr Padraig was seated in a faded armchair that looked like it had absorbed a couple of generations of dust. 'I can do that for you, but I don't think you did wrong.'

'I broke the law.'

'To save the law. There's a greater justice, and that's what you serve. That's what we all serve.'

'Without law—'

'That's true, Harry, but it's only part of the story. Look around you – the tempers unleashed, the conniving and the downright meanness. Look further, the corporations that plot their plundering, the governments that slaughter, the contempt for hope. Maybe in a thousand years – maybe in a thousand years we'll evolve into something else. Right now, look around – we're closer to the wilderness than to heaven.' He leaned forward. 'In the face of all that, our loyalty is to something greater than the law.'

'The law of God?'

The priest smiled. 'Do you see Him, Harry, hovering over us?' Fr Padraig joined his hands, held them in front of his chin, his thumbnails against his lips. He sat like that for at least a minute. Harry knew he wasn't expected to speak.

'Do you believe in God, Harry?'

'Of course.'

'I believed in God until I was thirty-eight, more than ten years older than you are now.'

'Father—'

'I'm a priest. I always will be. I wrestled with that for a long time. I was doing what I believed I should do with my life, but in here' – his clasped hands made a noise against his chest – 'it all just drained away. I didn't mean it to, I didn't want it to—'

'Father Padraig—'

'Religion doesn't have to be about God. Just like justice doesn't have to be about the law. People need something to look up to, and someone has to give it to them. We're barely sentient, Harry, the most sophisticated of us, at the mercy of temperament and greed. If people don't acknowledge that there's a force greater than themselves they won't recognise any limits to what they can get away with.' He shook his head. 'No better than animals.'

'That's what you do? Give them a force greater than they are?'

'The timid need assurance, the brazen need frightening.'

'I just—'

'What you did, Harry, you confronted the sins of a prisoner – a man who murdered a young policewoman – and you confronted the sins of his jailers. You achieved a form of justice, and that's as much as we can hope for.'

Harry Synnott realised that he was leaning forward in his chair, his hands clasped like the priest's. They both sat for a few minutes, then the priest went to the kitchen to get them something to eat. Harry Synnott stayed sitting as he was for a long time.

Fr Padraig stayed on past retirement age. The waning of the Church meant fewer young priests. The old ones had to stay on until they dropped or let parishes wither. One Sunday morning, in the vestry, preparing to say Mass, Fr Padraig fell forward onto his face. The stroke left him alive for the best part of a year. When Harry Synnott visited him, his old friend was barely able to speak a few words, his mind fitfully connected to his tongue.

Maybe in a thousand years.

Lying in bed, Synnott listened to the city sounds, the chugging noise of traffic mixed in with occasional catcalls and bursts of laughter. As he drifted towards sleep, individual voices, each with its own energy and purpose, blended into a muffled chorus, a refrain both solemn and threatening.

*

Dixie said, 'I'm sorry.'

Owen kept on walking, hands in his pockets, his face drained of expression, the anger displayed in the way he held his elbows clamped tight to his body.

'Owen!'

He ignored her.

Dixie screamed as a sharp pain cut deep into the calf of her right leg. She rolled off the bed, the shreds of the dream falling away. She stood on her left leg, just the toes of her right foot touching the floor as the pain burned relentlessly into her right calf. She made soft panting sounds as she forced her right heel down towards the floor, pushing against the twisted muscle defying her body's urge to go with the cramp.

A second after her heel touched the carpet the pain lifted, as she knew it would, and she let herself fall back onto the bed, half sitting, elbows behind her, wisps of hair clinging to her sweaty face. For a moment she thought she was back in a cell. Then she remembered that she was in Shelley's flat.

She let herself lie back. The pain was gone but the calf was fragile, the flesh still nervous. Her mind scrambled to retrieve the sensation of the dream. She couldn't remember Owen ever displaying real anger towards her throughout the four years of their marriage.

I'm sorry.

Dixie knew that when she felt this vulnerable she had to smother the self-pity that pushed and ebbed around her. To wallow in the permanence of the loss was to risk another loss, equally damning, the permanent loss of Christopher.

No.

She jerked her head sharply to the right, eyes closed, as though physically turning away from her body's urging that she go find the heroin in the living room.

Clear head.

After a while, her breathing was normal and her thoughts had settled into some kind of pattern.

Do something, fuck it. Do something.

MONDAY

35

It was tricky, because Christopher was still in junior school and Mrs Dobbs walked him all the way across the yard to the steps at the side entrance to the school building. It was two minutes to nine in the morning and Dixie Peyton, in a wine-coloured trouser suit and grey blouse that she'd borrowed from Shelley's flat, waited just inside the doorway. She found a niche where a teacher casually looking down the corridor towards the door was unlikely to see her. These days, you almost had to get a sworn affidavit from the Pope before a teacher would allow a child to break with routine. Christopher's teacher knew that he'd been taken away from Dixie – he'd probably met Mrs Dobbs when she'd started fostering – so any sight of Dixie would get him fluttering.

One side of the double door was open. There was a window in the centre of the other door, but Dixie decided it was too dangerous to look out. The drawback was that from the niche there was no way to see Mrs Dobbs and Christopher approach.

A steady trickle of kids came through the doorway, making their way up the corridor to the various classrooms. Among a group of three chattering girls, Dixie recognised one from Christopher's class. The kid hung up her coat, shouldered her school bag, smiled at Dixie and said hello. Dixie kept a stiff smile on her face as the three girls went up the corridor and into the second room on the right. If one of them said something to the teacher about Christopher's mammy being outside, it was all over.

Dixie turned and there was another kid coming in and she didn't recognise him until Christopher said, 'Mammy!' and Dixie put one hand behind his head and the other over his mouth. His eyes flared in terror.

She whispered, 'I'm sorry, I'm sorry, love, I'm sorry.' She bent over him, still breathlessly whispering, 'But we have to be quiet.'

She took her hands away. 'I'm sorry, did I frighten you? It's a game – we're taking a surprise day off school and we don't want anyone to know.'

Christopher looked at her, his mouth open, his tongue on his lower lip.

'It'll be great fun,' she whispered, 'just you and me, we haven't had a day out for ages.'

'Mammy?'

Dixie risked a glance out through the doorway at the schoolyard. Mrs Dobbs was taking her time waddling away.

'Mammy?'

Dixie took Christopher by the hand. She touched her lips with her finger, smiled and led him out the door and down the steps. In the distance Mrs Dobbs was passing out through the side gate. No reason for the cow to look back.

'Hi, Chris.'

It was a little girl, holding her mother's hand as she approached, smiling at Christopher.

'Hi, Greta.'

Dixie and the mother exchanged smiles.

On the way across the schoolyard, Christopher said, 'Mammy, it's art today. Could we have our surprise day tomorrow?'

'Then it wouldn't be a surprise.'

'Mammy?'

In the distance, out beyond the school gate, the cow was climbing into her Fiesta. Dixie stopped, waited. She took for ever to drive away.

'Mammy?'

'Yes, love?'

'I don't want a surprise day.'

Mrs Dobbs was gone. Dixie held Christopher's hand tighter as she smiled down at him and began walking towards the main road and the bus stop.

'It'll be great fun, love. It'll be great.'

*

When her daughter went up the steps and out of sight, Greta Flanagan's mother watched Dixie Peyton and her son leave through the school gates.

None of my business.

She knew about Chris's family troubles, about how he was being fostered. The children talked openly about that kind of thing and no family had a secret once a kid was aware of it.

Must have made an arrangement with the teacher.

Don't interfere.

Chris and his mother were out of sight now.

Greta Flanagan's mother stood there another full minute before she turned and went through the doorway and down the corridor towards her daughter's classroom.

*

When Rose Cheney arrived at her desk at Macken Road, carrying her first coffee of the day, she found a message there from Teresa Hunt, asking her to call.

Cheney told Harry Synnott, 'It may be she just needs to know if we intend to charge Max – some reassurance that we're not slacking.' Cheney knew that it wasn't unusual for a rape victim to need comforting at this stage. Had the police taken her seriously? Why hadn't she heard anything over the past five days?

Synnott made a gesture towards the papers and files on his desk.

'The sooner I get this stuff done – do you really need me there?'

Rose Cheney said, 'Boyce?'

'If we're taking him in today I want to be well grounded. You could do this one on your own, right?'

Cheney knew it made sense for Harry Synnott to concentrate on reviewing the files on the jewellery robbery before they arrested Joshua Boyce this afternoon. Material in a witness statement or the suspect file might well contradict something Boyce said in interrogation and there wouldn't be much joy in discovering that afterwards. Anyway, chances were that a meeting with Teresa Hunt wasn't going to lead to anything.

Cheney said, 'Comforting rape victims. I always get the fun jobs.'

Synnott smiled. 'Best if it's a woman.'

Harry Synnott was photocopying pages from the jewellery robbery file when he got a phone call from an inspector at headquarters. 'Deirdre Peyton? You know her?'

'What's she done now?'

'She's abducted a child.'

'Her son?'

'He's in foster care – took him from school.'

Synnott used his shoulder to clamp the phone to his ear and reached for a stapler.

He said, 'You need an address for her?'

'We've been there. Nothing.'

Synnott hit the stapler with the heel of his hand and stapled the pages together.

'She's got a brother in England – London, I think – she may have ideas about that.'

'Is she a danger to the kid?'

Synnott thought for a moment. 'I wouldn't say so.'

*

There were two middle-aged men on one side of the wide, long and very shiny table. They were seated side by side. Sitting a few feet to the left, Teresa Hunt looked inconspicuous. When Rose Cheney rang Teresa to agree a time and place Teresa asked her to come to the offices of one of Dublin's larger legal firms. The room was in proportion to the table, wide and high-ceilinged. And probably in proportion to the firm's fees and the expectations of its clients.

The younger of the two men, whose face seemed slightly familiar, rose and came to shake Cheney's hand. He introduced himself as Teresa's father. He introduced his companion, a solicitor, but Cheney didn't catch the name. Introductions done, Teresa's father returned to his seat and waved Cheney to a chair facing his across the table. 'I'm told, sergeant, that there's a Mr Synnott in charge of this case, a detective inspector.'

Rose Cheney put her face in neutral and waited.

The older of the two men had a voice with no edge to it. 'This isn't a question of gender, sergeant.' He might have been explaining the tooth fairy to a four-year-old. 'It's a question of rank. There has been a serious development and my clients—'

Cheney felt as though she was sitting slightly below the eye level of everyone else in the room. It was as though they'd had someone saw a couple of inches off the legs of her ornate walnut chair.

'My time is limited, I'm afraid,' Cheney said. 'Ms Hunt asked to speak to the police – I'm here to listen to what she has to say.'

Teresa looked to her father, who waited a few seconds, then nodded.

'It's nothing, really.' Teresa seemed to have found a spot on the table that needed polishing. She rubbed at it with an index finger, glancing up at Cheney every few seconds. 'A man came to see me, at Trinity. Friday afternoon. I was coming out of the Nassau Street exit, I was meeting a friend in Café En Seine, and this guy just came up to me.'

'Friday,' Cheney said. 'That was three days ago.'

The father said, 'She told her mother only yesterday.'

Cheney said to Teresa, 'Describe him.'

'Young, late twenties, wearing a suit, short dark hair – nothing special about him.'

'He said something?'

'He said he was a lawyer. He said it was terrible, what had happened to me, but he felt I ought to know what a criminal trial involved. A rape trial.'

She was looking now at her finger, rubbing the invisible spot on the table. She didn't look up. 'He mentioned two men, old boyfriends of mine. He knew their names. He said—'

Her father cut her off. 'It's intimidation. I know Hapgood – the father. These people think they can frighten—'

Cheney looked at Teresa. 'Did this man give you a name?'

'No, I don't think so. He just—'

'They want her to know,' the father said, 'that if she presses charges they'll drag up every—'

Cheney spoke to the lawyer. 'Have you a private room where I can talk with Teresa?'

The father took a deep breath and said, 'Sergeant.'

It must take a lot of practice, Rose Cheney thought, to be able to inject so much contempt into two syllables.

Cheney kept her gaze on the lawyer. After a moment he said, 'Perhaps it's best.'

The lawyer took them to a private room and when he left Teresa said, 'I'm sorry.'

Cheney said, 'Your dad means well.'

'In his world he lifts a finger, half a dozen vice-presidents are on their feet, telling him we've got that covered, J.P.'

J. P. Hunt.

That's why he was familiar. Cheney had seen the face in newspaper photographs. Hunt. John Patrick Hunt. 'My dad's in property,' Teresa had said at the hospital when Rose Cheney had asked about her parents. John Patrick Hunt was in property the way Microsoft was in software. Some of the best hotels and apartment blocks in Dublin, housing estates and superpubs throughout the country, half a dozen of the most imaginative property developments in London – if he didn't own them outright he was a pivotal figure in the consortium that did.

They were in some kind of conference room, long and narrow. The centre of the room was taken up by a long table and six chairs. There was just a single small window in the room, on the wall furthest from the door.

'You were coming out of the Nassau Street exit? Was there anyone with you?'

'I was on my own.'

If this creep had spent time hanging around, waiting to catch Teresa alone, perhaps he'd got in the way of a CCTV camera. It happened Friday – wouldn't they have reused the tape by now? Maybe not.

'He was wearing a suit?'

'He looked like a businessman – maybe he was a lawyer like he said. He was well-spoken.'

Cheney asked enough questions to get as complete a description as Teresa could give. She knew it was too vague to be of use.

Teresa said, 'Do they still do that, try to smear rape victims?'

'There won't be anything in the media – they're not allowed to report the victim's name. But, yes, the defence can try to use your sexual history to influence the jury. Mind you, they have to be careful. Juries aren't dumb, and they can react against that kind of thing.'

'Then—'

'I won't hide it, Teresa. These things are not pleasant. Even if you're giving innocuous evidence in a routine case, it can be intimidating. Sitting up in front of everyone in a courtroom, in a rape trial, being asked intimate questions by a smarmy lawyer who smiles and suggests that you offered to suck his client's cock – it's not a nice way to spend a morning. And what this bully is up to is letting you know that they'll make it as unpleasant as possible.'

'Would a lawyer – I mean—'

'Lawyers are supposed to try to get their clients off, using whatever material their clients provide them with. That's what they'll do in court. But I doubt if the man who approached you was really a lawyer. Just a thug for hire.'

Teresa was nodding. She moved her chair back and went to the window at the end of the room. Cheney sat where she was. Give the girl space. After a minute, Teresa said, 'One way or the other, I can expect a going-over.'

Cheney joined her by the window. There was a plaza six floors below – thin trees and a piece of bronze sculpture. Outside the entrance to the building across the way, three smokers were getting their fix.

Cheney kept her voice matter-of-fact. 'It helps Max Junior to portray you as the sexual predator, him as the innocent at large, accused of something he'd never dream of doing.'

'Are they allowed to – things I might have – what if they can prove I've had an active sex life?'

'This isn't about sex, Teresa, it's about beating you into submission. It's what rape is about and it's what Max and his yob friends are trying now. They might have got away with it in the old days, these days there's nothing that you or anyone else does in bed that a jury will see as justifying rape.'

Not strictly true. Cheney had seen juries do strange things after being fed the information that the alleged victim had a less than virginal history. A lawyer could employ no end of legal nods and winks in an effort to mine some reasonable doubt from a jury.

'These two men, the old boyfriends, don't contact them. We'll do that, to see if Max or his thug has been in touch. This may be no more than a wild swing by one of Max's friends.'

Or, given that Max had a history in which at least one other rape allegation was dropped, it could be something more serious.

'How are you holding up?'

'I'm fine.'

No, you're not.

Teresa's father was graciousness itself as he accompanied Rose Cheney down to the lobby.

'You have kids, sergeant?'

'Two.'

'Much younger than Teresa, of course, but you'll know how something like this affects a parent, so I'm sorry if—'

'Not at all, sir, it's the protective instinct.'

'Quite.'

In the lobby, J.P. Hunt held Cheney by one elbow and led her off to one side. They stood fifty feet from the reception desk, no one else around, beneath a twenty-foot-high painting that reminded Cheney of the pattern on her mother's dining-room curtains. Hunt leaned close. 'I want to make just one thing crystal clear, sergeant. Whatever happens with the police, I'm going after that little shit. Legally. I'll spend whatever it takes, I'll mount a private prosecution.' He couldn't help the changing pitch of his voice. 'I know the Hapgoods' business and I know what needs to be done so that anyone who chooses to employ Max Hapgood or anyone associated with him knows that they're making an enemy of me.'

He made a visible effort to bring his voice down a tone. 'And, sergeant, I am not a pleasant man to have as an enemy. I want you to know – and I want your superiors to know – that my lawyers will be keeping a scrupulous record of the police progress on this case.'

He held Cheney's gaze. 'Anyone slips up, there'll be a shit-storm of motions and injunctions and plain old damages claims heading your way.' He let go of Cheney's elbow and stood back. 'I want to thank you, sergeant, for your personal attention to my daughter. I know you'll do your best for us.'

36

Dixie bought sausages and chips for Christopher. She got a cup of coffee for herself. They were in a café in Mary Street, a busy place tucked away behind a cake shop.

'Do you remember the time we were in here before?'

Christopher shook his head.

'You had soup. You said it was the best soup you ever tasted.'

'Aunt Lucy makes lovely soup.'

Aunt Lucy Dobbs.

Ah, Christopher.

He ate the chips first and the ketchup went fast. He went alone to the counter to ask for more ketchup. He came back proudly clutching two sachets.

When Dixie asked her son how he was getting on at school he said he was doing OK. She reminded him that he was supposed to have a sleepover at his friend Willie's home and Christopher said he did, but he cried and Willie's mammy rang Auntie Lucy and she came and picked him up and brought him home.

'Are things OK now, mammy?'

'Of course they are, love – what do you mean?'

'Auntie Lucy says by and by things will be OK. She calls me chicken.'

'Does she?'

'She says just wait, chicken. Your mammy will be back when things are OK. Are things OK now, mammy?'

'Things are fine, Christopher.'

The boy held the knife awkwardly as he cut his sausages. Dixie watched his face, the lips pursed. He was wholly wrapped up in the task. The blue eyes, the soft cheeks, a tiny edge of his tongue peeking from the corner of his mouth. She could see Owen there still, somehow inside the soft little face. She felt a ripple of fear as she thought of Christopher at Owen's age, the dreadful possibilities that might hurt him as well as the lovely things he might expect.

She wanted to talk to him about his birthday party last year and the time they went to Howth and walked all the way out to the end of the pier. She wanted to ask him if he remembered any of the stories she'd told him about Owen and about how Owen was watching over him from up in heaven. She wanted to kiss him on the forehead and touch his cheek and whisper to him like she always did, 'You and me.' She wanted to tell him how much she missed him but she was suddenly afraid that he wouldn't remember anything she'd ever done with him or anything she'd ever told him.

Christopher put a piece of sausage in his mouth and said, 'Can I go home now, mammy?'

Dixie was about to tell him that they couldn't go home yet, that she was taking him on a little trip. Then it dawned on her that he'd said *I* and not *we* and she knew where he meant by home.

'I don't know, love.'

'Why?'

'We have some things to do.'

'Can I have an ice cream?'

'Later, love.'

They'd get the DART to Dun Laoghaire and find a B&B. In the morning they'd have breakfast, then do a flit on the ferry. There was no certainty about it, but a ferry port was a lot easier than an airport. Get through the ticket hall – sometimes the check-in was hectic, groups of Yanks milling around with their backpacks, going through on group tickets. Once you were through the ticket hall they didn't check you at the gangway. Shelley'd done it years ago, when she'd been young and game for anything.

It works or it doesn't.

Get to Holyhead – then what?

Onto the train.

Sorry – I seem to have lost the tickets.

It works or it doesn't.

London. Then what?

Step by step. She had enough for a night or two in a B&B. If one thing or another doesn't work out, improvise.

Stay here and – that's it, end of story. Christopher's gone.

Fuck it, go for it – nothing to lose.

'Mammy, I'm bored.'

'We're going now, love.'

'You said it'd be great fun.'

'We're going to take a trip on a big ship in the morning – how'd you like that?'

'Really?'

'Really.'

*

Garda Joe Mills wanted to get an early start, but the sergeant said there was no hurry. Mills said that if they started before dawn they might even reach Dublin early enough to get the business over with and get back to Galway that night. The sergeant smiled and said, 'I'll take that under consideration.'

They set off around lunchtime, the sergeant driving, Mills in the front passenger seat. He'd told the Chief Superintendent that he could make his own way to Dublin, but the reply was that he'd need his wits about him when he met the Assistant Commissioner. 'Sit back and let someone else do the driving.'

One week you're standing on the roof of a pub, trying to persuade a moody nutcase not to turn himself into a thick layer of strawberry jam on the pavement below. Next week the Chief Super has scrubbed you from the roster to allow you take part in endless conferences with lawyers and senior officers, and you end up being ferried to Dublin by a sports-mad chatterer.

'People who say he's a thug, they don't know football,' the sergeant said. They were two hours into the journey and this was the second time he'd taken the topic for a ramble.

'He's the best player this island ever produced. The difference between him and George Best is that Keane is a professional to his toenails. He's too disciplined to throw away his talent on beer and models.'

Joe Mills tried not to care, but he couldn't suppress the unease he felt. Halfway through a sentence, the sergeant would look across at Mills, and wouldn't turn his eyes back to the road until he got to the full stop. Quick glance at the road ahead, start another sentence, his head swivelling to the left again.

This is how I die. Fucking idiot driver. A wobble, a wallop, we go under a truck and as I'm crushed to mush in the back of a Primera the last thing I hear is shite talk about Roy Keane.

The sergeant made a scornful noise. 'It's called passion. Passion like he's got, it inspires a whole team. And passion like that, there's times he lost the run of himself and that's the price he paid. It's human nature. Passion and performance. You can't have one without the other.'

The sergeant left the occasional silence for Joe Mills to fill, but Mills had no opinion on the Roy Keane debate, nor on any of the subjects that had preceded it. He had no opinion on George Best, and he didn't know or care if D.J. Carey was a better hurler than Christy Ring, or whether Joe Louis could have beaten the crap out of Muhammad Ali. He had no opinion on the state of Irish rugby, the truth or otherwise about doping in Irish cycling, swimming or show jumping, the fixing of horse races or whether snooker was sport or show business.

Joe Mills tried to blank out the chatter. The dramatic moments and startling discoveries of the past five days played in his mind like a movie trailer.

'The Assistant Commissioner isn't into long reminiscences,' the Chief Super had told Mills the previous evening. 'He'll expect you to edit this down to the essentials. Facts, to the point, no opinions. What was said, what you saw.'

Wednesday the nutcase came down from the roof, Thursday they found the two bodies. Saturday his sister turned up in a taxi at her house in Bushy Park, back from a week in Amsterdam, and found out that her husband and son had been butchered by her brother.

'Woman?'

Mina Moylan didn't know what woman her brother might have been talking about. No one else lived in the house. Wayne didn't have a girlfriend in Dublin, as far as his sister knew. No, he didn't have a girlfriend in Galway. He'd had someone when he'd lived in England – the sister didn't know a name. He'd been living alone in Dublin for a few years. He came down to stay with her two or three times a year.

A detective sergeant did the interview. Joe Mills was allowed to sit in. Wayne Kemp's sister spoke slowly. It seemed like part of her mind was off somewhere else, and maybe it would stay there. Whenever she came back from wherever that was, she folded up, sobbing, her face wet, red and saturated with disbelief.

When she was coherent, she didn't have much to offer. Wayne wasn't the most sociable of people, yes, but she loved it when he came down to stay with her and her family. He was quiet, maybe a little distant, but he could be charming. No, he'd never received psychiatric treatment, and no, he'd never made any threats against her or her family. 'He's always been – I mean, even as a kid, he was a bit odd. Nothing violent.' She was hesitant, distracted, like she was trawling her mind for an explanation. 'Not as far as I know.'

'Any family tension?'

'He always got on with Davy and Joseph – he—'

Mina Moylan's eyes shut and her mouth opened and she made an involuntary sound. She sat that way for maybe a minute, her eyes tight, her cheeks wet, and when she spoke again her voice was quiet and high-pitched.

'Jesus, there's no reason.'

That's the way it stayed until Sunday.

'Wouldn't fancy that—'

The sergeant took his eye off the road and glanced across at Joe Mills.

'– one-to-one with the Assistant Commissioner.' He looked at the road again and shook his head. 'Could land yourself right in the shit. Make a bad impression, it goes in the file, twenty years from now they're still turning you down for promotions and transfers and no one'll tell you why and there's nothing you can do except go on delivering summonses until you drop in your tracks.' Another quick glance across at Mills. 'No, I wouldn't fancy your job today.'

Joe Mills looked out at the passing streetscape and went over his mental notes. Wednesday, the nutcase on the roof – keep it short. Thursday, they got the wallet, identified Wayne Kemp, found the bodies – again, it was all straightforward and the Assistant Commissioner would have a copy of the file. Saturday, the interview with Kemp's sister – she knew nothing about anything, Joe Mills could deal with it in a few sentences. All that was just a frame for the picture that the Assistant Commissioner wanted to examine in detail – what Kemp had said yesterday.

Mills had his notebook in his pocket, but he'd hardly need it.

Wayne Kemp, when he finally spoke on Sunday, had been plain and simple and matter-of-fact in his explanation.

'Hope it goes well for you'. The sergeant had taken his eyes away from the road again and was looking across at Joe Mills. 'Rubbing shoulders with the brass –' He shook his head.

The sergeant looked again at the road. Eighty feet ahead, a traffic light went from green to amber, which the sergeant seemed to take as a challenge. He gunned the engine. Joe Mills felt the acceleration in his back as the car jerked forward. His legs were rigid, his feet braced against the front of the footwell, as the car went through the red light.

'Yes indeed', the sergeant said, 'risky business, putting on a show for those lads'.

37

Garda Mickey Rynne was putting the frighteners on the street sellers on Henry Street. All he had to do was show up and word rippled through the pedestrianised street and the hustlers started shuffling off into the distance. Over by the pharmacy, one hurriedly closed his shabby attaché case. Around by Roches Stores two more covered up the contents of the tables that they'd propped on ramshackle buggies and shuffled out of his line of sight.

Mickey Rynne had no personal objection to unlicensed peddlers. If someone wanted to work long hours sourcing and selling fake Calvin Klein sweaters, phoney Gucci perfumes or bogus Versace jeans, more power to them. It wasn't like they were selling illegal fireworks to kids, or retailing cigarettes smuggled in by some bunch of thugs. That was different. If someone wanted to pay crazy money for real Gucci or Versace, Garda Rynne didn't see why that should stop someone else paying a fraction of the price for a good imitation. And he didn't feel strongly about protecting the copyright of some poncy foreign billionaires.

However, if he didn't show up to hassle the hustlers the shopkeepers got stroppy. So, at least twice in every shift, Garda Rynne got to stroll through the Henry Street shoppers, pretending not to notice the hustlers packing up and moving quickly away into the distance.

Past the junction with Liffey Street, coming into Mary Street,

Garda Rynne avoided looking directly at Jimbo Norton, shuffling down past M&S, pushing a makeshift countertop on a buggy. Garda Rynne slowed his pace. Jimbo was a decent, hard-working hustler, respectful of the police if not of the law.

Oh, you poor cow.

The woman might as well have had a neon sign attached to her head, a big red arrow blinking on and off and pointing straight down at her joyless face. This time of day, the kids were at school and if there was a woman coming out of a café holding a six-year-old boy by the hand there was a reasonable possibility that she was the woman mentioned in the abduction alert that had gone out around two hours ago. The wine-coloured trouser suit matched the description. What put the tin hat on it was the face – like she'd been carrying something very heavy and she hadn't set it down in a long time. Face like that, someone right out on the edge—

Look at the kid – Jesus, the way he's looking up at her. His hand, she's holding it so tight—

Her name – Garda Rynne was good at this. He could riffle the pages of his memory like a deck of cards.

Peyton.

Something Peyton.

He riffled again.

The woman saw him.

She stopped and stood there for a moment. Her head jerked to the left, looking up towards the Spire. Then she quickly glanced back inside the café, mouth loose, eyes wild.

Oh, you poor, poor cow.

Don't make it worse than it has to be.

Abduction cases were shit. Demented parents, mostly, custody disputes, foster care. Garda Rynne figured that when you got an abduction alert it started out like an all-points bulletin on the Lindbergh Kidnap but it almost always ended up with some poor bastard in a cell down the station, weeping into a pillow.

'Deirdre Peyton?'

Up close, he could see it was all over. Running wasn't an option, not with a kid in tow. The danger was that when the woman saw she was cornered she'd get hysterical, screaming and thrashing, all teeth and fingernails.

Then again.

He could see that she didn't have the spirit for that.

Her voice was thin. 'Let me say goodbye to him properly?'

Garda Mickey Rynne nodded. He fingered the radio mike at his lapel, turning his head down and sideways as he pressed the transmit button and quietly asked for a patrol car and a female garda to look after the kid.

The woman was hunkered down now, speaking quietly to the boy, long pauses between short sentences, one finger gently stroking his cheek. Whatever she was saying, the boy looked relieved.

*

The mobile phone was a stolen Nokia and it came in a plastic case. The keys were visible through a little plastic window. Matty said to Lar Mackendrick, 'You don't make any calls on this, you just take them. Just to be on the safe side, don't take it out of the case until we get rid of it. That way, no prints on the phone itself.'

As soon as it had served its purpose the phone would be chopped into a thousand pieces. No telecoms technician would ever link it to any call and there wouldn't be the slightest trace of physical or electronic evidence connecting it to Lar Mackendrick.

'What makes someone go like that?' Lar said. He put the mobile on the table, beside his Ballygowan. They were in the back garden of his home in Howth. It was a large villa-style house on a couple of acres of Howth Head, surrounded by greenery and with a view of the harbour. Nearly ten years back it had been owned by an undistinguished local councillor who suddenly sold off an extensive property portfolio and moved his family to Spain. The area closest to the house was a patio, decorated with a Mediterranean touch by one of Dublin's up-and-coming young designers. Lar had had a twenty-five-metre swimming pool installed, surrounded by decking. He swam there every afternoon, from early April to late September. He was wearing swimming togs under his fluffy yellow dressing gown.

'First time I met Dixie, at the wedding, I said to Owen, Jesus, that's some bird you've got. I mean, she was a knockout. They had it all. When Owen made a balls of a simple delivery job, ended up in a ditch, I could have said it's not my problem. Instead, I did the right thing. When she came looking for another handout, and I knew it was for shit to stick in her arm, I asked myself what Owen would want and I said no.'

Lar opened a palm to Matty. 'What makes someone betray someone who's been nothing but a friend to her?'

'Cunt,' Matty said.

Down at the end of the garden, Todd was using a Flymo to trim the grass edging. Lar liked the buzzing noise. Summery kind of sound, though it would be a couple of months before the weather made sitting out here as pleasant as it ought to be.

'You've put the number around?'

Matty nodded. 'About a dozen people, should be enough to let it ripple out. Far as anyone knows, when they ring the mobile they're ringing someone called Mr James. Anyone gets a sight of her, they ring Mr James. Two grand if she's where they say she is.'

'Owen was a nice boy. Bit of a dreamer, but a nice boy.' Lar shook his head. 'If he knew it had come to this.'

Matty said, 'Owen knew how the world works, Lar. He'd know it was the right thing to do.'

*

Mid-afternoon, they went in two cars. Harry Synnott and Rose Cheney in one, Bob Tidey and a younger detective in the other. A patrol car from Clontarf garda station met them two streets away from Joshua Boyce's house. A surveillance crew from the station had already reported that Boyce stayed home all weekend.

Tidey and his colleague probably wouldn't need the pistols they carried but they rechecked them, anyway. Joshua Boyce was unlikely to be fool enough to have a weapon in the house, but since the case involved firearms it was best to be on the safe side.

Walking up the path to the front door, Synnott said, 'What do you think of the aspect?'

Rose Cheney smiled. 'Place like this, we're talking maybe six hundred thousand. That's Northside prices. Same place on the Southside, you could add another three hundred thousand, maybe four.'

Boyce's wife answered the doorbell and when she saw Harry Synnott she said, 'He did nothing.'

Harry Synnott arrested them both.

'This is a stitch-up,' Joshua Boyce said when Bob Tidey hand-cuffed him. Boyce turned to Harry Synnott. 'You know that.'

Synnott told him that he had a right to remain silent. Rose Cheney took a number from Antoinette Boyce, then arranged for Antoinette's sister to come and collect the Boyces' daughter. Cheney then took Antoinette to the patrol car and had them drive her away. Cheney, Bob Tidey and his colleague gave the house a quick search and found nothing. Technical would arrive later to do a thorough job.

Halfway down the driveway, his hands cuffed in front of him, Boyce turned and showed Harry Synnott a smile. 'You losers don't have a case. You're chancing your arm.'

Synnott said, 'You keep telling yourself that.' He took out his notebook and scribbled a couple of lines.

Boyce said, 'You've got no evidence against me. You've got no one in the frame, so you're having a go at me.'

Bob Tidey arrived at Synnott's elbow. 'That's it – ready to go?'

Harry Synnott finished writing. Then he held up his notebook. 'Mr Boyce, I want you to sign my note of this conversation.'

Joshua Boyce's smile was wide. 'Go fuck yourself, loser,' he said. 'This really is a waste of time.'

Harry Synnott bit back a smart-arse remark. Anything he could say would only feed Boyce's sense of superiority. He stood in the driveway and watched as Bob Tidey took Boyce to his car and locked him into the back seat. When Synnott got to the car he said to Bob Tidey, 'I want you to make a note of exactly what you saw and heard since we arrived at the house, OK? Right up to this moment.'

'Soon as we get to the station.'

Synnott shook his head. 'Best you do it now. Anything you heard him say, put it in quotation marks.'

Tidey's young colleague was coming down the driveway. Synnott said, 'What's your name?'

'Purcell, sir, detective garda.'

'Get your notebook out, write down anything you saw or heard since you arrived at the house.' Rose Cheney was locking the front door of the house. Synnott gave her the same instruction.

It took them around three minutes to scribble their notes. Synnott stood with his back to the car. Behind him, looking out from the back seat, Joshua Boyce was still smiling.

They were on the coast road, almost into Fairview, Rose Cheney driving, when Synnott's mobile rang. It was a sergeant at Cooper Street station.

'You know someone called Deirdre Peyton?'

'This the child-abduction thing?'

'We picked her up – the kid's back with the foster-parents, no harm done.'

'She ask to talk to me?'

'She hasn't asked for anyone, hasn't said a word. I found your card in her pocket. Is there anything we should know?'

Synnott watched the car ahead, Tidey and Purcell up front. He could see the back of Joshua Boyce's head. The thief was slouching, his head resting comfortably against the back of the seat.

'She's just a tout I used to know. No big deal.'

38

'I honestly can't remember.'

'Bullshit.'

Joshua Boyce shook his head. 'I'm a busy man.'

'This is Monday,' Harry Synnott said. 'You're being asked to remember what you were doing three days ago, Friday morning.'

'Give me a minute.'

With a nervous suspect, Harry Synnott might display a sympathetic ear. *Get it off your chest. We know you didn't mean to do it.* Convince the suspect that he ought to explain how he's basically a good guy and he didn't mean to do whatever he did – let him stitch himself up. There were equivalent tactics for worming an incriminating statement out of loudmouths, smart-arses and mammies' boys, but a Joshua Boyce wouldn't fall for any of that. Boyce wouldn't feel any need to unburden himself of his guilt. He didn't need to boast or to explain himself. He knew it was his job to get into and out of Macken Road police station without giving the police a sliver of evidence to support their belief that he had committed a crime.

'What am I supposed to have done?'

'Friday – what time did you get up?'

'Far as I know, I don't have an alibi for whatever it was.'

'Let's take it step by step. You got up at?'

'I always get up about seven-thirty. Friday was a school day – we got Ciara up and ready, I suppose.'

'Don't suppose. You got up at seven-thirty, you got the kids ready for school.'

'Peter's working. Antoinette got Ciara dressed, I made breakfast – we were out of the house by quarter to nine. I drove Ciara to school, same as usual. Peter – Friday, he got a bus into town. Sometimes I give him a lift.' Boyce clicked his fingers. 'Friday – I remember – the bed.'

Synnott couldn't resist pursing his lips.

Here we go.

'What bed?'

'The missus wanted a new bed. I told her the old one was OK, but you know how it is.' This last was addressed to Rose Cheney, sitting beside Harry Synnott. She didn't acknowledge the remark.

Synnott said, 'You went shopping?'

'Perry Logan's, the superstore. Beyond the airport.'

'What time?'

'No idea. It was morning – maybe ten, more like eleven, whenever.'

'What did you do at Perry Logan's?'

'The wife's been looking to get a new bed since Christmas. Missed the January sales. I wouldn't let her pick it out herself – I mean, it's the kind of thing you'd want to have a say in, right?'

'You bought a bed?'

'It wouldn't have been my first choice – a bit too stately. But she liked it and I checked it was comfortable to lie on, so that was that.'

'Anything else?'

'Some bedding, sheets, pillowcases – figured we might as well push the boat out.'

'Then you left the store?'

'Yes, more or less. First we had a look around the furniture section – there was a sofa she liked, but it's only three, four years since we got the leather suite, so I said give me a break. That was it.'

'Then you left? This took what, an hour?'

'An hour, maybe more. It was – before we left, I forgot, we spent a bit of time in the electronics department, Antoinette wanted to check out the television sets. She's thinking of getting a little flat-screen set for the kitchen.'

'You bought one?'

'No, but when I got in there I spent a while looking at the computer stuff, came away with a photoprinter. Been meaning to get one for ages. Thing is, with a digital camera, it's not the same – looking at them on the screen, is it?'

'You have receipts?'

'Me? No. The missus usually holds on to stuff like that.' He turned to Rose Cheney. 'Bet it's the same in your house, right?'

Synnott turned to Cheney. 'Sergeant, I think it's about time for some coffee.'

Boyce gave Cheney a big smile. 'That'd be great. Black, no sugar.'

When she left the interrogation room Rose Cheney checked with Bob Tidey, who was questioning Antoinette Boyce. The suspect's wife said that they'd arrived at Perry Logan's sometime after ten-thirty. Which was around the time the jewellery shop was being held up.

Cheney found a number for the Perry Logan superstore on the airport road. An assistant manager used up some time admitting that he knew nothing about the CCTV set-up, and even if he did know anything about it he didn't have the authority to discuss company matters with outside agencies. No, there was no one more senior on the premises and they'd be closing up soon. Cheney bit back a comment and used a sweet voice to get him to phone a senior manager. Five minutes later the security director rang Macken Road and asked for Detective Garda Cheney.

Unless something dramatic happened, he said, a hold-up or someone caught shoplifting, the CCTV tapes at Perry Logan's were reused. It was more than forty-eight hours since the robbery, so there wasn't much chance that Friday's images had survived.

'There's always a possibility, but—'

Cheney had an image of a tape being at that moment erased. 'Please, check it right now.'

When Rose Cheney got back to the interrogation room she put on a big smile. Boyce smiled back.

'The coffee?'

Cheney raised her gaze to the ceiling, then smiled even more warmly. 'Silly me. Black, no sugar, right?'

*

The traffic was heavy on Infirmary Road and Joe Mills endured a final few minutes of sports chatter from the sergeant. When they parked the Primera inside Garda Headquarters the sergeant said, 'Welcome to the Heart of Darkness.' He headed off to the canteen and Joe Mills waited at reception until a superintendent arrived and took him across the courtyard towards the centre door in a long stone-clad building. They went down a couple of corridors and into a large room where the superintendent introduced Mills to Assistant Commissioner Colin O'Keefe. The Assistant Commissioner came around his desk, his hand out. 'Thanks for making the trip, Garda Mills. It's important that there's no mistake about this.'

Like I had a choice.

'Not at all, sir.'

'Hopefully it won't take long.' O'Keefe gestured to a chair in front of his desk. 'You haven't had time to eat, I take it?'

'No, sir.'

'Not to worry, we'll have a bite here while we talk – I'll order from the canteen.' Reaching for the phone, he said, 'They do a damn fine chicken sandwich.'

*

Rose Cheney said, 'To be honest, I don't see where this is going.' Cheney and Synnott were drinking mugs of coffee in the Macken Road canteen. Joshua Boyce was in a cell, having a meal.

A phone call from the security director at Perry Logan's had confirmed that the CCTV tape from Friday morning had already been reused. Cheney said, 'Even if they had the tape, and it showed Boyce's wife alone, that wouldn't have proved anything – he could claim he was elsewhere, out of camera range.'

'He wasn't there, he was in Kellsboro, shooting a security man.'

'His wife says she has the receipts.'

'She'll have them. They'll be time-stamped and they'll show that the purchases were made during that period. No signature on the credit card slips, all chip-and-pin these days.'

'He's got a workable alibi.'

'That's what he meant, in the driveway after we arrested him.'

Cheney looked puzzled. She watched Synnott flick through the pages of his notebook. 'I have the note here.' As he read the words, Synnott followed them with an index finger.

'*You losers don't have a case. You're chancing your arm. You have no evidence against me. I saw to that.*'

Cheney said, 'He said that?'

'Sneering, playing the big shot. "*You've no evidence against me. I saw to that.*" Bob Tidey heard me ask Boyce if he'd sign my notes, Boyce told me to go fuck myself.'

'One verbal. Is that enough?'

Synnott shook his head. 'We've got him for forty-eight hours. So far, we've nailed him to a timeline. Ten-thirty to eleven-thirty, maybe twelve. We find someone who spotted him somewhere else outside that timeline, he's ours. A busted alibi is worse than none at all. Give a jury an alibi, they're impressed. Kick a hole in the same alibi and they start to wonder why this guy needed an alibi.'

Cheney said, 'When will we put the verbal to him?'

'Tomorrow – he'll flip. It's the smart ones who can't believe they've been stupid enough to make a careless remark. He'll deny it. They always do.'

39

Past nine o'clock, Rose Cheney's husband was watching something on TV. The kids were in bed and Cheney had eaten the heated-up shepherd's pie that David had kept for her. Before leaving Macken Road she'd spent an hour making notes on the interrogation of Joshua Boyce and on her meeting that morning with Teresa Hunt and her father. A full day. Time to switch off.

David Cheney laughed softly. 'You've got to see this.'

It was a programme in which an assortment of young business people sought to impress a grumpy rich man with their business acumen. 'Look at the eyes,' David said. 'Naked greed.'

After Rose had watched for a while she wasn't sure if it was greed she saw in the eyes as much as desperation. She found herself feeling sorry for them. They were still recognisably human, but twisted into various shapes of avarice.

Cheney picked up the evening paper. The *Herald* had a very big headline over a very small story. She went to the kitchen and found the novel she'd put down two nights ago. She was reaching for the kettle when she stopped.

Worth a try.

The family computer was in a corner of the living room. While it was starting up, Cheney went back to the kitchen and made coffee for David and herself.

Hapgood and – what?

Max Senior, it turned out, was the principal of a thriving PR outfit, lately broken out of its niche market into the broader business world.

Hapgood and—?

When she got online she googled 'Max Hapgood' and found forty-three references and the top one gave her the firm's name. She googled 'Hapgood & Creasy', then went to the firm's website. It took another few clicks to find a page that listed the firm's partners and associates, topped by Max Hapgood himself. There were twelve of them, eleven male, each with a CV and a nice smiley colour photo. She decided that three of the men were too old, fat or bald. She saved the remaining eight male photos to her work file. She separately cut and pasted the personal details of each associate into a text file and printed it. Then she went offline and got a Pritt Stick from Louise's art box. She ran off a copy of each of the eight photos, on plain A4 paper. As each sheet came from the printer she cut out the appropriate personal details from the text sheet and pasted them onto the back.

Slumped on the sofa, Cheney's husband had turned up the television volume during the printing. On the screen the grumpy rich man was poking a finger in the direction of a squirming young woman. When Cheney was done David brought the sound down.

Cheney said, 'Sorry, love.'

David hoisted his coffee. 'Cheers.'

Leave it till tomorrow?

Or?

Cheney made a short phone call.

When David saw that she was wearing her jacket he said, 'This time of night?'

Cheney folded the photo sheets over and put them into her handbag. She kissed her husband and said, 'Won't be long.'

*

Harry Synnott, waiting for Dixie Peyton in a small room at the back of Cooper Street garda station, used a thumb and middle finger to rub his eyes. It had been a long day. Synnott thought of how much of his life he'd spent sitting across cheap, worn tables in one small room or another, talking to criminals, victims or witnesses, listening to lies and excuses, pleas and outrage. It had become a routine part of his life in the way that opening the bonnet of a car was a part of a mechanic's life. He'd come to accept the inevitability of moving on from this to whatever kind of police work became routine with Europol. Bigger rooms, perhaps, and bigger lies. Maybe the tables wouldn't be as cheap and as scarred.

When she came in Dixie seemed smaller, thinner than ever. Her face had a grey overlay that seemed to deepen the lines around her mouth. She sat down without looking at Synnott, her lips making nervous movements.

'How are you doing?'

She shrugged and sat sideways on the chair, her knees turned away from Synnott.

'Dixie?'

She ignored him.

'That three hundred? There might be a way. Maybe more.'

Dixie didn't look at him.

Bastard.

'Did you hear me, Dixie? There might be a way.'

Too late.

A few hours ago.

Now.

Fuck him. Bastard.

'Can't promise anything, but I've been thinking of a way to help.'

Dixie didn't respond.

'I'm not going to sit here for ever, Dixie. The thing with the kid – maybe it seems hopeless, but it's not. I'm here to help you.'

'What's the point?'

'There's always another chance.'

Her voice was sudden, loud and with an edge of harshness. 'There's no *point*.'

'In jail, Dixie, that's it – it's over, nothing but dead time.' Synnott reached across the table. Dixie's head jerked an inch as Synnott's fingers gently touched her chin. The fingers tenderly lifted her head. Her gaze came around to meet his. His voice was low, calm. 'Out there, some money in your pocket, maybe you have another shot at whatever it is you want to do, wherever it is you want to go.'

Dixie looked at him for a long time, trying to work out where this might be leading.

Synnott's voice was steady. 'A thousand. Free and clear. And that thing about you taking the child – the abduction goes away. No harm done. If it's put the right way, there's no one couldn't be persuaded to look at it as a family tragedy. And if it's a family tragedy, no need for charges. The mugging charge, the needle – there's no way they'll drop that, but it's a long time before that can come to court and I'll make sure it's even longer. Time enough for whatever you might decide to do. The people you mugged, they're tourists. Maybe they'll decide not to come back to give evidence, so the case fades away.'

Out of here.

A thousand.

Dixie looked up at him, thinking about what he'd said.

'*Maybe you have another shot at whatever it is you want to do, wherever it is you want to go.*'

Synnott watched her ease back into her chair, her body moving around until she was facing him.

'If it ever comes to court, I'll give evidence, tell them how you've been making great progress, coming to terms with your problems.'

A detective inspector telling a judge that the defendant was a changed woman made the difference between jail and a suspended sentence. *She wasn't herself, M'lord, when she committed the offence.* A widow, a young child. A custodial sentence might plunge her back into the depression that had caused her problems, while a second chance would allow her to pick herself up and make a positive contribution to society.

'It's the best offer you're going to get.'

Dixie sat there for half a minute, looking into Synnott's face.

'What do I have to do?'

'Where were you Friday morning? What did you do?'

Dixie looked blank, like she was trying to figure what day this was.

'Friday,' Synnott said, 'when you got out of custody. You got bail, you went – where did you go?'

'I went home.'

'Yeah, but take it step by step.'

'I walked down the quays.'

'Where to?'

'O'Connell Bridge.' She was remembering now. 'I was going to get a bus, but I didn't fancy standing there, so I walked.'

'Down the quays?'

She nodded. 'Over O'Connell Bridge, down the far side. Grand Canal, Boland's Mills.'

Synnott said nothing for a moment.

Try it?

Dixie Peyton?

Keep it simple, it'll work.

One step at a time.

'You crossed O'Connell Bridge? On foot?'

She nodded.

'Any idea what time?'

'No – maybe half-ten – whatever time I got out, then – whatever, maybe half an hour, three-quarters, give or take.'

'Between half-ten and eleven?'

'Yeah.'

'You sure?'

'I got home about, it was, maybe eleven, around that.'

As long as it's simple, it'll work.

'You saw Joshua Boyce.' It was a statement, not a question. 'He was crossing O'Connell Bridge, walking the other way. You passed each other.'

Dixie looked at him, puzzled.

'He walked past you.'

Dixie opened her mouth, then closed it again.

'You said hello, but he didn't hear you the first time, so you said it again.'

Dixie said, 'I said hello.'

'You said it again. This time he saw you, he smiled, he said "*Hello, Dixie,*" and then he was gone, and you went on your way. Down the quays, Grand Canal, Boland's Mills, home.'

Dixie sat there a while. Synnott held her gaze.

'You want me to – what – sign a statement?'

'More than that.'

'Give evidence?'

'You saw him, you said hello to each other – very simple, no one can say it didn't happen.'

'You said I could go wherever—'

'Months, that's all. We have him solid – the trial would be ready to go ahead in months.'

'And I just – wait?'

'Meanwhile, I get you into a programme, detox, visits with the kid, rehab, money in your pocket. Then there's a trial and you say what you saw, Joshua Boyce on O'Connell Bridge, and then you do whatever. Free as a bird.'

Sooner or later she'd start thinking that once she had the money she could change her mind, just do a runner.

'You sign a statement – you better know this up front.' Synnott was leaning across the table now, inches from her face. She had to strain to hear his words. 'You sign a statement and if you welsh on it there's no end of ways I can come back at you. You know what I mean?'

Dixie had to lower her gaze from his unblinking stare.

He said, 'I'm talking about Lar Mackendrick, Tommy Farr, Bill Ridley. You fuck me around, they find out where we got information that blew a hole in their operations. The names, the dates, the places. They'll be queuing up to take a slice of you.'

Dixie waited until she was sure that he was finished. Then, still looking down at the table, she said, 'Three thousand.'

40

When Rose Cheney got home her husband was asleep in bed. She checked the kids, then she went back downstairs and poured some Jack Daniels over ice. She sat at the kitchen table, enjoying the coldness of the glass.

It's amazing how dumb some smart people are.

Max Hapgood Senior was smart enough to run a successful PR company, making a fortune from burnishing the image of the entrepreneurial set. And determined enough to do whatever it took to repeatedly protect his darling son from the consequences of his own brutishness. And dumb enough to piss on his own doorstep.

Where does a man like Max Hapgood Senior find a presentable young thug to throw a scare into a young woman?

When Rose Cheney laid out the eight pictures she'd downloaded from the Hapgood & Creasy website, it took Teresa Hunt all of five seconds to point to the picture of the young man who'd approached her outside Trinity. Sitting in her city-centre flat, where she had been entertaining a girl friend when Cheney rang, Teresa tapped the photo and said, 'No doubt, none.'

'Take your time – look at each photo again, no hurry.'

Teresa nodded. She looked at the photo at the extreme left and worked her way through, spending several seconds on each. Again, she tapped the same picture.

On the back of the sheet Cheney had pasted the details of one Roland J.B. Jackson, B. Comm., M.P.R.I.I.

These days, even the hoodlums come with letters after their names.

Roland, according to the website, was a junior associate who specialised in corporate events. Which probably meant he chose the menu for company lunches when new products were being rolled out for key customers.

Little desperado like that, all Cheney and Synnott would have to do was cough and he'd roll over and give up his boss.

Cheney thought of ringing Harry Synnott, then she decided the hell with it. Probably in bed by now. Time enough in the morning.

The whiskey glass was empty. Too stimulated to go to bed, Cheney poured herself another drink. Then she sat in the living room, slouched in an armchair, thinking through the Hapgood case, looking for holes and deciding that there were none. The urge to contact Synnott had gone, along with an impulse to wake David and tell him about tonight. Instead, she just sat there and relished the feeling.

*

Harry Synnott was sitting at a desk in the incident room at Macken Road garda station. He'd gone there directly after talking to Dixie Peyton. On the desk in front of him was a statement, handwritten by Synnott and signed by Dixie. She'd have to spend the night in a cell but Synnott had promised to return to the station the next day to persuade the arresting garda that she was a deserving case. Before he left he had a word with a sergeant and told him this woman was being helpful.

'It would be a big plus if this thing stayed at this level. She's a good sort – she just got upset, wanted to see the kid, no harm done.' The sergeant said he'd have a word.

Synnott typed up Dixie's statement and produced a printed version to be signed in the morning. He made a copy of that and then made working copies of around a dozen statements from the files. It took him over half an hour to read them, marking sections with a red pen.

Macken Road was quiet. The shifts had changed and the debris from the post-pub fights hadn't yet been swept into the station. There were no detectives around and the incident room was dark except for a lamp on the desk where Synnott was working. It crossed his mind that he should call Chief Superintendent Malachy Hogg, keep him up with developments. But he decided it would be best to lay it all out for him tomorrow at the daily conference on the jewellery robbery and killing of Arthur Dunne.

The bulk of the file sent to the DPP would be supporting material – technical reports, factual statements from witnesses, an autopsy report that might clarify whether they could medically link the gunshot and the death. The evidence that would make it all work would be Synnott's own statement, about the conversation with the handcuffed Joshua Boyce in the driveway of his home. That statement was just a page and a half long, typed, and the only significant portion was a paragraph near the end.

When he saw that there was no one else within several yards the suspect spoke in a low voice. He said, 'This is all for show. You know you can't prove it.' I replied that it was early days yet. The suspect said, 'You're a loser, you don't have a case.' I replied that we would see about that. The suspect smiled at me and said 'You've got no evidence against me. I saw to that.' I asked if he was admitting the killing of Arthur Dunne and the suspect said, 'You don't really think I'm going to answer that'. I immediately made a note of this exchange and asked the suspect to sign it. He answered with an obscenity. At that stage we were joined by Sergeant Tidey and Garda Purcell and I asked them to make a note of anything they heard.

Bob Tidey's innocuous statement of what he witnessed in the

driveway would be helpful. Nothing incriminating, just confirmation that Synnott asked Boyce to sign his notes.

The clincher, when contrasted with the transcript record of Boyce's claim to have an alibi, was the witness statement signed by Dixie Peyton that destroyed that alibi.

> *My name is Deirdre Peyton. I live at 33 Portmahon Terrace, South Crescent. I wish to say that on the morning of Friday 15th April I was released from custody. I walked down the quays, towards home. When I was crossing O'Connell Bridge, at around eleven o'clock, heading in a southerly direction, I met Joshua Boyce, whom I have known since my childhood on the Cairnloch estate. Joshua was coming from the other direction. He was carrying a black holdall hanging from his shoulder. As we passed I said, 'Hi, Josh,' but he didn't hear me. He seemed to be in a hurry. I said hello again and he looked around and said 'Hi, Dixie.' I then continued on my way home. This statement has been read back to me and it is correct.*
> *Deirdre Peyton*

Harry Synnott considered adding some incriminating details to his statement of his interview with the security guard, Arthur Dunne. Boyce had a small acne scar on his left cheek. Maybe the security guard had seen that when he wrestled Boyce to the ground.

Too risky. Friday evening, he'd told Rose Cheney that the security guard had nothing useful.

There was a reasonable chance that the DPP could be persuaded that Boyce was the kind of gangster who would interfere with jurors. If so, the case would be tried in the Special Criminal Court in front of three judges sitting without a jury. Technically, the evidence was enough to convict Boyce. Whether it worked would depend on Harry Synnott's credibility in the witness box. And everyone knew that he was the man who told the truth.

Synnott stood at the window overlooking the front yard of Macken Road. A couple of uniforms were hauling a drunk out of a police car. The law could handle that kind of thing. In more complicated matters it was a clumsy, inefficient tool. Joshua Boyce had carried out five armed robberies that Synnott knew of, on each occasion using violence or the threat of violence. If Boyce hadn't killed the security guard on this robbery he'd have killed someone else on another robbery. This wasn't just about the law, it was about right and wrong.

Synnott took his jacket from the back of his chair and put it on.

The law is a flawed weapon against the cunning, but the power of the law in the right hands can achieve an imperfect justice.

It's the right thing to do.

Synnott leaned across his desk and switched off the light.

41

In reception at Garda Headquarters, there was a patrol-car driver waiting to take Garda Joe Mills to his hotel. Mills handed the garda his overnight bag and said he needed to take a walk. He was relieved that his meeting with the Assistant Commissioner was over and felt pissed-off on being told that he had to stay in Dublin next day.

'I want you here tomorrow morning, no later than eleven,' Assistant Commissioner O'Keefe told him. 'Then you'll be on standby for a few hours in case I need you in here again. Probably won't, but if we need you in a hurry you're bugger-all use to us halfway back to Galway.'

Shit. It'll be Wednesday before I get home.

The North Circular Road stretched ahead of him, from the gate of the Phoenix Park down towards Doyle's Corner and the city centre. Mills walked at a steady pace, his head down, paying little attention to the charm of the tree-lined pavements or the tall houses on either side of the street. After he left his native Navan, before he joined the force, he lived for a year in Dublin, in a flat off the North Circular and he knew well the neighbourhood's air of tatty elegance.

He could feel the tension of the day seep away with every step. It was a little more than twenty-four hours since he'd been called back on duty because the nutcase had again demanded to see 'the policeman from the roof'. Wayne Kemp had spent two days banged up in St Catherine's while a couple of shrinks tried to get into his head. Word had come from the police in Blackpool that they had no record of Kemp, but that he had a couple of convictions in Manchester for minor offenses.

Slumped on a chair in a bright room at St Catherine's, Kemp seemed to Joe Mills to be on edge. Some of the vagueness was gone. Every now and then he touched his face, his thumb and index finger making a pulling motion at his chin, like he was stroking an invisible beard. Sometimes, as though following a pattern, he made a wiping gesture across his forehead, then brushed something invisible away from his temple.

'You seem confused,' he said to Joe Mills.

Mills was tempted to make a crack. Instead he said, 'How so?'

'This woman thing.'

'It's what you said to us, Wayne, about hurting a woman – we still need to know where she is. Or are you making it up?'

'At first, what it was, I was just trying to scare her.'

'What's her name?'

'To stop her screaming.'

'Her name?'

Wayne Kemp shrugged. 'How would I know?'

'Did you cut her? Like the others?'

Kemp looked up. 'What others?'

'Davy and Joseph. Your sister's husband, her son – your nephew?'

Kemp looked away, his face blank, like he'd been reminded of an unwelcome chore he had yet to do. 'That was different.'

'How?'

Silence.

'Look, Wayne, we need to know. If you've cut someone else, if you did this to a woman, it's best—'

'I didn't cut her.'

*

'From the start, what happened? Where? An address?' Joe Mills was sitting now, his notebook open on the table, pen poised.

Kemp shook his head. 'Look, I'm trying to do the right thing – it's just, it's been so long and, I mean, does it matter any more?'

'When?'

'I don't know. Way back.'

'How long?'

'Oh, a long time.'

'In Galway? Dublin? Blackpool? Where?'

Kemp said nothing for a long while. When Joe Mills asked the same question again, Kemp looked up as though surprised to hear him speak. Mills wondered if maybe the cold, mad thing that he'd seen on the roof was paying Kemp another visit.

Then Kemp began speaking: one flowing sentence, a pause and then a rush of words, a cascade of fragments. Then it stopped.

Towards the end, as Kemp faltered, Joe Mills attempted to ask questions. Each time he tried to tie Kemp to a date or a location, to probe for a name or a detail, the nutcase stopped and tried to think and then seemed to drift off somewhere for a while before Joe Mills eased him back towards his splintered story.

It was the end of that story, just before Kemp closed up again, that was of most interest to Assistant Commissioner O'Keefe.

'Word for word, Garda Mills.'

Joe Mills had his notebook open. He went through the hair colour, and what Kemp remembered of the woman's size and shape – nothing remarkable. As Mills read from his notes, the Assistant Commissioner looked off to one side, his tongue agitated inside his cheek.

'She wouldn't shut up, screamed twice, three times – so Kemp put one hand over her mouth, she bit him, so he hit her, knocked her out. He said he didn't know what happened after that, until he looked down and saw she wasn't moving. He didn't remember messing with her clothes – what he said, sir – *her pants were down, I just looked up and the kid, the little boy – the kid wasn't screaming, just standing there, a few feet away, with his mouth open.'*

Colin O'Keefe's voice was a breath. 'Donny.'

Joe Mills looked up at the Assistant Commissioner. 'He didn't say a name. Last thing he said before he closed up again, sir—' Mills looked down at his notes and read aloud – *'Tiny little thing. Barely see it. A flower. Red flower. Thought at first it was a mole.'* Joe Mills looked up at O'Keefe, then down at his notebook again. *'Pretty little flower on her chubby little tummy. Pretty little rosebud.'*

TUESDAY

42

The first of five phone calls came shortly after ten o'clock and it was anonymous.

'Payback time, fuck-face.'

The voice was familiar.

'You piss on your colleagues, and when it comes your turn there isn't a hand that'll reach out to help, you *prick*.'

The answer machine was on, to filter calls while Synnott sat at his kitchen table and reviewed the copies of the statements he'd assembled the previous night.

'See how you like it, fuck-face, see how you like it when the screws are turning. When—'

Synnott picked up the phone.

'*Ferry?*'

'When you go down, fuck-face, there isn't a station that won't have a party.'

The phone went dead.

The second phone call was from a sergeant in Chief Superintendent Hogg's office. Synnott picked up. The morning conference on the jewellery robbery had been postponed; there would be a conference at 6 p.m., same as yesterday. That suited Harry Synnott. He was halfway through reading the statements, adding notes that might marginally increase the value of the file. The typed-up version of

Dixie's statement, slightly amended, was ready for her signature as soon as he finished here and got her out of custody. After this morning's work, he'd be equipped to recommend putting together a full investigation file for the DPP's office.

The third call was from Rose Cheney. Synnott picked up when he heard her voice.

She said, 'Taking the day off?'

He told her there'd been a development in the jewellery robbery. He was at home, working on statements. He had a witness who could place Joshua Boyce on O'Connell Bridge shortly after eleven o'clock – which sank Boyce's Perry Logan superstore alibi.

'Jesus, that's great! What's the witness like?'

'Dixie Peyton – a tout, she's given me reliable stuff before – grew up on the Cairnloch estate the same time as Boyce. It'll stand up.'

Rose Cheney told him she'd be spending most of the day in court. Then she gave him the good news about the Hapgood rape case.

'You won't believe what Maxie Senior did – pissed on his own doorstep.' Then she told him all about Roland J.B. Jackson, B. Comm., M.P.R.I.I.

Cheney was about to hang up when she said, 'By the way, there's something going on down here.'

'Problems?'

'The Chief Super was here until all hours last night. Lawyers in and out, two or three people from HQ – doors shut, not a word to anyone. This morning, the phone is hopping off the hook. At least two calls from the Commissioner's office, according to the desk.'

'Any notion of what it's about?'

'One of the lads heard there's a contingent up from Galway, talking to the Commissioner – and he's guessing it has something to do with the murders over there, the fella and the boy.'

The phone clamped between shoulder and ear, Synnott drew a line through several words on the copy of the statement in front of him. 'We'll probably read about it in the papers, so.'

The fourth phone call was from Michael. When Synnott's mobile rang he looked at the screen and saw his son's name.

Synnott put down the mobile and pushed away the file he'd been working on.

Later, Michael. Right now, the prospect of a ramble down some remote byway of his son's career fantasies, trying to display an interest in choices Michael might make in business careers that Synnott neither understood nor cared about, was too distracting.

When Michael hung up, Synnott crossed to the answer machine and checked that it was on. After a few moments the phone rang and the machine invited the caller to leave a message.

'Dad? You there?'

Synnott went back to the kitchen table and sat down.

'Dad?'

Later.

The fifth phone call came just after lunchtime, as Harry Synnott was coming out of the O'Connell Street branch of the National Irish Bank, having withdrawn €3,000 in cash from his account. He'd put the thirty €100 notes into an envelope along with the typed version of Dixie Peyton's statement. The envelope nestled in his inside jacket pocket.

'Detective Inspector Synnott?'

'Yes?'

The caller identified himself as a superintendent attached to the office of Colin O'Keefe. 'The Assistant Commissioner asked me to instruct you to report immediately to his office at Garda HQ.'

'What's going on?'

'How long will it take you to get here?'

Synnott said, 'I'm on my way to meet a potentially important witness.'

'Where are you?'

'O'Connell Street.'

'Assistant Commissioner O'Keefe will expect you within fifteen minutes.'

*

There was a young man sitting off to one side of Colin O'Keefe's desk. The Assistant Commissioner said, 'This is Garda Joe Mills – McCreary Street station, in Galway.'

The young garda nodded to Synnott. His lips briefly created an awkward smile.

Synnott turned to the assistant commissioner. 'Is there something wrong, sir?'

There was a formality to O'Keefe's manner that Synnott had never seen before. His bearing was impersonal, his expression detached. 'I asked Garda Mills to come up to Dublin yesterday to brief me on certain developments concerning the two murders uncovered in Galway several days ago, the man and the boy.' He nodded to Mills.

The garda picked up a notebook from O'Keefe's desk. When he spoke he addressed Harry Synnott.

'Myself and another garda, Declan Dockery, sir, we arrested a man, last Wednesday – an attempted suicide, on the roof of a pub. He was visiting Galway, he lives in Dublin. As a consequence of the arrest we called at a house in Bushy Park, where we discovered the two bodies. The man we arrested, Wayne Kemp, there's no doubt that he committed the murders – blood evidence, a verbal admission—'

O'Keefe said, 'And the man's clearly certifiable. To cut a long story short, there's no doubt that this Wayne Kemp will be a very old man before he sets foot outside the Central Mental Hospital. What complicates the case is that in the course of the investigation he made certain admissions.'

Garda Mills was leafing through his notebook. When he found what he was looking for he looked to O'Keefe, who nodded for him to continue.

'What worried us was something Mr Kemp said. *When it started out, there was no rough stuff. I'd never hurt a woman before.*' Mills looked up from his notes. 'For the next few days, we were looking for another body, a woman, maybe in Galway, maybe back in Dublin – maybe he made it up, maybe he had hallucinations, we didn't know.'

O'Keefe said, 'There was no woman. Not in Galway, not in Dublin – not now.'

Mills said, 'Mr Kemp told us – it took a while to get it out of him, he's not terribly coherent at times – that he killed a woman some years ago, in Dublin. He'd been living in Blackpool, then Manchester – he's not clear on dates – he was back in Dublin a short time. While he was in England he'd done a handful of burglaries, he did the same in Dublin, all in the one area. He couldn't remember where, though he lived in a flat in Drumcondra at the time and it was within walking distance.'

'Four burglaries,' O'Keefe said.

Mills said, 'It didn't mean anything to me, to be honest, sir, but my Chief Super, as soon as he heard the details – the little tattoo on the victim, on her lower abdomen, a rosebud – he made the connection.'

Harry Synnott said, 'Wait a minute—'

O'Keefe gestured for Mills to continue.

Mills looked at his notes again. 'Kemp was on the prowl, looking for a likely house, he saw a woman come home, go in, he went right up and knocked on the door, she answered, he pushed the door in—'

Harry Synnott stood up. 'Hold on—'

O'Keefe said, 'Thank you, Garda Mills. You may leave now – I'll send for you if I need you.'

O'Keefe sat silently behind his desk until the door clicked shut behind the young garda. Then he said, 'The Swanson Avenue case. Tell me everything.'

'There's—'

Harry Synnott felt the words melt from his tongue. He searched for a new sentence, something to say that would slow things down, give him time to match the past with the present, the assertions he'd just heard against the truth he'd known since he'd unravelled Ned Callaghan's lies. Truth and assisted truth coiled around one another, impossible to tell apart. Several combinations of words, half-thoughts, collided and he finally reached for words that he knew were inadequate. 'Sir, there appears to be a mistake of some—'

O'Keefe was staring down at the bare desk in front of him. 'And before you say anything, you should know that right now I've got a Chief Superintendent at the home of former Detective Inspector John Grace, interviewing him about his recollection of the case.'

43

A long silence.

'Harry, there's just you and me here – I have to know the lie of the land. This is off the record, so tell me.'

'Ned Callaghan murdered his wife.'

'That's not good enough, Harry.'

'It's what happened. I questioned him, so did John Grace. He denied everything. We knew from the kid—'

'The kid was three years old and he'd just had his head fucked up, watching the life battered out of his mother.'

'He said his dad did it.'

My daddy, my daddy—

'Three years old – the state he was in – he made noises to you, Harry—'

'I know what I heard. And Callaghan lied, repeatedly. His girlfriend, he suborned perjury. He made admissions.'

Harry Synnott's eyes were staring towards the assistant commissioner's desk, but they were focused somewhere in mid-air. He could see the dark patches of sweat on Ned Callaghan's light blue shirt. He could see the desperation in the man's eyes, he could see the patches of red on his cheeks, the broken veins beneath, he could see the man close his eyes, tilt his chin up, he could hear the voice so high in despair that it was almost a squeak.

'*Please!*'

Harry Synnott met Colin O'Keefe's gaze. 'The guilt and the shame was all over him. He killed himself. What more do you need?'

'I've checked – the detail about the tattoo, that never came out. This man Kemp, we already know him to be guilty of two murders, and he made an unsolicited admission about beating a woman to death, and he knew about the tattoo.'

Synnott said nothing for a while, then he said, 'That Galway fella, Mills – he said it took them days questioning him before he came up with this shit. How do we know – Jesus, Colin, you said yourself he belongs in the Central Mental Hospital.'

O'Keefe said, 'Remember the fingermarks found in the Callaghan house? This morning, we got a match with Kemp.'

Synnott said nothing.

O'Keefe's voice was flat. 'I had a couple of excitable chaps from the DPP's office in here an hour ago. This rape case, the Hapgood thing, they're extremely sceptical. They're dropping the charge.'

'Jesus—'

'And they want you off the jewellery robbery – they say that if it was Boyce who did it you've almost certainly contaminated the case already just by interrogating him.'

'That's bullshit.'

'This Galway thing is coming out, Harry. And what they don't want is you on the stand, against Hapgood or Boyce or anyone else, being cross-examined about what a suspect did or didn't say, with lawyers queuing up to rub your face in this fuck-up until every word you say stinks of Swanson Avenue. The DPP's office wants Boyce released. I've just given instructions to that effect.'

He leaned forward. 'Did Boyce, by the way, make any incriminating admissions to you?'

'He made certain admissions.'

O'Keefe said, 'I think you'll find it very, very difficult to get this one past the DPP, Harry, if there's verbal admissions involved. Do you have anything else on him?'

The envelope in Harry Synnott's inside pocket, the three thousand and Dixie Peyton's statement, felt like it had doubled in weight and volume.

It's not a runner. Not now.

With the police and the prosecution lawyers behind her, Dixie Peyton could hold up long enough to put the bastard away. With the same gardai and lawyers testing every sentence of her story there was no way she wouldn't crumble.

'He made certain admissions, sir – that's all we have.'

O'Keefe nodded slowly, like he'd heard something that was expected but still disappointing.

Synnott wanted everything to stop for a moment. He needed to think, to sweep away the extraneous detail and isolate the core of it all. What was certain? What was arguable? Where was there room to duck and weave, what were the immovable problems?

'By the way, Harry – word's been circulating about this since late last night. First thing this morning, the Minister for Justice was hammering at my ear.'

Synnott couldn't help smiling. 'He's reconsidering his offer?'

O'Keefe shook his head. 'He's already appointed someone else. A shiny young thing with impeccable party connections who'll do the country proud in Europe.'

'Fuck him.'

O'Keefe looked tired. 'Frankly, Harry, I'd have withdrawn your name, anyway. The last thing we need is to draw attention to you. By the time this ends, you might have a career left or you might not. Depends how the chips fall. We'll save you or we'll screw you – depends on what's best for the force.'

'Thanks.'

'No one asked you to stitch up Ned Callaghan.'

'No one cared how it was done – and you know how these things are done, and the politicians know how they're done – no one gives a shit until something like this happens.'

O'Keefe's face tightened.

'Don't play the martyr, Harry. We handled the heavy gang going around beating the crap out of suspects. We handled it when suspects were stitched up like chickens on a spit. And you, we'll handle you too.'

Synnott ran both hands back through his hair and paused a moment before he said, quietly, 'I'm fucked.'

'Maybe so. On balance, as long as you keep your head down and nothing else comes out, you just might shade it. Ned Callaghan's dead, Wayne Kemp's a nutter.' He paused before he met Synnott's gaze. 'I take it there's nothing else that might fall out of the woodpile?'

Synnott shook his head.

'OK. Then the best thing you can do is keep your head down. Word's already leaking through the force, it's only a matter of time before someone gives it to the media. Take a few days – let's see what it looks like when the dust settles.'

A mile or so from Garda HQ, Harry Synnott tasted the bile in his mouth and pulled the car over to the side of the road. He rolled down the window and took gulps of air. He had stopped by the side of the road in an isolated part of the Phoenix Park that he didn't recognise. He got out and walked some yards from the car.

Kill the statements.

Dixie's.

Mine. Do a new statement, lose the verbal.

He spat on the grass, but it didn't relieve the harsh taste in his mouth.

Have to stop somewhere, buy some mints.

Synnott took out his mobile and rang John Grace's house. A male voice he didn't recognise said, 'Yes?'

Synnott ended the call.

He had an urgent need for a piss. He walked away from the car, down an incline and towards the woods maybe fifty feet from the road. As he urinated against a tree, his back to the road, he remembered he'd left the car door open, the key in the ignition. He stifled a rush of anxiety that urged him to swing around. He forced himself to take his time, suppressing the irrational fear that at any moment he would hear the car being driven away. When he finished he turned and walked back towards the car.

No panic.

Think it through.

John Grace is retired – they've got no leverage, he sings dumb.

Swanson Avenue – it's a face-off between me and a lunatic who killed two people and tried to jump off a roof.

It's doable.

Everything else – this case or that, any other shit that was dragged up – without hard evidence it was nothing more than chatter, easily dealt with.

Take it easy.

Hold steady.

Do what has to be done.

Synnott could see a possibility.

Days, maybe a few weeks, of staying calm, taking any allegation head-on – *deny and challenge, make them work for every inch* – when it all blew itself out he could be still standing.

Nothing will be the same.

No promotion.

Ever.

Probably get shifted sideways to some backwater.

Quit?

Harry Synnott stood at the car, one hand on the roof, a fingernail tracing circular patterns on the blue paint.

I wouldn't know what to do.

44

At Macken Road, Harry Synnott unlocked the drawer in his desk and took out the folder of statements that he had compiled the previous night. He took out his own statement about his conversation with Joshua Boyce and the handwritten version of Dixie Peyton's statement. He drove to the city centre, parked, then walked to his flat by the Liffey and opened the copies of the files he'd brought home. In the kitchen sink he burned all versions of Dixie's statement, originals and copies, along with his own statement on his conversation with Joshua Boyce. He crumpled the ashes and ran the tap on them. He watched the black particles swirl around the sink until they disappeared.

Walking towards Cooper Street garda station Synnott made a phone call.

'Yeah?'

'Where are you?'

Rose Cheney said she was hanging around a corridor outside the Circuit Court, waiting while a judge listened to lawyers arguing a legal point very slowly.

'That statement I told you about this morning, from the tout?'

'Yeah?'

'It's not on. I talked to her again. She *thinks* it was Boyce she saw. Last night she said she was certain. Put her on the stand, let a lawyer at her, she'd fall apart. The statement's worthless.'

'That's a pity.'

'Not her fault, she was trying to help.'

'You OK?'

'Don't—'

'You sound tense.'

'Look, do me a favour – don't mention the statement to anyone. Cracking the alibi, then it falls apart – it's embarrassing.'

'Informers, that's how they are – these things happen.'

'Yeah.'

After a moment, Cheney said, 'You sure you're all right?'

'Fine. I'm fine. Just a bit disappointed, you know?'

It took no more than fifteen minutes to get Dixie out. The sergeant in charge at Cooper Street was indifferent and the arresting garda was a decent sort who felt sorry for the poor woman, barely his own age. Once he was assured that the kid she'd abducted had been in no danger, and that Synnott would ensure that she'd turn up for court proceedings, he nodded and that was that.

'Where to? Home?'

Dixie sat in the front passenger seat, mouth pinched, and Synnott had to ask her again. It took her a few seconds to focus on the question – then she shook her head.

'Just get me away from here. I'll stay in the city centre for a while. I'll – I don't know, I want to go somewhere, have a coffee, get my head straight.'

'We have to talk.'

Nervous.

Dixie had never seen Synnott like this. It was something about his facial movements – the way he moved his lips, rubbing the lower lip against the upper – something about the way his head kept moving slightly, turning just a little this way and that.

With Inspector Synnott, usually it was like he was carved out of stone.

He seemed as though he wasn't exactly sure what he ought to say next.

'That statement—'

The way he looks at me, it's usually like he's seeing right into what I'm thinking.

They were sitting on high stools at the little Croissanterie in the Ilac Centre, mugs of coffee in front of them, his head bent towards her, speaking low.

'The statement you signed last night?'

She nodded.

'Forget about it.'

As Dixie opened her mouth to speak he touched her arm. 'It's OK, you'll get your money. Things have changed. We don't need the statement, there's better evidence, we'll wrap it up without having to drag you into it.'

'I get paid?'

'A thousand.'

'We agreed three.'

'A thousand – for doing nothing. Don't be stupid, Dixie.'

Dixie stared at him. Then she said, 'OK.'

A thousand.

Enough.

Give it a day or two.

Lie low, at Shelley's place. No rushing things, suss things out.

Christopher.

Before the old Dobbs bitch knows I've got him we'll be in London, take it from there.

After a moment, Synnott said, 'This never happened, none of this. No statement, no money, we never talked about any of this – it just didn't happen.'

She met his gaze.

He did that thing with his lips again. 'Right?'

'Are you in trouble?'

'Fuck off, Dixie. This never happened, right?'

She said, 'Right. It never happened.'

'There are things I can do, you know that.'

'It never happened, Mr Synnott.'

There was silence for half a minute. Dixie finished her coffee. Synnott hadn't touched his. She put down the mug.

Why not?

'An extra five hundred?'

He stared at her.

'I'm not demanding it, Mr Synnott, I'm just asking. It means the difference, it—'

'Don't push it, Dixie.'

They went up in the lift to the third-floor car park and sat in Synnott's car. She watched Synnott take an envelope from his inside pocket. He held it so she couldn't see what was inside, then he counted out ten €100 notes and gave them to her.

Dixie said, 'Thanks.'

'Need a lift?'

'I'm OK.'

For a moment he looked like he was about to say something. Then he nodded and Dixie got out of the car and walked towards the exit.

A grand.

Lie low for a couple of days at most, work out how to get to Christopher. No point trying at the school again, the Dobbs bitch would see to that.

There's always a way.

No stalling, taxi straight to the airport, time it right, cut and run.

When she got to the ground floor, Dixie went out onto Henry Street and turned left, heading up towards Shelley's place.

*

Still sitting in his car, Harry Synnott rang John Grace's number again and this time Grace answered.

'You had a visitor?'

Grace said, 'Two.'

'Tough guys?'

'They wanted to be my friends.'

'What did you say?'

'I said I'd nothing to add to my statement of four years ago.'

'Do they still want to be your friends?'

John Grace didn't say anything for a moment. Then he said, 'Look, this is going to be difficult. They showed me what the fella said, the fella in Galway.'

'I know.'

'It's all there, pushing the door in, the tattoo, stuff he couldn't have known unless he—'

'A pissing contest. Two admissions.'

'His prints.'

'He could have been in the house a week earlier, a month. No connection with the killing.'

Grace said nothing.

'What we did was right, absolutely right – no doubt about that.'

Grace said, 'We did what we *thought* was right.'

Harry Synnott paused. 'That's all we can ever do.'

'Now it looks like—'

'John, you're retired – they can't do anything to you.' Harry Synnott felt a sudden revulsion at the pleading tone in his own voice. '*Fuck it* – we're not the bad guys, John, we're—'

'I know.'

'Just keep it together, whatever they do.'

'I said what I had to say about Swanson Avenue four years ago, that's all they'll get.'

Synnott realised he was about to say thanks. Instead, he said, 'We should have a drink some night this week, just – you know—'

John Grace said, 'Yeah.'

*

Shelley's flat was empty and when Dixie Peyton arrived she spent a while tidying up, thinking things through. No point waiting a couple of days before making another attempt to reach Christopher.

This is, what?

Tuesday.

Tomorrow – after school.

Every Wednesday since playschool Christopher would get together with his friend Willie immediately after school, at one or another of their homes.

Fifty-fifty.

The Dobbs's place or Willie's.

Tomorrow, if it was Christopher's turn to visit Willie at his home, that was where to do it. If it was the other way around, fuck that, the whole thing would have to wait a week.

I won't make it, not another week.

Has to be tomorrow.

Turn up at Willie's place, all concerned.

Christopher's granny, his dad's mother, she had an accident – fell down the stairs—

Jesus, that wouldn't work. Something a bit more—

His granny died this morning, suddenly, poor woman.

Have to take him home, sit him down, break it to him—

And if they ask—

Fuck that. She's dead – he's my son, I decide—

It'll work.

Dixie made a coffee and called Shelley's mobile.

Dixie could tell immediately Shelley was on edge. A clipped 'Yes?'

'You OK?'

'Fine.'

'Where are you?'

'Went to see Robbie.'

'Shelley—'

'He wants me out of the flat by the end of the week.'

'What?'

'All business. Sorry, love, client needs the place, money up front.'

'He can't do that.'

'What am I going to do?'

Dixie wanted to tell Shelley that she'd help out.

No.

Mention the thousand she'd got from Synnott and Shelley would want to know everything. Anyway, even if she gave Shelley a couple of hundred so what? It wouldn't do anything for Shelley's problems. And it wasn't like a thousand was such a big deal – once Dixie got Christopher across to England there were all kinds of emergencies could crop up and she'd need every cent.

'Jesus, Shelley—'

'I've a good mind to rat him out. The stuff he shifts, I know the where and the when. Just to see the look on his face.'

Dixie said, 'What're you going to do?'

'Come on down, I'm in Dwyer's – if ever there was a night for getting locked – come on.' Dixie wasn't used to the pleading tone in her friend's voice.

'Shelley, come home, we'll get in a couple of bottles, some food.'

Shelley said no, she couldn't stand being cooped up in the flat. 'Listen, Dix, what about you? I mean, this affects you – I'm really sorry. Will you be able to go back to your own place by the weekend?'

Dixie realised that she'd been picking at the corner of the wood-effect kitchen table. An inch or so of the side strip had started to peel away.

This isn't right. There must be something I can do for her.

Not now.

'I'll be OK, don't worry.'

Christopher comes first.

'I'm really sorry, Dix.'

When the call was over, Dixie pushed the strip back tight against the edge of the table. When she took her finger away it stayed in place.

Christopher, first.

Then, whatever—

45

Paddy Robert Garcia Murphy's face hurt. The jeweller was trying so hard to appear relaxed, an unconvincing smile fixed in place, that his facial muscles felt unpleasantly rigid. Across the restaurant his wife stood beside another table, leaning down, deep in conversation with a couple whose names Garcia didn't know. He realised that his tolerant smile had weakened to the point of vanishing, so he made an effort to restore it. He didn't want it to look as though her bad manners bothered him.

She was always doing this. Happening across friends and acquaintances, people he didn't know, and a nod or a hello wasn't enough, she had to yap endlessly. Leaving him hanging around like a spare prick at a wedding. It always annoyed him, but this evening he had expected more from her. Four days had passed since the robbery of his jewellery shop and Robert Garcia was feeling vulnerable.

The least she could do. Time like this. Bit of support.

He hadn't made contact with any of the owners of the jewellery taken from the floor safe. If they got the wrong idea—

Then, this morning, a phone call at home, at dawn. No name, but the voice was unmistakable.

'No problems, I hope?'

'What?'

'I saw from the newspapers, you had a wee spot of bother on Friday. Everything's OK, I hope?'

'Of course – yes – that was – look, I don't think we should—'

'Long as everything's hunky-dory.'

'Sure, no problem.'

They'd find out. The stuff was supposed to be on its way to Leeds before the end of the week. When that didn't happen—

From across the restaurant, the sound of his wife's laughter. Robert Garcia's smile evaporated. He no longer cared about concealing his annoyance.

He got up and headed towards the Gents'. His wife didn't notice.

He'd been standing at a urinal for a few seconds when the door opened behind him. A man came and stood two urinals away to his right.

'We meet again.'

Robert Garcia looked at the man. Grey suit, bright blue tie, short dark hair. Average height, average build, nothing familiar about the face. The man was smiling at Robert Garcia.

A customer, perhaps. They spend a couple of hundred and they expect you to remember them for ever.

'Hi,' the jeweller said.

As Garcia faced front again something clicked in his mind.

He's not pissing.

Garcia turned his head sharply and saw that the man was just standing there, his hands nowhere near his crotch. Garcia struggled to stop pissing, felt himself out of control for a moment, then he was pulling his zip up, stepping back from the urinal, and the man was also stepping back, making himself an obstacle between the jeweller and the door.

The man wasn't smiling now.

The jeweller said, 'Look – I didn't – it wasn't—'

Lying in bed after the phone call this morning he'd tried to work out what he'd say if he had to explain losing the special merchandise. Now he felt like his head was full of disconnected words.

'I swear—'

The man lifted his left hand and held his forefinger horizontally in front of his face.

Robert Garcia stopped trying to speak.

The man placed his finger in the space between his nose and his upper lip. Then he smiled.

Moustache—

The man said, 'You don't recognise me without a gun in my hand, right?'

Robert Garcia made an involuntary noise.

Joshua Boyce lowered his hand. 'It's OK, I just want a chat.'

The jeweller said, 'You bastard.'

'You're a businessman, there's business to be done.'

'Not with you.'

'I've had my own problems, these past few days.'

'You shot a man, you bastard. He died.'

'It wasn't supposed to be like that.'

The jeweller's voice was suddenly harsh. 'You've *ruined* me.'

After being released from police custody, Joshua Boyce had made three phone calls and confirmed what he suspected – the fence he'd lined up to buy the stolen jewellery was opting out. Two others asked if the jewellery was from the robbery where a security guard had croaked and when he admitted that it was they weren't interested.

One option.

'I didn't come here for a conversation. The jewellery from the floor safe, I know you can't report it missing. You've got to take the loss.'

The jeweller, despite his anger, felt a tiny flare of hope.

'I'll sell you the jewellery. One hundred thousand.'

The jeweller just stood there.

The merchandise from the floor safe was worth a quarter of a million.

Jesus. This could—

Robert Garcia said, 'Fifty thousand.'

The robber shook his head and Robert Garcia knew he meant it. The robber said, 'I can bury it, come back to it ten years from now.'

It would take a lot of juggling to raise a hundred grand, and the kind of debt he was in, this was just digging himself deeper into the hole.

Robert Garcia decided there were worse holes to be in.

'How do we do this?'

The robber said, 'I know where you live.'

'How do we do it?'

The robber held up a car key. 'I give you this, tell you where the car's parked. The jewellery's in the boot, you take it and leave the hundred grand in its place.'

Garcia was nodding.

The robber said, 'If I go there and the money isn't in the boot, or if the police are waiting, you won't live more than an hour.'

'I wouldn't—'

'Do we have a deal?'

'It'll take me a couple of days to get the cash.'

The robber moved his hand and the key was arcing through the air. Robert Garcia caught it. The robber said, 'I'll be in touch, let you know where to go.'

The robber had the door open when the jeweller said, 'Just one thing.'

Apart from his assistant, no one had known about the safe in the floor except the people who'd put it in and a couple of clients who'd insisted on knowing where their special merchandise would be stored. It wasn't that he could do anything if he found the culprit but he wanted to know.

'How did you find out about the safe in the floor?'

The robber cocked a finger at the jeweller and said, 'What you

321

need to worry about is what else I know, and how you're going to keep me sweet.'

When the robber left, Robert Garcia took a while to get his breathing back to normal. He felt a jolt in his chest when the toilet door swung open abruptly, but it was just a customer heading for a cubicle.

When he got back to his table his wife was sitting there, her irritation obvious. 'Where the bloody hell have you been all this time?'

46

The message from Chief Superintendent Hogg was delivered politely by a young detective garda named Mary something. The Chief Superintendent understood that Detective Inspector Synnott would not be attending the daily conference on the jewellery robbery, but he would be grateful if Mr Synnott would make himself available at Macken Road station in case the investigation team needed clarification on any aspect of the investigation.

Now, over an hour after the start of the conference, Synnott was still sitting at his desk, with no word from Hogg. It was getting dark outside. He decided that if he heard no word by eight-thirty he was going home.

It's not as though I owe them anything.

Synnott sat at his desk and leafed through a case file he'd been handling. An assault in which three teenagers from a prominent private college beat unconscious a pupil from a rival school and left him with a collapsed lung and a permanently droopy eyelid. The case was unlikely to come to court. Pay-offs and promises, private arrangements and class solidarity. Synnott had been reluctant to let it go. Now, he closed the file and threw it onto his desk. *Sweeping up the shit in the crazy house.*

'Thanks for coming in, sorry to keep you waiting.'

Detective Chief Superintendent Malachy Hogg was standing inside the door of the detectives' room, facing Synnott.

'No bother.'

Hogg came forward, pulled a chair from another desk and sat a couple of yards away. His voice was soft. 'Sorry to hear you've strayed into a spot of bother.'

Synnott nodded. 'I think I'll be OK.' Over the hours since the confrontation with Colin O'Keefe, Synnott had picked away at the details of his problem. If everything held together, the Swanson Avenue matter would remain a stalemate, a debatable clash of confessions – Ned Callaghan's suicidal guilt versus the suicidal killer from Galway. No other case was likely to come unglued. It was a pain in the arse to be removed from the jewellery robbery case. It was unfortunate that Joshua Boyce would dance free and Max Hapgood would slither out of a rape charge, but Synnott's anger had dimmed. He'd lost the promotion to Europol and he'd never again have the confidence of Colin O'Keefe, but to hell with that. No one could prove he'd done anything wrong. *Give it time.*

Hogg said, 'It's a tough business, and you're not the first policeman to find himself tripping over an ambiguous moral line.' Hogg leaned closer. 'I hope it works out for you.'

'Thank you, sir.'

Hogg said, 'I have to ask you about this tout. I'm told she gave you a statement that challenged the alibi of the suspect in the jewellery shop robbery.'

Harry Synnott stared back.

Hogg said, 'I understand the tout knows this chap Boyce, saw him somewhere, damaged his alibi?'

Bitch.

Cheney.

Fucking bitch.

'I'm sorry, sir – there seems to be a misunderstanding.'

Hogg's gaze was unflinching.

'Do you have a copy here of this woman's statement?'

'Sir – there's no statement. This informant, she's – she tries to be helpful, but there's times she hypes things. She thought she saw Boyce on the day of the robbery, but when I pushed her, when I tested her evidence – sir, that was the height of it. Happens all the time. She wasn't sure what day she saw him, she wasn't even a hundred per cent sure it was him.'

Hogg waited a moment. Then he said, 'I see.'

In the silence that followed, Harry Synnott found himself compelled to speak. 'There's no statement, sir.'

It sounded weak and he knew it. He recognised his own response from the dozens of times he'd let a suspect stew in silence, making them feel obliged to say something. He felt a flush of resentment at being the subject of such a cheap manoeuvre by a fellow officer. He stood up.

'Is that all, sir?'

'I'll need to talk to this tout.'

Harry Synnott stood there for a while, meeting Hogg's gaze. Then he pushed his chair back under his desk. He turned and walked towards the door, aware all the way that Hogg's gaze was fixed on him.

Five minutes away from Macken Road, Synnott pulled into a pub car park. He sat for a minute, then pulled out his mobile.

'Thanks a fucking lot.'

Rose Cheney said, 'Fuck you, too, sir.'

'I asked you, begged you, to keep the tout's statement to yourself. I told you it was embarrassing.'

'That's not what this is about, sir.'

'You went to Hogg, you tried to put me in the shit.'

'I was *this* close to putting that Hapgood bastard in jail for rape, not to mention putting his big-shot father behind bars for interfering with a witness – and you piss all over the work I've done.'

'That's not—'

'Hapgood's a serial rapist. We don't get him for what he did, and we can't stop him doing it again. Well done, sir. And maybe the next time the woman gets too stroppy and he kills her.'

'I did the Hapgood case by the book, every step –'

'It doesn't matter – you're damaged goods, and right now the DPP won't buy anything you're selling no matter what the price. Have you a notion of how hard it is to get a rape conviction in this country?'

Harry Synnott said, 'I did nothing wrong.'

Cheney made a noise. 'That's up to Hogg to sort out. Did you give him the tout's statement?'

'There was no statement.'

Cheney hesitated a moment, then she said, 'Last night, you told me the tout made a statement.'

Synnott said, 'She told me about seeing Joshua Boyce, I told you what she said, then she changed her mind. What you told Hogg was wrong. There's no statement.'

'When they talk to Dixie Peyton—'

Synnott felt a whiplash across his chest when he realised that Cheney remembered the tout's name.

'– she'd better back up whatever you told Hogg. Or you're fucked.'

'You sold me out.'

Cheney's voice was filtered through layers of ice. 'It's like you said – if you know about it and you stay silent you become part of it.'

*

When Shelley Hogan came out for a smoke, there was a loser standing outside the pub door, a pinch-faced gobshite with spiky, dyed blond hair. One of the worst things about the smoking ban, you come out for a smoke and the pavement's full of would-be Casanovas. Spiky Hair put on what he must have imagined was his playboy face and gave her a nod. Shelley ignored him and lit up a cigarette as she walked a few yards to the right. She stood, one hand across her midriff, cradling her other elbow, taking a second and then a third drag from the cigarette.

Her thumb was flicking at the bottom of the cigarette filter, shedding ash from the Rothman. She took another drag and watched the tip of the cigarette grow brighter.

Tight corners.

There are times when the corner's so tight you have to turn your face away from everything else and do what you have to do.

Spiky Hair was looking at Shelley's tits. She stared at him until he looked away, his lips sucking on the butt of his cigarette. Shelley took her mobile out of the side pocket of her jeans. She took a beer mat from her back pocket and checked the number scrawled on it, then she tapped in the number.

When someone answered, Shelley said, 'Is this Mr James?'

*

The flame from the candle made the heroin bubble and roll on the aluminium foil, the smoke rose in twisting ribbons and Dixie Peyton sucked it in and held her head back, eyes closed, as she felt the drug swaddle her mind.

Tomorrow.

47

Harry Synnott left the car's engine running outside Dixie's house in Portmahon Terrace. When Brendan Peyton answered Synnott's knock, he was on crutches.

'Is Dixie here?'

'Go away.'

Synnott hadn't seen Brendan Peyton for a couple of years. Whatever had happened to his legs, swathed in bandages below his creased and baggy shorts, had aged him by a decade.

'It's important.'

'I've no idea where she is and I couldn't care less.'

'What happened?'

'Goodbye.'

Brendan's hapless effort to shut the front door in Synnott's face caused him to drop one of the crutches. He winced as he hopped backwards, off balance.

Synnott held him by the shoulders, pushed him back against the hallway wall.

'Get the fuck—'

Synnott jammed his right forearm under Brendan's chin and forced his head back.

'Where is she?'

'I don't know.'

Synnott released Brendan and went further into the house. It took him less than a minute to check upstairs and down. When he returned, Brendan was sitting at the kitchen table. He slumped, as if something had broken inside him. 'I haven't seen her in days. I rang her mate's place an hour ago, when I got home from the hospital – someone answered and hung up as soon as I spoke. I think it was Dixie.'

'Her mate?'

'Shelley Hogan.'

'And Shelley Hogan lives where?'

'She did this. Dixie did.' Brendan gestured towards his legs. 'She ratted on Lar Mackendrick. Heard me talking about Lar's business – I didn't know she was touting – she never told me a thing about it. The bitch hung me out to dry.'

Brendan stared at Synnott, as if daring him to admit that he was the policeman who worked Dixie.

'You reckon she's there? This friend's place?'

'Hadn't the decency to answer me when I called, the cunt.'

'Lar knows she's a tout?'

'Brendan was silent for a while, then he said, 'They would've killed me.'

'Where does Shelley Hogan live?'

'Iron bars, they used. I didn't say anything at first, then I couldn't help it.'

'Where does Shelley live?'

'When Lar finds her, she's dead meat.'

'Where does Shelley live?'

After he got Shelley's address, Synnott put a hand to Brendan's forehead and pushed his head back until his face was almost horizontal. Synnott leaned down until his mouth was just inches from Brendan's ear.

'I didn't come here this evening. No matter who asks, no matter how this turns out, none of this ever happened. You, me, Dixie – one word to *anyone*, now or *ever*, and I put the word out that both of you – Dixie *and* you – were on the payroll.'

He released Brendan's head.

'Understood?'

Brendan said nothing.

Very gently, Harry Synnott kicked Brendan Peyton on the bandaged right shin. After Brendan finished screaming he moaned, 'I swear, I swear,' over and over. When he looked up at Harry Synnott there was nothing in his face any more except fear and submission.

*

Lar Mackendrick waited in the back of the Peugeot, parked down the street from the pub. Lar could see Matty standing in the pool of light outside the pub, talking to a bird with short dark hair. She was shaking her head. Then she took a drag on her cigarette and shook her head again. Matty turned and walked away and the woman said something. Matty went back and after they talked for a bit the woman took a pen from her handbag and wrote something on a piece of paper. Matty gave her something, then he turned and walked back towards the car.

When he got into the Peugeot he handed the piece of paper to Lar.

'Flat 48, in the Sunnyfield, near Gardiner Street. Fourth floor. That's the code you'll need for the front door into the building. She wouldn't give me the key to the flat itself, but that shouldn't be a problem if Dixie is really there.'

'The cow give you any trouble?'

'She wanted the two grand up front. I told her to go fuck herself, so she said she wouldn't tell me anything unless I gave her half up front. I gave her fifty on account.'

'Will she be a problem?'

Matty thought for a second. 'If it works out, we pay her off, she knows to keep her mouth shut.' He waited, then he said, 'We can do the other, if you think it's necessary.'

'Dixie's definitely there now?'

'They talked earlier. She's in for the night.'

'Let's go.'

*

Harry Synnott crossed the Liffey at Tara Street bridge. Traffic was in a tangle at Bus Aras, so he went the long way, up Amiens Street and around into Sean McDermott Street. Brendan Peyton hadn't been certain of the number of Shelley Hogan's flat – '42, 44 maybe – and there's a front-door code, so you'll need to press a lot of buttons before someone buzzes you in.'

There was no certainty that Dixie'd still be at Shelley's place. She might already have tried something, getting hold of the kid, taking him wherever. Whatever she tried, she'd fuck it up.

If she was taken in again, *Jesus.*

Five minutes it'll take, before she gives me up.

Synnott touched the outside of his jacket, feeling the bulk of the envelope in the inside pocket. Two grand, on top of the first one – that should be enough. One condition – she'd have to let him take her straight to the airport, this evening, see her onto a plane, off to hell out of here.

The kid, she could deal with that problem later.

Give it a week or two, Synnott would come to see her in London or wherever, help her get settled, sort herself out, help her get a job. After that, it would take a couple of months – then, quietly, she could begin the business of getting hold of the kid legitimately. With the money to keep her from going under – and it would cost more than the two grand in his pocket – she could hack it. Show that she'd made a life for herself, show she'd stayed clean. If it mattered enough to her, she could do that.

No guarantees. If anyone can fuck things up it's Dixie, but this is her best shot.

Synnott turned along Gardiner Street and a minute later he was in a narrow deserted road, Collier's Row. He pulled to the kerb about fifty yards from the Sunnyfield Apartments building and parked midway between two lamp-posts that gave out a feeble orange light.

Fourth floor. Time to start pressing buttons.

As he switched off the engine a black Peugeot turned in behind him from the Gardiner Street direction and swept past. It pulled into the kerb thirty yards ahead. As he watched, the back door on the left side of the Peugeot opened and a bulky figure got out.

Mackendrick.

Synnott could see the shapes of two others in the front of the car. He gripped the wheel and took a deep breath. Then he reached for the door handle.

*

Something made Dixie stand up. She pushed against the armchair and felt a weakness in one knee as she got to her feet. She was aware that she was swaying slightly, but she was steady enough to know she wasn't about to fall.

What?

There was some reason why she'd stood up.

She wasn't going anywhere, there wasn't anything she should be doing. Get something to eat? She wasn't hungry. Maybe she ought to have something to drink. She was thirsty.

Then the doorbell rang again and she knew that was what had got her on her feet. There was someone at the door.

48

The inner-city blocks of flats that Lar Mackendrick had known when he was young had had the smell of piss in the hallways. Teenage fuckers, they'd spend hours running themselves ragged kicking a football around, but expect them to walk twenty yards to their homes to use the jacks – why bother when there was a handy stairwell to piss in?

This place, this was more like it. The finish wasn't great, the materials were second-rate, the stairway was narrow, but it was clean. No graffiti. No smell of piss. Bit upmarket for the likes of Dixie Peyton and her mates.

Lar decided not to take the lift. By the time he got to the third floor he felt pleased with himself. The old days, he'd have been puffing before he got up to the first landing. Now, on his way to the fourth, he was keeping a steady pace. He could hear the flat tin box rattling in his pocket with every step.

She took ages to answer his ring.

When Dixie Peyton eventually opened the door Lar Mackendrick hit her in the face with his gloved fist and she fell backwards and slammed into the wall behind her. Lar stepped forward and held her upright against the wall. She was out of it, stunned by the blow, and halfway to heaven from whatever shit she'd been doing.

Lar let her slide down the wall, guiding her slowly. He put one hand under her head so that it didn't come down hard on the cork-tiled floor.

Lar closed the door and hurried down the short hallway to the small living room. There was a kind of kitchen in a nook and two bedrooms, all tiny and empty. The place was untidy and smelled of overcooked food. On a small table beside an armchair there was a candle and a blackened square of tinfoil.

Lar stood there for a minute, looking around him. Then he went out to the hallway and held Dixie under her shoulders and dragged her inside. He lifted her into the armchair.

She said, 'Lar.' Her eyes were open.

Poor dumb bitch. Out of it.

Lar took a moment to rate her. From the first time he saw her he'd reckoned Owen's bird was a looker, and even now she was tasty enough in the skirt and blouse she was wearing, her knees slightly apart. Pity she'd let herself go.

'Don't worry, love,' he said. 'You're all right.' He took the flat tin box from his pocket.

Dixie Peyton raised an arm. Weak as a windblown leaf, her hand brushed against Lar Mackendrick's shoulder, then hung there loosely in mid-air. Lar was holding up a syringe, studying it. He looked down at Dixie and saw her unfocused gaze drift towards the syringe. Her voice, when she spoke, was ragged.

'No, no, please, no.'

'It's OK,' Lar Mackendrick said. He flicked a fingernail against the syringe, as he'd seen junkies do, and the clear liquid shook. Something to do with dislodging air bubbles.

'Please,' said Dixie Peyton. There were tears on her cheeks and she said it again, this time in a sobbing voice that divided the word into several syllables.

'It's OK, Dixie, it's OK. It's for the best.'

'Oh, please.' Snot bubbled at one nostril. 'I'm sorry.'

'No need. I know how it is, you were in a corner.' Lar looked from the syringe to Dixie's face. 'Someone gets into a corner, they have to do what they can to help themselves. I don't blame you, Dixie. It's just, you had a choice. And you made it. And what it is, we all have to take responsibility for our actions. Otherwise—'

Lar Mackendrick's voice was low, gentle. He bent over so that his lips were almost touching Dixie's ear. 'The way to look at it – this is all there is for you, now. There's nothing left. No use to the cops any more. Nothing left except more of this. Hanging on from one fix to the next. This is all you have to look forward to, Dixie.'

The way Lar Mackendrick saw it, it wasn't like he was taking anything away from Dixie Peyton. A junkie is something that screams, begs, vomits when it can't get the drugs together. It's either that or it manages to get hold of the gear and it gets turned into a lump of nothing that ends up lying there, pissing itself because it can't be bothered to get up and find the jacks.

And a thing like that, when it knows things about people, it's dangerous and better tidied away.

Lar Mackendrick's voice became little more than a whisper. 'It's no life, Dixie.'

The stuff in the syringe, Matty had assured him that it was uncut. It would take Dixie higher than she'd ever been, past the clouds, around the stars and right through the gates of heaven. Lar wondered if, as she went, her vacant eyes would struggle to make a connection with anything real.

You're out of it, then it all just stops, you're gone – not the worst way to go.

He wanted to watch her eyes as she went. He'd watch a while, as long as it didn't drag on.

Dixie Peyton's right hand shot out and grabbed the syringe, the fist closing around it, the needle digging into her palm. It was as though she concentrated all the strength left in her body into that one sudden gesture. Her hand shook as it clung to the syringe and Lar's fingers, her arm rigid.

Lar Mackendrick reached for Dixie's hand and began to prise open her fingers. Dixie spat once, and again. Some of the spittle reached the front of Lar Mackendrick's shirt. He punched Dixie in the face and watched her head snap back and her hand let go of the syringe.

Lar Mackendrick, his breath now a little wheezy, said, 'Ah, Dixie.'

Dixie gave a small sob.

The syringe lay on the floor, bent near the top, useless.

Lar made a disgusted sound. He went into the little kitchen and opened a couple of cabinet doors, then slammed them shut. He bent down and opened a cupboard door under the sink. He pulled out a tool box.

When Lar returned to the living room he was carrying a hammer. Dixie was standing, moving unsteadily towards the door that led to the hallway. Lar led her back to the armchair and gently pushed her down. He knelt beside Dixie and made the sign of the cross.

'Oh my God I am heartily sorry for having offended thee.' His voice was low, gentle, and before he finished the Act of Contrition he saw that Dixie's lips were silently praying along with him.

He put down the hammer and reached for a yellow jacket that was draped over the back of a nearby chair.

Dixie made a noise, a long, liquid sniffle. Then she whispered, 'In the name of the Father, and of the Son, and of the Holy Ghost,' then she couldn't continue.

Lar Mackendrick said, 'As it was in the beginning—'

Dixie Peyton's eyes were closed now. She drew a deep breath and said, '—is now and ever shall be,' her voice barely there, 'world without end, amen.'

Lar Mackendrick said, 'Amen.' He draped the jacket over Dixie's head, picked up the hammer and hit the shrouded shape of the head very hard, several times. He paused. Then he did it again and again until he felt something give way under the yellow jacket.

He went over and stood by the window and after a while he noticed that he was breathing hard.

Down below, two middle-aged men were taking their time crossing the inner courtyard. One of them, his head thrown back, was passionately singing a song that Lar could barely hear and didn't recognise. His friend was keeping time with invisible drumsticks.

Lar went back and stood beside the armchair, looking down at Dixie. There was a blossom of blood coming through the yellow jacket. Lar lifted a corner. He looked at the mess underneath for just a moment, then let the jacket fall back. He looked down at his clothes. *No blood.* He checked around the room. There was nothing to worry about.

He went out into the hallway and very slowly opened the apartment door just a crack. No one in the corridor. He opened the door wide and listened. No sounds from any of the neighbouring apartments. He looked down and saw that he was still holding the hammer. He went back into the living room and put the weapon down carefully on the floor. He stared for a few moments at the heap that was Dixie Peyton, then he went back down the hallway. He went out and pulled the door shut behind him. It closed with a soft, resigned *click.*

*

It's too late now.

Detective Inspector Harry Synnott looked at his watch. How long since Lar Mackendrick went in?

How long did it take to make the decision, my hand on the handle of the car door, the inside of my head roaring with yes and no and what if—

Lar inside, taking the lift or the stairs.

Five seconds, ten, thirty.

Every second that passed, Lar was another few feet closer to Shelley Hogan's flat.

Watching Lar's two thugs in the front of the Peugeot.

When they saw Synnott get out of the car would they recognise him and rush to Lar's aid? Maybe they'd figure there was no percentage in that, maybe they'd just call Lar on his mobile and warn him?

If I call it in, get back-up—

And cutting across all this – the aftermath. The questions.

Think it through.

Even if we finesse this, get Dixie to England, what're the chances she won't fuck up?

Stand back.

See things as they are.

Two evils.

The lesser.

It means something, in the greater scheme of things.

Synnott made a brief involuntary noise.

What I do means something.

His hand relaxing on the door handle.

Feeling a surge inside his chest, realising the brief wail that filled the inside of the car came from his own lips. Then quiet.

Body slackening, yielding to the consequences of the decision made.

Synnott stared down at his knees, wishing away this moment, this hour, this day, this life. It was a while before he lifted his gaze to watch the entrance to the building, waiting for Lar Mackendrick to come out, his thoughts floating, each one disconnected from the one before.

No.

Don't try to justify it.

Jesus Mary.

Can't be justified.

Elbow on the steering wheel, fingertips rigid against his temple.

Just the way it has to be, that's all.

It took a while, then Lar came out and Harry Synnott released a long, slow, loud sigh. He felt like he'd been holding his breath for an hour.

Lar didn't look one way or the other, just walked quickly down the street. As he neared the black Peugeot the left rear door swung open and Harry Synnott could hear the engine start. As Lar closed the door the Peugeot moved off and screeched into an immediate U-turn, the nose of the car swinging around. Synnott slouched down in his car seat, his legs twisted in under the dash, knees against the wheel, his head below window level. He heard the rush of the Peugeot as it accelerated past him back towards Gardiner Street and he didn't sit up straight for at least a minute.

Too late now.

49

Garda Joe Mills moved away from the front of the pub. The smokers standing around the entrance were stinking up the air. He'd come outside because the noise was relentless, the crowd jabbering, the big-screen television blaring a replay of a two-month old football match. The sergeant who'd accompanied him to Dublin had linked up for a drinking session with two former colleagues who were now based in the city. Mills had been invited because the sergeant didn't want to appear unfriendly, and he'd gone along for the same reason. After almost two hours of strangers' nostalgic anecdotes he needed a break. He said he was going outside for some air.

Only once did the policemen's chatter touch on the episode that had brought Joe Mills to Dublin. One of the Dublin officers asked about this bastard that Joe Mills had arrested in Galway, the murderer the rumours were about. Was it true he'd got some Dublin detective in the shit? Mills said something non-committal about cookies crumbling. The Dublin officer nodded at Mills and said, 'All the same, next time you meet some guy on a rooftop, just give him a shove, right?'

The others laughed loudly and Joe Mills smiled. After a while, one of the Dublin pair stood up to order a round but Mills pointed to his half-full pint and said he was OK.

Outside now, three young women, all dressed in short skirts

and abbreviated tops, came up the narrow cobblestoned street. One of them, clutching a mobile and a small handbag in one hand, a glass of something in the other, looked at Mills, pursed her lips and discharged an inept wolf whistle. The two others shimmied and made lecherous noises and all three dissolved in laughter. Mills grinned and watched them repeat the gestures to other men as they moved on up the crowded street. Two young men responded with howls and rutting motions, then giggled as they moved on, neither of them able to resist a lingering glance back at the women.

It wasn't the Temple Bar that Mills knew from the year he'd lived in Dublin. And all the better for it. The lights and the sound and the bustle and the possibilities they held out made him wish he was a few years younger.

He was looking forward to getting back to Galway tomorrow. He had a couple of days' station duty and from next Monday he was rostered for a week of community liaison, giving talks at schools and community centres, a duty he enjoyed.

Some yards away, on a well-lit stretch of street, a young man in slacks and a rugby shirt was glumly pissing against the shuttered front door of a small shop that sold candles. Mills began ticking off the crimes the young man might be charged with. *Public nuisance, damage to private property, behaviour likely to lead to a breach of the peace* – and if he really wanted to screw up the kid's life he could add indecent exposure and risk getting him put on the sex offenders' register.

Mills turned a corner and walked down to the Liffey. There was a burst of cheerful noise from some young people on the boardwalk across the river. Mills decided that he wasn't going back to the pub. He'd walk to his hotel, let the air clear his head, be fast asleep by midnight.

For a midweek evening, O'Connell Bridge was busy, some people heading home, more moving from one attraction to another, couples linked, groups of youngsters dolled up and gelled for action. There was a buzz about the capital these days, no denying that. Something in the air, exciting and dangerous, as though at any moment there might be an eruption of merriment or savagery.